I0627757

A Spark of Darkness

Rebecca Maeve Hartwell

Content Warnings
WARNING: CONTAINS SPOILERS!!!

I wouldn't describe my stories as overall dark or grim-dark, but I address tough topics.

Depicted (on the page):
Death (adults human only), protagonists take lives/cause death, blood/gore/injury (nothing extreme), alcohol and substance consumption, fascist propaganda (not condoned or excused), attempts (unsuccessful) at coerced dating/relations, bigotry against a fictional nonhuman race, homelessness during civil unrest, insanity caused by brainwashing and abuse, bad parental relationships, use of innocent hostages, adult language, explicit sex scenes, brief suicidal ideation and metaphors, self-harm, vomit, use of a racial slur by a villainous character, kidnapping.

Mentioned (NOT on the page):
Child abuse, rape, abuse, abortion, nuclear weapons, loss of a sibling and best friend/grief, religious trauma and abuse, resource scarcity, religious mission colonization, firing squads, terrorism.

All of these are presented in ways meant to help heal from them and/or address them in productive and honest ways. None are designed to be traumatizing, triggering, or dismissive.

Bonus Material

To claim your free eBook copy of the prequel novella for the Unlocked series, *A Life of Stone*, scan the code below or visit:

www.rebeccamaevehartwell.com/a-life-of-stone

A Life of Stone

CHAPTER ONE

What had been a plume of smoke on the horizon the day before now cast an otherworldly amber patina over the high desert city Angie Forester navigated on foot, trying to remain unnoticed. The deep-orange sky overhead was so choked with smoke that the sun was little more than a red spark in the darkness, and her shoulders tightened. *I fit right in.*

Angie's aura swirled around her in thick, coiled layers of silver and blue, invisible to the stray passerby. Only one person reacted with a puzzled look to the smell of mahogany smoke clinging to her, subtly different from the thicker, more muddled wildfire smoke surrounding them all. Only adepts, those with magic, could see ordinary, passive magic. And even then, only when they tried.

She let go from holding her vision in the auric spectrum with a double blink, avoiding the headache she got with prolonged use of her auric vision. Half of the business fronts were boarded up, and none held a trace of the dusty-pink magic she hunted, or its owner.

Jasper Rose was hiding out in Nevada. Angie was sure of it. A true Seer had told her as much since the triumphant yet chaotic events of the summer solstice a few weeks ago, but she'd kept the information to herself. The former Councilor held the key to Eden, and Angie wanted to lay her claim to it alone. She needed to get to Eden. Whatever the old world orders were using to make it a utopia for the elite could be used for everyone in the real world instead. Either they'd agree, or the half-world would become one she owed a fiery and punitive visit.

A shout of pain nearby spurred Angie into a run, past the few other pedestrians also searching for the source of the sound. Glancing down each alley as she passed, she stopped when she saw an agitated cluster of people at the far end of one and ducked down it.

She reached the other end and stepped out onto what seemed to be the main street of the town, still uncertain who'd called out. Checking both ways for any cars—which were becoming increasingly uncommon since the solstice—Angie crossed the street, trying her best to look like she was simply aiming for the angry huddle gathered in front of a bank.

"Excuse me," she said, shouldering her way through the group to break them up, trying to act oblivious while quickly doing a mental tally. *One woman, five men—Or is it six?*

"No! Please! I need that money!" an elderly man crouched in the center cried out, barely visible, his distress clear in his deeply accented voice.

Angie pushed past the large woman standing over him and reached down to help him to his feet, but he flinched back. Raising her hands, she stepped back. "Hey, it's okay. I'm a good guy. Promise. I just want to help." She glowered at one of the scruffy-looking men hovering around them and grabbed the meager wad of cash in his hands. The redneck squawked in protest but didn't resist.

The Asian man licked his lips, squinting at Angie when she cautiously held out her hand once more to help him up, offering his money with the other. "There's no such thing." His chin quivered as he looked around, clearly wondering if she was yet another bully pretending to help so she could shove him back down. Scars peppered the skin left uncovered by his plain and worn clothes.

"I promise I am one," Angie insisted, crouching down to his level despite her self-preservation screaming at her to stay on her toes, the glares of the gang making her scalp prickle. "Were you a slave?" The man winced again, and Angie tried to give him a kind and understanding smile. "Well, you aren't anymore, by the looks of it. The empire has retreated back to the Roman Peninsula. You're safe now. You can leave now with your money."

"You're one of the shouters?" he asked, and Angie was confused until she saw that the man was looking at her dark-blue denim jacket, and he added, "That color. Like the ones who broke down the walls..."

"Yes," Angie said, smiling more authentically. She rubbed the sleeve of her late sister's jacket affectionately over the scar just above her elbow. "Like I said. Good guy."

The man nodded stiffly, and Angie helped him to his feet. "I doubt the world will have any of those left pretty soon." He looked around, as he shoved the money deep into his stained trousers, still looking like a cornered hare.

Angie stared down the least-committed looking man among those surrounding them until he half stepped aside, and the elderly man bolted through the gap, disappearing down another alley.

When she tried to follow suit, one man, who appeared to be the leader, blocked her path with a sneer which Angie matched. His show of bravado faltered, and he looked her up and down. "Not so fast. We only let him go 'cuz you look like more fun anyway." He reached for Angie's chin, full of smearing swagger. "You'll regret interfering."

The moment his finger touched her face, Angie dropped her stance and slugged him in the gut with her full weight. The man grunted and swung at her, but she easily ducked. She had years of gladiator training to her advantage, and more recent real-world chances to hone those skills, including her previous banishment out into the wildest half-worlds. This jackass didn't know what he'd started.

Angie caught his fist on his second blow, acutely aware that his friends may pile on at any second, and she shoved him back rather than countering. She raised her hands, turning in a circle, making sure her expression was an unmistakable snarl.

"Who the hell are you?" the leader asked, wheezing slightly, and Angie assessed his blue-collar clothes and the lump of chew in his lower lip. He was likely a farmer—and a bully—but not a trained threat. It was a shame she couldn't risk revealing her magic by Voyaging away to avoid conflict. Not in the center of a plebeian city.

"I don't want any trouble," Angie said, knowing she didn't sound like she meant it, and had just proved otherwise.

When the man's response was to raise an empty hand that began to glow slightly, Angie silently cursed her lack of care and double-blinked back into the auric spectrum. *Shit. He's an adept.* Angie glanced around at the increasing number of inepts, those without magic, gathering to watch the spectacle she'd become part of. She noticed with relief that the rest of the group whose cruel entertainment she'd interrupted were also lacking catalyzed power, their auras formless—only an otherworldly, colored light which seemed to shine on them alone.

She brought her aura of smoke into roaring flames in an instant, careful to keep them invisible to plebeians with a thought. Angie smiled darkly at the patrician before her, feeling the familiar, deep triumph of power rise in her chest. She could fight with magic as well as she could with fists.

Angie watched with satisfaction as the man blocking her path fell back half a step. "Stand down, asshole. If you want to test me, I'd be happy to put you in your place. But not in front of these people."

A rustle of motion behind her made her aura judder with a sickening, soul-deep lurch. Angie whipped around, certain there had been someone only inches away a breath before, but saw no cause as her magic warped against her control. "Fuck." It felt as if something had just untethered her magic, causing it to swell and yank against her intentions no matter how hard she tried to rein it in.

Angie turned back to the other patrician, suddenly feeling vulnerable as the little group around her broke apart with gasps. He was grinning like he knew something she didn't. It was decidedly time to leave. She tried to magically teleport away, despite the unrest she was sure such a demonstration would cause, but the Voyaging magic wouldn't catch.

She raised her hands in supplication to no one in particular as she watched her aura of flames and smoke gutter around her. It felt just like how her magic warped in some half-worlds. She reached for the ability to compensate which she'd learned during the seventeen months she'd spent surviving them in order to return from banishment, and found it rusty.

In the half a minute it took for her to haul her magic back under control, she became the center of a slowly growing crowd of men, women, children, and more shouting at her angrily, the bizarre light of the smoke-choked sky making their twisted expressions demonic. She briefly wondered if she had, somehow, Skipped into a half-world without realizing it, but her long-honed instinct for her native world quickly quashed it.

"Witch!" one shouted, other such accusations following it in quick succession from the jeering crowd.

"Get lost. You aren't welcome here!"

"Fuck off before you kill us all!"

"Run! Run before it's too late!" Angie saw the speaker of the last—a woman with bold features and gray-streaked hair—and took her advice without further hesitation, bolting through the first decent gap she saw. Several people cried out in pain as her flames brushed them, and Angie did her best to pull them back, spurred forward by the enraging laughter of the patrician man behind her whose unnecessary confrontation had pushed her to this display.

Two centurions, local law enforcement, blocked Angie's path as she ran for the side street where she'd parked her car, both drawing their weapons. *Fuck.* Angie stumbled to a stop, panting more from the mental strain of hauling her aura back from causing any more pain than from the physical exertion, and raised her hands. She closed her eyes momentarily, desperately willing her flames to shift back to smoke, and weighed her options.

Only a part of the mob she'd fled had pursued her, and Angie took off for a side street again as they neared, the centurions joining in and shouting commands. As she sprinted ahead, Angie tried to Voyage again—to anywhere she might lose her hunters—and this time, it finally worked.

She slammed into a brick wall and heard distant cries of surprise, fear, and rage. Angie turned her back to the wall, fished a heavy copper coin from the pocket of her light-wash jeans, and slid down to sit on the heels of her black boots.

"Jonathan," she gasped, looking around for any people or cameras that may have witnessed her abrupt arrival.

She held the coin tightly between her fingers, feeling the intricate, spiked-wheel sigil carved into it. "I need you..."

A ghostly form poured from the copper, ethereally wavering between light and mist, coalescing into a column a few feet away to form a man. "Angie," he said, tugging at the slacks of his azure suit and crouching beside her. "What happened? I only caught snippets." He reached out a tanned and calloused hand, which made no impression against her shoulder, his ice-blue eyes worried.

"I think I'm going to have a panic attack," Angie said, locking her attention onto the weathered face behind his black beard. "And this is a very bad time for that."

"Why? What are you feeling?"

Angie shook her head. "None of the usual warnings. My breath and focus are okay." She held out a hand in front of her, watching the smoke of her aura swirl around it. "But my magic warped when I tried to use it under stress, and a panic attack is the only explanation I've got. Well, at least the most likely one."

Jonathan's ghost took a deep breath, and Angie joined him, carefully checking her internal awareness for the panic she'd convinced herself must be there. Finding none was a relief, but a small part of her knew the absence of it raised questions about her warping magic she didn't want to acknowledge.

"I guess I was wrong," she said weakly, and Jonathan smiled, settling more comfortably into his kneeling position beside her.

"You're getting stronger. You're healing and learning yourself better. Things that would have triggered you in the past will keep getting easier to handle over time, even if not always in a smooth progression."

Angie nodded. She did feel a spark of pride that the panic hadn't come, but it was hard to cling to that feeling through the disappointment of having come so close yet again. "Yeah, thanks." She took several deep breaths and pulled herself back up to her feet. "I guess until then, I should just avoid angry mobs."

She'd intended it as a joke, but Jonathan frowned as he stood. "Did they see your magic? Is that what you meant when you said it warped?"

"Yeah. I tried to hide it, but they saw. And hunted me about five blocks. Had to dodge two centurions to get away."

"Why not talk this over with Dan? I don't have to talk to him to know he misses you."

Because I can't tell him about you, Angie thought, but didn't say. "I know. I really miss him, too." *Understatement of the century. I'm always thinking about him. Every minute.* "I don't want to bother him. He's got plenty on his own plate. Maybe I'll ask him about it the next time we catch up." She conjured a ball of fire in her palm, and the magic obeyed perfectly. "It was just something that adept was doing to mess with me." Angie didn't acknowledge the twist of doubt that accompanied the statement. Some part of her knew it wasn't true, but she didn't know what else it could have been.

Angie started walking, away from the distant cry she'd heard on arriving, knowing it came from her pursuers. Life would be easier with him, she knew. But she'd asked for the break in their relationship to figure herself out on her own for a bit, and constantly running to him felt like a betrayal of that.

"Which will be when?"

Angie gave Jonathan an exasperated sigh. "Whenever I'm done in this part of the world. Whenever I have something to actually show for all this, like Jasper or the Eden key."

"Do you want to reconsider hunting Jasper Rose and Eden, having now been hunted yourself for as little reason?" Jonathan's tone was every bit the careful, intelligent therapist he'd been in life, and when Angie glanced at him, his light-blue eyes were as cuttingly observant as always.

"No. I can keep things from getting more chaotic if I just find them. They were a Councilor. An established one. They can help us fix the unintended consequences of breaking all the language locks. And if I get control of Eden... Actually, I'm not sure. But she—sorry, they—can tell me why it's so special, and whatever it is, I'm sure we can use it."

She stopped when she finally caught sight of a street sign and turned back the way she'd come, orienting herself in case her Voyaging magic warped like her auric magic had. She held up the copper sigil coin Jonathan had made for her to protect against demonic possession, and his ghost frowned at it with a sigh.

Without protest, the ghost folded back into it, and Angie Voyaged.

She landed beside her plain blue hatchback and slipped inside, locking it and pulling down her cardboard window screens. If Jasper Rose was in Reno, they got to evade her another day. It was time for Angie to find a bolt-hole.

As Angie eased away from the curb, a black and gold centurion vehicle blew past her with lights and sirens, and she forced herself not to duck. She turned the way it had come from, not eager to see what unrest it was speeding toward—likely caused by her—and glanced at the digital compass built into her rearview mirror. She absently grabbed a smaller, newer sigil coin from the mess of change in the cup holder, fiddling with it anxiously.

In this direction lies home. Angie huffed ruefully as the song lyric played in her mind. The little ranch house tucked into the foothills of the northern Ruby Mountains hadn't been home in many years. And yet, the call of the familiar, endless desert highways was hard to resist.

As she followed the signs onto the freeway heading east, calm settled over her, and Angie promised herself she'd run for just a day before pursuing her quarry once more.

CHAPTER TWO

Daniel Fawl tapped his gloved fingers on the restaurant table he sat at. The space was lavishly decorated but sparsely populated. The waiter that had shown him to his table had barely spoken before hurrying away, and the few other dinner patrons—sipping wine from crystal glasses or eating off gilt porcelain plates—also seemed on edge. Perhaps they, quite rightly, worried that each outing would be their last taste of such a life.

"I didn't know I'd been invited here to meet a murderer."

Daniel looked up at the heavy set woman with olive skin hovering behind the chair opposite him, and stood respectfully, raising a gloved hand. Her last word was a knife into his heart, but he couldn't argue the truth of it. "Please, Miss Doukas. You know, better than most, why Milton Cartwright had to be removed from the power he held. You knew that even back when you helped vote me into the patrician Senate. All I'm asking for now is a few minutes of your time."

She and many others had watched him cross the line he'd long held himself back from, despite being happy to take credit for deaths he hadn't caused in the past.

The self-loathing that had coiled tightly around him in the weeks since squeezed a little harder around his lean chest.

Miss Doukas continued to look wary, only resting a hand on the back of her chair. "For what purpose?" Her thick Hellenese accent made the words sound heavy and round, and Daniel wondered why she didn't just use a layer of simple translation magic in her maroon aura instead.

"Dawn Renard sent me. Please. Just a moment of your time." Daniel sat, hoping the other adept would follow suit. "She simply wants to know if you'd be open to combining forces to help protect and provide for the massive influx of unlocked adepts that both your language and hers are struggling to awaken in time. An equal exchange of her resources and your connections into the last pocket of the empire."

A couple at a table nearby darted glances at the two patricians, and Daniel hoped it was because of his Caledonian accent in contrast against hers, and not for her agitated tone. Balancing the risk of exposure, Daniel extended his awareness to the shields of pale-yellow magic he'd built around the table, and did his best to add a layer that would obscure their words from eavesdroppers.

Miss Doukas took her seat, looking Daniel up and down. "She's the cause of the mess we're all in now. Her and Angie Forester." Daniel's Air aura shivered slightly at the mention of Angie, but he quickly soothed it to avoid revealing his intimate connection to her. "Tell me, what became of her since she destroyed the last Focal

Nucleus holding any scrap of magical order together? I hear many rumors." Daniel could only imagine and didn't volunteer any suggestions when Miss Doukas paused. "Among them, that your own sponsor's skin curse affected her once more at the solstice, and that some sordid dalliance with your first recruit was to blame. How are you remotely the kind of man deserving of my trust?"

Daniel poured her a glass of white wine from the bottle on the table. *No need to tell her the full truth.* "It's true. It appears the loophole Miss Forester and I had found in my skin curse closed for reasons I don't know. But I assure you, I never betrayed her or anyone else I called my friend, ally, or recruit. I've had very little contact with her in the last two weeks, and she has no part to play in Dawn's request for a simple, mutually beneficial alliance between the English and Greek language camps." Daniel lifted a toast. "The dregs of the empire need not be what they have always been."

Miss Doukas's eyes narrowed, first at Daniel, then at the wine he'd poured her, before sipping it. "So, what do you have to say about your latest recruit? Seth Laufey? The things he's been saying on the radio... Haven't you been listening?"

"No, I haven't." Daniel didn't want to attempt articulating the disgust, loss, and guilt that had kept him distant from such matters since the solstice and his best friend's death. "I've been otherwise engaged."

The former Greek Senator across from him sipped her wine more eagerly but regarded him with no greater fondness. "Well, he's changed his stance. He's now working directly for the emperor, by his own admission, and the same unhinged zeal with which he was threatening the remnants of the empire is now being aimed at its enemies."

Daniel, sadly, wasn't surprised. "All the more reason to help us infiltrate those halls of power before it's too late."

Miss Doukas swirled her wine, her maroon aura juddering with agitation, and drained it in one swig. "No, no," she finally said, pushing her chair back and standing. "I don't have the time, magic, or attention to spare for Renard or her people."

Daniel stood too. "Why not? Perhaps we can help. Raw resource production was unlocked when we broke the Latin lock in the Council world, and we have several people in the English ranks who are developing the skill. If you need food, building materials, golems for labor... what's holding you back?"

The Hellenese woman shook her head. "No more than all other languages are dealing with. We cannot get to all the adepts whose auras were unlocked when the Courts, Senate, and Council fell. Unless Renard is working toward building new locks to help stop the chaos, there's nothing the Greek speakers need from her."

"We could pursue that," Daniel said quickly. "The issue was never with the language locks keeping people's untrained magic suppressed. Only with the other, more malevolent purposes they had been corrupted to serve over so many centuries of the patrician orders forgetting that their purpose was to help all the people they ruled." He knew Angie would take issue with the statement, having heard her rant on several occasions about how unfair it was for potential adepts to be denied access to their magic, but he didn't care to share her stance at that moment.

"Yes? And how could that be pursued, as you say?"

Daniel winced. He had no idea. "I'm sure that finding and implementing the necessary information would go much faster in tandem than alone. And with your connections with the empire—"

Miss Doukas seemed to deflate and cut him off. "I'm sorry, Fawl. I really am. I'm just not willing to help people outside my own language until things settle down. I ask that you leave me alone to see to the needs of my people, and that you see to yours without me." Daniel dropped his head, scratching his short beard, and the other adept seemed to read his disappointment. "Even if I was willing, I don't have what you want in exchange." Daniel looked back up, and Miss Doukas looked apologetic. "I left what remains of the global empire before the solstice. I wanted no part in the measures for control they were preparing, which I doubt have been scrapped just because of their immense loss."

"Oh." Daniel felt his hopes sink with a chill through his aura. "I'm sorry, I didn't know." He took a deep breath and sat back down as Miss Doukas turned away from the table, his mind already racing with what his next moves might be.

"What I will tell you," the Hellenese woman added, stopping and halfway turning back, "is that the empire has every single soldier who hasn't defected guarding its nuclear weapons across the globe." Her maroon aura trembled, and Daniel could see her hesitant apology written in every inch of her posture. "We've tried to claim the one held in Patras, but they have enough magic bolstering their defenses that it was utterly impossible. If you have people, magic, or time to spare in the English camp, I strongly recommend that you spend them on that. Perhaps, since you were Laufey's sponsor, you're just the man to do what none of us can..."

Daniel shook his head, trying to imagine what speaking to Seth again would be like. "I'm not sure that's a good idea."

"Do you mean you've lost contact or goodwill with yet another former recruit?"

"He sends me letters." Daniel's lip curled, recalling the mix of threats and sycophantic adoration in the previous evening's addition. "Every single one demonstrates his volatility."

"Then I'd suggest you keep your distance." Miss Doukas turned toward the doors of the restaurant again. "More's the pity. For every innocent person on the planet. Trusting our fates to half-worlds is starting to look better by the day..."

—◦❖◦—

Daniel eventually found Dawn Renard picking her way through shards of broken glass in an evacuated airport and carefully dodged the other familiar, sullen patricians combing over the scene.

"Uncontacted adept?" he asked, glancing at the three body bags lined up against a row of black and silver chairs.

The rebellion leader nodded, one of her long, rope-like braids swinging free from its tie. "Yeah. Male, we think, mid-sixties. His fated moment seems to have been trying to fight his way into an already full flight, and we didn't get to him in time. He died from a centurion choking him, and his released magic killed two others when he did. Cleared the airport, going to clean up before heading back to camp." She stuffed her hands in her pockets, giving Daniel a hopeful look. "What of Miss Doukas? Any luck?"

Daniel shook his head, his tongue at the corner of his mouth. "No, I'm sorry. The Greek Senator won't help us."

Dawn's shoulders dropped. "Did you offer everything we'd discussed? I thought we had a real shot, with two Hellenians already providing mutual aid nearly every day..."

"I did. But like you'd said, I didn't mention Nikolaos or Demitria." Daniel glanced out through the shattered floor-to-ceiling window at a distant airplane with a distinct silver nose cone. "However, she did warn us that the emperor is putting a disproportionate number of resources into holding onto his nukes, and that Seth seems to have switched over to his side." He swallowed the fear that shaded his vision. "What can we do about that? Should we put people on it?"

Dawn huffed, and Daniel turned his attention back to her fracturing gold aura. She blew out a long breath, pulling a hand down her face, and her black brows knit. "How can I worry about nukes when every unlocked adept out there, in every language across the globe, is a bomb waiting to happen?" She waved at the scene before them with a dark hand, and Daniel wished he hadn't brought it up. "One percent of the population, as far as we can tell. Had I told you that?" Daniel shook his head, doing the math even before Dawn continued. "That's sixty million bombs that are also human lives, with very little idea of when they'll go off." Dawn wet her lips, and her voice dropped with her gaze. "I know I should care. I do. But I just don't have the capacity. I care for those I can see. If I reach for more, I'll burn out and can't help anyone."

"So, what should I do?" Daniel felt off balance, ready to do anything but stand still, but do what, he didn't know.

Dawn waved a hand, turning away. "If you want to chase it, please do, but leave me out of it. You've already made it clear you operate just fine on your own."

CHAPTER THREE

A piece of cottonwood fluff drifted past Angie's eyes as she stepped from her car, and she deftly caught it. In an instant, her past projected itself over her reality. Another gas station, years ago and two states away. She blinked it away, looking around at the small, forlorn place where she now stood, reassuring herself that it was different as hints of gasoline and burned rubber edged her smoke. This station, all yellow plastic and paint, stood in the heart of a small town. That other gas station had been the only change on an otherwise empty stretch of desert highway, the awning over the pumps a vivid pink. *I hadn't yet learned to hate that color back then*, she thought with a twist of bitterness.

She also noticed, with the usual twist of guilt, that the price for a gallon of gas was ten times what it had been on that fateful day early in her full ownership of magic. Even then, things had been desperate, and Angie pushed aside thoughts of the men who had attacked her.

Angie tucked the bit of fluff into the pocket of her jeans, feeling the same spark of life, of Wyrd, that she'd coaxed out of another just like it a lifetime ago—only days after the mugging and altercation she'd been so forcefully reminded of by catching it. Something nagged at the back of her mind, guilty and bitter, as she walked around to the door of the shop, but Angie wasn't sure which part of her resurfaced past the gap belonged to. She reached for it in her mind, but it slipped away.

Her stomach grumbled as she shouldered open the door, the jangling bell pulling her back to the present. It was a shame she'd shown no signs of the ability to produce or replicate food or other resources from nothing since she'd freed such powers from the patrician language locks. The thought of resorting to the ways she'd acquired food during her banishment didn't appeal.

The clerk was helping someone else, so Angie turned to the back wall, grabbing a large bottle of water out of the nearly empty coolers before turning her thoughts to food.

"Angelica?"

Angie looked up, instantly on edge. She cast around for the half-familiar voice in a place she didn't expect to be known, and when she saw the clerk staring at her, his jaw slack, she grimaced. "Hey, Garrett. How're things?"

Her high school ex swallowed, seeming to recover, and shrugged. "Better than some."

Angie nodded, hoping to end things there, and turned to pursue the sparse food options still stocked on the shelves.

"Why are you back here?" Garrett asked, and Angie groaned internally. "I thought you'd be exempt from the repatriation efforts as a patrician."

Angie blinked, glancing up at the young man with dark-blue eyes. "I am, but those restrictions were lifted a month ago. I mean"—she gestured vaguely around them—"who's going to enforce them or care now that the empire is gone?" Garrett's cheeks colored a shade, and he looked away, so Angie resumed her search for any food that looked not just edible but appetizing.

"So, you're a patrician?" Garrett asked, clearly not willing to leave her alone. "When I saw you in London with that Senator, that was real?"

"Yep," Angie said curtly, then reconsidered. "Why were you in London?" she asked, her hand pausing mid-reach for a bag of chips, realizing she'd never gotten a proper answer. "I remember you said you were there to interview in the Sen—I mean, in the Suardo Building, but you never said how you got the invitation."

Garrett shrugged as Angie feigned disinterest. "I met someone at my last job who got friendly with me and told me he could help me get ahead. His name was Milton, I think? Cartwright, for sure. He..."

Angie hid that the name made her breath speed up, but she wasn't surprised. She and Daniel had already speculated that the Councilor who had made both their lives hell for years had been behind several of their exes reappearing in their lives to throw them off their blackmail demand of the man.

"He told me about you, too." Angie arched a brow, glancing over her shoulder, but it dropped when Garrett asked, "Is it true you killed two men? And put another in a coma? That's what Cartwright said..."

Angie swayed. The mention of Milton Cartwright in connection with the mugging she'd been so forcefully reminded of just a few minutes before slammed itself against the nagging gap in her thoughts around the topic, and her head spun as a veil of fuchsia magic lifted from her memories. "He told me, too," she mumbled, and Garrett gave her a blank look. Angie cleared her throat, sorting through her newly returned memories of Milton trying to use the same information to blackmail her back in the cavern of half-world keys, squirming at the thought of his magic infecting her mind.

"Did he show you proof?" Angie asked in response, hoping to curtail the topic as she sorted through it herself. She grabbed a package of dried fruit, jerky, and a fresh sandwich from a cooler before dumping them all on the counter in front of her ex, who was regarding her with a squint.

"Yeah, I mean, sort of."

Angie braced herself, careful not to show her confusion or distress. Garrett started slowly ringing up her items between glances up at her. "He took me to a hospital in Reno where my last job was. He took me to see some guy he said was the only one who survived your attack on them and told me about the other two."

Angie scoffed, but her mind raced. Why would Cartwright have bothered telling a random ex-boyfriend of hers all of that? How did he think he would gain from that? "What was the man's name?" Angie asked as casually as she could, and Garrett shrugged as he stuffed her items into a flimsy plastic bag.

"Barns? Brown? Something like that. It was definitely the Order of Asclepius hospital there, though. Do you need gas, too?"

Angie shook her head, fishing cash out of her plain leather wallet and cringing at the rising costs despite her lack of financial distress. There were some mindsets she'd never be able to shake. She silently thanked Dawn for the enchantment that allowed her hatchback's tank to refill itself, although the magic had been proving iffy, and she'd still had to refuel every thousand miles or so. "No, I'm set."

Grabbing her bag of food, which should last her at least a full day, Angie turned to leave. She slowed when she saw a sign advertising strawberry milkshakes on the window beside the door, but decided that the nostalgia wasn't worth looking like she was finding an excuse to linger.

"Oh! Hold up!" Garrett said as Angie yanked the door open, and she paused. "Your parents are looking for you! They've been putting feelers out through everyone who used to know you."

Angie just stared, her brain grinding against the information. "Really?" Last she'd heard, her parents wanted nothing to do with her, and she'd never expected to hear from or see them again until she had to attend a funeral for one or both of them.

"Yeah." Garrett suddenly seemed unwilling to look Angie in the eyes, instead looking up and down her plain and worn clothes. "I may have told them you're a patrician now."

And the penny drops.

—◦✦◦—

Angie tossed the bag onto her passenger seat, slammed the door shut, and braced both arms against the upper edge, letting her head drop forward. She closed her eyes tight and just listened to the pounding in her ears for a long moment. A thousand thoughts tumbled over one another, each a bit less certain and more bitter on her tongue than the last.

When she straightened, it was with a long, pursed exhale. Her appetite was gone, and she needed to figure out where she was driving next. She stepped away under the small ribbon of shade beside the wall in front of her car and unclipped the sat phone from her belt.

She punched in a number and held it to her ear, smiling when a gruff Caledonian voice answered.

"Hey! Glad to hear from you. What's up?" Daniel sounded alert but wary, and Angie smiled.

"Nothing bad, relax. I just..." She trailed off, weighing how she wanted to broach a topic they'd yet to fully address between them, suddenly worried he might have as much reason as she did to avoid it. "I'm back in Nevada, not too far from where I grew up." Angie scuffed the dusty concrete with the toe of her shoe, wishing Daniel would fill the pause so she didn't have to. "I ran into someone I used to know, and he—they told me my parents have been trying to get back in touch with me, and now I'm wondering if I should go see them."

"That's wonderful!"

Angie could hear the smile in Daniel's voice, but it only lessened her frown. "Not really. I don't exactly want to see them, and before today I thought the feeling was mutual. Besides, I'm not just back here on vacation, I have work to do. Important work people like you, and Dawn, and Casey, and the rest are depending on. And even if I do allow myself a personal detour, I have much more practical options..." Her mind flitted to Milton and her muggers.

"Angie." Daniel spoke her name with a rush of static over the magically boosted satellite signal. "If your parents are alive and well, and wanting to interact with you, why would you say no?" A thousand old, deep, painful reasons swelled up in Angie's throat, but were stopped, unspoken, when Daniel added, "Take it from someone who no longer has that option, and never take that for granted. My parents are gone. Most of my aunts and uncles, too, my cousins spread out all over the world, including the area you're in now. I haven't spoken to any of those still living in decades, and I don't imagine I have to tell you what it's like to wish for one last conversion with someone once they're gone."

Angie turned to face the bare wall, away from anyone who might pull up to the gas pumps and see her as her unspoken objections hissed through her teeth. "Like Jonathan..." She pressed her free hand over the small lump in her jeans—the large copper sigil coin Jonathan's ghost was bound to—feeling the small stir of personality and energy within, so similar to how she'd sensed the demons that had, at different points, taken up residence in the silver key necklace hanging from her neck.

She wanted to tell him. To let him have one more conversation with his best friend just as she got to every day, but she couldn't. The longer she waited to go against Jonathan's wishes and tell him, the more it would hurt him. The more he would feel betrayed, and left out, and upset that she'd let him grieve every day that he did. It was a hole Angie knew she was digging deeper for herself every day, but that didn't mean she could stop.

Daniel was silent for a long moment before clearing his tight voice. "Yes. Like with Jonathan."

"Okay," Angie said, blinking away the sting in her eyes and wanting to talk about anything else as soon as possible. She wrapped her arm over her stomach, turning again to lean back against the wall. "How are things with you?"

Daniel cleared his throat once more, his tone light and detached. "Fine. Like I said yesterday, some new leads, but at the same time, not nearly enough to do with them."

Angie nodded, despite knowing Daniel couldn't see. The space and time she'd asked for between them—the break from being anything more than friends—felt heavy in the silences where Angie knew Daniel was choosing not to say something he might have a year ago. "Okay, well. Thanks for the advice. I'll consider it. And it was good hearing your voice."

"Yeah, you too."

Angie hung up before the shades of sorrow Daniel had tried to hide in his tone could hang in the hot, dry air around her as well. She flipped the sat phone over and over in her hands, staring without seeing at the quiet, nervous family filling up their overstuffed van at one of the pumps.

Swallowing hard, Angie dialed the only other phone number she had memorized, her anxiety mounting as the line rang over and over through the speaker held to her ear. When it clicked over to an error buzz, Angie felt relief wash over her. "Idiot," she whispered to herself, hanging up and clipping the phone to her belt. Regular phone lines were still down. That was the whole reason she had a sat phone in the first place. The landline in her childhood home obviously wouldn't be working.

Angie got back in her car, started the engine, but left it in park as she blasted the AC to make up for the few minutes she'd left it baking in the sun. Perhaps it was best she couldn't call. Her mind wandered to how she expected the call would have gone if it had connected as she sipped her blessedly cold water and nibbled on a few chips.

Her mother would have answered, never content to let her father take charge. If Garrett had been honest about their knowledge of Angie's rise in position and fortunes, Catherine would have then gushed about how long it had been, calling Robert from another part of the house to join the call. She'd prompt him to say something nice, and he'd grunt something unintelligible. Angie would ask how they'd been, and they'd complain about the farm, the livestock, the lack of rain, and just about any and everything else.

Cath would then ask Angie how she's been in return, and... Angie set her chips aside with a sigh, her stomach turning. And Angie would know without question that no matter how she answered, her mother would find some way of comparing it to the accomplishments of her sister. Angie could never measure up to the ghost of a daughter lost to tragedy years ago. The moment of awkwardness would stretch until Rob would grunt some remark about the family heritage going to shit, and they'd argue about that just for a distraction. Angie would know he was twisting the sigil ring of Silvanus he always wore as he spoke, passed down through his fathers for generations, without needing to see. Never mind the fact that he was the one who left the family logging business to die on the East Coast to live out delusions of being a cowboy in his youth.

Angie knew this cycle of theirs all too well and cursed loudly to break herself out of the spiral. "Pluto take them both," she spat as she slammed her car into gear rather harder than she needed to. Acrid sagebrush smoke filled the vehicle, and she rolled down a window rather than trying to rein it in. Ignoring her seatbelt, Angie swung out of the parking space recklessly, weaving around to the main road, and stopped.

Staring at the street signs across from her and glancing at the digital compass built into her rearview mirror, Angie hesitated. Everything in her felt pulled in two directions, rocking against each other as they tried to pull her apart.

She took a deep breath and clicked on her turn signal. Her parents weren't Daniel's, and if he remembered them fondly, they must have been a hell of a lot nicer than hers.

CHAPTER FOUR

When Daniel had Voyaged to Dawn's compound, hidden among towering redwoods on the Pacific coast, he hadn't expected to land nose-to-nose with Dawn's niece Léa. Daniel stumbled back a step to restore his personal space, glancing at the young, white-blond, tattooed Casey over her shoulder, who just scowled.

Daniel's brief call with Angie earlier that afternoon had left him feeling adrift, lost in memories. He'd intended to search out purpose—something to keep him busy—at Dawn's direction, but would have preferred to stay well clear of the young Seer, who he still harbored resentment for, along with pity.

The teenager was quite the contrast to Casey behind her. She was a full head shorter than him, her heart-shaped face and rich complexion hidden beneath a mountain of tight curls. Daniel double-blinked to activate the auric spectrum of his vision out of habit, hoping to understand this unusual greeting, and Casey's curry-yellow aura overlapped heavily with Léa's burnt-orange magic, both agitated.

"I warned you!" Léa rasped in a stage whisper, glaring at Daniel. Casey, just behind her, winced and placed a hand on her shoulder, which she shrugged off. "I warned you, and yet we are still on this path, and they're getting harder to see as the fabric unravels..."

Daniel stood frozen, torn between not wanting to deal with what he knew was coming, and not wanting to cause any distress to the troubled young woman before him by avoiding it. "I'm sorry," he said cautiously, but Léa cut him off.

"*An angel of flame and chaos brought an end to order. Water stood against the empire and fell.*"

He'd heard the prophecy many times, but never before in past tense, and the certainty which the shift lent the rest of the prediction he knew made bile rise in his throat.

Léa's eyes misted over with the magic of True Sight. "*Demons shall let the angel pass, leading them to the broken door. The Angel in the Forest. Two are one, one is two, all is nothing.* That's what you know?"

Daniel nodded and took a deep breath, believing her finished. But his gut dropped when she spoke new words onto the familiar lines.

"Then I ask you to understand. *Two that are one, you will not accept. One that is two, you will fight to reclaim. All power is nothing in no one's hands.* Write them down." Léa's tone turned stern as her magic left her eyes.

Daniel just blinked at the order, his Air aura beginning to blow around him. "I don't understand. That sounds like just more of the same riddle..."

She repeated her last demand with an edge of frustration, and when Daniel still failed to comply, her whole being shifted into desperate pleading. "Please write them down. If you know, if she knows, maybe a different path can be chosen..."

Stirring, Daniel pointlessly patted down his pockets before his brain fully engaged, and he summoned a pen and pad of paper from the Boston home he'd just left. He didn't need to write any of it down. The swirling mess of emotions in his aura, which he was straining to keep in check and away from the two adepts before him, should have made it clear that every syllable was seared onto his memory, but he obliged.

When Daniel held up the sheet of paper for Léa to see, each word of her prophecy written down in his messy scrawl, she visibly relaxed.

"Everything alright?" a voice behind Daniel asked, and he turned to see Mahina looking past him, concerned. "Oh dear," the Hawaiian woman tutted, giving Daniel a respectful nod before bustling forward to help Casey move Léa—now quiet and subdued—away toward a distant cluster of buildings. "Miss Renard told you to avoid using your Sight! That poor Hindustani girl is doing enough. You need to rest."

As they bustled away, Daniel looked around the small lawn at the center of the compound he'd arrived in, registering the other people present for the first time since his off-putting welcome. Not one face was friendly. He regretted coming.

Anthony Shupee peeled away from a group clustered near the common house, approaching Daniel with a tight smile. "Fawl. Anything we can do for you?"

"I came to ask the same," Daniel replied with what he hoped was a reassuring and friendly shrug. "Did Mahina just mention that Sakshi's been using her Sight to help you all?"

"Yeah," Anthony replied, shifting his weight from one foot to another and shielding his eyes against a spear of light through the massive redwood branches overhead. "Though it's taking a toll. She was eager at first, but the madness started building up faster. She said that she didn't used to feel the effect as bad, but it's worse now."

"Why? What changed?"

It was Anthony's turn to shrug. "The half-world Milton and his lot kept her in, maybe? Impossible to know for sure. So Dawn's told all the English Seers we have tabs on to stop using their gift if they can help it, but that young woman refuses to stop.

"Besides," he sighed, dropping his hand with his gaze, "according to Léa, the chains of potential cause and effect are getting harder to follow as the wider world becomes less ordered, so some are saying the True Seer gift might be all but useless soon, too, if things get worse." He ran his fingers through his steel-gray hair. "Maybe the old order was staunch about not allowing any chaos for more reasons than we thought." As if reading Daniel's thoughts, he added, "Nikolaos and Demitria left with Dawn to liaise with the Cantonese language leader. They'll be back soon."

"Listen," he turned to face Daniel more directly. "Don't know if you've heard, but Noah Byrne has reinhabited the English Conference site, and it's looking like he intends to burrow in. It's lucky that Miss Forester got in to snoop around when she did. Do you know if she found any of the Court's records or such? Anything we could use to try to get things back under control for unlocked adepts we can't get to in time, or... honestly, anything else?"

Daniel shook his head, wishing he had something more to offer the clearly worried man before him. "No, sorry, mate. She never mentioned finding anything apart from a trace back to the empty key vault."

Anthony looked defeated, and Daniel felt bad for just making things worse. "What about that ancient book Dawn said you and—" Anthony stopped himself, but the unspoken name still hurt. "That you gave Miss Forester to read building up to her first Victume Ceremony? Anything in there that might help?"

"Afraid not. It's more a collection of sagas than a manual of any kind. I've read it several times to be sure." *And because I've had fuck all else to do*, he thought to himself, but chose not to say.

Daniel was spared continuing by an appearance only a dozen paces away. Both he and Anthony backed away to make room as more people arrived, following a dark-skinned woman with long ropes of braid, dyed royal blue at the ends. Just seeing that shade of blue made Daniel's heart hurt. It was the exact color Jonathan's aura had been in life, and when Dawn turned, catching sight of Daniel, the same grief flashed across her face before it smoothed.

A tall young man with thick, curly black hair saw Dawn turn and followed suit, and Daniel found he couldn't look him in the eyes. Nikolaos looked far more tired than he'd seen him look before, and the way he held his slight, olive-skinned companion to his side—like she'd slip away any second—made Daniel ache for them both. As discreetly as he could, Daniel summoned a pair of leather gloves and pulled them on.

"Shupee, Fawl," Dawn called out in greeting, making the rest notice the two men and follow her over as the other people Anthony had been waiting with before Daniel's arrival also joined them. One of Dawn's wives, Olivia, peeled away from the group with several golems in tow, each carrying a large pack on its back.

"Boys, this is Xiao Sheng. Mister Xiao is the leader of the New Cantonese Uprising, as he'd dubbed it. We've just been delivering supplies to them as a gesture of good faith, since we were ahead of the curve on expanding our ranks a full two years before they were." Daniel doubted anyone else could see the shade of sorrow in Dawn's beaming smile. "It sounds like we may now be able to start building a more meaningful alliance."

Daniel extended a gloved hand, but the man's murky yellow-green aura rippled with disgust, and he stepped back.

"Fawl? Daniel Fawl?" Xiao Sheng's lips didn't match the words Daniel heard, indicating the use of translation magic on his end, but his disgust and contempt were clear in any language. He shook his close-shaven head exaggeratedly, the lines around his small mouth deepening as he grimaced.

Daniel just set his jaw as Xiao Sheng turned to Dawn. "I don't know what you're playing at, Fox, but if you're friends with a Councilor, allow them here to your home, call them yours... No, no, no. This is not good. There was already too much we disagreed on, and now this. I was mistaken. We cannot come to any agreement."

"Now hang on," Dawn said, only the faintest edge of sternness in her soothing voice as she ducked in front of the Cantonese leader when he turned to leave. "Surely you're well versed in double agents and moles. I assure you—"

"What you assured me," Xiao Sheng cut in in clipped tones, "was that you are and always have been the antithesis of the imperial powers which subjugated my whole continent for the better part of eighteen decades. That you weren't cowards like your predecessors. I only listened because our Hellenian friends, who have actually earned my trust, assured me of the same. This"—he gestured to Daniel with a calloused hand, and Daniel's lip curled at how much the gesture reminded him of Cartwright—"is the enemy standing proud within your walls. You've deceived us all. No. I wanted to be your friend, to return the help you've given and more, but no. I won't accept this. Any agreements are off."

"Wait," Dawn said, her deep-gold aura rippling around her with distress. "Please, I promise. I can prove you can trust us. I promise, just stay one hour. I'll explain everything."

In the tense silence that followed, the hair on the back of Daniel's neck prickled. He kept his eyes, like Dawn's, locked on Xiao Sheng, but he felt a hundred more watching him with a range of emotions that made his aura turn cold against his skin. Beside him, Anthony inched away from him, and Daniel double-blinked to deactivate his auric vision so he wouldn't have to see how the other man's navy-blue aura fractured with fear and unease any longer.

"Fine," Xiao Sheng said with the slightest hint of smugness, jerking a thumb in Daniel's direction. "But not if he stays."

Dawn nodded quickly, and Daniel signaled his intent to come with her without fuss when she hustled past him with a meaningful nod, brushing the arm of his shirt.

She waited until they were well out of sight on the path to the little-used front gates of the compound before stopping and turning to him. Taking several shallow, audible breaths, her dark eyes searched his before she shook her head. "You understand, right? This alliance, all the others we're working on..."

"Aye, of course." Daniel pursed his lips, dropped his chin, and folded his hands in front of him as he soothed his aura.

"We need all the help we can get," Dawn added anyway. "I can convince them all in time, but right now, we need their trust. Minerva help me. We just need a start..." Dawn's voice trailed off into a tight whisper. "We know the reputation you had to build to rise through the ranks of the patrician order. We know how much you dedicated and sacrificed to sell that ruse. And Dan, you know how well it worked." She smiled half-heartedly, and Daniel returned it with the same lack of effort. "Just for now, please, let us handle things from here. I'll let you know if there's something discreet that needs doing, but for now—I'm sorry Dan, but please stay away. Your presence isn't worth losing an ally like Xiao Sheng over."

Daniel's chest was tight, and his Adam's apple bobbed as he tried to respond. When he did, it was a croak. "Sure. Fine. I understand."

"Thank you," Dawn said, with no evident change in her demeanor. "To that end, I think we should start using code names. I can't have people balking when I mention your name. So, from here on, when needed, your code-name is *The Doctor*, and Angie's is *The Locksmith*, okay?"

It was anything but okay. Daniel's tongue worked against his teeth, wanting to argue that he'd never been a doctor. That he'd outright rejected the term from his army medic days in deference to his best friend, who'd earned it, but he bit back the words.

With a curt nod. Dawn Voyaged away back to the center of her compound, leaving Daniel alone between the last row of tenement houses in the camp.

One finger at a time, Daniel pulled off his leather gloves, fighting the urge to scrub the tainted residue of his own untouchable curse from his skin. Then again, what else did he have to do?

CHAPTER FIVE

Angie slouched in the stiff wooden chair, resisting the urge to prop her dusty boots on the pristine hospital blanket. The man in the bed before her lay still and silent. A dozen other coma patients shared the large room, illuminated by the fluorescent lights overhead and the large windows at the far end, but Angie was only interested in the one nearest the door leading out into the bustling hallway.

"Which one were you?" she mused, worrying her lip with her teeth and frowning. She replayed the fight over and over in her mind. Little by little, she worked through the fragmented memories from over three years ago until she felt they all fit together.

The first mugger who'd attacked her under that pink gas station awning as she and Daniel were making their way from Portland to Salt Lake had been the smallest of the three. He'd hung back when Angie had taken the crowbar he'd been wielding, but attacked her again with fists the moment he thought she was distracted by his companions. Angie swallowed as she recalled the way she'd swung his own weapon into his head, dropping him on the spot. For a breath, her heart kicked up, but she soothed it. She'd only been acting in defense. The person she was now had done worse—survived worse. Remembering that shouldn't bother her...

She remembered the largest mugger most clearly. He'd reminded her of her abuser, large and blond, and he'd been the last man standing. As best as Angie could remember, her last blow had been to his kidneys, while Daniel's Air aura had saved them both from choking on her smoke. He had fallen to his knees, coughing up blood, and the man before her certainly wasn't him.

Angie leaned forward, scrutinizing the placid, nondescript face before her. That only left the man who'd brought a gun but never fired it. Angie pressed her mind back. As hard as she tried to remember how this middle-aged man—now thinner and paler from years spent in this hospital—might have fallen to his current state at her hand, she couldn't account for it.

The door to the ward opened, admitting a burst of noise from the hallway along with a harried-looking nurse. "You getting on okay?" he asked, closing the door without glancing at Angie as he scanned the man and his monitors before looking over the others in the room.

"How did he end up in a coma?" Angie asked.

The nurse narrowed his eyes. "How did you say you knew this patient?"

Angie shrugged. "I was there when he was injured. At least, I think it was the same incident that landed him here." She did her best to look worried and gentle, glad the plebeian nurse couldn't read the dark twisting clouds of her smoky aura. "Another local told me what happened to him when I was forced back by the resettlement laws," she lied, adding, "I thought his worst injury from the fight was a bad blow to the nads. How'd he end up like this?"

Her explanation seemed to satisfy the nurse, who already had one hand on the doorknob. "Ah. Well, I only know what their charts say, but he sustained a diffuse axonal injury three years ago last March. If he was knocked down or fell and hit his head on a hard surface, that's a common cause. It's not always immediately apparent, so he could have succumbed to the coma hours or days later. Does that answer your question?"

Angie nodded with a polite smile, and the nurse disappeared with a soft click of the door. Angie tried to remember if she saw the man crack his head on the stained concrete of the gas station pad after she'd swung the crowbar into his crotch at full force, but she'd turned away almost immediately to deal with the more imminent threat.

Sighing and slouching back into her chair, her memories jumped ahead. The fact that Milton had told her of her muggers' fates and then erased her memories of him doing so unsettled her. She replayed the brief encounter in the cavernous hall of half-world keys the first time Milton Cartwright had shown it to them, recalling how he'd attempted to blackmail her with the revelation. She could rationalize him telling her, but why take it back with his magic as she left?

Angie scrunched her face and squirmed. She should have asked Daniel to meet up and check her mind for any more lingering magic from the dead Councilor after Garrett mentioned the muggers to her and the spell over the memory broke. The fact that Milton had told Garrett at all—let alone shown him the man before her—still didn't add up.

"I suppose I'll never know," she said when she eventually roused herself from her uncomfortable contemplations. She laid a hand briefly on the ankle of the prone patient, compelled by some lingering sense of responsibility and propriety. "May Asclepius watch over you."

As Angie turned to leave and reached for the door, she was so engrossed in her own past that she didn't register the latticework of bright-pink magical threads that faded into sight across the threshold until the latch refused to turn. The moment she did, her adrenaline spiked with a plume of fearful, sulfurous smoke. She tried to snatch her hand back, but it wouldn't move.

Angie attempted to take stock of her surroundings as her senses sharpened and her heart became loud in her ears, but she realized with a sinking swoop that she couldn't move. Her eyes widened, nostrils flaring, and she fought to stay focused through the panic swiftly falling over her.

Angie's breathing became labored, and it took her two more breaths to realize that it wasn't just her panic. The air was being sucked from the room. She watched in horror, unable to turn away, as tendrils of fuchsia magic seeped from the latticework surrounding the room to the edges of her peripheral vision through the doorknob she grasped. All around her, monitors began beeping urgently as their charges' vitals spiraled, but Angie barely noticed.

She screamed through lips she couldn't open as they sunk into her hand. Gasping for breath through her nose, she watched the tendrils sink beneath her skin, making her veins visible as a spreading pink web slowly climbed its way through them up her wrist and forearm. It seared like pure alcohol on a fresh wound with every millimeter it traveled.

Angie tried to Voyage away, but the magic didn't even think about clicking into place. She didn't doubt that the magic trapping her—freezing her and slowly worming its burning way toward her heart, making her sweat as it stole her air—was to blame. *Air...* The thought rang a bell in Angie's mind, and she scrambled to catch the spark of hope it offered before it slipped beneath her panic and pain. Removing her air was overkill, even by Milton's standards. *Air, what feeds my flames...*

A single tear fell from Angie's bulging eyes as she sucked down a pathetic, emptying breath, hyperventilating against the sensation. When she released it with another muffled scream, full of pain and terror, she flared her magic as hard as she could against the trap and poison overwhelming her.

The faint flicker of flames that flared briefly before falling back to smoke was a disappointment. Angie felt herself growing weak, the burning poison in her veins clawing its way through her shoulder. She was suffocating, helpless, utterly controlled and trapped, and as her vision began to fade, her last thought was to curse the lingering magic of the dead Transvaalian bastard with every scrap of rage she'd ever possessed.

She was shocked back into awareness when cold water drenched her from behind. She jerked, rattling the door she was still holding onto.

"Oh my Gods! Fire!" a muffled voice shouted from the hallway, and Angie blearily saw the same nurse from before grab an empty wheelchair, heft it, and chuck it straight through the glass window into the ward.

In the second the glass shattered, air rushed back into the room, and with the first breath of relief, Angie's Fire aura bloomed into an inferno. More calls of "Fire!" barely registered as the hallway became a mass of patients and doctors rushing to clear the area.

The magic holding Angie faltered a degree, and Angie opened her mouth, gasping down lungfuls of air, pulling back in her flames as the sprinkler on the ceiling continued dousing her. As she did, she saw the magical infection that made her bones ache with searing pain burn away in small sections along the veins it traveled.

As the restored oxygen hit her blood. Angie didn't waste her first returning burst of strength. She threw her weight back, finally ripping her hand away from the doorknob still soaked with the same orchid-pink magic that had entrapped her. One of her sneakers stayed put when she did, making her stumble, and Angie blinked. It was melted to the floor, and a glance down revealed that her clothes had burned in small patches as well, despite being magically fireproofed.

"What did you do?" Angie ignored the nurse as she turned her full concentration to her arm, pulling in her fire—fueled by anger and fear—so tightly that her skin began to redden. She clenched her teeth against the pain, both ongoing and fresh, as she set her magic against the lingering infection of Milton's until every last drop had been burned away. Only when she was certain the infection was completely removed did she look up and fully assess her surroundings.

Only two nurses lingered in the hallway outside, both shielding their eyes from the sprinklers overhead, and both looked horrified. Angie followed the gaze of one as it dropped and wished she hadn't.

The bed nearest the door was nothing more than a pile of twisted metal and ash. *That's three for three*, Angie thought, and guilt snaked through her, despite knowing that all three of her would-be muggers would have done the same to her for the little she'd owned back then.

"You killed him. That's why you came here. And the fire... You're one of them..."

No sooner had one of the nurses spoken than a burly, armed, and uniformed centurion of some sort stepped into view, raising his pistol at Angie's face. "Get back, get back now! Hands behind your head, step away from the door!"

Angie obeyed, moving slowly and carefully, as she tried to Voyage, or Skip, or beacon Daniel, all failing with almost nonexistent stirs in her aura, dampened and repressed by the woven strands of magic trapping her. "The air..." Angie muttered to herself as the centurion rattled the knob on the door. "The one thing his magic couldn't prevent me from using is my fire, which is why he took the air..." At least breaking the window had somehow restored it.

Angie glanced at the security cameras in the corner of the ward and in the hallway outside, assessing her options. Her magic was out—no question about it. And she'd never learned Daniel's skill for erasing such blunders from the record.

She fixed her attention on the latticework of magic over the door, and when the gun-for-hire succeeded in breaking it down, she saw what she'd hoped to and smiled. If Milton's trap had gone unnoticed for months or longer, waiting for her to step in and spring it, the permissions at the threshold must have been carefully crafted.

The centurion raised his gun once more, framed in the doorway. "Freeze! Don't—" his bullying confidence slipped for a beat, "Don't curse me."

Angie took her opening and launched herself at him. Her gamble worked, and it caught the burly man by surprise, knocking him backward with Angie clinging to the front of his uniform. As she'd hoped, the magic over the doorway tried to close between the plebeian and her, but her closeness allowed her to ride him through before it could.

Before Angie could scramble off the centurion, he had his gun pressed to Angie's temple as she lay prone atop him, and both froze. "Um."

Angie, too, wasn't quite sure what to do with the odd situation, but the sight of the lingering nurses dashing past into the coma ward and the sound of the centurion's gun clicking decided her next action for her.

She closed her eyes, flared her magic around her enough—she hoped—to melt metal without delay, and Voyaged, still horizontal.

Her palms landed on rough asphalt from a six-inch drop as the bulk of the centurion disappeared from beneath her. Her socked toes on one foot protested their lack of protection, and her eyes flew back open. Angie was on her stomach in a parking lot, tucked away between two cars. When she glanced up, the relief that flooded her was overwhelming.

Angie clambered to her feet, her breath finally slowing back to normal, and wiped her hands on the sides of her jeans. Whatever had become of the centurion, he'd deserved it. All bullies like him deserved it. Her time dating a centurion had proved it, and Angie didn't let herself dwell as she hastily unlocked her car and dove into the driver's seat.

When the door clicked locked behind her, she sat for a few long, deep breaths, just clutching the steering wheel and letting her mind catch up with everything that had happened. Her aura of smoke was still dark, and she watched the tangled patterns swirl around her, mentally combing out the denser patches until the smell of cigarettes and exhaust dissipated.

Remembering the security cameras all over the overworked, undersupplied hospital she'd just left, she didn't wait too long before starting the car and driving away. A small group of people gathered at the hospital's loading bay watched her go, pointing her out to others as she drove out of sight. *Damn.* She'd need to alter her license plates the first chance she got.

Blowing through a yellow light and turning past several large casinos as she headed south, Angie rolled up the window she'd left cracked open and tugged her sat phone off its charging mount on the console.

Punching in a number, she held it to her ear and assessed the damage to her clothes as it rang. Repairing clothes and other easy alterations of simple objects was a natural skill of Angie's, and she found herself actually looking forward to putting it to use. The shoes, on the other hand, she'd probably just have to replace since she'd left one behind.

"Hello?" Daniel's voice when he picked up sounded eager, and Angie smiled weakly, guilty that she was probably about to ruin his good mood. *I'd rather improve it*, she thought with a small curl of rosewood smoke in her aura as she heated with the thought of seeing him in person again after several weeks, but reined herself in.

"Hey! It's me. Listen. I—I think I fucked up pretty good."

CHAPTER SIX

D aniel hissed as he cut himself with the sharp kitchen knife he was using to chop onions. Rolling up his sleeves, he washed his hands well in the kitchen sink, wincing when the soap touched the cut.

It was his own fault for being so distracted. He'd felt like a caged animal, pacing around his clear, sleek home in Boston day after day, and it was getting to him. He'd spent the last week trying his best to be patient, but his call with Angie after her fiasco at the plebeian hospital had only heightened his restlessness and frustration.

Everything he tried to stay busy with felt hollow, only adding to his loneliness. And although he didn't want to admit it, his ability to concentrate enough to get his Scrying powers to work properly had been waning steadily in the months since Jonathan's death. And killing Milton. And Angie going off on her own. He couldn't even be helpful with one of his strongest natural skills, and that fact burrowed beneath his skin, heating his aura.

Holding his hand up and shaking it gently to dry it, he checked his phone for the hundredth time that day. Frustrated, he slid it across the counter harder than he intended. Still not one word from Dawn, or from any of her people, in a full week. He pulled a first aid kit from its brackets bolted to the inside of the kitchen cabinet. *Gods* he missed the easy texting of his modern cell, now dormant in the safe below with his other most treasured possessions.

As he carefully disinfected and bandaged the small cut on his left thumb, his mind ran through all the reasons Dawn might want to call on his help but be unable or un-willing to do so. Perhaps she'd lost his sat phone number and didn't want to beacon him for some reason? Perhaps the camp had been overrun, its members imprisoned or dead?

He repacked the med kit and returned it to its brack-et, and as he scraped the blood-flecked onions into the trash, those thoughts won out. He set his Voyaging inten-tion on the bustling camp before he could lose his nerve, pushing against memories of how he'd last departed and his agreement under duress to stay away.

When Daniel landed in a bustling camp green, alive with activity, he felt instantly gratified in his choice to come, but also wished he hadn't. People rushed past him carrying weapons, supplies, injured friends, shouting to others across and within the ever-expanding collection of buildings created to house and protect those dispos-sessed by their magic.

At the center of it all stood Dawn, the golden sun around which a thousand planets whirled. The toll of tracking, organizing, and marshaling so much complex activity was evident in the stress and exhaustion etched in every inch of her stocky body and face.

A frail, white-haired old man Daniel knew in passing, Frank, bustled past with an armful of towels, and Daniel gently caught his arm, pulling him to a stop. "What's going on?" he asked the old man as an injured woman nearby screamed in pain.

Frank's eyes had deep bags of papery skin hanging beneath them, and they wouldn't meet Daniel's gaze, darting back and forth among the throng. "Don't ask me. I only get rumors thirdhand. As best I can tell, that young Seer, Saki, or is it Sakshi, started rattling off imminent adept deaths she was seeing a few hours ago. Since then, we've been flat out. Someone said that loyalists to the empire attempted some sort of coordinated attempt to regain power in several major cities, and a bunch of folks who didn't know their magic had been unlocked were set to die in the conflicts. Ask someone who's been out with one of the squads if you want more."

Daniel released Frank's arm as he dove back into the fray with his towels. He scanned around, his adrenaline well and truly spiked. It only took a few moments for him to sort out the patterns. In the center of the green, skilled and able adepts were clustered in small groups of five to nine, each containing one of Dawn's followers he thought of as her lieutenants.

Some groups centered around a terrified person Daniel didn't recognize, the roiling, untrained clouds of colorful aura around them betraying them as the fresh recruits who had just been saved from a fated death in which their unlocked magic would have caused explosive damage in the moment of release. Others among their peers were being carried off to the outskirts of the green along the fronts of the original bunkhouses by the older, less sturdy, or healing-skilled members of the camp.

As Daniel skimmed over these outliers, he was dismayed to see a good number of adepts he recognized either writhing in pain or out cold. He didn't waste another second. He rolled down his sleeves despite the Pacific summer heat to avoid knocking anyone out on accident, and jogged over, his iffy knee protesting.

He knelt by the woman whose screams he'd shouted over a minute before. With a quick glance of approval from Olivia, who was trying to heal her, Daniel grabbed the back of the woman's neck with his bare hand. She passed out in an instant from the vibration of his skin, and Daniel carefully lowered her head onto a makeshift pillow of someone's folded jacket on the ground.

"Dive in," Olivia said gratefully, her shoulders dropping a centimeter, and Daniel nodded, old habits, skills, and versions of himself settling back into place with little effort. He quickly removed his many gold rings, dropping them into his shirt pocket.

"Medic!" someone cried a hundred yards away.

Daniel stood, summoning and pulling on a pair of rubber gloves over his bandaged thumb as he made his way through the chaos. He might not be able to heal magically, but he could absolutely stabilize a patient and relieve their distress until someone who could heal arrived.

—⊸⊷✦⊶⊷—

It took hours for the activity to die down. By the time it did, Daniel had lost track of how much shrapnel, blood, and tear gas particles he'd banished, or how many medical supplies he'd summoned since he'd arrived. He'd barely had time to think through it all, but he hadn't needed to. Years as a medic in the imperial army had trained him well.

When Daniel stood from one unconscious patient and realized there was no next one to get to, the spell broke. His senses to the outside world dulled a degree as he became aware of his own tense, aching muscles and labored breathing. Shucking off his umpteenth pair of rubber gloves, he banished any missed specks of blood from himself before wiping a tattooed wrist across his glistening face.

The end of the ordeal seemed to be unfolding in waves. Dawn no longer commanded her legions from the center of the green, which had been overtaken by the injured and scared. The recruitment squads, too, seemed to have disbanded, and Daniel searched for faces he'd been sure were among them, finding them in the crowds now attending to the wounded, and the bewildered and traumatized new recruits.

Casting around for where he could be of most use next, he spotted Dawn by the steps of the common house, engaged in what appeared to be a heated argument with several people he didn't recognize. He swiftly made his way over to them.

"I'm not trying to poach jack shit," Dawn spat as he arrived. "We were sent in by our Seer to spare innocent lives, plain and simple. I can't believe you're actually angry at me for saving the lives of adepts in your language instead of thanking me."

One of the young men Dawn was arguing with—Cathayan like Xiao Sheng, by the look of it—opened his mouth to retort, but stopped when he saw Daniel's glare. "Is that—" the man started to ask through the translation magic he was using, but Dawn cut him off.

"No. Look. I don't care what happens to them now. You're more than welcome to go around and count how many Cantonese speakers we grabbed, and take them back to your settlement now, or at any point in the future. I never intended to keep them here, as we're well over capacity with our own people alone. Tell Xiao Sheng the same. I'm his friend, his ally. All I want to do is help, and if he could assume I'm not trying to undermine him at every turn, maybe even more lives could have been saved."

The three men exchanged glances with each other, and when the one who had spoken bowed his head, the other two followed suit. With one last wary glance at Daniel, they scurried off into the crowd, and Dawn turned to Daniel.

"I thought you'd promised to stay away unless I called you."

Daniel huffed in disbelief, his aura teasing up. "Are you serious? You'd have more dead bodies on your hands right now if I hadn't come here today by sheer blind luck. If either of us has the right to get pissy, it's me for not being called in when you very clearly needed exactly the skills I have to offer."

Dawn closed her eyes and bowed her head, and Daniel's anger dissipated in a breath. He'd never seen her look so old and tired before, and guilt thrummed on his insides when she lifted a shaking hand to cover her mouth. "I know. I'm sorry. I just can't risk bad blood with Xiao Sheng over one person being seen in my compound. He's... Well. You know."

Daniel sighed through his nose, reaching out a hand for Dawn's shoulder as she lifted her head to look past him, but he pulled it back. "Listen. You're working yourself way too hard. You have good people around you who want to help carry your burdens. Let them." Dawn nodded almost imperceptibly, her lips tight as she crossed her arms over her denim jacket. "If nothing else, you really need to stop pouring your time, energy, and resources into people like Xiao Sheng. I mean, come on. He's a volatile bully."

"What the fuck would you know about alliances and diplomacy?" Dawn snapped back, her lip curling. "You're on no one's side but your own. You proved that last month when you killed your tormentor in a spectacle just because you could, and no one's going to forget that anytime soon. That's exactly why your presence here puts everyone who wants to trust me on edge."

Daniel clenched his jaw against arguing back, raising his palms in surrender. "All I was trying to say is that you have tons of people in your corner who are genuinely good and kind, so I don't know why you'd bother trying to recruit someone like Xiao Sheng. He will never be on your side as much as you're on his." He waited for Dawn to reply, but she stayed silent and unreadable. "Why are you trying so hard to befriend him?"

In the space of a breath, Dawn's whole being crumpled before his eyes. All of her commanding presence, strength, and posture seemed to slip off her like water. "Because I can't fight *everyone*, Daniel!" The words barked out in a sob, and Dawn clamped her hands over her mouth as more tears followed silently, her glittering eyes locked on Daniel. "Not now, not *everyone*." The words slipped out between her shaking fingers, and Daniel dropped his gaze to his shoes. "At some point, something I do has to matter, has to turn someone to a better path like *he* would have wanted, right?"

Daniel didn't have to ask who she meant. He only wished he knew what perfect, kind, uncomfortably observant thing Jonathan would have said in that moment to offer encouragement and comfort. But nothing came.

Anthony appeared at Dawn's side, wrapping an arm around her, and she turned into him, burying her face into his shoulder as her cries gained volume. Several people nearby looked up, all with pity, and Anthony called out to Olivia. She was there in a flash, pulling Dawn into her arms and giving Daniel a concerned, questioning look.

All Daniel felt in that moment was a yawning chasm between his grief and Dawn's, and when he spoke, he felt no resistance or hesitation. "I'm sorry. I won't come back. I know you'll always do what's best for you and yours. I'll stay out of it." Daniel turned away toward the front gates, not wanting his retreat to seem too cowardly, when a scuffle ahead made him slow.

A brown-haired woman was wrangling two small, squalling children along, a large pack on her back and a suitcase left on the wood-chip path just behind her.

"Hannah," Daniel breathed, recognizing Jonathan's widow, daughter, and son, feeling the world tilt beneath him.

He let himself get shuffled aside as people rushed forward to greet them, not wanting to be seen. Hannah had made her feelings toward him quite clear the last time they'd met. The Hellenes couple, Nikolaos and Demitria, elbowed their way to the front of the crowd, soothing the two children who were clearly familiar and comfortable with them as Hannah loudly asked what all the fuss in camp was about.

"We've got this, it's alright," Mahina said close behind Daniel, giving him an understanding look and a gentle nudge on his covered elbow. "I know the history there. Trust that we'll take good care of them."

He nodded gratefully, skirting around the edge of the crowd gathered to fold the returning family in with the other new arrivals waiting to be settled into the already overcrowded compound.

As he passed, he caught fragments of Hannah's voice. "That doesn't sound too bad... No, he kicked us out! I wouldn't stay with a close-minded sinner like him anyway... Oh no, those are just bruises, they're okay. He just fell..." He couldn't bring himself to process any of it, even as he caught a glimpse of the little boy's black eye.

When he reached the gate, he stopped just shy of the glowing, layered, magic shield that spanned the gap, unwilling to leave. The world inside that shield was the only purpose he had to hold onto. And yet, the thought of leaving for good felt strangely freeing.

The longer he stood there, breathing in the scent of pine and listening to the rustling needles that sounded almost like the ocean a few miles away, the more he knew it was time.

When his Voyaging magic deposited Daniel on the shaded, ocean cliff top, it took him a good minute to open his eyes. When he did, the white marble headstone stood out in stark contrast against the carpet of russet redwood needles. He closed his eyes tightly again as twin tears rolled down his cheeks into his short beard. Fighting the raw emotion that clawed its way through his being, Daniel walked up to the marker, sinking down and placing a trembling hand on it for the first time since the memorial service at which it had been erected.

Narrowing his attention to the smooth, cool surface of the stone and the crash of the waves against rock far below, Daniel spoke to the name carved into the stone as if it were the man himself.

"Perhaps it really is for the best. Maybe it's time I let go of... all that." Voicing that fact aloud ripped the last of Daniel's control from his grasp. He leaned against the stone, burying his face in his arms as his unrestrained Air aura lashed into a gale around him, whipping the trees into a roar and sending pine needles slicing through the air, nicking every inch of Daniel's exposed skin. He barely noticed, and his grief consumed him, bellowing in its vastness.

"I don't know what to do or where to go. The world is darker without you, and I can't see my way forward without your light."

CHAPTER SEVEN

"**I** wish I could tell him," Angie said to the ghost of Jonathan sitting beside her in her car as she tucked away the empty plastic bag from the last of her food. She turned on her blinker and pulled back onto the freeway from the shoulder, peering ahead at the sign counting down the miles to Las Vegas.

"I know. I'm sorry. But..." Jonathan trailed off, dropping his translucent, ice-blue eyes to the ghostly hands in his lap. "I'm not ready to handle that reunion. And I doubt Dan is, either."

As with every time Angie had asked him the same, she didn't know how to reply. She was constantly trying to figure out how much he remembered—or didn't—but he always shied away when she pressed. Her friend absently picked at the cuff of the rich-blue suit jacket his memory had been immortalized wearing, and Angie thought back to the vibrant aura of magic in a matching shade he'd had while living.

"Can you do magic in that form?" she asked, as much to fill the silence as anything. She double-blinked into the auric spectrum and glanced sidelong at him when he didn't respond right away, finding him carefully studying his palms.

"No, not in this form. But if things change, if, someday, I'm no longer bound to the coin..." His tan, weathered face may have paled as he trailed off and tucked his hands beneath his arms, but Angie couldn't be sure as the blurred flashes of clouds, hills, and telephone poles passed through his image from behind as they picked up speed. "How are you doing today around everything that happened at the hospital?"

Angie didn't address the blatant move to change the topic, frowning. "Fine."

"Really?"

She sighed. "Yeah, it's just..." Angie searched within herself for the words to describe the vague doubts and sense of failure that had been trailing her like less welcome ghosts for the last five days, eventually giving up. "I'm fine. Just still sorting myself out a little after... everything."

Angie cringed and eased off the gas when the car she had just blown past honked at her. "Sorry," she mumbled to the van shrinking in her rearview and hitched a breath, pulling herself out of the daydreaming that had left her driving recklessly on autopilot along the unchanging miles of highway. She missed having music for her long desert drives, but the radio was her only option, and the only station left—the imperial broadcast—had only been playing Seth Laufey's shitty religious cult music since he'd taken it over after the solstice a month ago.

She set her cruise control, not worrying about speed traps since local centurions had abandoned their imperial roles in favor of whoever would pay, and steered with her knee while taking a swig of water. Jonathan's ghost was once more dormant in the heavy copper sigil coin in the pocket of her sundress, and Angie begrudgingly turned her purposeful attention back to the road.

The moment she did, a misty, blooming vine of Jasper's dusty-pink magic caught her attention where it was wrapped around the legs of a large green sign ahead. She slowed further as she neared it, the same vehicle she'd passed a minute before honking once more as it sped past. Several tendrils of magic floated away against the wind, drifting down the freeway in the direction she was going. One led on as far as she could see, and Angie sped back up with a dark, triumphant grin.

She'd found what she was looking for. She had her path to Eden.

Angie double-parked her car across from Club Venus X in Las Vegas just after sunset, glancing at the clock on the dashboard before hurriedly turning it off and getting out. The tendrils of Jasper's magic were fading with the light, but they had left the roads for the first time in the hours Angie had chased them, so she knew she must be close to her quarry.

The desert night was hot and dry when she stepped out into it, a distant wildfire and nearby smokers staining the early dusk air with an acrid bite. Angie locked the car behind her and crossed the street, wishing she'd started her day out in jeans, but she'd had to drive flat out for three hours to keep up with the fading trail of magic leading her ahead, and couldn't risk a moment of wasted time.

As she rounded the front corner of the club, she nearly tripped over a man lying prone, his bloodied face pressed into the curb. Angie only paused for a beat before sprinting the remaining length of the building and whipping around the back corner, coming to a stop as a faint scream went up like a beacon behind the building.

Ahead of her, a small dome of dusty, pastel-pink magic surrounded an obscured figure hunched before a tall pile of black plastic trash bags, and Angie grinned, triumph coursing through her as cool relief. Angie broke into a sprint again, bringing up her flames, which held strong, and slammed into the shields directly ahead.

They buckled in an instant, and another shriek of pain rent the air. Angie readied a ball of fire in her palm, ready to attack the former Councilor if need be, to convince them to come with her. But as she raised it, Jasper Rose turned, their long, thick curls half-hiding their strained expression, and Angie saw the woman they were bent over just as the stranger whimpered, her eyes screwed shut.

"Get off her," Angie yelled, horrified, and she dropped her magic to yank the plump Councilor off the woman, afraid that any magic she hurled might hurt both.

"You idiot," Jasper snapped as Angie pulled them to their feet struggling against her grip, and only when the woman lying on the trash bags screamed at full volume did Angie see the blood on Jasper's hands, the wounds on the woman's temple and stomach, and her bright, chaotic aura of an unlocked but untrained adept. "I'm not hurting her, I'm healing and awakening her," Jasper hissed, their New Zealand accent twisting the words to Angie's ears. They pulled their arm from Angie's grasp, which had slackened with shock. "Give me light. Use your flames to help. How the hell did you find me?"

"You left markers and a trail," Angie replied, summoning a handful of flames to hold over the wounded woman. Angie dropped down beside Jasper as the former Councilor bent over the screaming woman and resumed what Angie now plainly saw was healing magic. Heartpine smoke expanded from her aura, tinged with worried cedar, and she wished she'd gotten good enough at magical healing to be of help. "I assumed you wanted to be found."

Jasper's lips pursed, shifting to make better use of the light from Angie's flames. "Those markers weren't meant for you." They glanced up at Angie unhappily, then past her, before returning their attention to their work.

"So, what happened?" Angie asked, searching for somewhere to look other than the gore and blood before her.

"Some bastard attacked her," Jasper explained, and seemed to hold back from saying more. "I believe he thought she was one of the performers." They jerked their head toward the strip club beside them. "And they didn't like it when she set him straight." Angie opened her mouth to ask more, but Jasper anticipated. "I came here to contact and awaken them. I was told their fated death wasn't until next week, but the predictions are getting sketchier." They finally turned their attention to her and away from their patient as their dusty-rose magic sank into the worst of the wounds, healing and calming the brand-new adept. "I'm not your enemy, Angie, if that's why you're chasing me. We might not see eye-to-eye, but I'm not your enemy."

Angie scowled, hiding how uncertain and confused she suddenly felt. "I'll decide that, thank you. We—I need answers from you, and when you're done here, you're still coming with me. You know about Eden, about who went there, and where the key went, and—"

"I'm not what you think," Jasper interrupted, their voice disconcertingly gentle. "And we can't leave her here to fend for herself."

Angie screwed her face up, stabilizing the flames she was holding with a thought when they flickered. They were right. With the way the plebeian world was reacting to magic as they became aware of it, leaving a freshly awakened adept with no training, guidance, or protection was a death sentence. That didn't mean she trusted Jasper, or could even let go of the long-held drive of pursuit and the triumph of finally having caught up to the other patrician. "Prove it. Why did you come looking for a fresh recruit?"

Jasper sighed as the injured woman's body slumped, falling unconscious as her wounds healed under Jasper's magic. "I, of all people, know what it feels like to be othered, to be mistreated. My bloodline is little else. I'd never leave someone to suffer, not when I could save them. I suspect you think ill of me for the titles I once held, but I assure you—I only played my part in the Council to pursue my own goals, just like Fawl did."

"And Cartwright," Angie sneered.

They shook their head of gray-brown curls. "Perhaps."

"What goals, then?"

Jasper took a deep breath, sitting up and finally removing their hands from the injured woman, wiping them clean on the hem of the long linen shirt they wore. "These days? To make sure that power falls to those responsible enough to control it. To stop the world from splintering further, and to instead forge new alliances, however unorthodox, to move our world forward toward restored order."

Angie considered for a long moment before letting go of her fistful of fire. Jerking her chin toward the alleyway she'd come down, she asked, "Did you kill that man?"

Jasper stood and Angie followed suit, braced for any sign that the patrician intended to flee. "Yes. When he attacked her." They gestured at the unconscious woman. "Her magic flared when he grabbed and kissed her, and he saw. Even as an inept. That's when he began beating her, and when I couldn't stand him down without reveal-ing myself, I took the necessary measures."

Angie nodded, but as she looked at the person standing mere inches from her, she still couldn't bring herself to trust them. Mentally shaking herself, Angie set her mind on the basement of Daniel's New York mansion, where he'd prepared a specially shielded room that they'd carefully built for this exact moment. All she'd have to do was Voyage in with Jasper, and Daniel's exceptional shield would keep them from leaving until they'd gotten the answers they needed.

"We'll see," Angie replied as she grabbed Jasper's arm and tried to Voyage. The magic failed, and Jasper's face twisted with contempt. Before Angie could try anything else to keep her quarry from getting away yet again, the older, nonbinary adept Voyaged away on their own and Angie's fingers closed on empty air.

"Fuck!" Angie whirled on the spot, mentally searching for a beacon to follow she knew wouldn't be there. She'd finally caught up with Jasper Rose after nearly a month of searching, and they'd slipped from her fingers. "Next time," Angie promised the space where Jasper had stood a moment before. "So help me."

Angie glanced down at the unconscious—but no longer injured—woman on the pile of trash bags as she turned away, but stopped when her chest tightened. She was older than Angie, with thin black hair and rosy, light-brown skin. She was dressed in the modest skirt and shapeless blouse of a lesser temple priestess, and Angie huffed. Of course the dead man had thought she was a stripper in religious costume. No one dressed like that was ever supposed to leave their temples, which, these days, were few and far between. Darkness and drunkenness must have hidden the modesty that was clear to Angie.

Remembering that Jasper's guiding markers had been intended for someone else, Angie decided not to wait and find out who. She wanted to go back to her car and at least park it somewhere safe for the night, but her conscience stopped her, and her chest eased. She'd never admit it, but the woman's thin black hair reminded Angie of her sister's. Kneeling beside the woman, Angie gently tapped her cheeks as the wail of a centurion siren drew nearer in the distance. "Hey, wake up, please. We should go somewhere safe."

The woman's eyes fluttered open, but when she saw Angie, her face warped with terror. "Get away from me," she shrieked, and Angie tumbled back as a blast of frigid, sky-blue magic slammed into her. *Another Air aura like Daniel?* The woman was scrambling back over the trash bags as Angie righted herself. Angie winced as the other woman stood and clutched her side, and the color drained from her face. "Oh..." was all she managed before she passed back out, and Angie caught her just before she hit the ground.

⸺❖⸺

After depositing the fresh adept in her car safely parked behind a factory a few blocks away, Angie tried to Voyage to Dawn's compound, but found herself deposited outside the multicolored shields. She frowned, offended. Hospitals were out of the question, as was trying to heal the woman's reopened wound on her own, and Daniel wasn't accepting her calls or beacons, leaving only Dawn's compound as an option for seeking a healer and someone to take the new recruit under their wing.

Angie pushed at the shield with her hand, but it was as solid and smooth as stone. She tried pushing her magic against it, too, but it made no difference. "Hey!" she shouted as loud as she could, the sound reverberating off the sheet metal bunk house nearest. "Why have I been locked out? Where's Dawn?"

Several dozen people peered at her from windows, some then disappearing as they jogged off or hustled to herd others out of sight. Angie knew a few would be going to get someone to fix the issue, and tapped her foot impatiently, wondering why she'd been blocked by the shields Daniel himself had helped set up, either accidentally or intentionally.

When a familiar face came into view, heading for the front gate, Angie's hopes dropped. The tall, skinny, brown-haired woman Angie recognized as Hannah Crowther, Jonathan's wife, wore a scowl as she approached, stopping a full hundred feet from the gate where Angie stood.

"Go away. You're not welcome here anymore, and if you don't leave, someone will make you."

Angie gaped, the smell of hot metal and burned hair swelling around her. "What? Says who?" In the space of two sentences, her confident ability to deal with the crisis that had landed on her shattered, and her shoulders tensed by degrees as her mind began spinning over what on earth she was supposed to do next.

"Me," Hannah replied, lifting her nose in the air, but dropped it again with a touch of color in her cheeks when Angie looked her up and down with a raised brow. "And Dawn."

"Let me talk to her."

"Hardly," Hannah responded, clearly trying and failing to give Angie the same withering assessment she'd just been on the receiving end of. "She's rarely here and has more important things to deal with when she is. Casey Easton has been put in charge of this camp and the Hawaii outpost, and the order stands through him as well."

Hurt and betrayal joined the mix of emotions spiraling through Angie's core and dark, thick aura, and she took a step back. "What? No. He'd never ban me like this. If I could just talk to him—"

"He said himself we can't trust you," Hannah cut in, and the rest of Angie's objections died on her tongue. "There's also the fact that we're full up. We literally don't have room for even one more adept to join the compound, least of all someone like you who'd be more trouble than they're worth." Hannah's light-red aura fluctuated around her in self-satisfied ripples, and only then did Angie notice the change in it since she'd last seen it.

"Your magic was awakened?" she asked incredulously, remembering how fervently Jonathan had argued in favor of keeping his wife's powers hidden from her.

Hannah grinned, and Angie found the odd spark buried deep in her eyes when she did so unnerving. "Indeed. I have claimed my divine blessing from my One True God. And I will make sure my children do the same, despite that bastard's attempts to keep us from what was ours by right. Jonathan never was a true believer." She must have seen the disgust on Angie's face at hearing her speak of her late husband in such terms, and her expression hardened. "Don't give me that look. A whore like you is the last person with any right to judge me."

"Excuse me?" Angie started, but Hannah's next words sent her reeling.

"I know you were close with him. Or more." She pursed her lips, tilting her head slightly. "You wanted him, didn't you? You were inappropriate together. I know there was nothing *pure* between the two of you."

Disgust and defensiveness rose in Angie like lava, but doubt doused it just as fast. *Do I really know? There must have been something that made her believe that. No, surely... I'd have known if...* She gaped, reaching for the copper coin in her pocket, but stopped short as Hannah's parting words barely registered, her mind reeling and heart racing.

"Get lost, Forester. Crawl back to the conference where the three of you hid from common decency every year if you really need someone to take you in. But you'll never be welcome here again."

As Angie turned away to Voyage back to her car, where a bleeding, scared new adept waited for her, alone in the world, she didn't know what other choice she had.

CHAPTER EIGHT

Daniel summoned his mail from the end of the drive the moment he returned to his Boston home. Despite the blank, fuzzy numbness that owned him after three long hours sobbing at the clifftop grave, when he unfolded his rectangular reading glasses onto his sharp nose and read the single letter, his stomach made a half-hearted attempt to flip.

There was no return address, no name signed at the bottom, and the plainly typed message was simple.

The empire's TV network is back up, with magical help. The emperor is looping a public announcement every fifteen minutes, starting at the top of each hour. You should watch.

Daniel glanced at the gold watch he always wore, the wisp of Angie's silver magic bound into it nearly invisible. Ten minutes to nine. Daniel examined the letter closely, finding nothing more, in or out of the magical spectrum.

When he tossed it into the wastepaper basket in the living room, his stomach completed its acrobatics. Littered beneath it were the dozens of letters he'd been receiving every day without fail from his most recent recruit since the day they'd last spoken. They ranged from threats, to pleading to meet up, to long, rambling outpourings of Seth's admiration and devotion, which made Daniel's skin crawl. The most recent had arrived five days before, and Daniel shuddered at his lack of attention. If he'd noticed the break in pattern before opening the mysterious letter, he would have been much more cautious in doing so.

To kill the ten minutes before the next imperial broadcast was scheduled to begin, Daniel confirmed that the large flat-screen TV in his living room was still connected and in working order despite its very rare use, and he shuffled into the kitchen, too numb to feel the dread at what awaited him that he'd feel under normal circumstances.

As he brewed himself a cup of tea and dropped some chocolate digestives onto a plate to satisfy his sweet tooth, what little emotions were left in him swirled instead around his departure from Dawn's compound. He regretted having pushed. He'd felt purposeful, needed, and more deserving of his new code name, The Doctor, than perhaps ever before, but then he'd gone and pushed the sore spot between him and his oldest remaining friend. And now he was certain he'd not be going back. No one trusted him with or to do anything, and he was done trying to convince them otherwise.

The empty, yawning space his new lack of purpose and direction over the last months echoed through him. It turned what had been a slow, steady drip of discontent and yearning for something more into a wave that had crashed over him at his departure and now held him down, suffocating.

Daniel grabbed five sugar cubes from the jar on the counter in his immaculate kitchen and moved his sorry excuse for a supper to the end table beside the white leather couch.

With neither excitement nor apprehension, Daniel settled himself and checked his watch once more through eyes swollen from three hours spent crying. With a heavy sigh, he used the remote to click on the television. For a few seconds, only static greeted him, and he wondered if his mysterious informant had been wrong.

With a pop, the static clicked over to a clear image Daniel had seen on many such broadcasts over the last decade. The emperor sat before the familiar backdrop of his palace quarters in Rome, a carefully contrived shadow across his deep-set eyes and a large microphone hiding what Daniel had always assumed must be a weak or unsightly chin, given that it was never seen.

Of far more interest to Daniel were the two figures standing respectfully behind the emperor, smiling confidently over his shoulders. Seth Laufey was sharply dressed in a conservative charcoal suit, black shirt, and white tie.

Marissa Hayward, his first recruit many years before, was his counterpart in an imperial-purple pants suit. Daniel hadn't forgotten that she'd been made the minister of communications by the patrician powers just before they fell, but seeing her on camera, showing her position off, did seem strange. He'd preferred just vaguely knowing she was the author behind the radio announcements that had been broadcasting since shortly after the solstice.

As the emperor began his speech, Daniel marked the way the raven-haired beauty seemed far more interested in stealing glances at the red-haired man standing with her than she did in what the leader of the empire had to say.

"Greetings to the globe. All my loyal subjects. I hail and salute you." Daniel snorted, then swallowed when the emperor seemed to respond to him. "To those who do not hear yourselves greeted in those words, I say this. The empire has not fallen. Our diseased and rotting limbs have been amputated to save the heart, the brain of our eternal regime. I assure you all, of any ilk, that the empire still holds ultimate power, and is no less capable of wielding it than we were the last time we cleaned and reabsorbed the many lands of this globe under one glorious rule. We shall do so again. Have no doubt. History shall repeat itself, as it always does, and Rome shall do so for a third and final time." Daniel nibbled a biscuit, unsurprised by anything so far.

"While you may all have been caught unaware, may have told yourselves and each other that you could not have seen the events of June twenty-first coming, I assure you the empire did, and has been strategically preparing for decades. We knew that as the last generation of brave soldiers and cowardly losers who remembered the Great Unification a century ago died away, the living memory of why the empire triumphed would die with them. The world would forget the might we brought to bear against New York, Los Angeles, Dover, Shanghai, Delhi, and other strategic locations to end the Great Unification. But we haven't. Nor have we been idle. We have grown. We have learned. And the weapons we will use in the next Great Reunification will be terrible. One bomb will wipe an entire city from existence, and the reclamation will be swift and decisive."

Daniel drew a whistling breath in through his nose. In all the drama and stress around Dawn and Jonathan, he'd nearly forgotten about the very real, imminent, and devastating threat of the nuclear bombs the empire had stockpiled across the globe. He reached for his old cell to jot down a note for himself to follow up on in the morning, hissing out a breath of frustration when he remembered he no longer used it.

"To that end," the emperor droned on, "I have been hard at work preparing my forces, and making sure that the empire is not only empowered, but well-governed. In efforts to revitalize our decadent and neglected might, I've sought out the best and brightest to serve at my side. As we progress, I will make more of these ministers and generals known to you. But for today, there is one that cannot wait. Seth Laughy has been appointed as my minister of information."

Daniel's aura buffeted out from him in cold, damp layers, and he placed a hand over his tea to prevent spilling it as the broadcast finally riveted his attention.

"He's already proven himself to me as a loyal and passionate minister. A spark of light for the faithful on our path forward together, and a wrath of darkness to any who defy the empire. I call on all my loyal citizens to follow his lead in all things. Lend solace and power to those fighting to regain and rebuild the empire, and give no rest, no quarter to those who make weak attempts at claiming scraps of our rightful power for themselves or support the traitors who do. Moving forward, I must devote myself without rest to leading and guiding this mighty empire of ours, and so, dear people, I must step back from the public eye. From this day forward, my most trusted minister, Seth Laufey, will speak as my own tongue and act as my own hand. So, I bid you farewell to attend matters of state, and I entreat the Gods to favor you as they favor and endorse the empire." Canned applause slowly faded up as the emperor waved, then back down as the image faded out.

The scene on the television changed to a closeup of Seth, now centered as the emperor had been before an impressive state backdrop, his red hair at odds with the imperial purple.

Daniel spared a thought to wonder which clip had been recorded first and noted that the symbols Seth stood before—a bundle of sticks crossed by two axes and bedecked by laurels—had been out of fashion since the end of the Unification. He didn't care to guess at what the emperor was trying to signal by choosing them.

"I'm honored. I thank the emperor for putting his faith in me, and I thank you, the people, for the same, which

I'm sure will come in time. I will do my duty by this sacred office to the extreme, and do so solemnly. We live in uncertain times, and many have suffered in the last few years from the random, unpredictable terror attacks that have spread across the globe since the solstice. We must stay vigilant. Given the nature of these explosions, which largely happen in crowded places in moments of high stress, we must be prepared for them in every moment we are fighting to restore law and order. Do not trust it will not be your neighbor whose death causes your own in a week, or a month, or a year. Those who wished to destroy the peace and order of the empire won't rest until the last of us who value justice, responsibility, and unity are dead."

Daniel shook his head, disgusted. People dying at their fated times, their unlocked but not yet awakened magic exploding out from them in the moment of release, wasn't terrorism. He couldn't deny that it was deadly and destructive, but hearing Seth use it so deftly to stir up fear and anger in a world already reeling from the slow but steady exposure of magic made Daniel's blood run cold.

"I call on all of you already acting as the empire's spies across the globe to continue in your right and patriotic duties. I commend you all. I also call upon you to recruit more and more to our cause, until there is nothing we do not know and nothing we cannot reach. In this way, it's you, not I, who will reunite all people under one flag, one law, one order. So go, my people. My friends. My trusted compatriots. Let me be the prophesied angel of chaos and flame against our enemies through you all, and let the glory of the empire arise stronger than ever through the trials and tests of the days to come."

More recorded applause concluded the speech, and the image changed again to one thanking the heroic loyalists of the empire as one of Seth's overly energetic cult songs Daniel had become familiar with during his sponsorship started playing over it, presumably to kill time until the broadcast repeated.

Daniel turned off the TV, letting the silence sing in his ears for a long moment as he pulled his dim, yellow aura back under control. Once gusts of wind no longer brushed his hair and face, he stood and took his tea with him to the piano by the window.

An obsidian mirror was propped against it, resting on the key lid, and Daniel sat before it. He sipped his sweet tea and pressed his hands flat before him, wincing when his cut thumb protested. He tried to calm and focus his mind. It wasn't racing like normal, not after draining himself so much on the clifftop in Oregon, which made him hopeful that after so many failures over the last month, his natural skill might finally work for him again.

It did not.

After half an hour of desperately trying to get the mirror before him to clearly pick up on the questions he posed to it about nuclear bombs, the emperor, and why Seth had ceased his obsessive fan letters, Daniel resigned himself to his exhaustion and stepped away. Cracking his stiff back, Daniel dropped his dishes back in the sink and jumped when his sat phone started buzzing from beneath the toaster at the other end of the counter.

Daniel felt the final straw of the jarring demand for his time, attention, and energy like a kick to the back of his knees. He screwed his eyes shut, bracing against the counter, and stopped time. The instant, silent relief of the magic working easily and effortlessly sent Daniel sliding to the floor, his back pressed against the cabinets, panting as his body tried to cry the tears he'd shed the last of an hour ago.

Some part of him waited to be intruded upon. For Milton Cartwright to come bursting in, spitting and purple with rage. But no such intrusion came, and even his panting ran out as Daniel realized he wished it would. That would mean he mattered. Mean that he still had some role to play in the world. That he had something to do.

As he sat in the still, utter silence of existing outside time, everything slowly settled together through his puffy exhaustion. No one but him was going to give his life meaning. He knew exactly the role of his to play that had always taken him where he wanted to go, helped him do what needed to be done. And the one path he had into the heart of the monster of the empire that refused to finish dying was slipping out of his grasp, or already had five days ago. Nothing was going to give him what he needed. But he could go looking for it, exactly where he now realized he'd always known he would find it.

Daniel stood, restarting time, and turned away from the sat phone, letting it ring out. Dawn had had her chance to include, use, or grieve with him. He was done taking her calls. He turned off the lights as he made his way down the hall past the stairs to his bedroom, bracing against the wall when his knee twinged from everything he'd put it through that eternal day.

Opening the closet, Daniel pulled out the cane Jonathan had long ago bound magic into to allow Daniel to change its appearance at will. He ran a hand along the plain wooden surface, and the instant he gave it a shake—turning it to sleek black lacquer with an intricate gold handle—the phone in the kitchen stopped ringing. Relief washed over Daniel like a sickly-sweet hit of a long-forgotten drug.

He was going to sleep until he couldn't possibly sleep any more, and when he was done, he was going to draw up a battle plan for stepping back into the lion's den.

CHAPTER NINE

"**C**ome on. Pick up, pick up, pick up..." Angie muttered into her ringing sat phone, beaconing Daniel yet again and having no idea if the magical signal for him to Voyage to her was even going through. She leaned against the open door as the line just kept ringing, looking down at the unconscious woman on the back seat of her car. She didn't even know her name.

Angie ground her teeth when it gave the electric buzz indicating that the call wouldn't go through, and she tossed it onto the front seat with a spark of anger in her dark, smoky aura. Angie barely registered it after three years of growing used to the ways her aura of smoke, ash, and flame expressed her emotions, thoughts, and intentions, but something was different this time.

A few of the small orange sparks that overlapped with the new adept's sky-blue Air aura flared as the rest went out, and curiosity stalled Angie's reaction. By the time she realized that the other woman's aura was fanning her flames outside of and beyond her control, they were spreading across Angie's whole aura and scorching the rubber seals of the car door within the sphere.

Angie backed away quickly, glancing over her shoulder to avoid tripping, until her back was pressed against the painted cinderblock wall of the factory she'd parked behind.

She considered Voyaging again, but as she reached for the magic to do so, the flames which had fed on the untrained adept's power dissolved back down to the thin blue-gray smoke of her aura, and Angie released a breath. She cautiously approached the car, closely watching both auras for a reaction, but the incident didn't repeat.

That clinched it. There was no way she could try to take on responsibility for this woman's magic training on her own. Not if their auras were inclined to react badly with each other. Faint memories of Daniel expressing matching concerns when she'd first met him, back when his magic was being repressed to a fraction of its full power and control, flitted across her thoughts.

Maybe going back to the first place she'd ever felt at home with her magic wasn't such a bad idea. Angie sighed, tugging the unconscious priestess to the edge of the car's back seat to hoist her up into a fireman's carry. They had no other options left.

As Angie tried to Voyage to the English Conference site in the Britannian Cotswolds, failed, and tried again, she whispered a silent prayer to Mercury and Vesta for easy travel to whatever home they might find.

—◦✤◦—

The woman woke up just as Angie landed in the cobbled courtyard of the English Patrician Conference site, and the scream that announced it made Angie's ears ring. Angie dropped her from the fireman's carry as gently as she could and backed away with her hands raised.

The sky overhead was only showing the faintest hints of morning, and she glanced up at it through the massive hawthorn tree under which she'd landed, half a planet away from where they'd departed. "Hey, calm down, it's okay. You were attacked, but I've brought you somewhere safe."

The woman didn't scream again, but her eyes remained wary as she very slowly pulled herself to stand. She pressed a hand to her belly, going pale when she undoubtedly felt the cold, slick wetness of blood, and pulled it away immediately to stare at the dash of scarlet that had stained it.

"You were hurt by that man. Do you remember?" The woman nodded. "My—" Angie paused. "My friend, I guess, saved your life. They tried to fix you up, but the wound seems to have opened back up."

Angie heard a shout from inside one of the classroom buildings nearby, and a moment later, a half-dozen adepts she didn't recognize poured out into the courtyard with a wash of yellow light. They all looked sleep-befuddled and alarmed, and two Voyaged away the moment they saw the scene before them.

"We need a healer!" Angie called out to no one in particular. "This is a brand-new recruit, and she's injured."

A third patrician Voyaged away as more began to arrive—magically and by foot—each stopping when they saw who had caused the commotion.

In front of her, the woman she'd brought looked like she was questioning her entire reality, and when someone behind Angie lit the courtyard with evenly diffused violet magic, what little color remained in her complexion drained away. Her sky-blue aura flared, and Angie backed away swiftly, bumping into someone who caught her with warm, bony hands.

Angie turned to see a Senator and former Judge she recognized, Barbara Collins, and almost laughed with relief. "She's an Air aura," she explained as Barbara stepped past her with her palms splayed. "My aura is reacting badly, but she needs help. She's been unconscious for the most part since her awaking, and—"

Barbara raised a hand, silencing Angie. The woman's serious attention was wholly focused on the woman before them, who was beginning to shake. "Hello. My name is Barbara, and I'd like to help you see to that wound, make sure you're safe, and answer any and all questions you may have. Would that be alright?" With a nod from the wounded adept, Barbara smiled, and Angie marveled at how not one strand of her mousy, graying hair was out of place. "Good. What's your name?"

"Lucia," the injured adept replied as Barbara carefully took her hand and steered her to sit on a stone bench in a little alcove against the garden wall. "Maiden Lucia of the Order of Minerva. I—where am I?"

"Get out." A booming voice with a Celtic accent distracted Angie from whatever answer Barbara was giving Lucia, and she turned to find Noah Byrne stalking toward her in a short robe and slippers. The large Celt was glowering behind his bushy beard, the setting moon reflecting off his shaven dome. "Get out, both of you," he repeated, stopping at the edge of the gathered onlookers, and Angie raised her hands in supplication.

"We can't," she said, disappointed to hear the honest way her voice cracked with desperation. "I had nowhere else to take her. Truly. I didn't go looking for a raw adept. I just stumbled across her," she lied, and a pang of guilt plucked at her heart at the thought of abandoning the woman to all these strangers. "She needs help. I'll go, but please, let Lucia—"

"No," Noah barked, but a hand on his arm stopped him, and Angie glanced at the blonde woman beside him. Noah seemed to gather himself, drawing up to his full height. "We can't take in more recruits. We're bursting at the seams, and the few experienced patricians we've got helping to train them are already overworked. And we only have one magical source for resource production now that we no longer have taxes or supply tithes coming into the patrician orders. You, of all people, are the last thing we need," he gestured at the hawthorn tree Angie stood under, "knowing your track record."

Angie swallowed, not looking at the tree she'd burned to ash and regrown during her first conference. "I know I've caused damage in the past. Like I said, I'll go, but please let Lucia stay."

"That hardly compares to causing this whole mess we're now cleaning up," Noah retorted, spreading his arms around the ever-growing collection of adepts watching them.

"Don't blame her," the blonde woman beside Noah said as she stepped forward, and Angie tried to place her familiar face. "Milton was warning everyone about the fall of the orders long before she ever came to magic." Angie's head tipped back as things clicked into place. Bailey had been among Milton and Noah's faithful entourage over the last conference that spring. "Did I hear you say she's an Air aura?" Angie nodded. "Well, then she needs another Elemental aura to train her. We only have one on staff, and they can't take on anyone else. But if you could stay to help them as well as your own..."

Noah seemed to back down in the face of Bailey's calm argument, and she smiled at Angie. "If you promise to stay to take on most of the responsibility for your recruit, and to help ease the burdens on the other sponsors here, then your presence would be a boon to us all, yes?" She looked between Angie and Noah, who both nodded hesitantly, and Angie finally dropped her hands to her sides. "Then do you both agree to these terms?"

Angie glanced back at where the head healer at previous conferences, Lady Braithwaite, was helping Barbara Collins to heal and soothe Lucia. She didn't want to agree. Not to an open, unknown time frame of being stuck in an overwhelming milieu of strangers who disliked and distrusted her at best. Not to being so fully derailed from her goals, and certainly not in a place where every inch reminded her of Jonathan, and Daniel, and Casey...

Angie nodded, trying to look like she meant it, but Noah's answering smile made her skin crawl.

"Beg."

Angie's jaw and fists clenched, her aura crackling into sparks and reeking of gasoline and cigarettes. Her eyes bored into Noah's, silently begging him to not make her hand over her last scrap of control. She mouthed the word *please*, but it only made Noah's smile widen.

Angie closed her eyes against the suffocating sight of hundreds of adepts watching her, judging her, as more arrived every second, and she listened to her heart pounding in her ears. Her throat tightened as she lowered herself to one knee, her fists stiff at her side.

"Please. Let me and Lucia stay if I take responsibility for her and help relieve your stress and burdens as much as I can."

Noah's smile shifted and darkened. "When you say that, does that mean you'll finally agree to—" Again, Bailey's hand on his arm stopped Noah mid-sentence, but Angie still felt sick from the request she knew had been silenced. A slight shift against the inside of his short robe confirmed it, and it took all of Angie's willpower to keep her lip from curling with revulsion.

"Beg like you mean it, and I'll agree."

Angie's mind spun over all the other options she'd pursued and exhausted, feeling her desperation grow with every blink until a tear escaped to roll down her freckled cheek. Angie lowered her other knee to the flagstones, tucked her rayon dress under her, and folded down as if in worship. Anger and shame heated her to a boil, but she repressed it ruthlessly.

"Please, I'm begging you, Noah. Please, please let us stay. Please, Last Lord High Supreme Justice of the English Patrician Court, let my recruit and I call this place our home."

⟶⟞✦⟝⟵

Angie kept her eyes down as she and Lucia spread out two down sleeping bags over thin mattresses in the common house just below the gardens that claimed the highest hill of the conference site. Whispers had followed them every step of the way as they'd been herded through the process of being brought into the fold.

Lucia had been healed and had taken the news of her unlocked and awakened magic much better than Angie would have expected for a temple priestess.

Angie flopped down hard on her new bed for the foreseeable future and watched her new charge gather a clean set of modest clothes she'd been given and hustle off to change from her blood-stained vestments.

She lay back, feeling the last hour swallowing up her energy reserves like a sinkhole to the underworld. Closing her eyes, Angie mused at how much religion had avoided her awareness for so long, and how it now seemed to be rising to the surface of her life. Like every child born since the Unification a century ago, Angie had been raised in the faith of the ancient pantheon of the empire, but she would never have called herself a believer. She wondered if that would change after sponsoring a priestess of Minerva.

Angie forced herself to sit up, knowing that if she gave in to her exhaustion now, the day to come would be impossible, and looked around. The common house was largely as she remembered it. There was the piano where Noah had first tried to woo her. There, across the room, the balcony where Emilia had learned to fly. Overhead, a wild collection of chandeliers and lanterns from every conceivable era of technology and fashion added their warm glow to the bright morning light streaming in through the long windows, draped with heavy curtains, that looked out over the sprawling gardens.

What had changed were the people. Angie watched Lucia return through the small collections of patricians who had set up camp among the sofas and armchairs spread out across the thick carpets. Sleeping bags, open suitcases, and stacks of books for makeshift nightstands denoted each person's claim on the space, and Angie realized she'd have to go back to her car for her basic possessions in the very near future. She'd also need to stash her hatchback somewhere it wouldn't get stolen or burgled.

"How old are you?" Lucia asked, returning and eyeing Angie shrewdly as she sat down on her own bed two feet away.

"Twenty-eight. You?"

Angie's answer seemed to displease Lucia, and her aura flared. "Thirty-nine."

"Can you feel that?" Angie asked, looking at the sky-blue cloud of magic around Lucia, but knowing she wouldn't know how to see the auric spectrum yet. "When your emotions flare, your magic does, too. And, especially for us Elemental auras, that can have unintended consequences if we don't learn to control it."

"I can control it," Lucia said in a sulking tone, and Angie just sighed, watching her aura slowly relax back to normal.

Angie wished the last day of her life had gone differently. As Lucia turned aside, carefully rearranging the bedding Lord Braithwaite had produced for both of them, Angie tried to focus on the positive. She'd found Jasper Rose and made contact. They might be more willing to help Angie and provide answers than she and Daniel had anticipated.

When Angie's thoughts turned to Casey, Hannah, and Dawn, she could find no silver lining, and so stuffed them back away.

She hugged her knees to her chest, feeling adrift in so many unexpected changes. She'd make it work. She had to. And when she got back to her car to stash it away, she'd talk to Daniel about it all, one way or another. If nothing else, she needed to reassure herself that his day hadn't gone as badly as hers.

Chapter Ten

D aniel felt ashamed as he ended his call with Angie, standing just inside his front door, already dressed in a black silk suit with a gold tie and jewelry. In retrospect, he couldn't believe that he'd blindly assumed it was Dawn calling him late last evening and not checked to see the half-dozen missed calls. When he'd called Angie back in a panic, worried that she'd needed his help with an emergency, the fact that he had to admit that he wouldn't have been much help even if he *had* picked up only made him feel worse.

When he Voyaged from his tidy home in Boston to a discreet alleyway in the heart of Rome, he promised himself he'd make it up to her. Just not right then. Daniel stepped out into an ancient piazza. A fountain burbled in the center, and he felt the hair on the back of his neck prickle at the lack of people anywhere to be seen.

With each tap of his cane across the rough cobblestones toward the looming imperial palace ahead, Daniel's unease grew. Only when he began climbing the long flight of stairs, his aching knee always trailing behind, did a dozen legionnaires appear silently from hidden alcoves along the piazza and from just inside the massive palace doors of reinforced steel. All wore smart gray uniforms and carried machine guns Daniel tried to ignore.

"Halt and present," the most decorated legionnaire said in Italian as Daniel reached the top, stepping forward.

Daniel smiled confidently, glad he'd thought to make use of translation magic for himself before leaving. He hooked his cane over his arm and pulled his passport from his breast pocket with gloved fingers, handing it over. The change in the guard's demeanor when he saw the imperial purple of the documentation inside was immediate.

"My apologies, Signore. Please step inside. I'll bring the minister of patrician affairs immediately."

Daniel followed him inside a lavish foyer as a clock tower nearby struck noon, glad to not be left to wait in the sweltering Roman summer day outside. The legionnaire was gone for less than a minute before he returned, stepping aside respectfully for a man Daniel recognized to pass before returning to his post.

"Senator Moretti," Daniel said with a bow, smiling. He doubted the former leader of the Senate liked him very much, but the man had always been fair in their dealings.

"Councilor Fawl. What can we help you with?" Moretti's mouth barely moved beneath his bushy mustache, and his rigid eggplant-colored aura betrayed nothing of his thoughts.

"That is rather what I came to ask the emperor."

Moretti frowned, looking Daniel up and down. "The emperor does not take visitors. However, if you're interested in aligning yourself with our cause, you may speak to Minister Laufey. This way." His accented voice was stern, and Daniel didn't argue as the former magistrate moved away.

The change in decorative style once they'd latched the first door behind them was noticeable. As they made their way along a spacious corridor of small busts on plinths, bathed in light from the windows all along behind them, Daniel was shocked to see two blank-faced mannequin golems uniformed in imperial purple. He opened his mouth to ask Moretti about the wisdom of using golems openly around plebeians but stayed silent when he saw that the guards flanking the far door had the richer auras of unlocked patricians.

Through more rooms and corridors, each embedded with the precious stones, metals, fibers, and arts collected by millennia of theft and exploitation, Moretti finally came to a stop beside a relatively unassuming door, carved with gilt-edged scrollwork. "I believe the minister is at leisure. Knock and enter."

Daniel did as instructed, openly appraising Moretti as he did so, amused by his careful formality.

"Come in," came the curt reply, and he opened the door onto an opulent, nearly empty office. "Fawl," Seth Laughy said, his face going slack as he stood from behind a baroque desk.

Daniel didn't have time to respond—or even decide how to—before another voice spoke from behind the open door, and he stiffened. "Daniel! I'm so glad you came."

"Fawl," he corrected Marissa Hayward for the hundredth time in their acquaintance. He closed the door behind him as his first recruit rose from a chaise longue. The rebuke had the desired effect of derailing the overly familiar hug the tan, raven-haired beauty had nearly reached him with.

"Yes, of course," she said, her smile vanishing. "Councilor Fawl. Welcome to the imperial palaces. I was so hoping you'd join us in time. Please"—she gestured to one of the three chairs arrayed before the desk—"take a seat. Tell us why you've come." Daniel took a seat as Marissa swayed ahead of him to drape herself on the arm of Seth's.

He glanced between them shrewdly. "I see you two have become quite close," he remarked without tone, and Marissa smiled.

"Indeed." She draped an arm over Seth's shoulders, which both men ignored. "And what of your own companion?"

Seth's eyes seemed to sharpen with the question, and Daniel didn't hesitate in giving the answer he was certain Marissa wanted to hear. "I have no idea. I've had no contact with her since the solstice. Nor have I tried to." He took no notice of the deep, rich texture of her blood-red aura, which wound around her in satisfaction, and spoke solely to Seth. "My reasons for coming are simple." He leaned forward, resting both hands on his cane before him. "I want to serve the emperor, just as I served the patrician orders with distinction."

Daniel chose not to elaborate just yet as the younger man simply tilted his head. It was true that Daniel had dressed in what he considered the costume of his other self, a mask he'd once fought to leave behind. But he secretly hoped that—just maybe—he could reach the emperor and remove the threat of nuclear destruction without having to fully act the part. How his initial offer was accepted would tell him if it was possible.

"Please leave us," Seth said, his gaze not breaking from Daniel's as he tilted his head up to Marissa perched beside him. "I believe you'll be needed in the radio studio soon." Her aura shivered unhappily, but she quickly and quietly stood and slipped through a side door with a soft click. "Serve the emperor," Seth echoed the moment Marissa was gone, reaching for a thick folder of papers on the desk before him and making a show of reading through them. "And what, may I ask, do you hope to gain from doing so?"

"Purpose," Daniel answered honestly, caught between relief and offense at Seth's apparent lack of interest. "I fought long and hard to serve the patricians, including sponsoring recruits and serving as a Judge, Senator, and Councilor. I was ashamed of my removal from those offices a few months ago when I was unjustly accused of sabotage by a jealous madman, but my desire to be of service has pushed me back into my true purpose despite that. If you'll allow me to plead my case, I'm sure I can convince the emperor of the value I could add to his endeavors."

"Madman?" Seth asked, bristling and glancing up from his papers, and Daniel pulled in his aura from expressing itself as he firmly decided on offense.

"Yes. And I have no doubt that I can be an even more effective agent and minister for law and order now that Milton Cartwright is no longer in the way. Not just for me, personally, but for the systems I wish to serve." Daniel watched Seth, wishing he had a better read on him. He needed to know how the younger man felt about Daniel's public execution of the other Councilor before he'd know if he needed to change tack.

Seth seemed to read his mind. "I agree that his death was helpful." His tongue appeared at the side of his mouth, revealing a canine. "I did intend to thank you someday for clearing my path to where I now sit, and for creating the circumstances that have allowed me to thrive by removing that fat, old man from the equation."

Daniel couldn't stop his yellow aura from darkening with relieved pleasure despite the discomfort he still felt about the manner and circumstances of taking Milton's life in cold blood, but it paled again almost immediately.

"That being said, Cartwright left quite the playbook." Daniel almost expected Seth to reach for a physical book and wondered if those were the pages the pale man was flipping through. "Only he had not the conviction to use it to its full potential... You opened the path for someone who did. Me." With the last, Seth fixed his full attention on Daniel with a disquieting smile, and it was all the older patrician could do to hide his uneasy disgust. "However," Seth sighed, returning to his papers, "I'm still disinclined to trust someone who murdered a peer."

"Twenty days of letters begging me to write back say otherwise." Daniel wished he'd thought about the argument before voicing it, but didn't for long.

Seth blinked. "Is that why you came? Because I stopped sending the letters?"

"Yes and no," Daniel admitted, the welcome ability to be so truthful despite his ultimately covert intentions putting him at ease. "All the other reasons I've named are true. However, realizing that you were doing what I was too cowardly to, like finding new purpose in the world, new powers to serve, was the wake-up call I needed to pursue them."

Seth seemed unconvinced but interested, and Daniel reached for what else might bolster his case. "I assure you. Cartwright was a traitor I dealt with in service to the Council and every patrician beneath them. I neither assisted nor condoned Miss Forester's acts of destruction or disruption, and I simply took advantage of her fondness for me in choosing to stay when the other Councilors were forced out. I truly believe that it's now my duty to help restore a system of order which can protect adepts from themselves. And to return to screening who is and isn't granted use of their magic to bring an end to the magical destabilization you expertly alluded to in your broadcast last night."

Seth's eyes narrowed. "Is that the only destabilization of magic you're worried about?"

"Yes," Daniel replied, confused. "Why?"

"Tell me, if and when you see Miss Forester again, will you be able to touch her?"

Daniel had no idea if Seth's question was supposed to answer his, but took a gamble on him wanting the same answer Marissa would, given their apparently close alliance. It still wasn't a pleasant half-lie to tell.

"No. The last time I touched her was when she returned to physical form at the solstice. The vibration of my skin curse affected her fully. Whatever loophole Marissa has likely told you of between me and Angie Forester seems to have closed."

Seth smiled. "Good." He tutted, pausing to pull a file from the stack, giving it a nod. "She's not someone I would trust." As Seth dropped the folder face up, Daniel caught the words REJECTED: DANGEROUS stamped across the top in big red letters, and he didn't bother asking how Seth had acquired Milton's file on Angie. If he got his way, he could find out later.

"So, may I offer my services to the emperor?" Daniel asked, trying to sound more confident than pleading.

Seth's reaction wasn't one he could have anticipated. He leapt to his feet, his folder of papers scattering, and Daniel followed when Seth screamed. "You should be asking if you can serve me!" He slammed a fist on his desk. "Anyone who wants to see the emperor goes through me, and I decide if they're worthy or useful!" Daniel brought his shields up as Seth's fine, ginger hair began to shift across his scalp with small licks of flame, and bright sparks lit in his pupils. "I don't need you. I have one Councilor in my pocket already. One who has promised me world-changing secrets that will stabilize our understanding of existence in a new form."

Seth raised an arm dripping with black soot, leveling it at Daniel's head as he stepped around the desk, papers curling to ash beneath his feet. "The only help or guidance I need are from my God and emperor, and both have made it clear that I am their chosen one. Chosen to enact their wills in this time of crisis and opportunity. I should smite you where you stand for not begging on your knees for my favor, you spineless, pointless, pathetic old man."

Daniel's frozen surprise snapped. After years with Angie, fireproofing had become second-nature to him, and he applied layers of the magic to his clothing and skin with a thought, stepping forward with a snarl. Grasping Seth's wrist in a gloved hand, he twisted it aside by the thumb until Seth gasped. "That's enough." The words growled between Daniel's teeth, and he brought his aura up with such force that the room groaned against the cyclone that sent every paper in the room spinning around them in a rattling cloud.

Not releasing Seth's twisted hand, Daniel yanked him in closer, standing tall as he used his magic to wrap the pale patrician in a frigid vacuum. "If you wanted to see exactly how this old man can put a spoiled child like you in their place, all you needed to do was ask." The show of force swelled in Daniel's whole being, burning away the month of self-loathing Seth's words had echoed. He'd been preparing to stand down a wildfire aura since he'd first laid eyes on the folder now spinning past him, and proving he could do so without injury was ecstasy.

Seth's fire and ash slowly receded, unexpectedly replaced with a wide smile and a natural—albeit unsettling—spark of madness in his eyes. Daniel released his wrist and the gale of his aura. Seth stepped back, cradling and rubbing his wrist as the papers drifted back to the floor. Daniel took a step to follow, leaning into the darkness inside that had turned the tables, and Seth yielded another step, raising his hands.

"It was just a test," the younger man panted, admiration and zeal blazing from him. "My whole act was just that. An act, a test. I had to see if you were still strong. Still worthy. Still the man I admire." Seth held out his hand, eagerness etched in every line of his face. "Please, yes, I'd love for you to join me. Share what you know, and in short order, I'll find a position worthy of you, I'm sure."

Daniel reeled from the turn of events and made a show of eyeing Seth's proffered hand warily. He couldn't back down now. He'd played his cards right, and if he let that success scare him away, then he deserved every name he could possibly be called, and more. He took Seth's hand with his own gloved one, pushing aside any emotion that tried to paint itself over his victory.

"I will. Thank you."

CHAPTER ELEVEN

"**G**reat! Very nicely done. Shall we leave it there for today?" Lucia nodded and, as Angie had taught her, lifted the lintel branch from where it sat across two slender birches and collapsed the swirling gray Threshold of magic stretched like a soap film across the opening.

The first two weeks of Angie's new life had passed in a blur. She deflated a degree as she and her recruit made their way around a small stand of evergreens toward the edge of the forest above the conference site. She was exhausted and sick of trying to teach someone who didn't seem to want to learn. Angie suspected Lucia's sheltered life in a temple was partly to blame, but there was more to it.

Lucia's head bobbed ahead of her down the path, her thin, black hair as wind mussed as always thanks to her Air aura. Every time Angie tried to guide or coach the older woman, she seemed to pull further away. She tried to give her newer adept the benefit of the doubt, but she couldn't ignore the ways she tried to mother Angie, and seemed to fully ignore half the things she said. Especially any advice.

As they stepped out into the upper reaches of the garden, down the path toward the central courtyard, Angie slowed. She tried to enjoy the slightly neglected flowers and shrubs, the light calls of birds in the gray, early-evening sky, but they all seemed distant. Instead, her mind filled with the deep obligation she felt to remain and settle deeper into the patterns she was already taking for granted.

Wondering why, Angie's thoughts flitted over another light-blue aura she'd known. And gotten killed. *No,* she thought to herself firmly, breaking into a trot to catch up with Lucia as they passed the Tudor manor house that had once held office spaces for the Judges of the English Court. *Don't go there.*

They parted ways at the massive, intricately carved brass doors of the Great Hall when Lucia's friends pulled her away, acting much younger than they clearly were as they gossiped about the grand party Noah had planned for the following weekend. Angie just nodded her goodbye before turning away and rolling her eyes.

"Angie, wait up." Noah's voice made Angie slow but not stop, and she glanced back to find him waving her into the great hall ahead of him. "You can help us set up."

Angie finally stopped, dropping her head a degree before pulling a fake smile onto her face and turning to step through the doors. She preceded Noah up the carved marble stairs to the main hall of the ballroom, feeling his eyes on her back with every step.

Lord Braithwaite had ensconced himself at the far end of the magnificent, mirrored hall, and dozens of golems scurried to and from him, bringing things to be altered or taking away the smaller baubles the harried man was pulling from thin air.

"Looks like you've got it covered," Angie said flatly, stopping at the top of the staircase to let Noah catch up.

Several dozen adepts, most of them fresh recruits judging by the untrained clouds of their aura, were also helping the gray-bearded man in the tweed suit, but Noah still shook his head. "You said you'd help."

Angie scowled, crossing her arms. "This isn't even a real conference. We aren't building up to a Victume Ceremony in three months, or even in three years. That's why there are no stress tests for these recruits, which I'm glad of, and no selection process for who's best or favorite. I don't see why we need a full-blown ball."

Noah didn't argue back right away, so Angie let her shoulders drop, grinding the heel of one hand into her puffy eyes and letting her exhaustion show. "I'm done with my obligations for the week. I helped all last weekend, and I will again next weekend with the party, but right now I need a few hours somewhere else on my own."

Noah caught Angie's arm as she turned toward the exit, but his expression softened, and he let go when she gave him a pleading look. "Fine, if you must. But don't shame us for wanting to feel happy just because you're bitter." Angie bit back her contempt again, moving for the exit, but Noah wasn't finished. "I'm sorry."

Angie stopped, turning warily to Noah a few steps above her. "What?"

The Celt was a caricature of disapproving pity. "I'm sorry if you've felt overburdened by everything here. I'm sorry for our tiffs in the past, and that we ended up on different sides around Ragnarök at the solstice." Angie didn't react, waiting unhopefully for Noah to address anything he'd actually done to hurt her, and he shifted uncomfortably.

"But you have to understand, you've made it very hard to defend or get along with you. I mean, just look at how much trouble and damage you've caused to this conference alone. There isn't even an English Court anymore! That's the only reason I'm hard on you. I'm trying to help you be a better person. Teach you responsibility. No one else is, apparently, and it's not easy for me, either."

Angie arched an unemotional brow, and Noah frowned. "I didn't have to let you bring your recruit here, you know. You really hurt me when you ended our friendship just because I was trying to help you see how you were refusing to take responsibility for your own shitty behavior in the past. And you have no idea how betrayed I felt when your traitor friends terrorized my attempt to rebuild what you'd broken."

Angie's auric expression slipped out of her control, heating the space around her with the smells of hot metal and burned plastic. She'd been right. He'd been wrong in every instance he brought up, and she wasn't about to apologize for any of it. She turned away, skipping down the stairs. "I'll be back tonight. Don't wait up." She heard

Noah sputter an objection, but she Voyaged away without acknowledging it.

She needed options other than being stuck with Noah Byrne indefinitely. Daniel had made it clear he had none to offer. So if Casey and Dawn were going to tell her that joining them wasn't one, they'd have to say it to her face.

It was all Angie could do to keep her angry aura under control when she returned many hours later. She'd been blocked and told off by just about everyone associated with Dawn or Casey at every turn. Only the Hellenians, Nikolaos and Demitria, had seemed sympathetic, but they'd been quickly silenced by their peers. Now, hungry, tired, and forced to return to the overcrowded, grumpy, superficial life she was begrudgingly becoming used to, Angie's aura was dark and interspersed with ribbons of red flames, and it stank of gasoline.

After checking in briefly with Lucia in the library, she was pleased to find the Roman bath house empty when she landed—a small gaggle of recruits with towels wrapped around them still making their way down the footpath toward the row of cottages along the stream. Angie wished she could still lay claim to the one she and Daniel had shared for the two conferences they'd attended together, but knew she couldn't.

The setting sun created wide stripes of gold and silver as it sliced through the worn stone column bordering the steaming turquoise water, and Angie fished her anti-possession sigil coin out of her pocket before sitting down on a dry bench with her back to it. A golem made from a gothic statue puttered nearby, scrubbing away at a wine stain on the ancient stones, but Angie ignored it.

She turned the coin over in her hand, willing the ghost held within to stay dormant while she processed the further accusations from his widow that she'd endured over the last hour. Try as she might, she'd never been able to think of a single instance where she'd shown the slightest bit of romantic interest, or more, in Jonathan Crowther, and yet his wife's insistence on impropriety between them, which Angie strongly suspected had been spreading like gossip since before she even heard of it, was unshakable. It made Angie question every moment of affection, support, and emotion from her dearest friend, and the complicated bitterness and distrust coating her insides was hard to wash away.

As Angie looked around at the calm, ancient luxury of the bathhouse, she realized that perhaps part of the reason she had been willing to beg to come back to the conference was to hide. From Hannah and her rumors, from having the privacy or time to talk through it with Jonathan, and from anyone like Daniel who might have answers she didn't want to hear. Maybe she was just like everyone else hiding there from the outside world and whatever troubles they'd left there.

Angie looked all around, making sure no one was nearby, and set up her shields as strong as she could make them before inviting the memory of her best friend out of the coin.

Jonathan's form expanded to stand before her. Half of him looked nearly solid in the shade of a column, the other nearly invisible in the warm rays of the setting sun. He smiled at Angie, his teeth bright against his black beard and tanned face, and she couldn't help smiling back as layers of stress slipped off her in his presence.

He looked around, walking to the edge of the pool before turning back to Angie. "I was surprised when you decided to come back here. We've been back here for a while, haven't we? Why bring me out now?"

"Long story," Angie replied. "Essentially, I ended up with a recruit and nowhere else to take them."

Jonathan's ice-blue eyes were as penetrating as ever, and Angie had no doubt that he saw through her discomfort and avoidance with ease. "Is that what you'd rather talk about right now, then?"

Angie nodded her head to one side before dropping her chin to her chest, absently watching the large coin turning over and over in her hands. She knew she couldn't bring herself to address Hannah's accusations with him. Not yet. But maybe just interacting with him again would remind her of their truth. "Yeah. I—I feel lost in trying to be a sponsor. I feel like I'm failing her, and like we don't even know each other. I was hoping you might have some advice. Might be willing to help."

"Of course," Jonathan said, sitting down beside Angie in the shade, and for a moment, Angie could almost convince herself he was still alive and real. "You know, Dan was saying the exact same things, not all that long ago, about you..."

—◦✤◦—

Angie's spirits were significantly raised half an hour later when she left the bathhouse, tucking the coin carefully back into her pocket. She still felt adrift in many ways, and as she processed what Jonathan had advised her about finding her own stability through rituals and habits, her thoughts overlapped with the topic of her recruit's faith, which had been on her mind since their meeting. Angie briefly wondered why there was no temple at the conference site, but didn't care enough to ask.

She stopped by one of the classroom buildings, which had been converted to store supplies among the cluster of larger buildings at the center of the conference, and grabbed some unpopular snacks before making her way up the hill past the white marble amphitheater carved into it.

Up through the garden, which seemed to be fraying slightly at the edges without the careful ministrations of Jasper Rose's green thumb, Angie paused again to pick a sprig of late-blooming lilac before continuing her climb up toward the towering yew tree at the forest's edge. It spread over a small, circular stone gazebo with thick, dark branches, and Angie smiled as she stepped into the cool, evergreen cave of its shade.

There were three matching benches along the sides away from the entrance, and Angie placed the food and flowers on the one straight ahead, kneeling. Trying to remember the proper way to worship instilled in her by her parents from a young age, Angie whispered a prayer to whatever Gods might grant her grace and lifted a fistful of fire to light the offerings and send them to the otherworld.

The flames spluttered out the moment they left Angie's fingers. Her jaw clenched, trying not to think about how it felt like the way her magic warped in half-worlds during her banishment. It took four more tries before her fire finally flared and lingered long enough to consume the offerings. Angie took no comfort in the success. Her magic felt like she imagined Daniel's had when it had been repressed. She just sat, staring at the pile of ash as it faded with the light, until her yearning for him—an ache that intensified whenever he entered her thoughts—became too much to bear.

When she stood to leave, Angie found Bailey Johnson waiting quietly and patiently a short distance from the gazebo, and winced at having been watched. When she saw Angie step out from under the spreading yew, Bailey smiled brightly and waved, almost ghost-like herself in the flat half-light.

"Hey, I'm so sorry, I didn't want to interrupt," she said, tying her blond curls back with a hair tie. She fell into step beside Angie as they walked back down toward the glowing cluster of larger buildings at the center of the site. "I just wanted to check in and see if you needed anything. Noah said you seemed to be having a bad day."

"No, I don't need anything," Angie replied, trying not to sound grumpy but not fully trusting one of Noah's many girlfriends.

"Not even a friend?"

Angie stumbled over a clump of woodchips, and Bailey caught her arm, steadying her. Angie was so thrown off by the cheerful kindness in Bailey's question that she didn't know how to respond. The blond seemed to grow uneasy the longer they walked in silence and stopped Angie before they reached the common house at the bottom of the gardens.

"Wait, before we go in..." Bailey chewed a lip, her pale brows knitting together as she glanced at the nearest group of patricians. "I was hoping to bring this up more subtly, but... Angie, you can't ask me how I know any of this, or from who, but you've been trying to get to Eden, right?"

Angie didn't hide her surprise. "Yes... Why?"

"Because"—Bailey looked around again, dropping her voice—"I know when another group is going through. I can tell you who to keep an eye on and follow, but I don't know where or when. I don't want anything for the info, either. Just call it a show of friendship."

Angie searched the woman before her for any lie but found none. For a heartbeat, she considered the costs—the promise of returning to the chase or declining it for Lucia's sake—and a smile slowly spread across her face. "I'd be very grateful. Thank you."

CHAPTER TWELVE

A little over two weeks after his meeting with Seth, Daniel wondered if he'd made the right move. Despite his initial eagerness, Seth had largely blown him off since, only agreeing to a one-hour meeting every few days—sometimes without warning—that were almost entirely spent pumping Daniel for information about anything and everything he'd learned as a Judge, Senator, and Councilor. Very few of Daniel's questions or requests for tasks with which he could prove himself had even been acknowledged, and almost none had been answered or granted.

Every time Daniel thought of Xiao Sheng in his place, having a home and purpose with Dawn and everything she was doing as he'd so dearly wanted, his bitterness only grew.

He'd moped around his New York mansion, wanting to play his part of former Councilor to the hilt, and not wanting Seth's presence to taint either of the homes he held more comfort in. It had paid off when his last conversation with Seth had come from an unannounced visit from the young man. By the end of their debriefing, Seth had asked Daniel if he'd be willing to host a feast for some wealthy plebeians he was hoping to convince to move to Rome in an effort to enforce the legitimacy of the last pocket of imperial control. Daniel had readily agreed.

It had been the icing on the cake when Angie had responded well to him reaching out to her, explaining that she'd been just about to call him herself, could finally leave her recruit for a night, and wanted to meet up. He'd suggested the day between the meeting and feast, as Seth was unlikely to visit, and had spent the day anxiously and distractedly awaiting her.

When he felt the tug on his shields that announced her arrival somewhere within the grounds of the large mansion, he looked up from the list of preparation tasks he'd been going over and folded away his reading glasses. He chose to stay seated, tempering his excitement to see her as he reminded himself of the current state of affairs between them.

"Hey!" he greeted Angie warmly as she stepped from the foyer into the large dining hall that dominated the first floor. She had dark bruises under her ocean-colored eyes, her freckled skin looked paler than usual, and her long auburn curls were pulled back into a messy bun.

When she saw him, she gave him a tight smile, walking past one of the many golems cleaning and decorating for the coming banquet.

"Hey. Thanks for calling," she said as she stopped a few feet away, leaning against the edge of the table and crossing her arms as Daniel stood.

Daniel nodded, not sure what to do with his hands. "Of course. Least I could do after missing so many calls."

He'd already told her of the preparations over the phone, and so offered no further explanations as Angie looked around at all the activity. The golems staffing Daniel's mansion had been made by Olivia, an Earth aura, and were primarily made from stone statues, both old and new, which were in plentiful supply under the global empire. Their blank, expressionless faces had been unsettling when Daniel first encountered them, but now even the act of using a scrap of his magic to bind his intentions into the stone had become mundane. "How have you been?"

Angie shrugged, folding her arms over her simple black dress. "Playing nice with people I don't like. Pretending I care about their issues, and pretending I don't care about my own. The usual."

Me, too. Couldn't have put it better myself, Daniel thought, but he didn't think saying it would help Angie's obvious bitterness. "Then hopefully ton—this evening can be a respite," he offered instead, feeling his cheeks heat slightly at his near slip up. Of course he wanted her to stay the night. But he had no right to assume that much.

Angie's shoulders dropped a centimeter, and she smiled more genuinely than when she'd arrived. "Yeah," she said, uncrossing her arms to brace them on the edge of the table she leaned against. "I hope so, too." Her gray-green eyes softened, gazing up at Daniel, whose heart leapt in response. "I need a change of pace, and I've really missed you."

Daniel couldn't help himself. A single step forward was all it took to stand over the ankles she'd crossed out in front of her. His knees brushed against hers through his slacks and her thin dress. He wouldn't admit it, but the more he slipped back beneath the mask he'd worn for Seth since their first meeting—one of brooding, reclusive detachment—the more it had festered behind his breastbone.

Holding his breath, he lifted tentative, slender fingers toward her bare arm, watching her face every second for permission. Her chest rose with a swell, her freckled cheeks flushing, and she gave the slightest nod. Daniel brushed her skin with his, and nothing happened.

He exhaled in a rush, gripping her arms with both hands. The loneliness of being untouchable eased instantly, and he trusted Angie to understand that as he closed his eyes to narrow his full awareness on the smooth, soft warmth beneath his fingers. "Angie," he whispered, the word shaking with need and longing.

When she didn't respond, Daniel looked up to find her flushed, her breath labored. "Daniel," she whispered back pleadingly. As soon as she stood up, pressed close against his chest, Daniel guided her arms up, and all thought left him as he claimed her mouth with his.

Any guilt or doubt was erased the moment Angie's hands on his back and neck pulled him closer. He wanted to ask if she was sure—what this meant for their break—but the sweet relief of falling into her silenced him.

Daniel trailed his hands over every inch of bare skin he could reach, caressing her face, arms, back, breasts... When she began unbuttoning his shirt, her hungry grin pulling the same from Daniel in response, he raised a hand to pause the delicious backslide in their agreements.

"Leave us," he called out to the dozen stone golems still going about their assigned tasks unbothered, sending the intention that they obey out through a ripple of his aura.

"No, wait," Angie said, her grin turning impish as she licked her lips. Her eyes scanned over the drones, now stilled by Daniel's indecision. "Let them stay. Make them watch."

Daniel moaned as his cock responded to the suggestion, swelling the last degree it possibly could. He latched onto Angie's neck, making her gasp, careful not to irritate the sensitive skin with his short, sandy beard.

"As you wish." He thought the command to the golems bound to his will, and with a faint shuffling of stone over lush carpets, a dozen blank faces gathered around the head of the long table, all turned toward them. It didn't matter. They were nothing more than animated shells.

Daniel's hands swept up Angie's thighs, lifting the skirt of her dress as she undid the front of his pants. He stilled, grasping her hips when her hand slipped inside and traced a finger along his shaft. "Angie."

"Yes?" she teased, grasping him, and Daniel's mind went blank. He pulled down her panties to her knees, let her pull his unbuttoned shirt away with her free hand, and found her hips once more.

He backed her against the edge of the table, lifting her onto it. Angie gasped as she settled onto the cold surface, her nipples rising against the fabric covering them. Daniel grasped one firmly as Angie tugged his remaining clothing down as far as she could, and she moaned as his erection sprang free.

"I missed you, too," Daniel said against her ear, certain that fact was evident to her in the raw need rolling off him. Her response was to press her lips to his neck and pull his hips in close with one leg wrapped behind his thighs.

Daniel dipped one hand between her legs, his teeth grinding when he felt how slick she was. Bunching her dress out of the way, he guided his shaft to her entrance, and his mouth fell open when Angie bucked her hips forward, pulling him inside.

His aura swirled around them in slow currents of deep-yellow light, twining in and out of the thin, silver cloud of Angie's rosewood smoke. It was all Daniel could do to hold himself back from his ravenous need as he pressed in and out to his limits several times, only speeding up when Angie gasped out a pleading "more." Daniel obliged and grabbed her shoulder to pull against.

For a second, Daniel thought Angie was going to balk at his stronger-than-normal grip, his gold rings pressed into her flesh. Instead, something darkened in Angie's eyes, and she raked her nails down his back. Daniel knew she'd drawn blood without looking, flinching from the pain. Angie just ground into the motion, oblivious, and Daniel placed a hand on her collarbone, gently leaning her away, not wanting her to do it again.

Again, Angie seemed to misinterpret. Her nails were crimson when she laid her hand over Daniel's, sliding it up to her throat. When she opened her eyes, deep and bright with lust, the shadows across them from the crystal chandelier high overhead and the color marking her fingers both reminded him so strongly of Marissa that he snatched his hand away.

Half a second later, he dove forward as Angie's eyes rolled back and she collapsed, unconscious, and he caught her before her head hit the polished oak table.

"I'm so sorry," Daniel said the moment Angie's eyes fluttered open, laid out in the imposing four-poster in the mansion's master bedroom an hour later. He swallowed hard against the guilt, shame, and self-loathing that had bubbled out of him sporadically as he'd initially panicked, magically cleaned them both, and carried her upstairs before sitting and waiting for what felt like an eternity.

"Don't be silly," Angie said, still sleep-muffled, as she pulled herself up to sit. "You barely brushed my neck. It was just the skin curse... I felt like I was going to vibrate apart."

Just the skin curse. Daniel couldn't bring himself to tell her that was exactly what he was apologizing for. Without thinking, he reached out to offer comfort, desperate for connection, but Angie shrank back an inch, and his insides turned to tar.

"I guess we should stick to the break, huh?" Angie asked with a cringing smile.

Daniel lifted his chin, dropping his gaze away. "Yeah. Suppose that was our reminder. Why—" he had to clear his throat before the rest of the question would come. "Why did it change so suddenly? The curse seemed to be fine for the first couple of minutes..."

Angie shook her head in his periphery, looking sad. After a long minute of silence, broken only by the rustling of silk and linen as both shifted uncomfortably, Angie sat forward and sighed. She started to say something, one hand reaching for her pocket, but stopped without uttering a single word.

"Will Lucia be okay overnight without you?" Daniel asked, scrubbing a hand down his face when he couldn't take the silence any longer.

"She'd better be. I'm not going back there tonight." Angie motioned for him to get out of her way, and he stood, letting her swing her legs over the side of the bed. "My new friend Bailey offered to sleep in my bed tonight to give me a break." She glanced up at him, her elfin features twisted with thoughts or emotions he couldn't read. "If you don't want me to stay here with you, I'll go sleep at the Cotswolds cottage."

"Why?"

"Because I need a break. From the people, from the noise, from being responsible for a recruit who resents me for being younger than her, and for not sharing her devotion to the Gods. From... everything. And everyone. So..." Again, Angie's gaze fell on him, then away as she dipped her head. "I'll crash at the cottage tonight."

"For the sake of the break, that might be best," Daniel said when she stood, hurt and betrayed by every syllable he uttered. "Have you had any more luck with Jasper Rose and all that since our last call?" he asked as she shifted to walk away, shameless in his desire to delay her departure.

"No. Still not even one key has been recovered." Angie's words dripped with bitterness, her aura dark and lethargic, leaking the scent of cedar smoke.

Daniel wanted to comfort her, but didn't move. "Well, I have a warded basement ready downstairs for when some do start coming to us. I promise it's only a matter of time." Angie just nodded, not looking at him as she moved to the chair where he'd left her panties and sandals. "What about your family?" Daniel reached for next, just trying to get her talking. "You haven't mentioned them again after that one call."

"I don't want to talk about them," Angie said flatly, sitting to put on her shoes. "I haven't spoken to either of them in five years, and I'm not going to start now."

Anger sparked deep within Daniel. At that moment, she was the same Angie who had acted just as sullen and closed off three full years ago when she confirmed she'd aborted her unwanted pregnancy. "Well, maybe if you tried being an adult about it and went to see them to talk through whatever happened—"

"Drop it," Angie warned, scowling, and the spark in Daniel winked out.

"At least tell me you've given them some sort of protection," he sighed, slumping to the edge of the bed Angie had vacated. "In these times, anyone we love, or once loved, might be used against us. I trust that you, and Dawn, and the rest can look after yourselves, but if my parents were still living, I'd have hidden them away long ago under fake names and strong shields." Angie's lip twitched, and Daniel rushed ahead before she could tell him to shut up again. "If you don't want to go, I'll go and do that for your parents for you. They don't even have to know of your involvement."

Angie deflated, closing her eyes for a long moment. "Thank you, but no. I genuinely want nothing to do with them, and don't want you to, either." She opened her eyes, and Daniel saw a shine of tears in them before it was blinked away. "They absolutely cannot be used as leverage against me."

Daniel sighed, dismissing the thought of trying to track them down on his own the moment it appeared. "If you insist. At least the absence of any trace of magic anywhere near them will go some way towards proving that to anyone who goes looking, and might dissuade them from thinking they could be used to coerce you. Complete separation and distance provides better protection than nothing."

"Great, then it's settled." Angie turned away, smoothing her thin black dress. "I'll find you after the Eden thing Nikolaos is helping me confirm to fill you in." She took half a step forward, paused, and whispered over her shoulder, "Good night, Daniel."

The image of her face lingered for him even after she Voyaged away, her sad, distracted eyes the last to fade. "Good night, Angie," he whispered back to the empty room, and lay back into a fretful night of regrets and self-loathing.

CHAPTER THIRTEEN

"There it is." As she peered around trees at the familiar Threshold built in the center of the large clearing below, a thrill rushed through Angie, overriding the lingering shame and frustration from her last encounter with Daniel. "Go tell the others, but don't bring anyone in until or unless I beacon for you, okay? Thanks again for helping me confirm who was coming and follow them. Give my best to Deo."

Beside her, Nikolaos nodded, his handsome, youthful face unreadable in the heavy darkness. "Of course. Deo wanted to help, too, but Hannah has her watching the kids this weekend. Just don't tell Dawn you were involved if I do bring them to break this up, please. She's... well. You know."

Angie nodded that she did, and the Hellenian Seer Voyaged away, leaving her alone on a densely forested hillside of his homeland. She crept down toward the gathering below, shielding her eyes against the fat drops of rain dripping from the branches overhead with a shiver. At least she'd worn her dark denim jacket.

She wondered if she should try using the uncomfortable phase-walking skill she'd needed when she, Daniel,

Dawn, and others had attacked the same Threshold to stop Ragnarök from happening a month and a half ago, but decided against it. The shielding around the clearing now was nothing in comparison.

Angie had waited until everyone else at Noah's ball was well and truly sloshed before sneaking away, changing, and meeting Nikolaos to chase the Eden move Bailey had warned her was coming. Familiar, capable power coursed through her nearly making her lightheaded as she drew a steel sword from the belt holding her field jacket closed.

Carefully gathering the dark smoke of her aura, Angie willed it into the visible spectrum, even for those who hadn't activated their vision to see magic, wrapping it around her like a shroud. She'd learned the trick during her long banishment out in half-worlds, inspired by the mysterious figure who had followed her from world to world from the beginning. Concealed by the darkness of her own power, Angie was able to get a hundred feet from the freestanding Threshold at the center before she was noticed.

"We have company!" someone unseen shouted, and Angie dropped her smoke with a wicked grin as every-one who was ferrying goods and supplies through the dust-pink film of magic abandoned their loads and looked around wildly.

"Surprise," Angie growled. Her eyes darted over the gathered patricians as they scattered. She was watching for whoever might have the key that had opened the Threshold to Eden, but no one stood out among the wide-eyed, expensively dressed patricians.

A bolt of magic glanced off Angie's shields, and she Voyaged to the man who had tossed it in an instant, her gladiator sword at his throat before another bolt could form in his fingers. "Who's in charge?" she hissed into his ear, and with a bob of his Adam's apple, which scraped his skin raw against her blade, he pointed a trembling finger.

Angie looked where he'd pointed and shoved him aside with her shoulder. "Stop!" she shouted to the people about to step through the Threshold. Two were supporting a third between them—an ancient and frail old man wearing the loose, flowing garb of the Arabian Peninsula. Angie recognized him in an instant as one of the former Councilors who had so happily subjugated a whole globe to feed their greed for eons. She cursed when her Voyaging magic refused to carry her into their path.

Someone lunged at her from the side, and Angie darted forward, dodging them and keeping another at bay with a wide swing of her arm-length blade. She let out a shriek as she tried to hurl a ball of fire at the Arab ex-Councilor, but instead, it blasted hot and dry in her face, singeing the hairs in her nose and temporarily blinding her.

When she was able to open her eyes again against the blistering air, it was just in time to watch the three figures at the Threshold disappear into its depths. In a flash, Jasper Rose appeared silhouetted against the luminous film of dusty-pink magic. Angie had barely drawn breath to shout or rush them when they touched something to the Threshold and it winked out, plunging the scene into darkness.

Angie flared her flames before her eyes could adjust to the dark, and was rewarded with a clear, bright, almost slow-motion glimpse of the object she'd been chasing for months and across continents. The large jade key Jasper pressed into someone else's hand pulsed with maroon, yellow, and white magic, dancing around it like light on the bottom of a pool. A second later, the person Jasper had handed it to was gone, and Angie screamed with frustration.

All around her, patricians were Voyaging—some carrying possessions they'd been trying to take with them on their retreat from facing the consequences of the world they'd built, and some empty-handed. Angie swung at one who passed dangerously near, reaching to grab another, desperate to not come away empty-handed yet again, but she missed her grab when Jasper Rose Voyaged between Angie and her target.

"Angie, stand down," they said loudly, raising their hands and skipping back out of Angie's reach. "Ragnarök isn't back on. Eden is just still a calm, safe, beautiful world these people have every right to choose to move to."

"Not those cowards. Not if they're fleeing the world they built and mined until it collapsed down around their ears. Not bastards like you." Angie watched as the last few patricians Voyaged away, realizing she wouldn't even know what to do with one if she managed to catch them. She'd come for the key, and that was gone. She raised her sword, holding it steady at Jasper's heart. "Where's the key? Who did you give it to?"

"Grow up," Jasper replied, their brown eyes invisible in the near-total dark. "I'm acting in the best interests of humanity. If you can't see that, that's on you. I'm just trying to help those who need it and reduce suffering in the most effective ways I can."

"Like what?" Angie spat.

Jasper lowered their hands slowly, their dusty-pink aura thick but passive, and their voice was hesitant but firm when they replied. "I'm not hoarding the keys I grabbed from the vault when the Council fell. I'm not. I'm slowly disseminating them to those I think will do the most good with them, and passing along the secrets of the old order along with them."

Angie drew breath to ask why, if that was true, neither she nor any of those she considered friends had been included, but Jasper seemed to anticipate. "I don't mean people I like, or who like me. Or even necessarily people I agree with." The comments felt pointed, and Angie bristled. "Just people with a history of being lawful and loyal, and who, unlike you, have a track record for preventing more chaos than they've caused."

"And the secrets? The information you hold? You want me to believe that hoarding that information somehow makes you noble and just?" Jasper's aura juddered, and Angie held her breath for the answer.

"No, you're right. I'd intended to only spend my time teaching leaders who could then pass the knowledge on..." Jasper's aura twisted and writhed, before calming with a sigh. "But if you need a show of good faith to stop hunting me, I'll make an exception." Jasper shook their long curls. "You need to stop seeing me as your enemy, Angie Forester. The Eden key, which is protecting those who sought peace and safety from the uncertain chaos this world is falling into, isn't a price I'm willing to pay to earn your trust, but my time and knowledge are if you're willing to learn in good faith, despite our differences."

Angie examined Jasper's expression, noting their wary concern and honest sincerity, as she considered their response. She needed the key to Eden. The fact that her grab for it had failed sat heavy on her mood, but another part of her had to admit that being one step closer to someone who'd held it was better than nothing. "Give me something I can run with now, and I'll think about it."

Jasper's chest lifted and fell with exaggerated slow-ness, and Angie wondered if the weight in their words that followed was contrived or authentic. "Not all demons are mindless. Some are sentient, like us. And I'm working on, hopefully, opening the way for alliances with some that may be able to help stabilize our world before it's too late." Angie blinked, thrown for a beat, and missed the glance Jasper threw past her shoulder before adding. "I won't tell you more about that until you've proven I can trust you, but if you wait patiently, I'll teach you about other things I know you want to learn. Go cool off, work on seeing past the end of your own nose, and I'll be in touch."

"*Páfsi!*" a loud, male voice called from the edge of the forest nearest the Threshold, and Angie jumped. Jasper was gone before Angie had even registered the black-clad special forces unit advancing from the trees, automatic weapons trained on her through the dead and empty threshold.

"Halt," the same man, apparently their leader, called again in English as Angie backed away. "Wait. I just want to talk. You are a patrician, yes? My name is Ezio. I just want to talk." He appeared to be a tall, stout Romani with a shaved head and an unreadable expression, and as he drew closer, raising his hands without touching the trigger of his large pistol, Angie could see a pre-Unification Hellenian flag embroidered on his armored vest.

Angie's desires fractioned in the time it took her to draw breath. Chase Jasper, or Eden, or the key, stay and fight on her own, call for Nikolaos to bring in a band of fighters and leave it to them, or just accept the loss?

"Fuck," Angie cussed, and Skipped out into a half-world, chasing Eden, before she heard what the soldier said next. At least the familiar, heightened rush of that silenced her mind.

She was empty-handed, tired, and injured from run-ins with demons, but back in control when she returned to the English Conference site in the wee hours of the morning. After a quick stop with Lady Braithwaite in the infirmary, glad the stolid patrician didn't ask about the cut down Angie's back that she'd gotten from a nasty slide down sharp rocks in a half-world, Angie was deeply ready to crawl into her sleeping bag bed and fall asleep. Too bad she'd likely be surrounded by drunk adepts fucking. But she'd made a commitment to Lucia, and however badly she wanted to, this meant she couldn't go sleep in a cozy cottage bed with Daniel for a night instead.

Bailey was waiting for her on the steps of the common house when Angie Voyaged to it, standing when she appeared. "Are you okay? I was worried when I couldn't find you after the party."

"So you stayed up until this ungodly hour to check on me?"

"No," Bailey said with an embarrassed smile, the slowly forming friendship between them dulling the edge of Angie's annoyance at the delay. "I've only been waiting about ten minutes. The party only ended then. Listen, I know this probably isn't the best moment, but I know he's distracted right now, so..." Bailey glanced around nervously. Happy to not be asked where she'd been, as she was dressed for combat and half-world exploration, Angie waited patiently. "Is it true you did a magical abortion on yourself as your power demo three years ago?"

The question caught Angie off guard, and she nodded before her tired brain could stop her. "Um, yeah, sort of. Why?" A dozen possible reasons bubbled up in her mind, each with a healthy note of sympathy. But no sooner had she spoken than Angie saw Noah Byrne and Lucia round the corner behind Bailey, and she raised a hand to silence her as subtly as she could. Bailey followed where Angie was looking, and when she turned back to give Angie a curt nod before scurrying away, her expression struck Angie as very odd.

Angie turned her focus to Lucia, hoping to ignore Noah in the process, but the Celt stopped them both. "Here you are," he beamed, nudging Lucia ahead of him toward Angie. "Your wise and caring mentor. I'm sure she'll help contain your aura while you sleep it off."

Lucia swayed slightly in place, her lip curling. "I'm a grown woman, thank you," she slurred, turning up the stairs into the common house with a huff. "I'm her elder, for Minerva's sake. It's stupid she gets to boss me around." Angie didn't move to follow, closing her eyes for a long moment. She didn't have the bandwidth to deal with this, too, right then.

"Listen," Noah said, his cheeks faintly colored by wine, but not nearly as tipsy as Angie would have expected him to be after such a party. "I know we've tiptoed around this in the past, but..." He took a deep breath, the nervousness radiating from him almost endearing for a split-second. "Would you like to hang out, just the two of us, some time? I mean, would you like to go on a date with me? Or, if that's not your style, just, like, start dating each other, whatever that looks like?"

A hot, grossed-out retort rose to Angie's throat, but with a glance where Bailey's blonde curls had bounced out of sight, she swallowed it. *If Bailey, who's already dating him, is clearly scared of him, the last thing I should do is make him mad and send him home to bed with her.*

"No thanks, I'm all set." She expected Noah to wheedle, threaten, or the like, but wasn't prepared for what actually came.

"I miss who you used to be. I really liked that Angie. I hope someday you realize you used to be nicer, and sweeter, and change back."

The words cut deeper than Angie could have expected, and she tried to cover it. "Yeah? Who exactly do you miss?"

"The girl who loved listening to me play piano. Who enjoyed parties, and dressing up nice, and happily showed the world how special she was without making it anyone else's problem. I just have to wonder if your old friend Crowther would approve of the bitter, sulking person you are now."

"You don't know a single damn thing about what he would or wouldn't approve of," Angie snapped, her aura flaring with cedar smoke and sparks.

Noah eyed her suspiciously. "Easy there, no need to fly off the handle. Unless, of course, the rumors are true, and you and he—"

"They aren't. They are complete bullshit." Angie's breath came faster, and the half-disgusted, half-satisfied smile that twisted Noah's face in reply made her want to punch it so, so badly.

"Methinks she doth protest too much."

Angie turned, stomping into the common house as her aura threatened to slip out of control. "If you'd say so. You can't conceive of not fucking every friend of an acceptable gender you make."

"So that's a no, then?" Noah's voice was maddeningly teasing.

"That's a hard no," Angie snapped, and slammed the door behind her.

CHAPTER FOURTEEN

The feast was so uneventful that Daniel felt adrift in its wake. Not one of the wealthy plebeians had been interesting or kind, and Daniel had reached the end of the evening barely remembering or caring about the preceding hours, having let himself operate without thought as his old familiar Senator character.

The one good thing to come of it was Seth assuring him that after such a success, as he saw it, Daniel's probation of being debriefed at arm's length from the emperor would draw to a close.

Five days later, Daniel couldn't wait to finally break out of his monotony. Seth had agreed to see him that Sunday evening, but Daniel had watched the grandfather clock in the feast hall slowly tick away the hours long after the minister had promised he'd arrive.

"Sorry I'm late," Seth said, striding through the double glass doors from the foyer and stirring Daniel out of his reverie where he sat along one long side of the polished oak table. "I was delayed." Seth looked unkempt and flustered, the first time Daniel had ever seen him in such a state. The redhead slumped in the chair opposite his former sponsor, leaning his head back and closing his eyes. "Nothing too sinister, I hope," Daniel replied, mentally readying himself for the usual debriefing of their last few private meetings.

Seth roused, scratching his jaw and flopping a brief-case onto the table, which he then simply stared at. "The emperor is displeased with me. I—" he glanced up at Daniel, seeming to rethink whatever he'd been about to say. "We have found the first point upon which he and I see things differently, and while I don't think my cause is hopeless, it will take some doing to bring him around to seeing things my way on this particular matter."

Daniel nodded sagely, internally wondering what fresh hell Seth could be dancing around. He didn't even bother hoping that he wouldn't be the person responsible for dealing with whatever it was.

"On top of that, we're having trouble with a Hellenian plebeian general who's been stirring up trouble. Etsio, or something like that. Apparently, he even just now disrupted a group of patricians attempting to establish contact with the Eden half-world. The emperor instructed our network to put extra effort into finding a way to control or eliminate him, but they've had no luck, and the emperor is running low on patience." Daniel stayed silent, acutely alert as Seth vented, both triumph and wariness at the apparent increase in his security clearance making his aura tug against his mental control.

Seth huffed. "I'm sure all of this must bore you, being a military man yourself."

Daniel was caught off guard, given that it had been many years since he'd last casually thought of himself in such terms. "Not really," he replied, summoning over a golem that had been standing motionless by the doors to the kitchen. "The machinations of command were a far cry from the concerns of a medic like me. Would you care for coffee? Something to eat?"

Seth shook his head, glancing at the attentive golem. "No, thank you. I'm not staying." Daniel arched an inquisitive brow. "I've asked you every question I can think of, and you've passed with flying colors. If there's more for you to tell me, you can bring it up to me as you think of it. I'm happy to make that call at this stage." Seth stood and Daniel followed suit, excited triumph heating his aura, which he did his best to mute. "We'll have the phone networks back up in a day or two, and I want you to be a part of things in the capital when we announce it."

When Seth pulled off his suit jacket and draped it over his arm, it took all of Daniel's giddy self-control to not roll his eyes and laugh at the perfect print of lipstick revealed on his shirt collar. It was unmistakably Marissa's shade of red, and couldn't possibly have gotten there in pristine precision without contriving to do so.

Half-turned away from his seat, Seth paused and looked back. "Could I ask your advice about a delicate matter?"

"Of course," Daniel replied, eager to step back into such a role for the man paving his way to the emperor.

"I'm not sure if I'm doing the right thing with the emperor and..." Seth sighed, and Daniel's eyes narrowed a fraction at the slightly exaggerated air of dejectedness the younger man exuded. "Well, you always seem so sure of your convictions. Even when, to me, they seem to contradict themselves in how you act on them."

Daniel considered for a moment, knowing that this was more a test of politics than a request for advice, since no clear question had been asked. "If you ask me," he started slowly, "if your goals are, as you say, to bring the globe back under the empire, then there are a few thoughts that may help guide you to do so in a manner I'd choose."

Seth cocked his head, and Daniel proceeded, the rush from the balanced gamble he was taking swift in his veins. "First, people are far more willing to peacefully abide under an empire they didn't watch slaughter their loved ones. An empire that didn't wipe entire cities of innocent civilians from existence to make a point."

Daniel licked his dry lips. "Whatever steps can be taken to recruit and persuade, rather than attack and punish, might be a good place to put your energy until forced to do otherwise."

A slow, disconcerting smile spread across Seth's face. "When the head dies, the body follows..." The words were barely audible, and Seth seemed to shake himself and his voice cleared. "Yes. Yes, you're right. You have something there. Thank you, Mister Fawl."

Daniel bowed his head graciously. "I'm glad to be of service. To that end..." Seth again paused as he turned to leave the table. "When might I be granted an audience with the emperor to offer the same to him in person?" Seth's face darkened, and his whole aura began leaking great plumes of soot-laden smoke, which stained the coffered ceiling high overhead. "Or," Daniel said quickly, switching to his backup approach, "when might I be allowed to start pursuing a solution to the problem of unlocked adepts through imperial channels and research sources?"

The shift in topic seemed to please Seth, and his aura eased around him with a deep breath. "Soon. I'll be in touch."

Seth hefted his briefcase and walked back along the table toward the door, pausing when he reached it. "One last thing," he said with a hint of slyness, and Daniel groaned internally, wishing he'd stop beleaguering his departure. "I know you were once close with Dawn Renard. I have need of a mole within her little band of traitors and terrorists. Who would you suggest I approach? Who would be most open to defecting to our cause?"

Daniel's mind spun into hyperdrive, and he did his best to hide that fact from the man scrutinizing him a dozen yards away. If he gave an answer, it would be a confession of his rebellion ties. If he didn't, all of his efforts to get to the emperor through Seth might have been in vain. With a blink, Daniel ran through every person he knew to be there, briefly considering Milton Cartwright's ex-husband, Anthony, before his mind landed on another name, and his traitorous mouth blurted it out before he could stop it.

"Hannah Crowther." He quickly reached for a lie to cover why he'd have her name, and be willing to give it. "I had the same idea, and was given that name by a neutral agent I'm still in contact with from the solstice. Hannah shares your cult—faith, shares your faith, and is likely looking for someone to talk to about that. Her magic was repressed, keeping her from knowing about it or using it even after the English lock broke, and she harbors bitterness over that. I'm told she only ended up in Dawn's camp because she and her children wouldn't have been welcome at the conference, and Cartwright was targeting them, too. I suspect she'd jump at a chance for everything the emperor could offer her, as I have, once my role in defeating Milton was finished."

It was Seth's turn to blink. "Crowther? The late Dr. Crowther's wife?" Daniel nodded, and a twisted smile claimed Seth's handsome features. "Throwing your best friend's wife to a wolf like me... Perhaps I misjudged you."

Bile rose in Daniel's throat, eager to spill over. Not trusting his open lips as his eyes stung, Daniel held his breath and nodded with a tight smile. The moment a tug on his shields told Daniel that Seth was fully gone, he gasped and clung to the back of the nearest chair until guilt stopped threatening to drown him.

Straightening and collecting himself, he let his eyes linger on the trail of scorched footprints burned into his carpet before glancing up at the streak of soot overhead. He motioned to the waiting golem to fetch a ladder and start cleaning, noting, not for the first time, that Seth's Fire aura had no discernible smell. Not even in outbursts.

In his mind, he sent up a Voyaging beacon to the first person he had to warn, but a full minute stretched past with no response. He knew what he needed to do next but hesitated. Less than a month ago, he'd sworn he'd never go back. *So much for that.*

Daniel tuned out everything beyond his laser focus the second he landed at the edge of the compound shields. Unsurprisingly, they refused him entry, but Daniel bypassed them in under a minute, forcing his own powerful tendrils of magic into their workings.

He ignored the adepts who called out to him in offended tones, even those who tried to block his path as he strode on steady legs toward the little green at the center of the compound. He left those who only shouted untouched, but the few who reached out to stop or attack him were dropped with a quick brush of his hand on theirs, or left gasping for air in his wake.

"Fawl." Anthony Shupee and Olivia moved to intercept him as he reached the green, and he finally slowed. Both adepts looked concerned, and Daniel did his best to hide the raw emotions fighting to lash out of him, whether or not the target was deserving.

"I need to speak to Dawn urgently. Like, in the next five minutes, max. She's not answering my beacon, and she hasn't answered my calls in over a month. I had no other choice. If you want me to, I'll wait out of sight in her office, but you need to bring her here now."

Both Olivia and Anthony nodded, tight-lipped, and Anthony led Daniel up to the common house and through the front doors, shooing away the two adepts going over lists of food items in Dawn's office just inside. They left without protest, and Daniel found himself standing alone. His fists were balled at his sides, and the world around him sounded like he was underwater.

Jonathan's wife. Daniel knew Hannah's had been the right name to give, but the role she held in those two words drowned it out. He knew the practical reasons he shouldn't feel as bad as he did. As far as he knew, theirs had never been a marriage of love, at least on Jonathan's side. Hannah wasn't particularly kind, or loving, or compassionate to her friends, or kids—least of all to Daniel. His rational mind and breaking heart were at war, and he barely blinked when Dawn strode through the door behind him.

"What the hell were you thinking showing up like that and demanding—"

"I had to give Hannah to Seth. He's going to convince her to defect, and she's going to become a spy and possible saboteur within your walls." Daniel turned to find Dawn's heart-shaped face slack, her hand still on the knob. Swallowing, she very slowly and deliberately closed the door behind her, her deep-gold aura fracturing around her.

"Right." They both stared at the other for a long moment until Dawn turned to walk around Daniel to the battered cabinet along one wall, bracing against it. "She's here right now. No one can make a move on her until she steps out for some reason, so we have time."

"Are you absolutely certain?"

"I spoke to her five minutes ago. And since Seth Laufey didn't help build the shields protecting us, I doubt he can walk right through them like you." The words held none of the accusing anger Daniel would have expected them to. "Tell me more."

Daniel cut to the chase. "We have a dilemma. Either we warn Hannah and tip our hand that I warned her—through you or directly—or we let him make his approach and risk her actually betraying us."

Dawn shook her head, her long, blue-dyed braids swaying. "Damnit, Daniel! Why do you always end up in binds you could have just stayed out of." She pulled a hand down her face, a gesture Jonathan had once shared, and exhaustion seemed to fall over her like a veil. "What do we lose with option one?"

"A mole in the heart of the pocket holdout of the empire, our only real chance to stop nuclear measures being taken against us, and possibly the information we need to slow or stop the tide of adepts dying without ever learning to use or understand their magic. Causing mass damage, death, and disruption in doing so."

Dawn swore, dropping into a chair. "Well if you put it like that." She let out a shaky exhale which Daniel silently joined. "Okay then, Mister Fawl, what the hell is your plan for option two? I hope you at least have one?"

Daniel's cheeks pulled up. "Sort of. First, I can modify her memories slightly to limit the damage she can do if she does flip. Second, you keep her sidelined and warn folks not to tell her too much, if anything. Third, we try to come up with some reason for her to leave camp regularly so Seth can actually have a chance to contact her. Beyond that"—he shrugged guiltily—"we'll have to see."

Dawn rubbed her nose. "I hate this. I hate everything about this." She looked up at Daniel, her eyes worried, and shook her head. "I can handle warning other people in camp, and send her on the weekly runs into town for news, easy enough. But dammit, Dan, this had better not come back to bite us all." She stood, and when Daniel reached for something more to say, nothing came. "Just do your part, and for Mercury's sake, don't miss when or if she successfully starts helping the God's-damned empire."

With that, she left, and Daniel tried to gather himself before facing the revolting task of breaking into Hannah's mind to limit the damage she could cause if she chose to betray her late husband's closest friends. Summoning his phone, Daniel punched in Angie's number, relief easing the knots in his shoulders when she picked up almost immediately.

"Hey. What's up?"

"Would you meet me in an hour?" Daniel asked without preamble. "I'm busy here for another hour or so"—*and might need at least one more to collect myself*—"but I'd really like to see you in person again. Please."

Chapter Fifteen

When Angie landed in the large, comfortable, dark front room of the Cotswolds cottage, the clean, soft, and quiet familiarity washed over her like a balm. She took one deep breath after another until the last few hours had been washed away. Not to be forgotten, but to be dealt with at some, *any*, other time.

Not waiting for Daniel to join her, Angie took the stairs two at a time, shedding her clothes the moment she got to the bedroom, swapping them for a house robe, and stomped into the bathroom to use every single scented, soothing product she'd left behind to live in her car and chase Eden.

A little over an hour and a half later, she opened the door once more to let the perfumed steam roll out, very carefully teasing up her aura around her just enough to dry her hair. She didn't want to think about the red welts on her left hand and wrist where her own fireball had burned her. Thankfully, as she watched her auburn hair closely in the mirror for any damage, her flesh and hair seemed to be once more impervious to her own flames.

"Angie?" a welcome voice called from downstairs, and Angie grinned before stepping out into the spacious bedroom.

"Yes! Up here!" She pulled aside the curtains to reveal the dark night beyond, opening the window beneath the thatched roof to let in the refreshing Britannian breeze. When she turned away, Daniel stood in the doorway. "Oh, hey. Where were you?"

Daniel was dressed as if for patrician matters, but the pine needles caught on the cuff of his trousers told her otherwise. He nodded, rolling his shoulders and looking away. "Dawn's. I know, I know, but something came up which I had to go back to... deal with." Angie's dark mood returned just a fraction, and she apparently failed to disguise it.

"What? Why that look?" Daniel asked.

Angie shrugged, not wanting to dwell on the topic, and tried to let go of the bitterness that had risen in her throat. "I haven't been welcome there since the solstice nearly two months ago. Not a big deal, it just... doesn't feel great." She wanted to say more, ask if he knew why Casey had shunned her, but didn't.

Daniel released a heavy sigh as he leaned against the dresser opposite the large, perfectly made bed from Angie. "Yeah. Same here." He crossed his arms across his trim waist, and Angie tried not to notice. "Don't take it too personally. I think a lot of it has to do with all of them mourning Jonathan, like we are, and they might be looking for someone to blame so it hurts less. However," he added quickly, grimacing. "I'm not saying either of us are to blame! Not at all." He rubbed a hand across the back of his neck, and Angie couldn't make herself meet his eyes. "Cartwright is the only person with any blame, and well, he got his."

Angie's eyes darted to her jeans, left on the floor at the foot of the bed, the heavy copper sigil coin still in the pocket. She colored when she realized the tiny action would have just given away her biggest secret if Daniel had known what to watch for. She nodded distractedly when Daniel didn't go on. She was almost certain that wasn't why Casey had blackballed her. But that didn't get her any closer to knowing the real reason.

"I miss him, too," Daniel said, his voice tight, and Angie finally looked up, only getting a glimpse of the deep, raw grief on Daniel's beautiful face before the sight became too much. "If you ever want to talk about it, about him..."

"I'm fine," Angie said, trying to find somewhere reasonable and bland to look as she belted her soft robe tighter around her.

"That's what worries me." Angie knew what was coming next, but that didn't ease the sick twist under her crossed arms that accompanied it. "You've been fine for weeks now. Not mourning, not grieving. It's like you gave yourself the first week after we lost him to feel it all, and then just stopped. Angie, please look at me." She did, and he shook his head, looking lost. "It's not healthy."

"I know," Angie said around the lump in her throat. She did. Jonathan himself, or at least his ghost, had told her the same several times. "It's just"—*now or never*—"I don't feel like he's really gone. Not emotionally, not in my soul.

I know it." Angie pressed her fingers to her temple, then over her heart. "But I don't feel it. In fact, there's a chance that if you wanted, I could help you—"

"That's exactly what I mean. That denial isn't healthy."

"No, you don't get it," Angie said with exasperation. "It's sort of like with the demons I've hosted in my necklace…" Angie trailed off when Daniel's whole aspect darkened. *Literally*, Angie thought numbly, *thanks to his aura of light*. Her fingers twisting the silver key hanging from her necklace. "Never mind," she mumbled, feeling like she needed to backtrack. "I'll think about all that. Thanks."

Searching for the nearest distraction to hand, she moved to perch on the end of the bed and twisted toward Daniel. "I do have news on the Eden front." Daniel didn't move, still frowning, and Angie trailed off uncertainly when he stayed frozen. "I didn't get the key. But I saw Jasper again. They… they told me something about some demons being sentient, and I saw one of the old Councilors go through. The oldest, the little old man."

Daniel's aura flashed cold at the mention of Jasper's hint about demons, and Angie could see the way he mentally fought his way out of the dark humor before he sighed, dropping his tense arms to his sides. "Well. Assuming he was the only one to go through, that leaves only three more in the wind, including Jasper. I never did learn his name. I don't expect to find the Slavic general unless he wants us to, but I've been waiting for the Frankish woman to pop up again. She didn't seem the type to stay quiet or unseen for long."

He pushed away from the dresser and moved to sit on the side of the bed a few feet away. "Angie, I heard about what happened during the move out to Eden you interrupted. Please, the next time you find them, promise me you'll take things slow and easy. Attacking them isn't working, so you should really try something else. Please." Angie nodded, then cringed when Daniel added, "And if Jasper tries to bait you with demons, supposedly sentient or not, run. Don't trust them, don't be curious, just run. I don't want to discourage you from chasing Eden and whatever else Jasper was involved in, but please..."

"I will," Angie promised quickly. *Unless it seems safe*, she told herself, but knew Daniel didn't want to hear it.

"So how have you been recently? Just on your own?" he asked, a film of stress and hesitation coating every inch of his angular face and lean body.

"Frustrated. Mostly from everything around Jasper and the conference. And..." Angie drew breath to ask him if Jonathan had ever said anything to him about feelings beyond friendship with her, to ask about how the two men had gone from lovers to friends, to brothers. She wanted so badly to ask, but as she reached for the concentration and energy she knew it would take to have that conversation, the weight of it swamped her. As the breath left her silently, her force of will followed, and Angie surrendered to her baser motives. She tucked everything else away in the back of her mind and leaned toward Daniel. "Tired. Very tired."

Daniel gently bumped his shoulder into hers, his Caledonian voice a soft rumble. "Anything you want to talk about?"

She shrugged, sitting back up straight and cracking her back. "The conference, or whatever it should be called now that it's permanent and unorganized, just isn't the life for me." She let go of her careful mental blinders around exactly why, and Noah's cutting remark bubbled to the surface. "They don't want me there, either. The established adepts. Noah told me just tonight that he missed who I used to be. That he missed—that I've changed."

"People are supposed to change, Angie," was Daniel's simple reply, and Angie felt the sting of Noah's words melt away as she smiled at Daniel's gentle sincerity. "Those who love you will change with you to keep loving whoever you become." Angie hungrily scoured him with her gaze, lingering on his dark eyes, sharp nose, and the sliver of his lean, muscled chest visible at his unbuttoned collar. He held out a slender, strong hand covered in gold rings. "I know we're on a break, but that doesn't mean I can't offer comfort if you need some. There's no shame in that."

Cautiously, Angie brushed her fingers against his open palm. The sigh of relief she breathed when the vibration of his skin was barely noticeable released tension throughout her body she hadn't been aware of until it was gone. *Fuck the break*, she thought to herself, grasping Daniel's wrist over his spiked-wheel tattoo and pressing her thumb to his pulse. "I'm sorry I ever asked for the stupid break," she admitted, her throat tight as new, more immediate tension replaced the old, and rosewood smoke rose in her aura. "Can we please officially pause it for one night? I know I started it, and it's not fair to keep yanking you around, but I really, really need..." Angie's throat closed off, and she couldn't finish the thought.

"On one condition," Daniel said, making her heart soar. "Be whoever you are, whoever you need to be. But please, let's keep things light and sweet?"

Angie nodded eagerly. "So *we don't get a repeat of last time*," went unsaid. She'd barely drawn a breath when Daniel's lips met hers. Soft and tender at first, she let herself melt into the taste of him. Time dropped away, and Angie let go of every scrap of thought or emotion not tied to the moment she existed in.

It didn't take long for the way they were leaning toward each other to become uncomfortable, and Angie wrapped the arm she'd been propped on around Daniel's neck, laying back onto the thick, soft duvet with a sigh and pulling him with her.

Lithe as a cat, Daniel landed on his elbows over her. His eyes were dark and heavy with lust, and when he resumed his kisses, they were deeper, more urgent, and Angie matched his energy with gusto. One of Daniel's hands slipped easily into the front of her robe, massaging and gently pinching her breast, and Angie replied with a soft gasp of pleasure.

Reaching down between them, Angie's fingers found his cock already hardening beneath the fine wool of his slacks. No sooner had she brushed along his length than Daniel wrapped an arm roped with lean muscle beneath

Angie's back and half-lifted her, shifting her fully onto the bed, and laying himself close along her side from shoulder to ankle. Her robe had only halfway come with her, and Daniel delicately shifted it apart the rest of the way, his grin as he did so making Angie melt further.

When his fingers slipped beneath her thighs, Angie's breath juddered. Daniel's mouth fell to her neck, and it wasn't long before Angie was desperate for him. "Daniel," she panted, rolling toward him enough to separate them an inch, and she undid his buttons and zip. He paused his ministrations to help remove his clothes, standing to peel away his trousers and socks, and Angie took the opportunity to slip the robe fully off her shoulders.

When Daniel climbed back atop her, Angie's heart skipped a beat. He was beautiful. Elegant and predatory, his attention fixed on her with such restrained ferocity that her blood instinctually retreated, then rushed back up to meet him. Again, his fingers reached into her, his gold rings cold against her heat, as he kissed up her neck. "Are you ready?" His breath rushed against her ear. When she nodded, parting her legs wider for him, his fingers spread her slickness and were replaced by the slow, indulgent thrust of his shaft, making them both shudder.

Angie's mouth fell open and she relaxed into the sensation, letting Daniel set the pace. Part of her wanted to grasp, to scratch, to reach for the demons of darker lust that rose in her mind, but she breathed in the smell of Daniel's skin—beeswax and frankincense—and let them fall away again as he settled into her.

They went slow, closely entwined. Angie caressed every inch of Daniel's skin she could reach, feeling the slight buzz of his skin lessen the more she let go into the moment, the sensation, and the blessed, joyful closeness of him. When the pace began to feel too slow, Angie tugged at Daniel's thigh, and he pulled hers up over his shoulder, reaching down with his other to gently tease her clit.

She moaned his name, and he echoed with hers, picking up the speed of his thrusts with matching circles of his thumb. His beard tickled her neck as he buried his face there, his back arching. "Fuck," he swore, the muscles in his shoulders rolling, and Angie stopped breathing as a shift deep within her core began to build. Reading her silence, Daniel maintained his pace and patterns, the hand he braced himself on gripping her shoulder.

Everything fell away—no thoughts except for her own pleasure stretching across her mind, and when her pressure broke, Daniel was only a moment behind, shuddering into her as his hand on her clit slowly stilled.

Only when Angie had stopped convulsing did Daniel still, lowering himself to Angie's chest with shaking arms. Angie held him tight to her, not wanting to part yet. He kissed her temple, and she nudged his head aside to do the same, grinning. She felt at peace, and when her thoughts cleared enough to remember that the bliss would have to end sooner than later, she did her best to pretend otherwise.

"Thank you," she whispered into his sandy hair as he nestled into her, still panting.

"I love you," he whispered back, his low brows slightly drawn but his smile at ease. "All of you. Whoever you are, and however you might change."

Sneaking up to the steps of the common house at the conference a few hours later, Angie stilled as Noah Byrne pushed away from a shadowed section of wall beneath a tree nearby.

"You're a liar."

Her happy, satisfied contentment faltered, and she fought to hold it intact. "Lucia was asleep before I left, and I left extra protections in place around her. I made sure everything was totally taken care of before I left. I'm not a prisoner here." Angie tried to keep her exasperation out of her voice, crossing her arms as he approached.

"Not about that," Noah scoffed, waving a hand, his words slurring slightly from whatever he was clearly intoxicated by. He looked her up and down, and Angie could see his cheeks flush even in the faint, night-light glow through the windows behind her. "You've just come back from fucking him, haven't you?"

Angie rolled her eyes, too tired and, for once, happy, to let his words get to her again. Anything she said would risk confirming his accusations anyway, so she just shook her head, turning back toward the common house.

"Is it the others? Is that why you won't date me?" Noah asked, and Angie merely stopped with a frustrated sigh. Before she could answer, Noah took another step closer and added, "I'd dump them all and be monogamous with you, if that's what it takes. You can do way better than that old man, trust me."

"I hope you don't mean you," Angie shot back, turning back as her contempt won out. "And no. I wouldn't consider 'dating you' even if you weren't poly. Stop asking." She mockingly emphasized the words she echoed back to him with her fingers, her aura darkening with disgust at what she knew he actually wanted from her. "That's not what I want, not something I'd ever ask for from someone who was poly, and it wouldn't say good things about me if I did. Or you if you did it."

Noah's hand shot out, grabbing her shoulder, and Angie barely had to think to make her aura blister his skin where it touched hers as she bared her teeth in a snarl. He yanked his hand back, his eyes going wide, and cradled it against his chest with his other.

"I *have* changed," Angie said with bitter pleasure, reflecting on seventeen months of banishment and everything else that had shaped and strengthened her since she'd first met the Celt standing before her. "And I'm glad of it. You, on the other hand, haven't. And there's no way you ever could, no version of you that you could ever become that would make me even think about crawling into your bed."

"Go fuck yourself," Noah spat, his expression caught between fear and anger.

"Happily." Angie looked him up and down, her lip twisting. "Given the alternative." She expected her chest to heat with emotion, but the deep relief of her time with Daniel seemed to act as a resilient buffer.

As she turned away, determined to accept no more delays on her path to sleep, Noah asked behind her, "So, are you still fucking Fawl?"

"We are on a break," Angie said exasperatedly as she mounted the stairs. "But that doesn't mean I'm remotely interested in dating anyone else. And in case you have any big ideas about why I'm staying here," she added, yanking open the door, "Lucia is the only, I repeat *only*, reason I'm not running away from you as fast as I can Voyage." *Well. That and waiting to hear from Jasper...* "Go fuck one of the girlfriends you already neglect."

Chapter Sixteen

"Fawl, Minister Laufey has specifically request-ed your attendance at the recording of today's broadcast." Daniel looked up through his dark shades at Marissa striding toward him, and disengaged his aura from the shielding he was working on by releasing the clear, solid tendrils of magic back. Her stiletto heels made her wobble slightly on the uneven cobbles of the piazza, and he summoned his cane from the bench where he'd left it nearby to meet her halfway and reduce the chances of her falling.

The Mediterranean day was sweltering, without a cloud in sight. It took Daniel little effort to cool the air around him with his aura, but Marissa Hayward looked damp. A year ago, he would have extended his Air aura around her as he drew near, but now he kept his magic slightly hardened from overlapping or mixing with hers in the slightest. He'd paid too dearly in the recent past for letting her magic infect him.

"How is it going?" Marissa asked as she turned back the way she'd come, and Daniel fell into step beside her. When her shoes caught between two paving stones, she flailed briefly, and Daniel made no move to steady her.

"Well. If any rioters or armies make it into the city, the defenses around the palace will hold out for a few extra days. Less, if there are patricians among them, but they'll still buy the emperor time. What news from him?"

"I believe Seth would rather tell you himself." Marissa slowed as they climbed the steps. "He's rather marvelous, isn't he?" she cooed, pulling her aura into the shape of a blood-red ribbon, which she wound through her fingers in a girlish way, ill-befitting her age. "So commanding, intelligent, and passionate..."

He knew she was baiting him and debated whether or not he should pretend to care. Daniel kept the knee that had spent many years possessed stiff and trailing behind him as he climbed the stairs, despite it not actually paining him that day. It helped with his persona. "Indeed" was all he settled on.

They passed through the entry hall, and Moretti gave them a small bow as he exited the way they'd come. "You know," Marissa said, glancing at Daniel sidelong with a sly smile, "he's really being such a good boyfriend. I can't believe he's promoted me so fast from writing radio broadcasts to now appearing on TV. Generous, too. And in more ways than that." She laughed a girly trill. "I mean, we're both busy, obviously, but just last night, in bed, he must have gotten—"

"Well," Daniel interrupted swiftly, feeling nauseous, "you clearly have a different idea of what dating looks like than I do." Marissa blinked at him, frowning but looking pleased with herself as they turned a corner toward the large room at the back of the palace. "For the three years Angie and I were together, not even once did I go to a meeting with lipstick on my collar, and I simply can't imagine her ever describing our activities in bed to someone who had long ago told her that they were uninterested in such topics being raised between them. It's almost like you and Laufey are putting on a show of it all."

Marissa's mouth fell open, and she looked hurt. "Do you hate me?" she asked, sounding much younger than her forty-something years, and Daniel came to a stop a stride ahead of her when she fell back.

He blew out a long breath before half-turning, not looking at her but at the oil painting of some long-forgotten battle on the wall. "I don't care about you in the slightest—not even enough to hate you." He'd already told her as much a few months ago at the closing ball of the English Conference, but saying it here and now somehow felt crueler. More deeply meant. "But if you ever attempt to control or deceive me again, I will ensure you pay dearly for it."

Marissa's caramel skin paled. "Then, those little indiscretions in my past you once held over me..."

Daniel huffed, remembering when they'd hoped to use blackmail to keep the world from tipping over into the chaos now slowly eroding it. "Are forgotten until, or unless, you give me a reason to remember."

Marissa yielded a step beneath his glowering stare, and he turned away, reaching the end of the hall and carefully stepping through an unassuming door into the bustling newsroom beyond.

A large backdrop of rich imperial imagery dominated one wall, and lights hanging from rigging overhead made up for every window in the room being boarded and heavily curtained. A dozen patricians Daniel barely recognized—or didn't recognize at all—buzzed around four large film cameras, doing he-didn't-know-what with the machines and the banks of monitors and switches connected to them by a jungle of cables under foot.

"Fawl, over here!" Daniel found Seth already seated behind the large, immaculate desk in front of the backdrop, a sickly-looking young woman tapping powdered makeup across his cheeks. "Thank you for coming. I really wanted to have you here for this."

Daniel gave him a politely quizzical look as he picked his way through the cables, and Seth's answering look of bright, sycophantic zeal made him slow.

"Thirty seconds," a black man nearby announced to the room, and the makeup lady scurried away.

Seth tapped a sheath of papers on the desk before him, beckoning Daniel closer. "Please. I want you nearby. I think you'll like today's broadcast, and I have a surprise for you. Would you please stand just there?" He pointed to a spot at the end of the desk.

Daniel did his best to look more supportive than worried, despite his deep unease, and did as directed. Thankfully, every camera arrayed before him was pointed squarely at Seth, and he was confident he'd be fully out of shot. He folded his gloved hands across the head of his cane as the lights dimmed, leaving only the stage illuminated.

"Greetings to the globe," Seth began, his voice changing in quality as he addressed the camera directly before him. "All loyal subjects of the empire, I hail and salute you. Particularly those of our mighty network of informants and fighters who are keeping the spirit of the empire alive in far-flung lands. I know that the last two months have been filled with pain, fear, and uncertainty for many of you, but today it is my great honor to bring you glad and triumphant news from the emperor. First of all, we are delighted to announce that, with the help of expert patricians in the emperor's service, all landline and cell phone connectivity across the globe has, as of this moment, been restored."

Seth raised his hand dramatically with a wide smile, and Daniel saw Marissa, back at the banks of monitors, grumpily press a large button with a manicured nail. An odd, artificial electrical noise accompanied it, dimming the lights for a breath, and Daniel pursed his lips at the theatrics.

As Seth rambled, praising the might and wisdom of the empire, Daniel surreptitiously summoned his old sleek cell phone from the safe in his Boston kitchen straight into his pocket, his heart swelling at the familiar, missed weight of it as it appeared in his hidden hand. He pressed and held the power button without needing to look, but even as it buzzed silently upon waking, Daniel's excitement soured. "*With the help of expert patricians...*" While Seth wouldn't announce it to any and all, that statement meant magic was involved in restoring that infrastructure. And that, in turn, likely meant he couldn't consider the use of his deeply useful cell to be safe anymore.

He banished it back to the safe with a sour taste on his tongue as Seth paused and shifted. "Now, I hope your appetites have been whetted, because I have even bigger news to bring you, which I hope will greatly ease the stress you all feel in these uncertain times." Daniel shifted his cane to one side, leaning his hip against it. "After much consideration and a great deal of careful planning, the emperor wishes to announce that, as a gesture of good faith to every citizen across the globe, he's committed to disarming, dismantling, and disposing of all nuclear weapons stockpiled since the Great Unification. Such weapons will never be used on his future subjects, in hopes of minimizing bloodshed as we reunite all of humankind under one just and righteous rule."

Daniel nearly fell over as recorded applause filled the room. Standing back upright and gripping his cane, he couldn't help smiling as his mind raced. It was a thousand times better than he could have hoped for. He wondered how much of this decision was primarily aimed at keeping opposing factions from stealing and using them against the empire, but the results were exactly what he'd spent sleepless nights praying for. The shocking revelation that they'd paid off made him lightheaded.

"I fully believe that I have acted for the good of all in encouraging the emperor in this decision, and we will continue to strive to reach the many faction leaders emerging across the globe, and to face them, not on a field of battle, but at a negotiating table. I know that to some of you, this may seem to contradict the previous position held by the emperor and shared by me, and I would like to acknowledge that both the emperor and I were swayed in this."

Daniel tilted his head, hoping whoever the influence was would be named. They were undoubtedly someone Daniel needed to contact, but none of the patricians who had joined Seth in flocking back to the heart of the diminished empire seemed likely candidates as he mentally reviewed the ones he knew.

Seth went on, "I have the great honor and privilege of being advised by a courageous and measured man, whose kind advice has helped me see not only what would benefit the empire as it is, but also what it someday could be. My one-time adversary, who has become my idolized mentor, and a level-headed military veteran whose subtle, calculated intelligence will undoubtedly be a vital element to the Reunification, balanced against the passionate zeal of his own in the wise hands of the emperor—Daniel Fawl."

Daniel couldn't hide his deep shock and mentally grabbed his aura to pull it back under control as it buffeted wildly with hope and apprehension. This was the share of power and prestige he'd been chasing, but he'd always thrived in the shadows, not in the limelight.

Seth had turned to look at him and was clearly waiting for some signal. Glancing at the cameras that stayed trained on the younger man, Daniel swallowed. He was a man of shadows. Keeping out of sight in pursuit of his goals. *To be named so publicly, let alone to be shown...*

Daniel nodded curtly, and pressed a tight smile to his lips as two of the cameras panned to him. He raised a gloved hand, nodding once more, and breathed a silent gust of relief when they turned back to Seth. Thank the Gods he hadn't been expected to say anything.

Seth continued, but Daniel barely listened. The broadcast would be repeated all day long, so he wasn't worried about missing anything more in the moment. If what his former recruit said was true, that meant the emperor must surely know of him by now and was open to being heavily swayed. And, as Daniel replayed what had just happened, he felt the weight of being invited to appear on camera, as well as his permission to do so being waited for, settle with warm triumph through his core. He'd won.

Are both the emperor and Seth now my unexpected allies? Just the emperor, and Seth was playing along? Just Seth, crediting the emperor for things he never said? Whatever the answer, the possibility of recruiting the emperor as an already-converted ally made Daniel's whole being buzz with excitement.

Chapter Seventeen

Angie wasted no time in following Jasper's Voyaging beacon after two and a half weeks of waiting. She'd been lounging in the library at the conference site, avoiding Noah and being avoided by Lucia when the signal had pinged in her mind, and she'd known in an instant where to find the former Councilor, and that they were waiting for her.

The first day of September was cool and slightly overcast, and Angie was dressed in the black linen dress she'd modified too many times to count since Daniel had first given it to her the day after they'd met. In fact, she doubted he'd even recognize it as being the same. Not wanting to waste time changing, Angie simply handed her book to one of the leathery golems that staffed the library and brought up her shields and magic before Voyaging to Jasper's beacon.

The cautious hesitation Angie suspected had caused the delay in them meeting again was etched in every line of their body, and Angie momentarily panicked when she realized they were underground. She knew the chamber well, despite having only visited it once before. It was circular, doming overhead. The walls were lined with sheets of copper, silver, and gold, which had been hammered thin and polished until they shone and reflected the light of several magically maintained torches placed in sconces along the walls.

"Angie. I hope you're well."

A stone threshold, complete with a slender, carefully balanced lintel stood in the center, and a tunnel just large enough for two people to walk abreast twisted out of sight behind Jasper. The dull rumble of the slow-moving cars overhead was far more sporadic than it had been last time.

"Stonehenge?" Angie asked, looking up and behind her where she knew the monument stood on the surface.

"No," Jasper replied, pointing at the inactive threshold between them with a chubby hand. "For today's lesson, the well-worn Threshold is all we need. Any would do, but I'm fond of this one."

Angie arched a brow. "Lesson? I'd started to think you weren't going to keep your promise. And who were you trying to lead to Lucia in Nevada? I want to know who you trust, if I'm supposed to trust you."

Jasper ignored her, fishing in a pocket of their long shirt with an exasperated sigh. When they pulled out what was clearly a half-world key, Angie had to hold herself back from snatching it away and running.

In an instant, all of Angie's reservations seemed unimportant. *One key at a time. Anything to get to Eden.* She sighed with wary surrender. "So, what am I here to learn then?"

"Basics. And then, if you're willing after I explain, I have a favor to ask. In exchange," they added before Angie could express her contempt, "for the exact kind of payment you've been chasing me for two months to find. I'll take you to visit Eden."

Angie saluted Jasper with exaggerated pomp. "Yes, Councilor." Jasper shot her a reproachful look, and Angie sheepishly stuffed her hands into the pockets of her linen dress, wrapping her fingers around the copper coin and sat phone held within. "I do already know some basics. What did you plan to cover?"

"You know how to build them in the normal way?"

"Yes. Just using intention, then checking if you got it right before locking it in. I also know how to use a key."

Jasper looked surprised. "Really? How?"

Angie shrugged, deciding there was no longer a reason to keep her actions from two years ago to herself. "I've used two before. To find the English Court's Seer when Cartwright tried to illegally cut Daniel's Wyrd thread short. And then again from there through to the Norns' world to bargain with them."

Jasper nodded, and Angie got the impression that they resisted the urge to detour down that topic, sniffing and shifting a long gray curl out of their face. "Right. Well, were both of those two-way Thresholds?"

Angie nodded, then stopped. "Yes, but the banishment Threshold Cartwright shoved me through wasn't. There was no other side to it when I landed in Discordium."

Jasper swallowed hard, and Angie didn't hide her bitter smile. Occasional reminders that she was the only adept ever known to make it back from banishment were also good reminders of just how much she had, and could, survive. Perhaps, one day, she should record what she'd seen there, since all keys to Discordium had been destroyed and none other could ever report on it.

"Yes, well, then you also already know that Thresholds can be built either way. And that choice can be built into the keys themselves, so any gateway opened with them is always one or the other." Angie nodded, her senses sharpening. She hadn't realized she'd known that before now. Had never given it much thought. "You also know, I presume, that Thresholds can only be built from this world? Regardless of keys or kinds?"

Angie nodded again, swallowing in turn. She could picture Jonathan telling her all about such matters in the drizzling woods behind the conference site like it was yesterday. She gave the coin in her fist a squeeze, grief unexpectedly welling in her, and pushed the memory away. As she did, another replaced it. She'd stepped through her first keyed Threshold thoughtlessly years before, running into Sakshi's world in a blind attempt to save the life of Daniel who was writhing and dying in her arms as his life thread was ripped away. She'd taken the key and closed the Threshold behind her without thinking. She suppressed a shudder. "Yeah. Come on, you aren't teaching me much so far. In fact, I've already taught my recruit, Lucia, most of this myself..."

Jasper only seemed mildly annoyed by Angie's needling. "Do you know how to collapse a keyed Threshold?"

"By using the same key in it again?" Angie wished she sounded certain, but she'd only done or seen it once, and, in retrospect, had done so very foolishly.

"Yes, that's one way. Or, another key can be used on an active Threshold to change which world it leads to. The only other way"—Jasper looked up at the narrow stone lintel balanced on its pillars—"is to break the frame the magic is built into. Unlike ordinary Thresholds, keyed Thresholds cannot be collapsed any other way, such as pulling the magic away, which can take time. Hence the lintels we can knock aside in emergencies."

Knowing that made Angie uncomfortable. Half the frames she'd seen keyed Thresholds built into had been doors in walls with no removable lintel. What if they had never been closed properly? What if something had happened to the person holding the key? "Noted."

"Now," Jasper said, and Angie's aura flared when they lifted the key they held to eye level. "As you know, the basic magic of a key is to prevent a specific half-world from being Skipped to, and to ensure the exact same world is always reached through the Threshold. It's not inherent to the half-world magic bound to keys, but many also have practical magic layered on top. Such as restrictions on summoning them, or the like." Jasper tipped their hand, and the key vanished. When they held it palm up once more, it reappeared. "Have you learned to add or remove such magic?"

"No. I know about it, but summoning isn't something I'm very good at, and I've never learned those kinds of wards."

Jasper nodded, seeming pleased. "Well, that will take a great deal of time, so let's plan on that for our next lesson."

Angie gave them a skeptical look. "I haven't learned much in this one yet."

"Well, you clearly know more than I expected." Jasper dipped a gracious nod, and Angie assessed yet again whether or not to believe the seemingly kind and gentle nature of the adept before her. "But I'm glad you do. That means I can cut right to the chase." They stepped forward, placing the key they held into a small hole in the stone doorframe, clearly made for that purpose, and a dusty-pink membrane of magic stretched across it, adding a slight pastel glow to the chamber. "I called you here today," Jasper said, stepping back once more, "because it's time for me to make first contact with the Inferi, and I need backup."

"Woah, hold up," Angie said, raising her hands. "Inferi? And when did I agree to be your backup?"

"Inferi is the word, I believe, that the old texts used to refer to demons with more human intelligence than the others. And I'm asking you, specifically, to play a part in trying to contact them because you, more than anyone else I know of, might believe me—and believe that an alliance might be possible."

"Demons are all—" Angie realized the retort she was about to give was Daniel's words more than her own, and cut it short. The idea of it made her squirm, but she wanted to be open-minded. "I never really thought of it that way—animalistic versus sentient. Just demons who all wanted to hurt me the moment they knew I was there."

Jasper watched her silently, one of their plump hands rubbing nervous circles on the other.

"I guess there were a few worlds..." Angie eventually said, frowning as she replayed old memories in a new light. "Ones with houses, abandoned cities, plenty I assumed were just trying to mimic the true world in some way." Angie reached for a coat pocket she didn't have without noticing. "There was even one where I landed in a war-torn city. It even had air-raid sirens. A lot of the supplies that kept me alive came from there. And there was this shrouded man..." Angie swallowed, feeling vulnerable as more memories of being stalked through world after world rose too fast to stop. "Fine. I'll believe you for the moment. But I'll still need proof."

Jasper grinned. "You'll get some. I promise. But for today, it's really me who has to put a great deal of trust in you, whether I want to or not. I can't take the key with me, as I can't risk it being lost forever if going there kills me," they explained when Angie gave them a skeptical look, "but I need to leave it guarded in this world, as I've been worried for a while now that you aren't the only person following my movements."

They turned to face the Threshold fully, and Angie followed suit. "I need a lookout. If the gateway is closed behind me, I'm lost for good. I don't yet know if this key is even two-way, so perhaps I'm lost regardless, but I need you to hope and trust for long enough that I stand a chance of coming home."

The last two words struck a chord in Angie, and the stubbornness in her that had been about to decline to help shrank away. She'd fought so hard and long to return from banishment. She couldn't stand the thought of putting someone else through the same. "What's through there?" Angie asked instead.

"I'll let you know." Jasper pulled a small imperial coin from their pocket, tossing it at the membrane of magic. It bounced off and rolled to fall beside Angie's foot. "Debris, and atmosphere, and the like can't pass through Thresholds. Creating them in the first place would be far more dangerous if not. Only living beings, and whatever they're carrying, can pass through. Otherwise, we'd risk things like radiation, poisoned gasses, or floods by opening Thresholds to unknown destinations. The only way to learn what's on the other side is to step through.

"One last question..." Angie nodded for them to ask it, and they looked at her sidelong, seeming to hold their breath. "Is it true you know how to remove demon possessions, and have even successfully done so?"

Angie smiled darkly. "Yes. And yes, more than once."

Jasper sighed happily. "Excellent. I hope I won't need to ask you to use those skills for me, but it's a great further comfort. How, may I ask, did you learn?"

Angie tilted her head back and forth. "Just instinct. Honestly. I'd barely learned to use my magic, and Daniel let me just feel it out with the demon in his knee." Angie winced, realizing that he probably wouldn't thank her for revealing how long he'd kept that event a secret from everyone, including Jasper. "If you're worried about possession," Angie added, barely thinking, "Jonathan created sigils designed to prevent—" She stopped herself short, the coin already in her fingers as she lifted it from her pocket, realizing there was no way she was willing to part with it.

Between her and the undulating Threshold, Jonathan's ghost took shape. His eyes opened, widening further when they landed on Jasper, and Angie quickly willed him back into the coin. He looked at her for a piercing moment before obeying, and Angie couldn't bring herself to look at Jasper standing beside her as she desperately tried to think of a plausible explanation.

"Interesting." The word was barely audible. "So is it true, then, that he and you—"

"I'll do it," Angie said quickly to change the topic. "But I want keys as payment." Perhaps, if she got her hands on any of value, she could use them as a reason to make Dawn—or, more importantly, Casey—talk to her again.

"I understand." Jasper's tone was pitying, and Angie didn't want to think about the double meaning in their response. "I cannot, will not, give you the Eden key, as there are far too many innocents living there that I wouldn't trust you to safeguard. At least not yet. But I have many others I've left with a trusted confidant. However," they interjected, raising a hand when Angie drew breath to make further demands, "I'll be holding off on handing over any of them until I return safely. Knowing you could take this one and run away, I'll risk on trust. But the others I'll keep as insurance against that."

Unable to come up with a convincing argument, Angie stuffed her hands back in her pockets. "Fine. I'll stand guard for as long as I reasonably can, and if you get possessed, I'll help you with that too. In exchange for *valuable* keys to locked half-worlds." *In exchange for Eden, and the better world that could be built here instead,* she thought, but didn't say. There was time to earn Jasper's trust.

Jasper smiled gratefully and strode through the Threshold they had opened. Angie shifted uncomfortably in the solitude left behind. She'd expected the older adept to grab supplies, or tools, or weapons before stepping through. Angie circled around the Threshold, which was invisible from the back as all Thresholds were, before planting herself back in front.

Jasper reappeared less than a minute later, outlined by the stretching magical membrane before breaking through. Their eyes were bright, and their plump cheeks were flushed with excitement. "Thanks for waiting so long. It's the right world, and they seem open to helping us, or at least talking. Oh this is wonderful." They clapped, and turned right back to the Threshold. "Please wait a few more hours."

Angie gaped as they passed right back through without waiting for a response. Apart from the shock that Jasper appeared to have been right about sentient demons being real, Angie hadn't been waiting long at all. *Must be a faster timestream there.* Jasper must have also been confident in their abilities, and not wanted Angie to have time to argue, leaving her no choice but to stay. Deciding to settle in, she looked around the small, isolated chamber. There wasn't much to see.

She wandered toward her own reflection in one polished wall, but before she could sit down on the smooth, solid stone floor, another beacon lit in her mind—wild, strong, and full of fear. *Not from Jasper, but from Daniel.*

CHAPTER EIGHTEEN

D aniel was quietly wandering through the massive, winding warren of the imperial palace in Rome, searching for the emperor's private rooms, when someone grabbed him from behind and Voyaged them both away.

Without even needing to think, Daniel held his breath and willed his aura to remove any and all oxygen from the surrounding area as he steadied himself with his cane. He'd landed in a familiar white marble amphitheater and summoned a pair of dark shades to protect against the glare of the sun off the stone. He put them on in the second it took him to turn in a full circle, realizing whoever had brought him to the English Conference site had left just as fast.

"Angie?" he called out, releasing the aura from his attempt at stalling an attack, and stripping off his leather gloves with a growing sense of unease. Whoever grabbed him had felt much larger than her, but he couldn't think of who else would take him there. He was surprised the shields around the space would even allow it.

"I knew it. I fucking knew it."

Noah's voice was close behind Daniel, and he turned to face the Celt, holding back his magic but not his ire. "Excuse me? I don't know who you think you are, but I assure you, you'll regret bringing me here in such a manner."

Noah's reply was high-pitched and mocking. "We're on a break." The absurdity of it made Daniel blink, but Noah's voice returned to normal as he shifted into a rant that made Daniel's sense of danger prick. "I should have known. You're just stringing her along, aren't you? Promising her your little 'break' can end once the political heat around her dies down, right? Well I can see through your lies. And it's time to dash those false hopes for her. It's time for her to move on, time for her to give someone better a chance."

Daniel checked and reinforced his shields with a thought, shaking his head with a show of disappointment and tutting at the bald, bearded Celt circling him. "My, my, you have gotten yourself worked up. How, exactly, do you plan to force this stance of yours onto Angie? I assure you, she's not one to let anyone else decide her fate."

"Through you." Noah stopped before Daniel, squaring off uncomfortably close. "Tell her off. Tell her she's never, ever getting back with you. Tell her you hate her and make her believe it, or I'll take matters into my own hands."

The suggestion made blistering rage course through Daniel's limbs, and he leaned in, staring up at Noah with unflinching defiance. Some old part of him that would have taken the threat and demand to heart rose but was quickly silenced. Daniel readied himself, his bare hands, sharp cane, and charged aura all at his disposal. "Make me."

Noah's answering smug grin was expected. The man had always had more balls than brains.

The resounding crack that completely broke Daniel's shields in a blink was not. Daniel dodged the fist that swung at him, utterly thrown by the awful turn of events. Swearing, Daniel hobbled back, half-falling, and tried to Voyage away, but nothing happened.

A blunt bolt of Noah's beige magic slammed into his solar plexus, dropping Daniel to his knees and knocking the wind out of him. When he tried to scramble back to his feet, he found every scrap of strength sapped from him.

Noah hadn't moved, standing firm at the very center of the circular, white stage, framed by the mounting layers of seats beyond. "Being Supreme Justice of the English Court has its perks," he said, cracking his neck, and began walking toward Daniel with maddening, menacing slowness. "Even more so when my mentor, the Justice before me, took the privileges of that office to new heights, and prepared me well to follow in his footsteps after he was gone."

Daniel's whole attention was held by the spiked, glowing barb of magic growing around Noah's fist. The younger man was tall and stocky, and Daniel doubted he could take an unenchanted punch from him, let alone one delivered with the magical brass knuckles shedding heat-waves over him. Daniel tried to stop time, tried everything he could think of, but everything failed utterly.

As Noah raised his fist, his face screwed with intent, Daniel threw every scrap of dwindling magic he could into a wild and desperate beacon, hoping that, even if he died in a few seconds, Noah wouldn't go unpunished for it.

Angie appeared before him almost instantaneously.

Noah's raised fist jerked as he pulled the punch back the moment it started. Angie's stance dropped an inch, but didn't move. Daniel watched, astonished, as the heel of Angie's hand slammed into the center of Noah's chest with a roar of flames, sending him skidding backward across the smooth marble.

The impact of the heat blast made Daniel shield his eyes as he instinctively scrambled backward. Someone grabbed him under the arms, hauling him to his feet as they both stumbled back. When Daniel's vision cleared, Marissa Hayward was beside him, looking pale and wide-eyed. She let go of him once he steadied, her attention locked on the sphere of flames centered in the amphitheater.

Others besides her had already arrived, more appearing every second. Barbara Collins, the Braithwaites, Anthony Shupee, and more—all faces he knew. When Dawn appeared, flanked by Xiao Sheng and Miss Doukas, her hands were already crackling with whips of deadly gold magic. It only took her a few seconds to make eye contact with Daniel, see his small warning shake, and Voyage back away with the Cantonese and Greek leaders in tow.

A cannonball of tan magic aimed at Daniel slammed against the inside of the sphere of fire, barely missing Angie, and several people gasped. "Shan should have killed you when she had the chance," Noah bellowed, and Daniel doubted anyone but him could tell Noah's eyes were locked on *his* face, not Angie's standing between them.

Angie's aura flared, forcing everyone back another pace from the blistering heat. Thick, roiling clouds of putrid smoke seemed to leak from her skin, gathering in her hands.

When she pointed one at Noah's head, he instantly gasped, retching and choking as his knees buckled. "No, please, no, stop." His features were swallowed by the smoke Angie was attacking him with, and as she spoke, Daniel thought he heard the Celt's coughing turn to sobs.

"How does it feel? To be robbed of control? To be at my mercy? To be forced to endure, to have your objections ignored, even if you manage to voice any. To have another person take delight in your suffering…" Angie's voice was raw with emotion. "I tried to tell you how it feels. Do you remember? In the gardens just there. But you told me I was crazy. Told me that I was stupid and selfish for calling the abuse I've endured exactly that. Now you'll have some small taste of it for yourself."

Daniel's aura flared, released from whatever control Noah had exercised over it. Gasping from the relief, Daniel steadied himself and gathered it around him into an arctic shield. With his cane tapping on the marble, he walked carefully forward, inching deeper into the inferno. When he reached the edge of Angie's visible shields, he tested them with his hand and yanked it away when his skin instantly flushed with a burn.

"Angie," he called out, raising his voice over the dull roar of flames rushing around him. "You promised. Keep them all out if you need to, but not me." The woman before him didn't move an inch, but a ripple passed over the shields before him. When he put his hand forward again, they let him pass.

"Please, please stop," Noah cried out in anguish, clawing pointlessly at the smoke engulfing him.

When Daniel's aura brushed against an outlying tendril of the same magic as he stepped up behind Angie, he stumbled. The smoke was heavy with visceral, vivid memories that Daniel had glimpsed when Angie's trauma had been unintentionally revealed to him through scrying three years ago, along with more he hadn't meant to see. He balked from the wave of helpless, frozen trauma that coursed through him, his shields snapping shut against the magic carrying it. The sensation faded almost instantly, but the memory of what he'd felt lingered. He mouthed the air wordlessly, trying to comprehend. Angie's magic was carrying the past she wanted Noah to feel, to torture him with, and somehow Daniel doubted she even knew what she was doing.

Noah was shaking hard from head to toe, hunching over his knees where he knelt. Angie raised her other hand, seemingly grasping something from his now unrestrained and wild khaki aura that fractured around him.

She fell back half a step as Noah shuddered, dropping whatever she'd reached to do, and her smoke wavered.

Taking his chances, Daniel stepped up right behind Angie, careful to avoid the magic streaming between her and Noah. She glanced over her shoulder, her expression shifting from unreadable horror to cold anger as he settled the length of his body along hers, but she didn't shift away as her attention returned to the Celt.

"Angie, that's enough," he said against her ear, wrapping an arm across her chest and shoulders. His bare hand on her arm didn't seem to affect her, but the shields surrounding them both darkened and broke from flames to smoke. His heart ached for her, and he pressed every drop of love, admiration, and sympathy he'd ever held for her into his voice and embrace. "You can let go now and be done. Let go."

"I couldn't let him hurt you."

Daniel squeezed her a little tighter, turning his face against hers and closing his eyes as her words sank through him. "I know. And you saved me. I'm just fine. You've done enough." Daniel felt Angie's chest expand, only realizing in contrast how little she'd been breathing through the ordeal. Her fingers wrapped around his bicep and wrist, and he didn't need to look to know that her memory-infused smoke had dissipated.

"Oh my Gods, Noah, Noah!" a voice shrieked, and Daniel released Angie as a blonde woman, not much older than her, came barreling toward Angie's spark-filled shields. They disappeared just as the woman reached them, and she dove to the ground where Noah lay curled, frantically checking him over. "Noah, Noah, it's okay, I'm here, it's okay." The large Celt just whimpered unintelligibly, hiding his face with his arms.

"Are you sure you're alright?" Angie asked, turning to face Daniel, and their noses nearly brushed.

His heart skipped a beat. He hadn't seen her ocean-colored eyes in sunlight in far too long. "Yes. I'm sure."

"I have to go back," she said in reply, walking backward and pulling a large copper sigil coin from her pocket. "I'll explain later, but I promised..." she fumbled the coin and caught it with a gasp before it hit the marble stage. When the insubstantial form of Jonathan Crowther sprang from the coin at Angie's touch, Daniel thought his heart might stop for good.

"Not again," the apparition said with gentle, apologetic disappointment, his voice a flawless match to the one Daniel still clung to in his dreams. "We really must—" He stopped short, and the ghostly mirage of his tan, lined face paled. "Dan..." A breath later, Angie Voyaged away, taking the coin with her, and the apparition vanished.

It wouldn't register. What he had just seen and heard refused to sink into Daniel's understanding, even as it fanned his aura into a confused, tumbling mess of hot, cold, dry, and damp around him. The world kept spinning, building with emotional babble and tussling from the onlookers, but he was deaf and blind to it all.

"Did you just touch her?" Marissa's hissed question in his ear snapped Daniel back to reality. "The smoke was thick, but it looked like... And she didn't react..."

Daniel reached for his magic, ready to stop time, Voyage, or both, but a late arrival just behind Marissa forced him to reconsider. Seth looked smug, taking in the now strangely empty scene with apparent indifference. Daniel wanted to run, to hide, but knew he must play his hand differently with Seth as witness.

"How did you get her to do that for you? What are you hiding? Did you lie about you and her?" Marissa demanded, and the forty or so adepts who had witnessed the altercation seemed to quiet as swarms more began appearing from the conference buildings down the hill.

Daniel glanced around, glad his sunglasses hid his eyes. He saw Casey and Olivia, Moretti, and many other faces he recognized, looking cautious, angry, or disappointed. He briefly wondered just how wild or warped his beacon must have been to call people he didn't even know, and how many had been summoned by secondary beacons sent out by others when they arrived.

"Then you must have seen wrong," he replied, loudly enough that it carried. "I was kidnapped and brought here by Noah Byrne. My former recruit, who is a sponsor herself now, defended me. I didn't ask her to do so, and I considered it no more than my duty to stand her down when she exceeded her purview."

Moretti stepped forward, his eggplant-colored aura quivering in time with his mustache. "I saw Dawn Renard come to your summons. How do you explain that if you're not sympathetic to her cause or in league with her, as you claim?"

"It wasn't my beacon," Daniel said, thinking fast. "Angie must have summoned her after she arrived. Before today, I hadn't laid eyes on either since the solstice."

A babble of jeers, questions, and arguments broke out among the adept leaders and agents present, and Daniel sought a reason to ignore them. He made for Noah, still curled on the ground, people staying out of his path with looks of disgust at his bare hands. Kneeling, he gave the teary blonde woman leaning over the Celt a kind but firm smile, and she got out of his way. Noah stilled the moment Daniel's fingers touched his temples.

He closed his eyes, pressing his magic into the man's dormant mind, barely hearing the young woman he guessed was a girlfriend of Noah's as she held back someone who approached them, yelling. The effects of Angie's magic were evident, the forcefully imparted trauma she'd rammed through Noah's mind, coating every surface of his thoughts. Daniel didn't want to undo the healthy dose of imposed empathy she'd delivered. But neither did he want to give the imperial loyalist reasons to come after him for his part in hurting a centrist, neutral agent with connections in their party. So, he compromised. Angie's experiences, imparted to Noah imperfectly through her magic, had left a swath of trauma in their wake. Daniel soothed only the most jagged edges, settling them into a deeper layer of Noah's mind.

"What are you doing here?" a woman shouted, and Daniel stood, turning. To his surprise, former Senator Utley was glaring not at him, but at Seth, who merely shrugged with a smug smile.

"I didn't want to miss the show. And, as for how I knew to come, the empire—through me—has agents *everywhere*." He emphasized the last word with a glimpse of his canines, spreading his hands at the gathered crowd before folding them neatly before him. Bickering and quarreling exploded from all quarters, everyone present turning on their neighbors in defensive distrust. Seth just smiled, his eyes shrewd and darting, seeming to drink it all in.

"Is that why you came? To rile everyone up?" Lord Braithwaite asked, half-shielding his much shorter wife behind him. His hunter-green aura was held stiff around them both in an obvious shield.

"Not at all," Seth replied, the hubbub easing to hear his response. "I'm here as a humble mediator, to ensure peace and lawfulness."

"Bullshit," Casey Easton spat, shaking off Anthony's arm when the other man fearfully tried to tug him away. "We've all heard you on the radio calling yourself an angel of chaos, the prophesied end of days, promising to cleanse the earth of anyone you disagree with."

Seth's smile only widened, his soot-black aura placid. "My friends know that I speak those words to the enemies of the empire, not our own." His response made Daniel uneasy, a feeling clearly shared by others as the arguments that had broken out died down almost entirely. "Besides," Seth added, examining his own soot-stained fingernails, "you must have missed the last nine or ten daily broadcasts. I've had a change of heart, and am now, in fact, spearheading the efforts to ensure none of you find yourselves atomized for pissing off the emperor. You should all be thanking me."

The gathered adepts shifted uncomfortably, and Karen Utley threw her hands in the air, her expression of furious contempt half-hidden by her chin-length hair. "I don't have time to deal with this juvenile bullshit. I only came because Moretti called me here, and I don't think you have anything to actually offer us, like you claim."

"Just a moment," another woman said, stepping forward. Barbara Collins was one of the few former Senators that Daniel held any true respect for, and he shifted a few steps to one side to see her better. "Please, Minister Laufey. If, as you say, you're working to help reduce harm and prevent destabilization, then would you be willing to help us with that where we need it most at the moment as a goodwill gesture?" Seth tilted his head, unreadable. "Did the Council's records, or perhaps the Latin Language's documents, on how to rebuild the locks that could slow or stem the tide of uncontacted adept deaths fall into the hands of the empire?"

Seth bowed his head graciously. "Indeed they did."

Barbara stiffened, and whispers passed through the crowd like a swarm. "Then why, may I ask, has that information not been passed along? Doing so could have spared countless deaths, destruction, and unrest among the plebeians these last few months…"

Seth's dark-blue eyes scanned over the patricians watching him with bated breath, his aura swelling with deep-red sparks. Daniel suppressed a shudder of unease as his gaze lingered on him. "I'll think about it."

"That's insane." Casey's voice was full of disbelieving desperation, and Seth's expression darkened at the words. "You must be batshit crazy to let everything keep falling apart—letting people keep killing their loved ones with magic they don't even know they have—when you could just tell us how to stop it!"

Everyone looked to Seth for his response, and Daniel sprang into action, pushing his way through the throng the moment he saw how the minister's chest heaved. "What did you call me?" The reply was so faint people on either side of Daniel leaned in to hear as he passed them, jumping back away when Seth repeated it as a bellowing scream. "What did you call me? How dare you call me insane!"

The whiplash shift in Seth's unhinged demeanor sent people scrambling and Voyaging away even before his Fire aura bloomed around him in angry red flames. Seth's face was twisted with rage, spittle flying from his thin lips as he screamed hysterically at the fleeing patricians. "You dare to call *me* crazy? I am your better! I am the chosen one, your leader, your God made flesh!"

Daniel reached the front of the crowd as it retreated past him and was glad for the chilly shield he hadn't released entirely after Angie's outburst. For a moment he considered trying to contain the situation, but one simple thought—heavy with betrayal, exhaustion, and loss—held him still. *Why bother?*

Seth screamed a laugh that sent a shiver down Daniel's spine. "Run, run, run! That's all rats like you ever do." He seemed feverish, scanning over the backs of those fleeing, and Daniel was relieved when Seth didn't linger on him but turned away. "Run away! All of you. Run from what you cannot face!"

Daniel glanced behind him as three adepts carried away the unconscious Noah. He had no doubt that the shields around the conference site would once more bar his entry as soon as Noah woke, but he didn't much care.

All he needed or wanted as he Voyaged away were answers from Angie about how a living likeness of his dead best friend ended up in her hands.

CHAPTER NINETEEN

When Angie returned to the underground chamber, her heart dropped into her shoes. Beside her, Jonathan's ghost was silent.

The Threshold was dead and dark, and the key was gone.

Angie grasped the silver key necklace at her throat. She felt paralyzed by disbelief. She'd only been gone a few minutes. She'd abandoned her promised post for only a few minutes, hurrying back as soon as she could. And yet both her brief teacher and the coveted half-world keys they'd promised her were gone without a trace.

Sparks peppered through her aura, filling the underground room with the smell of struck matches. She turned in a circle, casting about for any clue or indication of what had transpired in her brief absence, but found nothing. She stared at the empty stone doorway once more, reaching out in her mind for a beacon, anything that might indicate that Jasper had returned and taken the key, but found nothing. She then tried beaconing for them to come to her, her intentions narrowed and strengthened by desperation, but felt no answer. She didn't even bother trying to summon the key she knew was warded against it.

"No," Angie sank to the floor, releasing her necklace, and felt all of her heat seep away. She knew in her bones that Jasper hadn't returned through the Threshold before it was closed, and Angie had no idea who may have done so and taken the key. They were lost out in some unknown half-world with unknown demons, or Inferi, as Jasper had called them, until or unless Angie or someone else used that key once more to help them back across.

"Angie," Jonathan said in a gentle rebuke. "I told you I wasn't ready to see or speak to anyone else. Why call me up in a setting like that?"

Angie scoffed, her eyes starting to brim. She suspected he was trying to distract her from the crushing weight of what had been lost by abandoning her post, but it only made her feel worse. "I wasn't calling you. You misread my intentions sometimes when I touch the coin, and I can't help that. Go back to sleep."

"Angie," Jonathan said kindly, crouching down beside her, appearing fully solid in the half-light. "I do have some small awareness of what happens around me when I'm dormant in the coin, and it would have been hard to miss your heat flare. As far as I can tell, Daniel would be dead or in a bad way right now if you hadn't left your post here. You made the right call, and I'm confident Jasper would agree."

"I've lost them," Angie said, and something more than her voice broke deep inside. "They were my only lead. Getting to them, getting them to work with me, was the only thing I knew for sure I could do to help. To do something, anything, to fix... everything." Tears she didn't want to explain welled up, and the world seemed to wrap in close and dark around her as hopelessness blanketed her heart. "Please, Jonathan. Just let me grieve."

Angie didn't know how long she sat in the silence only broken by the occasional faint rumble of a car overhead. Jonathan had disappeared back into the coin in her pocket at some point before she opened her eyes to stare blankly at the empty threshold. She didn't know what to do next. She'd had no backup plan.

Guilt writhed through her when she remembered Lucia. Her recruit, blameless in the bitterness Angie felt toward her commitments as her sponsor. But Lucia didn't feel like a backup plan, or a consolation, or even a silver lining. Remembering her only added weight, tethering Angie down and making sure she couldn't fly away and try to find something else worth chasing.

Lucia was also the reason she'd have to face Noah again. Sooner than later. She didn't want to think about what that would look like. She dropped her gaze to her right hand. There'd been a moment, when he was already incapacitated by her magic, when she'd felt something odd in his aura. Almost like she could feel his Wyrd thread, his life force, through his magic. She'd only ever felt the sensation through physical contact with living things in the past, and never with the same sense of magic that filled her mind—more than just life. But when she'd reached for it, trying to grasp and understand it, a sickening sense of foreboding made it slip back away.

Angie jumped when the sat phone in her pocket buzzed against the worn stone floor. She scrubbed her eyes in a weak attempt to wake herself up from her daze and frowned at the unknown number on the small readout when she pulled it out. Hope flashed through her when she realized it might be Jasper calling to say everything was fine, but it winked back out just as fast when she answered. "Hello?"

"Angelica? Is that you? Oh my, oh thank the Gods." The woman's voice was achingly familiar and faded out briefly while Angie was still trying to process. "Robert, it's her! The number went through!"

"Mom?" The word felt foreign on Angie's tongue, and she pushed herself up to stand, the instinct to run away tingling at the base of her skull. "How..."

"Oh Angelica, I'm so glad we reached you!"

"No really, Cath," Angie insisted, her mother's first name slightly more palatable. She gripped the phone to her ear with both hands. "How did you get this number? Who told you how to reach me?"

"We got a letter," Cath said happily, and Angie faintly heard a rustle over the line. "It says, 'Dear Mister and Missus Forester. I heard you were trying to get back in touch with your daughter, Angelica, and feel it my duty to help since I'm able.' Then it gives your phone number and is just signed 'A good Samaritan.' What does that even mean?"

Angie knew the answer, thanks to her religion studies in school. It meant that one of the two Christians she knew, Hannah Crowther or Seth Laufey, had been behind it. "Nothing, just—nothing." Angie pinched the bridge of her nose, where a headache was already starting. She didn't want to ask. She really didn't want to know the answer, but she had to. "Cath, why were you and Dad trying to find me? The last time we spoke, you told me you never wanted to see or speak to me again, and I've respected that."

Some part of Angie desperately wanted her mother to admit it, to apologize and beg for forgiveness, but reality was far more predictable than that. "Don't be silly. We heard you were doing quite well for yourself these days, and we just thought—"

"Put Dad on," Angie interjected, partly because she knew Cath could ramble for ages, and partly to avoid hearing her greedy reasons for calling, which Angie should have expected from the start.

"Angelica, don't be rude. I was just saying—"

"Put him on."

A great huff of static rushed down the line, followed a moment later by a gruff, "Hello."

Angie found she couldn't speak. Her father's sigil rings tapped in a steady, demanding rhythm against the receiver he held. It was an old habit she doubted he even knew he had. The familiar sound loosened her grip on the present. The words *I'm sorry* rose in her throat, but she bit them back. "What do you two want? I'll hang up if it's about... her." Angie swallowed, wishing she'd worn her sister's dark-blue denim jacket that day, just to have the comfort of it at that moment.

Rob harrumphed. "Nothing too much. Nothing you can't afford now that you're a patrician." He paused, but Angie refused to take his bait and let the uncomfortable silence stretch. "It's a shame you never reached out to offer. You know the ranch has struggled these last few years. All we want is a little repayment for raising you, for putting you through school, getting you on your feet working in that textiles factory—"

Angie dropped the phone from her ear, gripping it so hard her knuckles were white, and ended the call. Every fiber of her being wanted to throw the phone as hard and as far as she could. To let the pressure filling her at hearing those voices again explode out of her in any and every way possible. *I owe them nothing*, she reminded herself, screaming the words inside her own head, then aloud when they still didn't catch. "I owe them nothing! Piously self-centered, insufferable, greedy, immature..." Old, deeply buried scars ripped at her heart as they were poked again so directly after so many long years.

When the phone rang again, Angie did throw it. Hard and fast, straight at the wall. The damn thing bounced off, unharmed, and continued to buzz. Angie was drawing back a ball of fire which spluttered and wavered, intending to melt it into oblivion, when Daniel's careful, faint Voyaging beacon touched her mind.

Angie closed her eyes, breathing hard through her nose, and let her fireball dissipate. Wrapping the key at her throat in a fist, Angie poured her excess heat into it until the three interlocked rings at one end glowed harmlessly against her impervious skin, and the demons in her soul quieted.

She reluctantly walked over and picked up the phone just as it stopped buzzing, seeing that it had, in fact, been Daniel calling and not her parents. Having a pretty good idea what was about to come, Angie slipped the phone back into her pocket, gathered her composure, and braced herself for the worst before following Daniel's beacon and Voyaging away.

CHAPTER TWENTY

"W hat the HELL were you thinking?" Daniel demanded the moment Angie appeared. They stood in the center of another large, circular stage, this time indoors. Daniel watched, his chest heaving with barely suppressed emotion as Angie took in their surroundings, clearly stalling her answer.

Daniel's aura rippled the five-story-tall gauze curtains that hung from ceiling to floor in four columns around them, partially obscuring the private theater booths, replete with finely set dining tables. He'd expanded his magic as large as he could in the hopes of diluting the turbulence in it that he couldn't control, having chosen the lavish imperial Boston Coliseum for that very reason.

"Show me," Daniel demanded, the leather of his gloves squeaking against the gold-handled cane he gripped before him.

"What?" Angie asked, finally turning her attention away from the props of blood-red silk littered all through the circular orchestra pit surrounding them.

Daniel barely contained his desire to slam his cane into the pristine white stage on which they stood to snap her out of her childish stalling. "You fucking know what. Show. Me."

Every muscle in Daniel's body ached with taut strain as Angie ducked her head, averting her eyes, and fished a large copper coin engraved with a spiked sigil from the pocket of her black linen dress. She turned it over in her hands several times. Frowning, she darted him a guilty glance before muttering to the coin, "No really, I'm inviting you out this time."

Jonathan appeared between them, dressed in a royal-blue suit, his dark hair and beard neatly groomed. When he saw Daniel, he covered his mouth with one hand, his eyes brimming in an instant. The two men just stared at each other for a long moment. Daniel double-blinked, activating his auric vision, but the only magic he saw around the apparition of his friend was the clear heat haze of Angie's magic. Anger and grief won out over the momentary shattering relief as two tears fell down the illusion's cheeks.

"Dan." The illusion seemed unable or unwilling to say more, sorrow pouring off it.

"Why the hell did you keep this a secret?" Daniel asked Angie past the apparition, but the not-Jonathan answered.

"It's my fault," it said, holding out an imploring hand to Daniel and a silencing one to Angie. "I—I'm so sorry. But I knew that seeing you or Dawn again... Seeing either of my dearest, most loved friends again, knowing you'd both been grieving my death..." his voice broke, and more tears fell. "I knew it would break me." He seemed to search Daniel's face for understanding, but Daniel instead searched Angie's.

She seemed guilty and hurt, her smoky, bruise-colored aura pulled in tight around her. "He asked me not to tell anyone," she said softly, shifting under Daniel's charged, unblinking stare. "And then it started feeling like you'd be more angry than happy if I told you anyway, and things just kept getting"—she glanced at the apparition before dropping her attention to her shoes and hiding her eyes by scratching at her hairline—"more complicated."

"What are you?" Daniel asked the illusion of his dead best friend, the overwhelming, raw and biting emotions roiling through him kicking up another notch, and the curtains around them billowed.

"I'm Jon," it replied, looking hurt.

Daniel bared his teeth, scanning down its slightly transparent body. "Not who, *what*. Jonathan Crowther is dead. I carried his lifeless body myself." His voice quavered, then broke. "Saw him buried. I want to know *what* you are to mimic him so closely, to desecrate his memory, and to dare to try to convince me you're real, as you clearly have Angie, who I'd hoped wouldn't have been so gullible."

Angie looked offended, stepping forward. "Now hang on. I found him in Jonathan's office. He explained that Jonathan, the real, living Jonathan, made a backup of himself and stored it in the coin. That's all it is—"

"There's no such magic," Daniel snapped, glaring at the imitation man. "Jon told me about Léa's insistence that he look for a way, and he also told me there was no magic that could do that. I even poked around in the Court, Senate, and Council records I had access to for him and found nothing. So, what"—he lifted his cane beneath the chin of the illusion, which swallowed and eyed it—"are you?"

The illusion looked between the two living adepts, lingering on Angie with a pleading look. Closing its eyes and bowing its head, it seemed to collect itself before answering in a low whisper. "You'd call me Inferi. A sentient demon."

The cry that ripped itself from Daniel's throat was primal. He threw himself at the illusion, pulling his blasting, frigid aura back in close around him. Angie stepped between them, pressing her hands against his chest through his black shirt and jacket, and his gloved fingers slipped through the apparition like mist. The flare of rage faded back down to a simmer as disappointment washed over him, Jonathan's expression of deep, compassionate pain and sorrow breaking his momentum. *Not Jonathan's expression,* he reminded himself, feeling like the short-fused, Glaswegian teenager he'd been long ago as he stepped back on the balls of his feet. *That thing's.*

Daniel wanted to yell at Angie for being taken in by a demon, for trusting it and bringing it into contact with who knew how many people it might have tried to kill or possess, but the shocked hurt on her face as she, too, inched away from the illusion made him set that priority aside.

"Are you from a mimic world?" Daniel asked, banishing his cane and peeling off his jacket, not bothering to restrain the buffeting, indecisive wind his aura lashed around them.

"No," the demon said, seeming to take a deep breath before clasping its hands behind him and planting his feet like a man before a firing squad. "My people simply have a unique gift for taking on the forms of others. It gives us form in return. The coin gives me a home so I can survive in this world, and keeps my appearance and consciousness stable."

"Why this form?" Daniel peeled off his gloves and rolled up his sleeves. He didn't know why, but it felt like preparation, like being proactive as he fought the urge to run fast and far from any demon, especially one speaking in his dear, lost friend's deep voice and watching him with piercing ice-blue eyes it had no right to look through.

"Your friend, Jonathan Crowther, asked me to and allowed me to copy his memories, his emotions, his personality onto myself."

"All of his memories and the rest?"

"Yes, though with the same fallible subjectivity his true, human memories were subject to."

Daniel's jaw worked beneath his short beard. He wanted to ask why, then, it hadn't asked immediately to be returned to Jonathan's wife and children, but he had to begrudgingly admit that the choice not to was a point in favor of it telling the truth. Hannah wouldn't have coped well, likely treating the illusion of Jonathan as poorly as she had his living counterpart. As for his son and daughter, he'd heard Dr. Crowther talk about the healthy processing of grief enough over the course of their long acquaintance to make an educated guess that staying away in his intangible form was for their long-term benefit. *Its. Not his.* "Fine. Let's say I believe you. Why agree to it?"

"Curiosity. And compassion."

Nothing had prepared Daniel for that answer, and nothing in all the worlds could make him believe it for an instant. "No. I'm asking the demon, not Jonathan. What do you, demon, get out of agreeing? Did you want access to our world? To find more people to copy, or earn Angie's trust so she'd let you possess her willingly? Why?"

Angie was silent beside him, and the demon looked sadly between them both.

It sighed, one cheek lifting in an expression of reconsidering so familiar Daniel's aura dropped a degree. "Those are my answers. Both as who I am now, and who I used to be. But if you cannot accept them, then perhaps you can believe me when I say that I didn't particularly like who I used to be and was bored of the world I'd lived in my whole life. When Jonathan offered me the chance to be exactly the kind of strong, kind, intelligent person I'd always wanted to be, and to see glimpses of his vibrant, varied world, I jumped at it."

"*Person* you used to be? *Person?* A demon is just a fucking demon." Daniel turned and paced away, pulling a hand down over his mouth and beard as he tried to stay calm. Or at least something resembling it. As much as he wanted to dispute the claim more, he understood the desire and temptation of choosing to be someone else, someone better, all too well. And being Jonathan was the best choice he could imagine ever being offered.

Daniel turned back, waving a hand with exaggerated disgust. "Go away. Fuck off and disappear back to wherever you came from. Angie, destroy that thing."

"Daniel, it hasn't done any harm." Angie was meek and quiet, turning the coin over and over in her hands. Daniel almost wanted her to be angry instead. Fiery and dangerous and sharing even a scrap of the betrayal, horror, and anger making his hands shake.

When Daniel just shook his head at her, full of everything he felt toward her and the demon watching him with infuriating pity, she turned toward it and held out the coin. They exchanged a long look Daniel didn't try to interpret, and watched, disgusted, as the demon collapsed down invisibly into the coin.

Exactly how the demon that had painfully possessed his knee had miraculously left him to reside in the key necklace he'd bought Angie only days after they'd met.

When she slipped the key into her pocket and turned to him with pleading blue-green eyes, his anger faltered. Her fist stayed in her pocket, and when Daniel saw her dark-gray aura harden around her as shields, he double-blinked once more to stop seeing auras and magic. "What are you going to do? Going forward, around Seth, and Marissa, and the rest?"

Daniel hissed through his teeth, searching for anything to look at besides her, and chewed on the blatant change in topic. "The only thing I can do." He forced himself to take a deep breath, dragging up such practical matters through the sludge of emotions clinging to his thoughts. Through them, his roles and goals he'd clung to since... he didn't even know when, seemed childish and oversimple. But he clung on all the harder for it. He needed simple. "The only way I can do what needs to be done is without directly challenging the power I wish to influence." Saying it out loud felt like blasphemy, and he swallowed. "So what I do going forward is make apologies and excuses, throw someone else under the bus when I have to, and pray that I at least see it coming when it eventually stops working."

Angie nodded, drawing herself up. She half-smiled, and the cockiness in it ground against the careful path for self-preservation he'd literally just handed her by stating his intent to adhere to it. "Well, I—"

"Will continue acting rashly and without caution," he snapped. "Trusting situations and people you shouldn't, at least without serious questioning, and acting without thinking again when they inevitably come back to bite you."

"Look, Jonathan hasn't given me any reasons to not—"

"I'm not just talking about that!" Daniel interrupted again, gesturing at Angie with frustrated incredulity. "I was actually thinking of how you walked right into a trap set by a dead man, surrounded by stressed and scared plebeians, baited with nothing more than your insistence on not letting go of your own past, and ended up killing *a man in a coma* with little to no care!" Daniel felt shades of his own murderous guilt paint themselves onto his accusations, and tried to keep his focus narrowed.

"Not to mention how you ended up with a recruit you can barely be bothered to care about, whose aura is a serious problem with yours by nature, and who may very well have been a blatant trap for you. Which you've never once questioned or assessed, despite listening to me process my exact same concerns about you being assigned as my recruit three years ago, so you have no excuse."

Angie was silent and unreadable, and the small relief of finally spilling all of his worries stopped Daniel from stemming his outpouring. "You went looking for trouble in taking Lucia to Noah's conference. And again in screwing up with Jasper, and who knows what other powerful and experienced patricians at the Eden gate, and yet again, just today, in not grabbing me and running the moment you stopped Noah. You keep looking for trouble with no plan of how to handle it, and making things worse with your rash actions when it inevitably goes south."

Daniel shook his head, ashamed by everything he was saying, even as vindictive satisfaction eased his heart. "Gods know what you did to Casey to have him blackball you. Undoubtedly more of the same." Daniel felt the line as he crossed it as a stumble in his confidence, and the way Angie's expression darkened across the white stage confirmed it. "Sorry," he muttered, dropping his head as his stomach followed suit. "Low blow."

"No shit, prick." Angie was glowering at him, her arms crossed, and Daniel just accepted the insult.

"But seriously, Angie." Daniel's head throbbed with a distant, pounding ache, and he massaged his temple. "I don't want to hear about you getting in any more trouble or causing any more harm to yourself or the rest of us because you go into things with zero plan and act without thinking."

"Then you won't." Angie's response was sullen, edged with pain, and Daniel turned away, not having it in him to try to talk her around after everything. After learning of the dangerous secrets she'd been keeping from him.

He tried to Voyage away, but his concentration slipped for one non-magical step after another, until Daniel stopped, his jaw clenching. In a last-ditch effort to clear his thoughts enough for the magic to work, he restated what the darkest parts of his heart were screaming. "I have more important shit to deal with, and more real, physical problems to spend my time and attention on than ensuring you won't fuck up my life. I can't deal with this, too."

He regretted his words the moment his traveling magic deposited him in the foyer of his New York mansion.

He didn't go back.

CHAPTER TWENTY-ONE

A ngie Voyaged away the moment Daniel disappeared, the hurt retort she'd been going to fire back withering on her lips. The last time Daniel had been properly angry with her had been after her first full fiery outburst during her first conference. She'd been so young and naive back then. She felt so again now in the wake of Daniel's rebukes. The sound of his voice echoed in her ears. His beeswax and frankincense smell, strengthened and spread by his upset aura, lingered in her breath.

A raindrop hit Angie's nose, and she looked up at the sky, only then realizing that the trees she stood beneath weren't at the edge of the garden and forest at the top of the English Conference site as she'd intended. Instead, she was flanked by tall, brambled hedgerows bordering a narrow Britannian road. Angie's heart sank even further as she placed a hand against the massive dome of magical shields which arced up and away over what appeared from the outside to be a muddy field of grazing and sleeping cows. *Not again.*

Angie jumped back when two shouting figures appeared seemingly out of nowhere through the shields where they overlapped with a wooden gate. She yanked her aura back under control, not letting it heat even enough to evaporate the rain starting to fall. Lucia stumbled as Noah shoved her ahead of him. He threw down two full trash bags as a store mannequin golem stepped wordlessly through the barrier behind him with another pack and two sleeping bags.

"You don't get a say," he shouted, his face flushed, as Lucia opened her mouth to speak. "Your worthless bitch of a sponsor broke several major rules of my conference, including a malicious attack on the Supreme Justice, and even if she hadn't, I'd still kick her out just because I wanted to. As her recruit, you go with her, which I promise you she knew quite well before getting in my way and torturing me."

Angie stepped forward, and both other adepts turned toward the motion. Noah's face went white, and he turned, tight-lipped, and disappeared back behind the shield without a word to her. Shame kept Angie from calling after him. Not that she thought it would do any good. She took the sleeping bags from the golem, handing one to a shocked-looking Lucia, then accepted the pack from it as well. Rain dripped down Angie's face as she watched the golem silently disappear back through the shields she doubted would ever let her back in.

It was honestly more than she'd expected that Noah had bothered to pack their things, and had possibly even waited until Angie had returned to kick Lucia out. Maybe he'd learned a tiny bit of compassion from their altercation after all? She'd dearly wanted him to, but had no idea how she might have accidentally managed it.

"What now?" Lucia asked, tears brimming in her eyes, and Angie realized that the natural Air aura might be affecting the weather through her magic, if not controlling it outright. *I'd know if she had that skill, wouldn't I?* Angie didn't ask for fear the answer would deepen her shame.

"Um. Well…" Angie felt hollow and lost. She needed to process. Needed to think things through, and get her bearings again, take stock, and make a new plan. But life always seemed to get in her way. She shifted and bent to pull the pack onto her back, picking up one of the plastic garbage bags and nodded for Lucia to do the same.

For a moment that seemed to make the world zoom out around her, Angie considered running away. Just abandoning her obligations, her promises, and any sense of restriction. But even as the sweet call of wild, capable, limitless running with nothing more than what she could carry had her shifting her weight to Voyage or Skip, it was doused. That would be acting rashly. That would be acting without thinking and without thought of the consequences. And the more Angie looked at the ice-blue aura of the woman before her, the more she couldn't stomach the thought of leaving her to fend for herself.

"We could go back to my convent," Lucia offered with little conviction, hugging the rolled sleeping bag to her like a stuffed animal.

The thought of going anywhere near one of the rare pockets of such devoted worshippers, let alone asking to sleep in a temple, made Angie's skin crawl. From what little Angie knew of the traumas in Lucia's past that had catalyzed her magic, she was surprised the other woman even suggested it. "No, I don't think that's our best option."

Lucia nodded, both adepts thoroughly soaked as the rain increased every minute. For once, she seemed to be completely content to follow Angie's lead and direction, and for once, Angie wished she'd take on the role as the "elder and wiser between them" as she'd commented on several occasions.

"I think our best options are hotels or my car. At least for tonight." Angie craved the easier, dryer, more convenient option, but also yearned for the freeing, mobile control of her car. She flipped through every other place she might once have turned in her mind, quickly discounting each. She doubted she'd be welcome at any of the homes she'd recently shared with Daniel after the revelation of Jonathan's ghost. The house in Hawaii had become an extension of Dawn's camp months ago, and neither would grant her entry.

"Let's go to my car and drive to a hotel for tonight," Angie said, settling on a compromise. "I'll go first. When you feel it, follow my beacon like I taught you."

Angie waited until Lucia was asleep in their musty motel room before rising and trading her nightgown for her black linen dress, now dried by Lucia's efforts earlier in the evening. She couldn't even think about sleeping herself, and she dug up her dark denim jacket just for the comfort of it.

It wouldn't be safe for them to stay long. Angie had a decent stash of cash, but no way to replenish it, and costs across the globe were rising exorbitantly every day. Not to mention that the check-in clerk had been deeply suspicious of them, likely because there wasn't a cloud in sight, and when pressed, had mentioned that a magical explosion had killed four people in the neighboring town a fortnight ago. If their magic was seen, which was likely with the unhappy way their auras sparked off each other under confined stress...

She knew it was only a matter of time before she felt the loss of Lord Braithwaite's resource production skills, but for the moment, their bags had been well packed. Angie pulled on her sister's old blue jacket, leaving behind the rest as she Voyaged away.

Angie looked out over the waves far below the clifftop she stood on, letting the sounds of water against rocks and wind through the pines wash over her in the faint light of the nearly perfect full moon. Only when she felt ready did she step back from the edge and pull the sigil coin from her pocket.

As in the colosseum, the ghost within seemed hesitant to come to her call after two accidental appearances, and so she spoke aloud. "Come out. We need to talk."

Jonathan appeared before her, the moonlight making him look more ghostly than ever before. Angie wanted him to say something to make it all better. To take back what had been revealed, to prove it was all a lie. But the longer he stayed silent, looking sad, the more foolish the desire seemed.

Angie paced back and forth, her arms hugged tightly over her middle, carefully avoiding even glancing at the slab of white marble a dozen steps away at the edge of the trees. She knew all it was doing was getting her more and more worked up, but didn't care.

"You're a fucking demon?" she finally lashed out, and Jonathan winced. Should she even still be thinking of it as Jonathan? Or more as the animalistic creature of basic instinct and fear she'd hosted in her jewelry in the past?

"Inferi, yes. Demon only in that I'm from a different world than you. But unlike the demons you likely know, I am conscious. I have self. Even a soul, maybe, as Jonathan would understand things through his faith."

"You stole his soul?" Angie asked, her aura swirling with a shower of sparks. She knew the question was unfairly obtuse, but needed the excuse to release more of the betrayal steaming through her.

"No, and you know the truth of how I came to be me, be Jonathan. Who he was, pressed onto a blank soul."

"Blank?"

Jonathan didn't reply, and Angie shouted her wordless frustration, unshed tears blurring her vision. Resuming her pacing, she clutched the coin that had meant the difference between life and death countless times during the never-ending nightmare of her banishment. The faint ridges around the edge pressed into her palm, her thumb rubbing circles against the face.

"Why didn't you let me tell Daniel right away?"

"Because I didn't want to lose him."

"Why didn't you tell me you were a fucking demon?"

"Because I didn't want to lose you, either."

Angie's breath panted out of her on the verge of tears, and the fever that consumed her as her flames turned inward—fearful of the dry summer forest beside her—blurred her thoughts.

"Well guess what?" she yelled, her voice screeching as she threw months of stress, anger, and loss behind it. "I don't fucking care. I kept your secrets, and now I've lost Daniel, too. You might not have lied to me outright, but you lied by omission for too long." Angie's voice broke, and as her tears followed, she wound her arm back, ready to throw her weight into an action she regretted even before she did it. "Well guess what, asshole, doing so lost me, too. I hate you."

Angie hurled the coin as high and far as she could toward the sea, wishing she could call it back as it spun overhead. "I'm sorry," she whispered, her eyes wide and fearful with regret, as the coin plummeted between the setting moon and Jonathan's dear, grieving, kind face. He lingered for a moment before the coin fell too far, dragging him with it, and his deep voice was nearly lost to the sound of the deep-blue ocean below.

"I know."

Falling to the carpet of pine needles, Angie doubled over and retched, her hands grinding fistfuls of them beneath her as she screamed in great, choking sobs. "I'm sorry..."

CHAPTER TWENTY-TWO

*H*ow am I any better?

Daniel sat in the attic of his Boston home, surrounded by every paper and book he'd grabbed from Jonathan's home when legionnaires had tried to deport his family, and from his office at the English Conference site when Angie had returned from it maddeningly empty-handed. He hadn't wanted to return to the space that felt so much like his dearest friend could appear at any moment, but he couldn't bear the thought of any scrap of it being thrown away. Perhaps he should give some of it back to Hannah, now that she fully accepted her magic and might not immediately burn it. But the thought of her passing it right along to Seth soured that idea.

The stillness surrounding him under the eaves, his raging winds long since blown out, was oddly lonely. Perhaps, in a different frame of mind, he could have named the way his magic was yet another constant companion now absent.

"What would you think of me now, old friend?" He tried to not guess. Jonathan hadn't lived long enough to see him kill Milton Cartwright in cold blood. Hadn't witnessed Daniel cross the line he had so carefully maintained for his belief in his own goodness for so many years. Nor had Jonathan lived to see any of the lesser sins that had followed. He didn't want to admit it, but he understood why Angie had simply tucked the coin back away, holding onto the ghostly demon within. If he let himself truly believe even for a minute that any real part of his comrade turned lover, turned friend, turned brother still lived on in any form, he'd cling to it just as tightly.

By the dim light of the single lamp he'd brought up, Daniel lifted a sheaf of papers, his mind lingering more on the familiar handwriting than the words they strung together about astral navigation. When Daniel realized the topic was being recorded in the context of navigating half-worlds, he had to set it aside. The topic was too raw.

His mind flitted briefly to the ancient gold astrolabe Milton Cartwright had always kept in a place of prominence during his years as an English Judge, but pushed the memory away. Someday he'd be ready to read further. But that day hadn't yet arrived.

As Daniel reached for a stack of loose papers, he paused. Beside them lay one of Jonathan's personal journals. Perhaps now was the right time for that. Daniel drew a deep breath and held it as he picked up the journal reverently. It shook as he exhaled, and his spent aura raised a few pages by their corners before quieting once more.

A note on the flyleaf noted the date range of the journal, starting from the winter before Angie's first conference. Daniel summoned cushions from downstairs and settled himself, stretching out his once-possessed knee in front of him. The ache in his chest eased as he began to read, and let himself fall back into a now-lost time.

Now and then, a certain passage would pull him out of his exhausted reverie. The first was an assessment of Daniel through Jonathan's eyes, calling his careful, reclusive existence through the years before Angie as him "hiding from the world that still wants him vibrantly in it." It made Daniel squirm. It wasn't a surprise. Jonathan had more or less told him as much to his face. Reading on, "I wonder when he'll stop always trying to find an oblique way to influence the struggles he needs to face, and paying the price to his sturdy sense of justice," provided a deeper swoop for the rollercoaster in his core than the first.

If I'd been more direct sooner, if I'd killed Milton Cartwright when I should have, when Angie first told me we should, Jonathan would still be alive. He was too tired for the thought to spear him as deeply as he knew it would in the morning. He'd deal with it then.

The next passage that jarred him was an early mention of Angie. "I'm glad the stars finally aligned, and Daniel is no longer alone. Angie seems like she might actually bring the man I once loved, and still love as a brother, back to life within the shell Cartwright has made of him." And, in an entry on the next page, "Despite Dan's grounded fears, I think Angie is the best thing that could have happened to him. She seems far more capable of self-control and mentally stable than Fire auras have a grounded reputation for being. Her maturity in handling stressors and relationships has room for growth, but that can come with time, and I believe Daniel will be an excellent influence in that regard."

The feelings that weakly swirled through Daniel's aura were too complicated, too biased and blurry for him to untangle. Seth was everything he'd expected Angie to be. And yet, he would go running back to the first in the morning, having shunned the latter. "I have no other choice," Daniel said to the cobwebs and dust, trying to convince himself.

Daniel read until sunrise crept ephemeral fingers through the small window set in the attic roof. Across three such journals, nothing else had caught his eye, but every line had brought him peace and pain in equal measure. He didn't know how falling back into the words, thoughts, and feelings of the living Jonathan affected how he felt about the demonic imitation.

The weight of it all draped across every inch of him, every hair, and it wasn't with hesitation that Daniel finally shook himself free and crawled out from under it down the attic steps. He needed to breathe clear of the cloying memories. His empty stomach grumbled, and he reluctantly turned on the glaring overhead lights as he made his way to the front of the house.

He didn't know what light he was chasing anymore. But he knew he couldn't linger in the dark.

—◦✦◦—

He arrived in Rome an hour later, blinking against the bright midday light. The piazza he always aimed for when Voyaging to the imperial palaces was as empty as usual, and Daniel didn't bother summoning sunglasses for the short walk up to the reinforced steel doors.

Knocking, Daniel braced himself for as many of the worst-case scenarios running through his overtired mind as he could. Something clicked deep inside the door, and a smartly uniformed legionnaire pulled it open for him. Daniel stepped through, his eyes slow to adjust to the gloomy interior, and he tensed when Seth's voice spoke from the hallway off to one side.

"Ah, Fawl, good." Seth looked disconcertingly cheery. He was striding toward Daniel, shrugging on a fresh linen blazer, a much more somber-looking Marissa trailing in his wake. "Good God, man. You look awful." He stopped in front of Daniel, openly taking in the bags under Daniel's red eyes and his unkempt beard.

Marissa stopped beside Seth, who beamed at her, holding out an arm. She took it with a perfect crimson smile that didn't reach her eyes. "Go home. Get some rest. Marissa and I are off to the games. The emperor is pleased with the developments your stunt at the English Conference set in motion." Daniel blinked, barely comprehending—let alone believing—the unexpected luck that somehow failed to lift his mood.

"How so?" he asked.

Seth just waved a pale hand. "More people are reaching out. Movers and shakers, you might say. People with influence." He looked Daniel up and down with a tilt of his head, his expression sympathetic. "Now go home and rest. I mean it. Take a few days if you need. You, of all people, have earned it."

As Seth led Marissa past Daniel out the door, she shot him a regretful glance, and Daniel didn't even think about arguing. He had somehow twisted things to his advantage. His bed was calling like a siren from the deep.

Perhaps tomorrow he'd care enough to learn what price he'd have to pay for living in the halls of the empire one more day.

CHAPTER TWENTY-THREE

"C asey! I know you're here. I just—just come talk to me!" Angie stepped away from the small dome of shields surrounding the large house perched on the tropical mountainside above Lahaina. Trying to gather her magic around her fist like a glove like she'd seen Noah prepare to use against Daniel, Angie threw her weight and gladiator training into a punch against the barrier. Her magic spluttered out completely just before impact, and Angie yelped with pain when her bare knuckles connected.

Shaking out her hand, she turned her attention to the seemingly dilapidated mansion beyond, knowing it was an illusion. "Please. I can help. I need help." Bitterness replaced the words she wished she could add—offering keys, and knowledge, and a former Councilor to help and teach, all of which had now been lost to her.

The weight on her chest lifted when Casey stepped through the shields, seeming to materialize from thin air. She stepped back to give him room, grinning, but her smile faltered when she saw his scowl and the two stone statue golems that stepped through to flank him.

Casey's young face was stern and wary beneath his tousled white-blond hair, and he raised a tattooed hand to stop Angie when she moved to hug him. "What help do you need? We don't have much we can offer."

Angie searched him for any hint of the energetic, optimistic kindness she was used to finding in him, but found none. "My recruit and I need somewhere to stay. I need help training her, need..." Angie swallowed, feeling raw and scared. "We need friends. Please."

Only his curry-orange aura betrayed a ripple of whatever emotion he felt for her pleas, but Angie couldn't decipher it. "I know. I saw why. And I'm certain that we can't help you."

"Why not?" Angie asked, trying to keep her helpless distress at bay for fear of seeming childish.

Casey shook his head. When he spoke, he seemed to gather momentum with each sentence, his expressive face finally betraying his inner turmoil. "We already have far too much on our plates with new unlocked adepts, helping other languages with the same, and more folks pouring in as the world out there goes to shit." Casey gestured down the mountain toward the sea. "You have no idea what we're dealing with. If you did, you would have been helping us since the beginning instead of always, *always*, running off on your own, only showing back up again to cause chaos." Casey's labored breath became noticeable, but he plowed on. "Magic is seeping into the plebeian world. Inepts are starting to attack people they even suspect of being adepts. And we're so busy just trying to protect and care for our own that we can't even start to think about helping everyone else."

Only when he seemed done did Angie dare speak, needing to ask about the hint she'd finally gotten about why her one-time friend had iced her out. "Is that why? Because I keep..." She resisted the urge to subtly defend herself, or to explain and excuse, and instead carefully used the same word Casey had. "Because I keep running off? I swear to you, Casey, I never try to. I never want—well, I never do so intentionally. Is that really why you hate me now?"

Anger dashed across Casey's narrow face, fading into exhausted disdain. "I don't hate you, Angie. I could never hate you." His eyes glittered with something sadder, but his tone became harsh. "But even knowing that, saying that, I can also see, and know, and say that trying to keep you in my life hurts a lot of other people I care about. It's better for my world if I let you go. If I sacrifice how I feel about you because I know what needs to be done."

Casey turned away, but Angie tried to stop him. "Wait, please! Casey..." She wanted to make things right. She wanted to feel safe and welcome, and to have people to turn to, to ask questions, to help... But when Casey turned, waiting for her to say more, she couldn't speak over the possibility that he was right.

When she said nothing, Casey shook his head and disappeared back into the shields. The two golems took a step closer to each other, blocking Angie from even touching the shield she couldn't pass. Not that Angie intended to. Instead, she Voyaged away back to the last person left she could talk to.

—◦✦◦—

Lucia returned to the small motel room shortly after Angie, her thin black hair wind-tossed. "Wait, slow down," Angie said when Lucia's aura flared, and a spark of bitterness in Angie's aura caught on the rich oxygen. Angie backed away toward the door, trying to pull her magic back in and away from the damage it was doing, but the more she tried to get a grip on it, the more it resisted control.

"What are you doing?" Lucia asked, wide-eyed, also backing away.

"There's something wrong with my magic." The moment Angie said it out loud, the truth of it buckled her. How long had she been trying to ignore or gloss over that fact without realizing it? *This isn't the moment to go there.*

Angie turned and unbolted the motel room door, quickly stepping out and slamming it behind her. She skipped backward, unnecessarily checking that her aura came with her, and only stopped when she could place a steadying hand on the sun-warmed hood of her car. She glanced around, desperately hoping that no one had seen, and saw no witnesses.

"You okay?" she called out to the curtained room before her, every second a tense eternity before Lucia pulled the curtain aside and cracked the window to speak.

"Yeah. But..." She trailed off, her lips a thin line. "Look. I can only do so much when it's your aura causing problems with mine. I know you're trying, but you just don't have the control or maturity I have, so it's not a surprise this happened. Perhaps it would be best if you sleep somewhere else tonight?"

Lucia's words rolled off Angie. She'd stopped caring about such jabs a month ago. The only reasons she hesitated to take the permission to leave for good and never come back was the dark chasm of loneliness that Lucia was the last guardrail against. "Yeah. Sure. Um... Go in the bathroom while I grab my stuff. I'll shout when I'm all set. And I'll come check back in tomorrow. You have enough money for the moment?"

Angie had driven until the sun had gone down, pulling over at a remote pit stop that was little more than a parking lot and a poorly cleaned restroom. She'd settled back into living out of her car, and without anything else to distract or occupy her, had sought sleep without delay. Laying in the dark, she'd tried to calm her unrelenting stress by fiddling with the smaller, new sigil coin Jonathan had made many of shortly before his death, but it had done little more than remind her of what she'd lost with its predecessor, and she tossed it away after only a minute.

When someone tapped on the back window, Angie jumped. Carefully folding back a corner of her cardboard privacy screens, she was shocked to see none of the people she'd hoped for or expected, but Bailey Johnson.

"Sorry to disturb you," the blonde said, stepping back and wringing her hands when Angie unlocked the back door and stepped out. "It's just that I *really* need to talk to you, and this seemed like a decent time."

"How did you know? How did you find me?"

Bailey shrugged, shoving her hands into the pockets of the oversized letterman jacket she wore. "I'm a decent scryer. I set things up so my absence wouldn't be noticed for a day or two, and it took some doing, but I eventually saw you here. Did I misjudge?"

Angie crossed her arms. "So, the fact that Noah and I are no longer remotely friendly isn't something you considered?"

Bailey responded with something between a smile and a wince. "He and I aren't one person," she explained. "And I thought you, of all people, would get that. I mean, from what I've heard about your first conference and such, if you'd only talked to people who liked the man you loved, you would never have had a single friend." Angie dropped her gaze, appropriately chastened, and the last of her suspicious dislike melted away when Bailey added, "Please. I really do consider you a friend, and I really need some help only you can give me."

"With what?" Angie consciously uncrossed her arms, closing the door to the car and leaning against it more casually.

"I'm pregnant," Bailey said, barely louder than a whisper, nervously placing a hand over her stomach. "Not far along. And I really, really don't want to be, but don't want Noah or Lady B to know."

All of Angie's lingering stresses and worries slid away in an instant in favor of proud, eager determination. This was magic unrelated to her aura. Deep, calm magic of Wyrd that Angie doubted would be corrupted in the same way her flames had been of late. She recalled the deep relief, comfort, and freedom she'd felt when she'd pulled away an unwanted, barely started life growing in her own belly years before, and the thought of gifting the same to someone else brought her heart happiness and peace.

"Yes, of course I'll help. Come on, let's settle in comfortably. This is going to take a long time."

Chapter Twenty-Four

T he next day found Daniel kneeling in the hallways outside the emperor's private suite, picking the ornate silver lock keeping the double doors secure. It was proving far more difficult than anticipated since his picks kept melting in the lock, and Daniel hadn't yet managed to sufficiently fireproof his tools or remove the invisible scrap of Seth's magic he knew must be embedded inside.

He glanced over his shoulder, back down the hallway. He wasn't sure his planned excuse of adding extra shielding to the emperor's quarters would hold up if he was caught. But his shielding concentration was poor these days, and taking the more direct risk was worth it. At least, that's what he'd convinced himself of over his much-needed day of rest. He just needed to introduce himself. Earn the emperor's trust. From there, influencing him away from war with the rest of the globe and getting access to the wealth of information the empire must have collected and hidden away over the centuries would finally be in his grasp.

Daniel was so distracted by his thoughts that he didn't notice the dark spark of magic eating its way out of the lock until it touched his hand, making him gasp. Daniel stood, his aura flaring, and tried to shake it off. A moment later, he felt a sickening lurch in his aura, and watched in horror as the spark multiplied, fizzing off in every direction, leaving scorched, soot-black trails in his pale-yellow magic.

Daniel stopped time in a heartbeat. To his great relief, the infecting sparks stopped too. Gathering a fistful of icy, oxygen-devoid aura in his fist, Daniel pressed it against the spark that had dropped from the silver lock to his hand, letting out a long breath when it finally winked out. One by one, he gave each spark scattered through his magic the same treatment, until no sign of the infection remained. When he cautiously felt through his magic for any he had missed, he found none.

Perhaps... Daniel didn't release the fistful of icy void he'd created with his Air aura, and instead turned back to the silver lock standing between him and the leader of the last pocket of the patrician Order Daniel had worked so long and so hard to dismantle.

A footstep behind him in the hallway made Daniel guiltily drop the magic, whirling to see who had caught him. A vacantly smiling marble golem carrying a tray of food walked steadily toward him. Seth Laufey rounded the corner a moment later, slowing and frowning when he saw Daniel, who silently lamented not having Voyaged away the moment he'd heard the sound.

"Fawl? What are you doing here?" The minister seemed to search Daniel's aura for an answer, and Daniel carefully smoothed it. *No sparks to see here...*

"Moretti suggested that my skills with shields might be used to bolster the emperor's protections, but I can find no fault or flaw in the current security. I was just going to report as much back to him." Seth nodded, his eyes narrowing, and Daniel did a double take at the golem. It hadn't been enchanted to look like a living human, and the implication that the emperor might be used to it bringing his meals—and was therefore aware of magic—gave him pause.

"Right. Well. Best be on then. And no reason to check again. I've told you how much the emperor values his privacy." Seth's calm tone was betrayed by the streamers of black ash that fell from his hands through his aura of thin red flames.

"Of course, Minister." Daniel didn't waste time striding past Seth down the hall.

The soft chime of a text alert from behind him was closely followed by Seth barking, "Wait," and Daniel obeyed. Seth's attention was fixed on the cell phone in his hand, and Daniel viscerally missed his own sleek and modern cell for a disconcerting moment. He swallowed when Seth smiled, the expression at odds with his words. "Hannah's in trouble at Renard's compound. She's reached out to Marissa, and has either just been exposed as a mole, or is about to be." He glanced at the golem and the door to the emperor's suites. "Do me a favor?"

Daniel nodded, trying to hide the way his thoughts and heart sped up at the mention of her name. *So, Hannah had been successfully turned...* He'd failed to keep tabs on that, and hoped that Dawn hadn't.

"See if you can find out which," Seth instructed Daniel, still typing on his cell. "If she's still under cover, go attack her or whatever to sell that she's our enemy. Obviously, don't hurt her too badly. If she's been caught, attack the compound. Make a show of it. Distract Renard and her people enough for Hannah to get away." He put the phone away, raising his hand when Daniel shifted to leave. "When you're done, wait for me in my office. I was going to call you after I met with the emperor to discuss the storage of the half-world keys his network has been collecting." Seth's chest puffed with pride, and Daniel's sunk an inch. "I have something to show you when we're both ready."

So that's where all the keys went... Daniel wondered if he should stay and try to take those powerful bargaining chips by force, but Seth's close, frowning inspection of the silver lock he made no move to open decided the matter for him.

Daniel Voyaged not to the heart of Dawn's compound, as he once would have, but to the small clearing in the redwood forest outside the gates. Instead of tranquil stillness, his arrival was met by a cacophony of shouting already well underway from just inside the tall wooden walls, and Daniel barely registered that the shields let him pass without protest as he jogged through them, readying his own.

A hundred people or so were gathered just inside the gates, all shouting and jeering except for Hannah, who stood closest to him with her back turned. The crowd didn't seem to notice or care that Daniel was there, and he briefly scanned for Hannah and Jonathan's two small children but didn't see them. Dawn shot him a glowering look, and Daniel raised his hands, willing his shields to render him invisible.

Dawn was at the forefront, her face twisted with anger, and the first words Daniel understood clearly made him feel sick. "I don't fucking care if you thought it would give them magic, and I especially don't fucking care if you thought it would come directly from your sadistic bastard of a nameless God. You don't fucking abuse your children in my camp just because some full-blown nutjob told you magic is catalyzed by trauma!"

A suitcase was thrown at Hannah's feet, and she snatched up the handle, her voice shrieking with anger. "How dare you speak of the One True God in that manner? Or of his living prophet?" Her light-red aura shook with her hands. "They are my children to do with as I please. If Jonathan were still alive, I'm sure he'd—"

"Hate you for hurting them to the depths of his soul," Dawn cut her off in a dangerous growl. Her long, blue braids, the exact shade Jonathan's aura had once been, quivered, and her fists were clenched at her sides. "Get the fuck out of my sight. And if you ever go near those poor kids again, I'll personally show you what it's like to be in their shoes. What it's like to be tortured by someone older, smarter, and stronger than you."

None of it felt real to Daniel. The horror of what he'd clearly missed left his aura utterly uncertain of what it needed to express. The lurching lulls of it echoed in his heart when Hannah failed to even try to defend herself or fight to stay with her kids.

Daniel sensed Hannah preparing to Voyage away, and he stepped forward, almost without thinking, touching a tendril of his magic to the back of her head. If this was it, if she was leaving Dawn's compound fully and for good, there was no point in letting her take her memories of it—or of any of the good people living there—back to Seth. He barely got his intentions narrowed and concentrated on the thoughts he wished to take from her mind when she vanished. *No way to tell if it worked...* The glimpses of code names, locations, and favors promised that he'd tried to grab from her memory were concerning.

Xiao Sheng, the Cantonese language leader, stepped forward, his eyes glittering with muted triumph as he stared at the spot where Hannah had Voyaged from. "The Hellenians have the children. They're hurt and upset, but it doesn't seem that either's powers were catalyzed. Shame." His lips pursed as he folded his arms. "We need more soldiers."

Dawn closed her eyes, and Daniel's long familiarity with her showed the deep regret, anger, and fear she was clearly trying to fight back and hide. "Good. We'll take care of them. But please, *please*, Mister Xiao. Don't let word of this get out." She turned away, and the crowd followed suit, only a few darting glances at where Daniel had momentarily appeared through the shields. "What we need more of is peace."

When Daniel was left alone, he realized that he couldn't take the time to process, or calm or steady himself. If his attempt at modifying Hannah's memories had failed, it was imperative that he reached Seth first.

When Daniel got to Seth's office, it was empty. The twenty minutes he had to wait were torture. The room's clean, bright, baroque lavishness only added to his stress. He'd thought, leading up to the solstice, that he'd be done lingering in extravagant halls of power, waiting for corrupt leaders who could destroy his life. He'd hoped such rooms would be emptied...

"Well?" Seth said, striding past Daniel and sitting behind his desk. The door clicked closed softly.

Marissa Hayward, in a too-short dress, draped herself on the arm of Seth's chair, greeting him before he could respond. "Hello, Doctor."

Daniel ignored her and the small smirk she wore with her use of the title he'd shunned for years. "She was gone by the time I got there." The lie took little effort. "I think they kept her kids, though. I didn't stick around to check."

Seth just stared at him for an inscrutable moment before sighing. "I know. My—The emperor's network picked her up at her brother-in-law's. Marissa will debrief her tomorrow. Unfortunately, it seems that her memory was extensively wiped before her departure." Seth's eyes narrowed. "You wouldn't have anything to do with that, would you?"

Daniel let his surprise show. "Me? Of course not. Like I said, I never even crossed her path." *How does Seth know of my ability to meddle with people's memories?* When Seth failed to reply, Daniel failed to hide his discomfort. "How did things go with the emperor? What news of the half-world keys?"

Seth leaned back in his chair, and Daniel wondered if he was intentionally trying to copy Milton Cartwright as he folded pale hands over his stomach. "Such matters aren't yet within your purview, Fawl. Don't go poking your nose where it doesn't belong."

Daniel's jaw clenched. He looked at Marissa, who smirked back. Her blood-red aura was shapeless, shifting unhappily around her. "What is my purview, then? I believe I've been told to keep my nose out of matters of governance, military operations, plebeian relations, pursuing new locks to stem the tide of adept deaths, and, as of today, shielding and half-world keys. What does that leave? What did you want to show me?"

As he'd hoped, the question seemed to spark Seth's excitement. He leaned forward, faint embers burning deep in his eyes. "Yes. About that." He pulled a file from a drawer, skimming it across the polished desk to Daniel, who caught it with a gloved hand. "Take a look."

Daniel obeyed, allowing himself a disbelieving smile when he found reports of disarmament and disposal of nuclear weapons inside, neatly stapled to photos of people in hazmat suits carefully pulling apart the casings and inner workings of massive missiles. "The decommissioning work?" he asked unnecessarily, trying to judge the authenticity of the deeply relieving proof he'd just been handed. The sensation didn't last.

"Yes. But the emperor has changed his mind." Seth steepled his fingers, and it took all of Daniel's self-control to hold back from lashing out and demanding an end to the games. "He will not, as previously announced, be ending the empire's nuclear capabilities. We will, of course, continue disposing of any and all warheads kept in territories no longer under imperial control and recalling the troops guarding them. But the emperor has decided to keep a few untouched within the borders of the peninsula we still occupy."

But he promised, Daniel almost argued aloud, catching himself before something so childish could part his lips. He tossed the folder back on the desk, his teeth grinding. "Of course. Whatever he deems best. But this is hardly the olive branch he'd promised the plebeian forces and civilians across the globe in an effort to reunite peacefully."

"Peacefully?" Seth leaned forward against his desk, and Daniel instinctively braced against an unhinged outburst like the one he'd witnessed after his nearly deadly confrontation with Noah Byrne a day and a half before. "Peacefully was never on the table. We were always going to have our war, our rapture. We still hope to even the scales in our favor by reducing the public reasons the stupid, huddled masses have to rally against us, but the goal was always primarily to keep nuclear weapons from falling into our enemies' hands. The choice they face hasn't changed. Bow to the empire or die. We simply wish to keep ourselves equipped for the latter should they fail in the former."

Daniel hid the way his fear and sorrow rose at the words and chastised himself for not questioning the empire's supposed kindness more. He knew he had to reply, to show that he was, as always, a loyal tool in the emperor's hand, and recalled a portion of the latest propaganda broadcast he'd witnessed. "I see. Very wise. The emperor is indeed a man of 'action and conviction' as you've said."

Seth's eyes were still bright with an edge of madness. "He's not alone. I shall be his foremost weapon in the coming war."

When Daniel looked at Marissa, wondering how she could attach herself so closely to such a man, her careful, perfect smile faltered, and a flash of fear and regret poked through. Daniel tried to count his wins, such as not getting arrested for his attempt to reach the emperor, and for his apparent success at minimizing the damage Hannah could do to Dawn's people and efforts. A glimmer of triumph warmed his cold aura as his thoughts flicked to Jonathan's children, now free of their awful mother, and when Seth spoke again, his intensity all but gone, the glimmer shone a little brighter.

"But we're not done trying to collect more agents to our side in goodwill, and that is something you can help with. Tell me more about why you believe the world needs to rebuild the locks you helped destroy at the solstice. The emperor is ready to listen."

CHAPTER TWENTY-FIVE

"Thank you," Bailey whispered, running the glowing strand of colorless magic through her fingers. The untouched, unrealized Wyrd thread of a life no longer growing inside her.

Angie nodded happily. They both sat on the back seat of Angie's hatchback in the gentle light of the rising sun. There was so much she could say. Could explain and ask and suggest. But none of it was asked for, so she offered none. Whatever further burdens or joys came from their night of meditation and magic were Bailey's to bear, not hers. "See, like I said. Painless."

Angie almost objected when Bailey slipped the thread into her pocket and reached for the door. She hadn't consciously expected to keep the thread she'd created at Bailey's request, and yet it felt odd to let it go. What was she going to do with it? Angie's thoughts flitted to the Norns she'd once paid with a thread just like it to lengthen Daniel's life, and to promise to stop serving the patrician orders. The key to their half-world was yet one more she needed to find before it fell into the wrong hands.

Bailey seemed to anticipate her as Angie climbed out of her own door, stretching and swaying slightly. The last time she'd done such magic, it had taken a day and a half, and she'd passed out upon completion. At least it had proven easier on a second try.

"Here," the blonde said, and Angie's grogginess evaporated. Bailey walked around the back of the car and dropped something into Angie's hand, which she barely caught.

It was a key. It was tarnished brass, small and unassuming, but when Angie double-blinked, the multicolored magic bound to it was unmistakable. "Where did you get this?" Angie asked, her face slowly breaking into a smile as her heart thudded.

Bailey smiled back. "Through Noah. Who got it through Cartwright. Who got it through... who knows who. He's got a bunch stashed all over. I don't think he'll notice that one's gone for a good long while. It's the least I can do to repay you."

"Where does it lead?" The magic of it against her palm had her itching to try it right away.

"I'm not sure," Bailey admitted, chewing her lip. "But when I asked my scrying mirror what key you needed most, it showed me that one, and where to find it. It was shielded, but I got Noah drunk and was able to bypass it."

"Thank you so much." Angie gave Bailey a delighted grin, barely registering the odd glint of darker triumph in the other woman as she turned and Voyaged away. A dozen wonderful possibilities raced through Angie's mind, not the least of which was the possibility of finding Jasper once more or offering the key for a chance to make things right with Casey. Before she could know the true value of what she held, she'd have to go through and see where it led.

Angie got in the driver's seat and started the car. She'd just tell Lucia where she was going, make sure she was settled for a few days in case it took Angie a long time—or if the time stream was much slower than the true world—and then she'd be off.

"Don't be silly," Lucia said, stuffing the last of her belongings into the plastic trash bag neither had bothered to replace. "If I have to leave anyway just so we aren't facing the risks of staying in one place for too long, then I might as well leave with you." She slung it over her shoulder, tucking her sleeping bag under one arm. "We're a team. At least that's what everyone kept telling me. And if you want to go to another underworld, then two demigods to keep the demons at bay are better than one."

Angie groaned, defeated. She would never have used Lucia's terminology, but she couldn't argue with her logic. "Fine. Load up. But I have conditions."

When Angie stepped through the makeshift Threshold she'd built behind a dilapidated train station, her heart was in her throat. What if the half-world she stepped into was Carens Animus, or another anti-magic half-world and the Threshold was one-way? What if it deposited her straight into lava? What if, what if, what if... All her fears from countless experiences Skipping through half-worlds during her banishment piled on top of each other. She just had to hope the insane luck that had brought her home from that ordeal in one piece would hold.

When the pressure of the veil lifted from Angie's ribs and she found herself in a fairly tame looking landscape of giant blue ferns, she breathed a sigh of relief and awkwardly thanked whatever God or Goddess had her back.

She beaconed for Lucia and watched as the woman appeared in silhouette before breaking through the rippling sheet of marbled-gray magic, standing disembodied in the half-light of the half-world.

Angie had chosen to take the key with them into the half-world for fear of someone doing to them what had been done to Jasper, but she was still nervous about moving away from the Threshold. Tucking the key into her pocket, she also touched the one at her throat. If she concentrated, she could feel the wisp of Daniel's magic bound into it, along with the spider-web thread of her own bound to his watch, which had led her out of banishment, back toward the true world. She took a calming breath.

"Right." Angie turned toward the thick, towering ferns that grew several stories tall all around them. Her hand itched for a sword, and her back felt dangerously light without a pack of supplies. "Not sure what we're looking for. Bailey just said this was the world I needed to come to, according to her scrying magic. If anything happens, stay close to me."

Seventeen minutes later, they'd Voyaged to yet another random location in the world, finding nothing but more ferns when the hair on Angie's arms prickled. Instantly on high alert, she scanned their surroundings. "Lucia, come here, right next to me." Angie shifted to the dead center of the small clearing they'd landed on, her senses sharpening. Lucia ignored her, so Angie raised her voice. "Get away from the ferns. Lucia, now."

"Why, is there something there?" Lucia said, clearly not noticing—or not caring about—Angie's shift in mood. She looked up at the dense green clouds overhead, as if expecting something to swoop down, backing away under the deep shadows of the nearest giant fern.

Angie swore. Cover was never the right call until you knew what kind of demon was chasing you. Half the time, the cover itself wished you harm. "Lucia, I said—" Angie stopped short when a shift in movement past Lucia made her blood run cold.

"I've asked you not to use language like that in front of me." Angie swore again, even louder, and Voyaged to Lucia's side, hauling her with all her might to the center of the clearing.

"Damnit, Lucia. Look." Lucia turned to look where she'd been cowering, and both women backed away as a foot the size of a car stepped down silently where Lucia had been standing a moment before. Looking up, Angie saw a massive being formed of green clouds, vaguely resembling a six-legged reptile, slowly walking toward them. "Voyage. Now. Anywhere. Then Voyage to my beacon."

Angie Voyaged away and sent up a mental beacon without waiting for a reply. More ferns surrounded her, but thankfully there were no cloud beings in sight. Every second that ticked by without Lucia joining her made her heart pound harder. When, after an interminable minute, Angie felt Lucia's beacon calling her, she gathered what flames would bend to her will and Voyaged, aiming to land a short distance from the signal.

Lucia stood, wide-eyed and still, right where Angie had left her, one hand raised to the sky. Before Angie could move, a great misty maw descended, seeming to close around the adept before lifting away again, and Lucia screamed.

Angie darted forward, skidding to a stop when she saw the carpet of green fog surrounding Lucia's feet, but not bleeding out further.

"I'm sorry," Lucia whimpered, her hand still raised, and her eyes fell on Angie. "I thought because it was a cloud, I could just dispel it, or blow it away, or..." Lucia screamed again as the insubstantial beast took another bite around her, and this time Angie saw a chunk of her sky-blue aura ripped away with it. The sight was viscerally sickening, and Angie's heart constricted. She couldn't let it happen again. *Not to Shan*—The mistaken name in Angie's mind distracted her for one vital second, and several things happened too fast to fully follow.

She tried to step forward but found she couldn't. Looking down, she saw a single wisp of smoke wrapping itself around her ankle, and when she tried to look back up, even that was beyond her control. Likewise, when she tried to Voyage away to take a different approach, the magic wouldn't catch.

Only able to move her eyes, Angie strained them to look up at Lucia in a panic. The older woman's aura blossomed out from her—fractured, frantic, and torn to ribbons—and as the great cloud beast descended on her once more, her final scream seemed to untether it from her as she collapsed.

Angie wasn't watching her own aura, but when the paralyzing magic holding her in place seemed to ease, her awareness snapped back to it. Down where the mist wrapped around her ankle, a single glowing spark in her terrified aura had caught on a quickly fading ribbon of sky-blue air, which the green mist retreated from.

The moment Angie could, she lifted her head, her heart dropping with a sickening lurch. Lucia's body lay crumpled in the clearing between the massive blue ferns, devoid of the magic Angie had never seen her without. Angie wanted to run to her, to beg forgiveness from the vacant flesh, or try to atone by returning her recruit to her temple for a proper burial... All such thoughts were forced aside when the last scrap of Lucia's magic burned away, and the green fog reached for her once more.

Angie Voyaged away before it could reach her, back to where the Threshold should be to take her home, away from the nightmare. But there was nothing waiting. Angie cast around, the panic, loss, and trauma of the last few minutes threatening to break free from the shock holding them at bay. Nothing. Angie wondered if she'd simply gotten the location wrong, but when she reached for the key in the front pocket of her jeans, she had her answer. It, too, was gone.

As Angie Skipped away, following the faint tether in her magic and instinct back toward home, she screamed with everything eating through her just like her own magic had consumed that of the recruit she'd just gotten killed.

World after world sped by. Oceans of freezing darkness that tried to drown her, deserts of burning glass that left her knees and palms bloody, and a thousand worlds too bizarre or ordinary to cling to her memory. With each step, she felt herself drawing closer to the pulsing beacon of home nested at the very core of her magic and intuition. *Gods how much she'd missed it.* Angie pushed the feeling aside, hating herself for the relief she felt as she Skipped, never sure of her next footfall, letting each new terror wring her dry of every burden she carried in her heart.

When she landed back in the true world, Angie scrambled to her feet, panting in ragged gasps. With a thought, she Voyaged back to her car, and looked, dismayed at the empty makeshift Threshold beside it. When Angie tapped her empty pocket, her heart dropped another impossible inch.

She closed her eyes, letting the confirmation of the betrayal overwhelm all else. She didn't even know when Bailey had summoned it back. The bitch was almost certainly safely back behind the conference shields with who knew how many half-world keys, a potent, untouched Wyrd thread Angie had helped her make, and, given her abilities with scrying, probably the satisfied knowledge of what Angie had just lost.

One more piece that didn't fit into the machine of lingering injustice and the scattering of chaos she'd thought she'd been trying to fight but could no longer even name. Without a clear monster to fight, without a tangible beast to slay, she was nothing. She couldn't fight what she couldn't touch. Couldn't name. Couldn't spear through the heart.

And if she couldn't fix her world, if she didn't even know how, what was the point of surviving when her actions caused others to die?

Angie turned away from the dead threshold, her panting taking on a new quality. *No. Not now. Not again.* She practically ran to her car, falling into it and locking the door behind her as the panic attack came on fast. *No, no, no.* Angie tried to push the hopeless thoughts aside, her shame only compounding as she tried to convince herself it wasn't her fault. That two years ago, Shan had been a willing volunteer, Cartwright the only one truly to blame for her death, and that Lucia and Bailey now held the same responsibilities.

As her hyperventilating deteriorated into sobs, Angie reached for Jonathan, for his comfort, and kindness, and wisdom, but the coin was nowhere in reach. She let her thoughts scatter, words and actions abandoning her, and wished she had anywhere left to turn.

CHAPTER TWENTY-SIX

The silver lock snapped open with a satisfying click. Daniel's nostrils flared, and he let go of the handful of frigid vacuum he'd created with his aura. Carefully sliding the handle of the lock out of the door, Daniel stood, stretching out his protesting knee, and let the excitement coursing through him brighten his aura and strengthen the shields rendering him invisible to anyone who might approach the emperor's chambers.

It had been nearly two weeks since his last attempt, and the extra planning and preparation had paid off. He thought of how he'd share the good news with Angie once he'd met the emperor, but realized with a small twist of shame that it had been nearly as long since he'd heard from her. *The break was her idea*, he told himself firmly as he checked the door and frame one more time for any traps or shields against his entry. *If she had a reason to call me, she would.*

"Hello? Your majesty?" Daniel said through a wisp of translation magic, nudging the door open just enough to slip through and closing it behind him. "Your majesty, my name is Daniel Fawl. I believe Minister Laufey has mentioned me to you?" The chambers were dim, barely lit, and as Daniel's eyes adjusted, his lip curled with disgust. The floor was littered with clothes, torn papers, food, and suspicious, unidentifiable lumps Daniel didn't want to guess at. When he took a nervous step forward and the smell hit him, he didn't have to.

Daniel pulled out his blue silk pocket square and held it over his nose and mouth until he was able to craft his aura to filter out the gagging stench, and even then was hesitant to pull it away. "Your majesty? Do—do you need me to get help?" He was about to run and fetch Seth, certain that the horrendous state of the royal suite must have a recent and concerning cause, but stopped when something moved on the other side of two large stone columns dividing the small room by the doors from the larger chamber beyond.

A store mannequin dummy shuffled into sight, its featureless face unsettling in the dim light cracking through distant, heavy curtains. It bent and picked up something that dripped through its stained fingers back to the floor with wet plops, and placed it atop a plastic trash bag already stuffed to overflowing. Daniel momentarily considered banishing all the stinking filth away, but stopped himself. Doing so would betray his intrusion.

A whimper from a far corner tore Daniel's attention from the grotesque sight, and he carefully picked his way through the mess toward the sound. Once past the columns, Daniel could see the rich, sumptuous backdrop that he'd seen the emperor make television speeches in front of, complete with a desk, chair, and huddle of microphones. The little tableau was spotless, and when

Daniel looked more closely, he could see the faint, multi-colored shield of magic around it, undoubtedly denying access to whatever had trashed the rest of the room, and possibly the rest of the palace wing beyond.

Another whimper accompanied the sickening sound of metal against bone, and Daniel turned to see the back of a man huddled in the deep shadows behind a large conference table as filthy as the floor beneath it. "Your Majesty?" Daniel asked again, now hoping for a different answer than he had upon entering. When he came around the side of the table and flared the light of his aura to see better, his jaw and stomach dropped in unison.

The man before him was indeed the emperor, his familiar face pale, scared, and gaunt beneath an unkempt beard. He looked at Daniel with the eyes of an animal and, without looking away, jabbed a fork into the top of a foot that had clearly already withstood innumerable such blows.

"No," Daniel said, horrified, and lunged forward to grab the emperor's grimy wrist in a gloved hand as he raised it for yet another jab. "Please. Your majesty... Gods..." His mind struggled to comprehend that the gibbering, bleeding beggar before him was the most powerful man on earth, even after the fall of the global empire.

"I want to be powerful again," the man said with fervent emphasis, his words out of sync with his mouth as Daniel's magic translated them to English. "Powerful like them. They tried to hide it from me." He giggled, and Daniel let go as visceral disgust pushed him away from the sound. "How to get power. But I heard it. Very quietly. When they were telling me other secret things to say."

Realization slowly dawned through Daniel's mind, and he swallowed the bile that rose with it as the emperor once more drove the silver fork into his mangled foot. Daniel twisted his aura into tangible tendrils that reached out and held the other man's wrists still while a third touched the center of his furrowed brow. It smoothed slowly as Daniel pressed into his mind, careful not to further disturb what he found. As he'd expected, blood-red magic faintly twined with soot black was tangled through the emperor's mind, as far and as deep as Daniel could reach.

Drawing back mentally, but not releasing the emperor to move, Daniel's aura yanked free from his control with a fierce, frigid surge of disgust and anger. The idea that Marissa Hayward could play any part in such an atrocity sickened him. Daniel turned aside, retching onto a pile of equally disgusting garbage, and quickly pulled a filtering layer of his agitated aura back over his nose and mouth.

He banished only his own sick, carefully leaving no trace that he'd ever witnessed the contents of the Royal apartments, turning back toward the emperor with a lump in his throat. The man before him was powerless. A used and abused puppet, his every thought infected by the magic stitched through him. Daniel felt foolish. He'd known the rumors—that the emperor was nothing more than a puppet of the patrician powers—and chided himself for blindly believing otherwise since their fall.

Perhaps, if his stint as a Councilor had lasted long enough to get to such matters...

Still holding his blue silk pocket square over his face, Daniel reached into the emperor's mind with his aura, careful not to touch the other traces of magic embedded there, scouring for anything useful. He found nothing.

Daniel weighed his options as he crouched before the emperor, careful not to touch a knee to the filthy floor. "Can you hear me? Do you understand me?" he asked as kindly as he could, and the emperor nodded with a slight, confused smile. "Good. I promise you, you'll never get magic that way." He pointed to the wounds in the other man's feet, and the emperor looked down at them sadly.

Daniel probed his mind once more, assessing if there was any way he could help the traumatized man regain his sanity, but the damage was too extensive, too complete. "Would you like to have magic in your dreams, and dream forever?" Daniel asked, disgusted by his own intentions, but the wide, childishly bright smile that lit the emperor's face eased it.

"Oh, yes please! That sounds lovely."

Daniel stood, trying to offer a comforting smile from behind the cloth that now felt like an executioner's hood. He didn't want to think. Didn't want to acknowledge the truth now staring him expectantly in the face.

The emperor could give him *nothing* he'd hoped for, and that dropped the last scrap of footing Daniel had been balanced on out from under him. Seth was the true head of the beast, and he didn't even know how to approach that. The only thing he knew for sure was that none of the tried-and-true strategies his mind raced to produce stood a chance.

As Daniel reached into the emperor's mind, ready to cut it loose from its mooring and yank away any possible trace of the cause, he almost considered trying to control the man to his own ends. He heaved at the thought and dismissed it. *I have time,* he reassured himself. Seth was gone for business and hadn't mentioned including Daniel until the equinox feast just over a week away. *I have time to make a plan.*

Daniel closed his eyes, unwilling to witness the results of his actions, and with a thought, gave the emperor the eternal dreams of magic and power he'd promised, freeing him forever from the cruelty he'd been embedded in.

When Daniel Voyaged to the hallway outside, he replaced the ornate silver lock, hating the sight of it and everything it had revealed. He checked that he'd left no trace and Voyaged away, his lunch once more forcing its way up.

CHAPTER TWENTY-SEVEN

A ngie had been on her own for two and a half weeks when she hit her breaking point. She'd cried all she could cry, barely slept, and eventually locked herself in an empty, crumbling parking garage in Salt Lake when missing Daniel, Jonathan, and Casey—and guilt over Lucia and Jasper—had all become too heavy to bear. Unable to function, to care, she'd Voyaged away now and then to see to her necessities, but on that warm, mid-September Tuesday when she emptied her last bottle of water, something finally shifted.

She hadn't told a soul about Lucia's demise, and the loneliness of that threatened to swallow her whole. She pulled her dark-blue jacket a little tighter around her, despite the heat.

Anything is better than this. The thought clattered through her, making her blink. With it came the image of her childhood home, of her parents, her sister, the secret little corners where they used to play, and for the first time in many long years, they didn't sting against the contrast of the rest of Angie's state of being. She tried to smile wryly to herself but didn't feel her face move. *What do I honestly have to lose at this point?*

She was seated in the open trunk of her car and tossed the empty bottle over her shoulder. She'd parked diagonally in the very center of the second-highest level of the parking garage for no reason other than she could, and when she closed the trunk, locking it with the fob in her pocket, the beep echoed through the empty space between the asphalt slab and low ceiling.

Houseless folks would sometimes carve out little corners of the ground level for themselves, but hers was the only car in the whole building. She'd ensured that by welding the front gates closed with a spark of heat. She doubted any would climb up and burgle her car, but just to be safe, she gave a halfhearted attempt to leave her car shielded from notice before Voyaging away to a driveway she knew all too well.

It was far more overgrown than she remembered. A massive bower of yellow roses obscured the yard to the side of the century-old farmhouse ahead, and what she could see of it looked streaked by decades of dust-laden rain and in poor repair. Swallowing her pride, she walked up to the unassuming front door, wiped her boots on the worn brush bolted to the bottom step, and took a deep steadying breath.

When she knocked, barely rapping against the peeling paint, it was yanked open in seconds by a middle-aged woman with chestnut hair and a deeply practiced scowl.

She seemed stunned to see Angie, and Angie felt genuine relief so deeply she almost cried when Cath smiled.

"Angelica!" She stood aside, beckoning Angie in and folding her into a crushing hug the moment the door was closed. Her eyes lingered on the dark denim jacket Angie wore, and her eyes misted. "I'm so, so glad you came back. Your father will be, too." The inside of the farmhouse was warm and smelled of old wood and vinegar, and Angie tried to ignore how awkwardly she returned her mother's hug. "Robert!" Cath hollered up the narrow stairs as she led Angie into the tiny kitchen. "Angelica came to visit! Change into a nice shirt and get down here."

Angie settled herself on a chair at the low table tucked against one wall without even thinking, and the nostalgia that washed over her was a palpable sweetness on her tongue. Cath put a lid over what smelled like vegetable stock simmering on the stove, and Angie pushed the lump that rose in her throat back down. "Are you and Dad getting by okay?"

Her mother huffed a long-suffering sigh, and darted Angie an odd glance that put her on edge. "Hardly. Better than some, with the garden and animals, but with prices for everything going through the roof?" She made a disbelieving sound. "I genuinely don't know how the Fawls are keeping their ranch afloat. They don't even raise beef, and yet they somehow—"

"The Fawls?" Angie asked, shocked.

"Yes. Nice family, if a bit odd. I only mention them because they're doing better than most. They live off towards Lamoille. Caledonian, I think. Or at least he is.

Not that you can tell from his accent. But like I was saying, looking at them, you'd think everything in the world was still roses."

Angie couldn't formulate a reply. Daniel had once told her he had distant family somewhere in the western Americas, but the fact that her parents knew them refused to sink in.

"Hey, sweetheart," Robert said, creaking on the bottom step behind her.

Angie was certain she'd never heard that word in her father's voice before in her entire life. Her guard rose, painfully and protesting loudly, against the gentle comfort she'd found for almost a full minute. She didn't turn, and her father walked over to join her mother, still tucking in the tails of a clean and mended work shirt. "Robert. I assume you two have kept trying to reach me, but I, um, lost my phone. What do you want?"

"Well," Robert exchanged a loaded look with his wife, and leaned against the counter beside the sink, crossing his arms. "We did start to explain on the phone before you—" He seemed to chew the words he thought better of saying. "Before we got cut off." Angie ignored him, blatantly looking instead at the faint dusting of white in his once-black hair.

"We just want to reconnect," Cath said sweetly, pulling a glass from a cupboard. "We—we worried that you lost your way. Lost your faith." Angie glanced at the small shrine to various imperial Gods and Goddesses in the sitting room beyond. She didn't want to tell her mother she'd never truly shared her faith. "Or"—Cath drew herself up—"had forgotten your duties as a good and pious daughter." She glanced at her husband. "But I'm sure you haven't. Right?"

Cath set a cold glass of water on the table next to Angie with a couple of broken cookies, and guilt over her parents' meager attempt to win her back put her further on edge. "I'm sorry," she said, pushing her chair back and standing. "I shouldn't have come here." She reached for her wallet, pulling out the few hundred dollars she had with her. "I somehow got convinced I was supposed to because you were family, but we both know that hasn't been true since—" Angie's throat didn't want to let the name pass, and her eyes didn't leave the cuff of her precious jacket as she held out the wad of imperial bills. "Since she died."

Cath put a hand over her mouth, her eyes suddenly bright, and Robert wouldn't look at Angie as he stepped forward to take the money she offered him, counted it, and folded it away into his back pocket.

"Is that it?" he finally said, and Angie replied before he'd finished, eager to leave as soon as possible.

"Is what it?"

"You're a patrician now, aren't you? We need more help than that, and from what I've heard, you can easily afford to give it."

"Heard from who?" Angie asked with a sneer, which faltered when her father replied.

"Garrett. That young man you dated for a bit. We were reaching out to anyone we thought you might have stayed in touch with, and he told us you were a patrician when I ran into him a few months back. Then after we got that letter with your phone number, he called and told us more. Told us you could take us somewhere safe, somewhere where all you rich folks are going to wait things out until they get better." Reality felt a degree off-kilter for Angie as Robert added, "He called it Eden."

"Is that how you know the Fawls?" Angie demanded, and her mother looked taken-aback.

"The hell do they have to do with anything?" Robert asked both women, stepping between them. "Look," he said to Angie when neither answered. "You know what's going on out there, you know what we're trying to get away from. We're just asking for your help."

Angie shook her head, backing away. "Bullshit. This is a setup. Who actually told you how to reach me? Told you I was a patrician? About Eden? Garrett said you were looking for me before you talked to him." Her smoke juddered sporadically into flames around her, reeking of cigarettes and burning rubber, and she hoped her inept parents couldn't see it. "Was it Milton Cartwright? Seth Laughy? That—that evil bastard of a centurion I told you never to speak to again?"

"It's true? You know the minister?" her mother asked quietly, going starry-eyed like a schoolgirl at a mention of their crush, but her husband ignored her.

"I have no idea what you're talking about," Robert said gruffly, and Angie couldn't tell if he was covering a lie or just uncomfortable with her not instantly caving to his demands.

"I don't believe you." Angie turned to leave, her vision blurred, but Cath stopped her.

"What, you mean, you won't help us?"

Angie turned back at the tremor in her mother's voice. She buttoned her dark denim jacket closed over her churning stomach and hardened her expression in reply. "You blamed me for my own sister's death. Not because I did anything wrong, but because I chose to go live my own life instead of staying here with you like she did. You told me you never wanted to speak to me again, and that I'd never again be welcome in your home. I didn't hear one word from either of you for years. And you thought you could break that silence just because you heard I'd done okay for myself, and I'd just roll over like I used to as a kid?" Angie wrapped her fingers around her silver necklace, sinking the heat of her emotions into it as she forcefully reminded herself of the adult she'd become. "Fuck off with that."

Beside her offended mother, Robert twisted the large gold ring on his pinky finger. "Running away like that, betraying your legacy..." He frowned, still spinning the family heirloom carved with the axe and branch emblem of Silvanus. "Hell, even shaming us by doing gladiator sports in school instead of something more appropriate for a girl. We didn't want to disown you, Angelica. And we don't want to now. That's why we're giving you a second chance. But if you don't want to be our daughter, don't want to do your duties as one, we may have no choice. Do you want to be the reason our long family line ends?"

The deeper cut in her father's words bled years of long-held bitterness as her answer spilled out. "You ended the family legacy the day you left the logging business they handed down to you to come play cowboy, making the rest of us miserable with you when you learned it wasn't as easy as it looked. This family ended the day that drunk piece of shit killed the only good thing about it." Angie forced herself to not look at the photo hanging on the wall beside the narrow staircase of her smiling, black-haired sister wearing the jacket Angie now claimed. Grief swelled in her as raw and overwhelming as the day they'd gotten the news of the cattle truck running off the road by the lower pasture.

Angie reached for the comforting, familiar weight of the copper sigil coin, and when she realized it was absent and remembered why, her tears broke their dam, hot and angry. Angie raised a hand when her mother moved toward her, and her grief was momentarily derailed.

Her fingers faded away to wisps of smoke at the knuckles.

Her parents clearly noticed in the same moment Angie did, and both reached for each other as they took a step away. Angie stuffed her hands in her pockets and closed her eyes. No, *no, no. I'm not falling apart. I'm okay. I'm fine. Hold it together.*

When she opened them, she found she couldn't speak. So she took one last long, pained look at her frightened parents, turned on her heel, and Voyaged away the moment the front door closed behind her.

—◦❖◦—

When Angie got back to her car, she slammed the heel of her hand into the hood, a blast of heat shedding off her with the blow. She didn't want to cry. Didn't want to grieve any more for the people she'd lost. Didn't want to risk losing herself to do so...

"Fuck!" Angie shouted to the empty garage, the word reverberating beneath her skin. "I can't fix it," she said to herself much more quietly as she turned in a circle, feeling the world press in on her as she searched for something to make it stop. "There's nothing I can do to fix it..."

Angie leaned on the hood of her car, unwilling to name the hot, wild, desperate call in her heart. But the longer she ignored it, the more it itched at her need to move, tugged at her sense of direction, and stirred the core of her magic, burning with the breath of every demon her heart held.

Pushing off with new, untested determination, Angie's emotions faded back down as she unlocked her car and opened the trunk. Only anger lingered as she dumped out her rucksack and quickly repacked it with the essentials for a different kind of life. As she gathered each piece, digging under seats and into suitcases, she marveled with some chagrin that she had, without noticing, collected every essential tool of her banishment back around her without realizing it. *Perhaps it was always meant to come to this.*

At last, Angie pulled the sword she had kept since the day she'd blooded her abuser with it to ensure his continued residence in prison, retrieving it from under the back seat of her hatchback and slinging it from a belt at her hip. She closed the car, locked it, added what magic she could to the shields around it, and set her mind out in the direction of the wildest half-world that might be waiting for her. *If this world doesn't want me, I'll find one that does.*

CHAPTER TWENTY-EIGHT

"**T**he emperor was nothing but your puppet, wasn't he?" Daniel whispered in Seth's ear as the two men stood, watching uniformed golems set the massive dining hall with solid gold wares. "And I suspect I don't have to ask how he learned that magic is born of trauma, pain, and suffering... You were careless."

"You did that?" Seth hissed, whirling to Daniel with a burst of flames that the older patrician deftly anticipated and redirected harmlessly.

"Prove it," Daniel said with a sneer, and Seth eyed him with the wary respect Daniel had hoped for. He'd spent the last week weighing the gamble, having left himself the option of plausible deniability, but he didn't know how to move forward without revealing what he'd learned.

"I can, if I'm pressed to," Seth replied, "and the price you'd pay for *killing* the emperor would be steep..." A small smirk told Daniel all he needed to know about the unexpected detail, and he swallowed.

He shouldn't be surprised Seth would just kill the emperor once he was no longer pupetable, and frame someone for it. He wondered if the lock he'd opened to reach the poor man held the damning evidence, but otherwise ignored the threat. "You aren't the right hand of the empire," Daniel continued, circling around Seth, his cane tapping on the marble floor. He dropped his voice as Moretti scurried past with another patrician, discussing a recent disturbance in the plebeian quarter of the city. "You're the head."

Seth replied with a small, slow nod as Daniel stopped before him. Daniel smiled and bent into a deep bow. When he straightened, Seth looked wary but flattered, and Daniel leaned in conspiratorially. "Then I will endeavor to be the best right hand to *you* I'm capable of being." Daniel saw the minister's aura ripple into flames and raised his Air aura in a great sphere around it, prepared to contain or smother them as needed.

Seth glanced around at the glimmering membrane of lemon-yellow magic, and his flames subsided into smoke. "And how, pray tell, do you propose doing so?"

Daniel brushed a nonexistent speck of dust from the sleeve of his black silk suit, weighing his answer carefully. Some part of him knew that he shouldn't get too cocky just because his approach and confession had paid off perfectly. But the taste of that success was so sweet. So tempting to reach for more. "To be your loyal follower," he began in a light and measured tone, watching Seth's expressive face closely, "and to lend my talents, knowledge, and experience to your causes in any way I'm able. To begin," he added, feeling the rush of the gamble rustle through his aura as a dry chill, "I thought I might offer to help collect, identify, and protect the half-world keys I understand have been finding their ways into your coffers."

Seth's tight smile made the muscles in Daniel's back tense. "I don't need help with these things," he said coolly. "They're perfectly well protected without your help, and I have a more experienced and knowledgeable Councilor ready and willing to help sort and identify them all once they're done seeing to other matters. They were even directing centurions in my network to recruitable new adepts for a while." Daniel frowned slightly, wondering which Councilor it was before catching himself and smoothing his expression under Seth's scrutiny. "As for collection, my network of loyalists have proven themselves to be more than adequate. I'll find other, less, shall we say, *delicate* uses for you."

Daniel exhaled audibly, chewing over the arguments he wanted to make and the fawning compliments he knew he should offer.

Nearby, Marissa was running a perfectly manicured finger along one crisp linen tablecloth as she marshaled and directed the legion of golems. Seeming to sense the tension between the two men, she glanced up and handed off her clipboard to Moretti before joining them. She took Seth's arm, giving both men a nervous and inquisitive look, and Seth sized her up before returning his attention to Daniel.

"Speaking of keys," he started, and Daniel's hope rose cautiously. "I've heard rumors through my network that a few keys that were making their way to me may have been, unfortunately, *diverted.*" Daniel arched a brow. "In fact, I believe a dangerous one may have, sadly, found its way into the hands of a relative of yours."

Daniel didn't need to fake his barely bothered reaction. "Oh? Who?"

Seth gave him a wicked smile. "Your cousins in Nevada, in the Americas. They have two young daughters, don't they?" He tutted through his teeth, and Daniel's blood heated. "Who knows what sort of damage a key like the one I lost could do in the hands of anyone so uneducated." He checked his nails for dirt, glancing at Daniel sidelong. "Especially an unlocked adept that young. No idea how it might have been waylaid so very far."

Daniel didn't like the idea of a child being used as a pawn to manipulate him, but hardly thought showing it was worth jeopardizing everything over. He turned his attention to Marissa, wondering if he could read more about the obvious bait in her aura or demeanor. "Why should I care? Did you think that would be a new button of mine for you to push?"

The smile which had started to creep across Marissa's elegant features faltered just as quickly, and Daniel knew he'd got it in one.

Seth, on the other hand, seemed pleased by Daniel's lack of emotion and needled him. "Aw, Fawl, have you really forgotten what it means to care about family? Or what it's like to have family to care about you?" Daniel gave him a withering look, which only added strength to Seth's goading. "You've gone soft since your military days. Perhaps that uniform you wore to my first ball with the English Conference *was* just a costume, like everyone said."

Daniel wasn't sure if he should play along or push back and decided on simple bluntness in place of either. "Do you want me to go get the key back for you, Minister?"

Seth's expression flipped from teasing to rage in a beat, and Marissa jumped away from him, bumping into Daniel and grabbing his wrist to steady herself when orange flames began to lick from his skin. The massive clock tower in the piazza struck six times, and Seth waited until the final chime before pulling his aura back under control and spitting a trite "Yes. If it's not too much trouble" at Daniel's feet. Daniel twisted his wrist out of Marissa's grasp, and she tucked her hands into the folds of her emerald taffeta dress as Seth pulled her aside, muttering, "Give the signal. We move ahead as planned."

Daniel Voyaged away to Moretti's office at the front of the palace, and after running a gloved finger down a list of addresses pinned to the corkboard inside, Voyaged again to another office he'd never been to before. The population registration office for the Nevada province was, as Daniel had hoped, empty at nine in the morning on a Saturday and global holiday, so he took his time finding the name *Fawl* filed away in the wall of cabinets.

Seth's last words to Marissa nagged at the back of Daniel's mind, and even with the needed address in hand, he hesitated. Reaching beneath his short jacket, he unclipped his sat phone from his belt and dialed Angie's number. He listened to it ring over and over, frustrated. "Come on. Pick up. I really mean it this time." He'd been trying to reach her for days to fill her in about the emperor and make sure that she was okay—maybe even to apologize, if he was honest with himself—but even his Voyaging beacons had gone unanswered.

When the line clicked over to a grating buzz, Daniel swore and clipped the phone back to his belt. Pushing thoughts of Angie aside, he carefully read the address on the sheaf of papers he held and willed his magic to deliver him to the little girl who he'd ensure would no longer be a pawn in whatever game or war Seth was about to set in motion.

CHAPTER TWENTY-NINE

The first half-world Angie landed in was a familiar one, where a sweet-smelling, teal prairie stretched impossibly far to a nonexistent horizon. The massive red sun overhead illuminated the lumps of earth that swelled at her arrival, and Angie Skipped away before the humanoid or beast-like demons could form.

The next world resembled earth, complete with the parking garage Angie had left from in the true world, and she Voyaged around it several times, until the city park she'd landed in started closing in around her. Angie Skipped away, not sure what else she was searching for, but knowing that a mimic world that would try to trap her wasn't it.

Skip. A dark world with a glowing, fetid shoreline strewn with luminous seaweed.

Skip. Towering sandstone mountains carved into sleeping faces, weathered and warped by the howling winds Angie shielded her eyes against.

Skip. Tiny creatures, more plant than beast, scattered beneath her boots when she landed on a world she towered over.

Angie felt for her sense of home, the tethers and instinct pointing her back in that direction. Over and over, she ran away from it, yearning to get far enough away that her sense of the true world faded. As she did, she pondered the fact that, despite the infinite number of half-worlds she might encounter at any given layer, she could only flee her reality one layer at a time. Or return one layer at a time, should she change her mind. *One layer. One move. One small step at a time.*

When Angie landed in the first world that warped her Skipping magic, she felt no terror, but the intoxicating exhilaration she'd craved. She tried to Skip away a few times, feeling the magic start to catch before failing with each attempt, and took in the half-world of short-shorn grass she'd landed in. Darkness hovered only a dozen paces away on all sides, looking like a solid dome barely blurred at the edges, and Angie could see no light source to explain why it didn't engulf her.

She walked forward, drawing her sword, and the little bubble of flat, inexplicable light stayed centered on her. Smiling darkly, the adrenaline in her veins fresh and welcome, Angie dropped into a run, and the darkness parted before her.

As her body and mind settled into the familiar, acute awareness of sprinting toward unknown dangers, thoughts rose through her mind as if finally shaken free from the depths where the cares of her ordinary life had held them down.

One small step at a time. The thought wouldn't let go and slowly morphed. *No matter how hard I tried, I couldn't have gotten here in one Skip. I couldn't have gotten home from banishment in less than thousands.* Naming what she already knew poked at something she didn't want to think about, and Angie ran harder, trying to Skip again with no luck. *One foot in front of the other.*

Angie nearly missed it when the short-shorn grass within her bubble of light changed as she sped past, but she skidded to a halt, doing her best to turn back exactly the way she'd come without any point of reference. She retraced her steps, panting and begrudgingly acknowledging that she was no longer in the peak physical condition she'd been in the last time she'd run wild through half-worlds.

If I'd thought it only took one Skip to get home back then, I never would have made it. Hopelessness squeezed at Angie's lungs as she imagined what it would have meant to think that back then, and the layers of it, added to the hopelessness that had been growing within her since the solstice, since Lucia's death, seemed to bind together like poison to a poultice. *But I didn't,* she reminded herself, buckling her rucksack across her chest. *I knew the truth.*

When she saw the tuft of taller grass she'd run past, Angie smiled. As she walked up to it, she could see it was the edge of an untouched field beyond the mown one, extending who knew how far past the wall of darkness. The moment Angie stepped into the taller grass, her Skipping magic caught, yanking her away once more.

Angie Skipped over and over and over. She didn't know which or how many had slower or faster time streams than her true world and didn't much care. Each step took her further away from everything she'd lost. Eventually, Angie slowed, exploring each world in more depth until boredom or danger pushed her on.

When she realized she could no longer sense the direction of the real world through her instinct and magic—only through the tethers bound to her heart and necklace—a bitter note of shame twisted her reckless triumph. *Was I wrong to run? Does running away make me a sellout?* Angie ducked her head, remembering how she'd once heatedly accused Daniel of being the same for capitulating to the prices his world demanded of him in exchange for the stability he needed.

Angie Skipped to a world waist-deep in snow, and away again as quickly as she could. Pausing in a dense evergreen forest, she cursed as the wet cold seeped into her jeans and socks. Her aura refused to flare to dry and warm her for several tries as she mentally tried to adjust against the warping properties of the half-world. When it finally obeyed her will, Angie breathed a sigh of relief and didn't catch the shift of motion in the corner of her eye until it was too late.

A sharp prick on Angie's wrist made her yelp, and she snatched it away from the pine branch which had left a spot of blood on her skin. Angie Skipped away instantly, back toward her true world on instinct, and was glad she did.

In the bright, sharp light of a thousand fluorescent bulbs hanging from an unseen ceiling over a geometric tile floor, the dark shadow wrapping itself around Angie's wrist was evident, and she dropped to her knees as her head spun. "Oh fuck."

Angie batted at it, but it didn't care. In a panic, she flared her aura as it gathered close to the break in her skin, screaming in pain as it sunk into her wrist, possessing her.

She reached for the copper anti-possession sigil coin that had kept her safe from demons throughout her banishment, but she knew she didn't have it. Knew it was too late. She was on her own, unprotected, and would have to figure it out on her own.

Gritting her teeth against the sharp, throbbing pain, Angie grasped the arm the demon had claimed, wildly coming up with a dozen possible solutions and rejecting them all just as fast. Her panic, but not her pain, eased when she realized the demon wasn't trying to spread up her arm as she'd expected, and even seemed to be condensing itself into the screaming joint of her wrist.

When Angie realized that the bright light around her was dimming, she decided on a course of action. Hauling herself to her feet, Angie Skipped. She didn't even pause to see where she landed before Skipping again, and again, and again, always back toward her true world where she knew she stood the best chance of surviving, or getting help, or coaxing it out of her flesh. One step after another back toward a reality she no longer resented.

⸺⋐✦⋑⸺

When Angie landed on the bare asphalt beside her car, she cried out with relief. She'd returned to her world in the middle of a bustling street in Hindustan, but Voyaged back to her sanctuary before the large, brightly painted truck trundling at her had a chance to honk. She stripped off her sword and rucksack one-handed, bracing her back against her hatchback as she gripped the site of her possession once more.

Lifting her possessed wrist to grasp the silver key at her throat felt like placing a gun under her chin. Breathing hard, half from the pain shooting up her arm and half from panic, Angie squeezed her eyes closed and turned every scrap of intention she could muster to the shadowy demon in her flesh. "I've done this before," she told herself when her sense for the demon failed to sharpen into focus. "Daniel's demon was just the same. Just focus."

Little by little, Angie's mind became more acutely aware of the animalistic mind of the demon. Each throb of pain it shot through her forced her to lose, then reclaim, a layer of her focus. When she finally felt her attempts to reach it acknowledged by a flare of fear in its emotions, it burrowed deeper into her wrist and a bolt of pain shot clear through her shoulder and chest, making her heart skip a beat.

"Please," she gasped, desperately pushing her feelings into the thoughts and intentions she pressed toward the demon in her mind. "Please. If you stay in me, we both die. I know that as a fact, and you can sense that in me, can't you? Look." Angie squeezed the silver key necklace tight, picturing the demon that had long possessed Daniel sinking into it in her mind's eye. "You can live in this instead. It's worked in the past. You'll be safe there. Immortal." Angie sobbed, shaking. "Please."

When the pain in her wrist eased, Angie opened her eyes to see the shadowy demon wrapped around not just her wrist but the silver poking out of her fist with tentative little motions. Angie held her breath, trying to heat the silver to entice the demon in, and cautiously fumbled with the chain clasp behind her head with one hand.

The chain fell away, slithering into her lap, and Angie's heart leapt when the demon condensed and sank into the silver key, releasing her wrist. She threw the key as far as she could with her stiff and shaking arm the moment her pain eased. The key clattered across the black asphalt as she scrambled to her feet, and the demon reared from it.

Angie dug her car keys out of her pocket with throbbing fingers, unlocking the driver's door and yanking it open. Her instincts screamed at her to not turn her back, but she dove for the loose coins in the console, shouting with relief and triumph when her fingers closed on one of the smaller, newer anti-possession coins Jonathan had mass-produced leading up to the solstice. She couldn't believe that she hadn't thought to take it with her when she'd gathered her belongings to Skip again, and the terrified hindsight made her nearly faint.

An unworldly scream rent the air just behind her, and Angie scrabbled across the front seats before turning, wide-eyed, to see what the demon did next. It stretched and expanded from the silver key laying only a few yards away. When it broke free altogether, it screamed again, and Angie clutched the anti-possession coin for dear life.

The demon could clearly sense that it could no longer return to her, and Angie watched, aghast, as it began vibrating, darkening, and with one final, earsplitting scream, shattered into a thousand wisps that quickly dissipated into nothing.

Angie didn't move an inch for an eternal minute. When she hauled herself back up and out of the car, every joint and muscle ached. She bent and picked up the chain, then walked over to the silver key and, after making sure it was vacant, retrieved it as well. It was so cold to the touch that Angie worried her skin might stick to it.

She breathed on it, trying to warm it with her petulant magic, threaded the chain back through it, and returned it to its comforting place around her neck.

As Angie lifted her rucksack to set it on the seat, the sat phone on the console buzzed. She looked between the two, each promising a different path forward, a different next step to take, and when she hefted the pack onto the back seat and answered Daniel's call, it was with a rush of solid, certain relief.

"Yes. Hello. I'm here."

Chapter Thirty

A little earlier...

Daniel was truly, properly angry. Seth had put a powerful and dangerous tool in the hands of a literal *child*, designed to hurt her and her family, just for some murky power play against him. It was a miracle she'd handled it all well, and it had been a relief to see in her unlocked magic that she had decades before her fated death when her magic could be awakened.

He tossed the key in his hand, standing in the driveway of the large house tucked away in its own little green valley, watching it from behind his shades. Small and gold with a filigree design at the handle, it looked more like a plaything than an object of power. But the rainbow of magic bound through it that Daniel could see through his auric vision revealed the truth.

Among the magic was a thread of black that Daniel felt through his magic as much as saw, and he stood stock-still in the late-morning birdsong for a long few minutes, carefully and meticulously teasing it out from where it had been bound into the other magic. The last thing he needed was to have the first half-world key he had managed to acquire summoned away from under his nose. Once it was done and the scrap of Seth's magic dissolved, he replaced it with a thread of his own, binding it to his aura so that he alone could summon or banish it in the future.

With a wave of his hand, Daniel banished it away to the carefully prepared stash he'd created months ago for just that purpose. Looking back at the house, Daniel built a large shield around it, careful to make sure that only other patricians would be barred from entering, with his cousin's adept daughter the only exception. When he was satisfied, he turned his back on the distraction and, with a crunch of gravel beneath his cane, took one step forward and Voyaged.

Daniel landed back in the feast hall in Rome he'd left from with a snarl. He'd only been gone ten minutes at most, and Seth seemed to shrink back from his arrival, standing at the far end of the hall, speaking closely with Marissa, Moretti, and several other guilty-looking patricians.

"Fawl," he said, his voice unsure, though his expression was irked. "I didn't expect you to return so soon. Perhaps you could give us a few more minutes."

Daniel just bared his teeth and let his anger bleed into his aura with every slow, echoing step he took down the center of the long room. "You crossed a line, boy." The face of the little girl reluctantly handing him her key with a brave but unhappy expression flitted before his eyes, and the tablecloths between him and Seth fluttered nervously. "No one, *no one*, tries to play me like that without paying the price."

Daniel could feel the added strength of the equinox in his blood, the time of power feeding his recklessness. Seth's companions scattered away from him as the minister's fire flared, and Daniel batted aside the bolt of flames that hurtled in his direction with his aura-wrapped cane. It slammed into the windows along one wall, shattering them out into the piazza below with a crash, but Daniel's attention didn't waver.

Banishing his cane to free his hands, Daniel gathered an armful of arctic wind, compressing it down until the pressure was immense, and released it to hurtle straight for Seth's face. The other man had been preparing more flames—the floor, walls, and ceiling around him scorching—but when the blast hit him, they reverted to smoke as his head slammed into the door behind him.

Daniel broke into a run, ignoring the protests from his bum knee, and before Seth could regain his bearings, the Caledonian snatched the air from his lungs and slammed him back against the door by the throat. "You. Crossed. A line." Daniel knew the intensity of his outburst didn't match his true, more measured feelings about his family, but he had waited so long to stand up to someone—anyone—who thought he would roll over under their attacks. A decade of pent up, defensive anger was stored in his aura, and it was all he could do to hold himself back as much as he did.

"I'm sorry," Seth rasped, his skin darkening with soot as Daniel deprived it of oxygen.

"I don't care," Daniel said, his face inches from Seth's. "I don't care about the cousins you tried to hurt me through. I don't care about anyone in this whole wide world but myself, and the people I think have something to offer me." When Moretti stepped forward, clearly intending to intervene, he didn't take a second step when Daniel turned his face a degree toward him in warning, keeping his eyes locked on Seth. "What I won't stand for is being played for a fool." Daniel pushed away from Seth with disgust, as he released his neck and the magic suffocating him. Seth slumped to his hands and knees, gasping down air, and Daniel looked down his sharp nose at him. "You know who I am. What I am. And you most certainly know what I'm capable of."

When Seth looked up at him with reddened eyes, it was with a mirthless smile Daniel almost stepped back from. He stood slowly, sliding up against the charred wall, his hands raised, and his aura agitated but meek. "You're right. I should have known better." Daniel found his unreadable smile maddening. "Would you believe I just wanted to see if you still had enough fight left in you to be of use to me?"

"No," Daniel replied flatly, not reacting when Marissa approached from his flank, a spear of blood-red magic resting unused in her hand.

"Fair enough." Seth wiped the back of his hand across his mouth, leaving a streak of soot. He glanced at Marissa, and with an almost imperceptible shake of his head, her spear disintegrated. "The truth is, I didn't think you'd approve. But I thought if I could just keep you away until it was done, that you would once you saw the result..." Daniel let his anger flair through his aura, and Seth made a mocking show of wincing. "I'm not," he said with a manic laugh. "I'm really not playing you for a fool, Fawl. Do you want proof?"

"That would help," Daniel sneered, stepping out of Seth's personal space when the younger man beckoned for the patrician onlookers to come closer.

"Magistrate, what was I trying to keep Councilor Fawl from knowing about until it was done?"

Moretti scowled, hanging back. "Are you sure?" Seth nodded, and the magistrate then turned to Daniel. "Very well. Minister Laufey has, for some time, been liaising with every known leader of adept communities across the globe. He has, in secret, been working to bring them all together to reinstate a Focal Nucleus lock to help stabilize the disruptions caused by uncontacted adepts meeting their fated end. He's been successful, and it was expected that we would all be assembling in the Council world at, well"—he glanced at his watch—"we're already late."

"Go in my place."

Daniel turned to Seth, surprised by his emphatic suggestion, and his face was bright and earnest.

"As a gesture of good faith from me to you," he insisted, taking a half step toward Daniel. "Go ahead of me, in my place. Represent the empire under *your* power, not mine. Take credit for this unifying return of control, of leadership, to the faithful. Spearhead the expansion of our righteous networks into every magical community under the sun. Isn't this what you want?"

Daniel weighed his options and what he stood to gain. "All leaders?"

Seth nodded. "Yes. Well, I mean, everyone from me, to Noah Byrne, to Dawn Renard. But none of the plebeian leaders fighting to steal what they can never have, like that Hellenian general."

Daniel turned to Marissa. "What say you, Marissa? Am I being gotten rid of, or honored as he says?"

"How dare you question the minister?" She looked affronted, only a slight twist of her painted lips betraying the coy act.

"Cut the shit," Daniel snapped, and she blinked. Daniel moved in close to her and saw a mix of reactions swirl with confusion across her face and aura. "No one believes you two are actually dating. Not in the way real people do. And whatever little jealousy-baiting game you're playing at isn't working on me. He can have you for all I care." Marissa looked wounded, and Daniel shook his head, remembering the blood-red magic bound through the emperor's self-destructive madness to stop himself from feeling pity. "You've lost yourself, Marissa. And if you don't start questioning the actions of your beloved minister soon, I fear you'll be the next to pay for the oversight. Now. Should I go to this meeting?"

Marissa swallowed, placing a gold-encrusted hand to her chest. She looked between Daniel and Seth, her sculpted black brows knitted, but she nodded jerkily. "Yes." Her voice dropped, and for a moment Daniel glimpsed the scared recruit she'd once been to him. She touched her other hand to her ear, her brown eyes clearly trying to impart some meaning. "But your enemies will be there among your friends. So please, be careful."

Daniel rolled his shoulders, pulling himself up to his full height, and looked around at the gathered patricians of the empire in exile. His gaze lingered on each until they looked away—except for Seth, who held his stare. "I accept."

"The Threshold is above the English Conference site. Neutral ground."

"And the rest of you?"

"Will prepare to join you. And see to our other equinox endeavors." Seth's eyes slid from Daniel to Marissa. "Go sit on our Hail Mary, will you?"

"What's that?" Daniel asked, tensing for another outburst as Marissa Voyaged away.

"Don't worry," Seth said, dusting himself off and coating the floor around his feet with a fine layer of ash. "If things go wrong at the meeting, it's an insurance policy. If all goes well, I'll show you after. Go with God."

Daniel resisted the urge to roll his eyes and Voyaged a good distance from the edge of the English Conference shields in the woods above the small village, carefully checking that no one else seeking the Threshold had had the same idea. He pulled out his sat phone and dialed.

Angie picked up on the third ring. "Yes. Hello. I'm here."

Daniel stifled the way his aura warmed and brightened, and tried to keep emotion out of his voice. "Angie, just listen. I have no time. Seth targeted my family and may do the same with yours. Hopefully the distance you kept from them will discourage him from targeting them. I think he did it to get me out of the way for something he's ramping up, but I may have foiled him and gotten invited into whatever it is anyway. I'm heading to a meeting Seth set up in the Council world. Something is happening, and it might be a trap. Stay alert, stay safe, and keep an ear on the radio."

CHAPTER THIRTY-ONE

"I understand. Be careful. I—" *I miss you. Please let me come with you.* "I'll catch up with you later.

Angie hung up, locked her car, and Voyaged straight back to her parent's house. Daniel's words rang in her head. *"Hopefully the distance you've kept from them will discourage him from targeting them.'"* How had she forgotten that keeping her distance was keeping them safe? What damage might her visit have caused, given that it had never occurred to her to leave any protection in place?

Angie burst through the front door without knocking, and for the minute it took her to check the dining room, mudroom, kitchen, sitting room, and every room upstairs, she tried to convince herself that it was fine. That they were out running errands or doing ranch work. A check of the vehicles and farm equipment still sitting in the driveway, and a glance through to the garden and orchard disillusioned her of that idea.

Another search of the house revealed that their essentials—like toothbrushes, carved idols from the altar, and her sister's photo from the wall—were all missing, which only complicated Angie's sense of guilt. *I can't save the world, but I should have saved them. They can't have gotten far.* She knew she was grasping at straws, but she had no other choice.

Angie Voyaged to the roof, scanning all around, but saw no sign of life apart from the herd of black angus cows dotting the distant horizon. She Voyaged again in intervals down the road in one direction, then the other, with no luck.

Angie realized with a sickening lurch that she wasn't following any of Daniel's advice, and Voyaged back to her car.

She quickly unlocked it and got in, started the engine, and peeled off for the ramp down to the lower levels. As she descended, Angie clicked on the radio she hadn't touched in recent memory and tuned it to the imperial station.

"Equinox parties are expected to continue across the globe despite rising tensions since the nonviolent collapse of imperial governance and trade systems three months ago."

Angie tuned out the reporter droning on about the emperor's party in Rome and slowed as she neared the bottom of the parking garage. Carefully steering around a tent set up in the shelter of the ground floor, she stopped just inside the gate, ignoring the man shouting questions at her about why she had a car.

Angie had welded the gates wide enough for cars closed when she'd taken up residence, and the longer she tried to melt them back apart so she could leave, the more frustrated she became at her failure. As the home-less man finally approached her directly, she shouted in frustration, releasing any and all control of her magic, and hoped the raw expression of her emotions might do what her will couldn't.

The metal beneath her hands melted like butter, and Angie shoved the gates open, pushing them out into the nearly empty street. The man fell silent, wide-eyed, as Angie jumped back into her car and sped off in the di-rection of her childhood home in Nevada, turning up the radio over the grind of her engine.

Forty minutes later, as she maintained a dangerous speed along the straight freeway lanes cutting through salt flats, Angie's attention was pulled back from her speedometer by a change in tone from the radio an-nouncer just as she was passing a small rest stop and out-look anchoring the expansive miles of flat, white noth-ingness.

"This just in as a breaking bulletin. The empire is on the lookout for a Locksmith from north-eastern Nevada, rumored to have started several fires after returning from banishment."

Angie slammed on her breaks, crossing the median and circling back toward the rest stop at a much more distracted speed. He was talking about her, she was sure of it.

"*The aura of danger that they are creating must end by sunset tonight.*"

Sunset where?

"*In other news, efforts to disarm nuclear warheads across the globe have reached their end. The last two intact are being kept here in our own fair city of Florence. Minister Laufey is personally overseeing the final stage, under the watchful eyes of The Doctor in charge of nuclear research.*"

She was certain that was code for Daniel.

"*The doctor is quoted as saying that time is of the essence in these matters, and that bringing them to a close is a matter of following the bonds and conscience of his heart. Follow the watch—I'm sorry folks, there seems to have been a slight glitch with the end of the bulletin there.*"

Angie frowned at the clock built into her dashboard. What time was she supposed to be watching for? Or was the last line of the announcement not the mistake the announcer had believed it to be? She turned off the radio so she could think better as she jerked to a stop haphazardly in a parking space, shifted into park, and tapped her fingers against the steering wheel.

In truth, she had no idea why she was driving back to her parent's house. Even if her parents had left willingly—which was unlikely given Daniel's warning—the chances of her passing or finding them by car were just as slim as with Voyaging. She'd just been driving because sitting still in her car to listen to the radio as instructed would have been torture.

She was acutely aware of the knot of guilt, obligation, and longing for the family she'd lost tucked in tight behind her breastbone. *Lost? Never had, more like.* The thought unraveled it, making her gasp, and the more Angie let herself consider abandoning the search for the parents who had never once acted like they loved her as much as they loved controlling and using her, the more the knot broke apart, lifting weights from Angie's soul she'd stopped noticing decades ago.

She was glad they'd finally moved on from the suffocating little life they'd brought her into. It was only right that she did the same.

Angie turned off her car, stripped off her dark-blue denim jacket, and carefully tucked it beneath her seat before getting out. Out of what was quickly becoming a habit, she put up the window shades, locked the doors, and did her best to shield it from notice.

Closing her eyes. Angie focused on the scrap of her aura bound into Daniel's gold watch just as his was bound into her silver necklace. With silent hope that she'd interpreted the cryptic radio message correctly, she Voyaged away.

CHAPTER THIRTY-TWO

D aniel had managed to slip through the Threshold of soot-black magic onto the pebbled beach of a matching shade with other stragglers, using a layer of his aura to avoid notice. He realized as soon as he arrived that he was ill-equipped to step into the role Seth had offered him.

Only when Dawn and Noah arrived did he step out of his concealment, all heads turning to watch. The late-evening sun was warm overhead, and the waves that lapped at the wide beach beneath the towering obsidian cliff were the only sound besides the crunch of pebbles as the three met in the center of the piles of rubble that had once been the Council thrones.

"Fawl," Dawn said curtly.

Noah shifted, clearly not wanting to appear associated with either of the other two, his khaki aura lethargic. "Where's Laufey? He'd promised all factions would be here. Rebel"—he gave Dawn a wary look—"neutral"—he placed a hand on his chest and looked Daniel up and down—"and imperial."

"He's sent me in his place," Daniel explained, aware that the moment wasn't right to address his last meeting with the Celt, and keenly grateful for Dawn's and Casey's presence among the gathered adept leaders.

Again, he reached for what he was supposed to do or say next, realizing Seth had sent him in with no preparations. Quickly assessing everything he had gathered in the half-hour since he'd learned about the meeting, he pulled together an explanation for the many listening patricians, who were trading untrusting glances with each other, and hoped he wouldn't be proved a liar. "He'll join us once he's seen to other matters and bring with him the information and tools we need to stabilize all of our communities under democratic control. For the moment, we just need to wait patiently and do our best to get along."

So wait he did.

Tensions rose as the following hour passed, ratcheting up with each degree the sun sank toward the tops of the vertical obsidian cliffs. The black Threshold of glass-like obsidian at the shoreline stood unchanging—a reminder of what failed to step through—as the shadow from the clifftops inched across the hundred or so agitated, whispering adepts toward its base.

When the shadow began creeping up the still-vacant Threshold, the tension snapped.

"Where the hell is Laufey?" Xiao Sheng shouted, and many of the onlookers nodded. "He'd promised us we could use the power of sunset on the equinox to rebuild some sort of lock. That's the only reason I agreed to come here in peace. We don't want to wait any longer."

"He'll come," Daniel said, loud enough to be heard by all, but his own confidence in the statement wavered.

"Do you know how to rebuild a Focal Nucleus?" Dawn asked, and Daniel felt the weight of countless eyes on him.

"No. I wish I did. I know how important it is to stem the tide of new adepts. So many that we can't collectively get to them before the magic released at their deaths causes further fear and harm. Not to mention needing to curb the damage the exposure of that magic is causing in the non-magical world. But I haven't been able to find how that might be done, and Minister Laufey hasn't trusted me with whatever solution he's promised us all."

"He's not coming at all, is he?" someone shouted, kicking up a general babble.

Dawn raised her hands, turning in a circle. "Calm down, everyone. I'm sure there's a reasonable—" Whatever more she had to say was lost beneath the babble of anger and fear that swelled over her words.

She tried to shout over the roar as everyone turned on each other and the three disparate leaders standing in the middle, but when no one listened, she seemed to deflate. She looked so tired. So much older than Daniel wanted to see her as.

"This is a setup!" a man nearby shouted, and Daniel tried to see who'd spoken with magical volume to be heard. Noah flinched, as if to protest his innocence, when Daniel's attention lingered on him. A man with a graying buzz cut stepped into the central circle of rubble where the Latin Focal Nucleus had once stood, holding the empire together. "This is a set up. You brought us here to kill us. If we all die, so do our causes. When the head dies, the body follows."

He was speaking to Daniel directly, and Daniel's eyes narrowed. "Quite the accusation coming from another former Councilor. And one that fought to hold their seat against these good people"—Daniel spread a gloved hand to the shouting onlookers—"when they made their first bid for an equal say."

Daniel doubted even half of the gathered adepts heard his reply, but a moment later he regretted ever having spoken.

"You." Xiao Sheng hurtled past Daniel, hurling himself at the Slavic Councilor, the two men instantly locked in a fierce fight of fists and magic.

Dawn made an attempt to stop him, but her gold magic faltered in her clearly exhausted state, breaking with her grip when she tried to pull him away. "Fuck!" she shouted, but whatever more she said to stop the unprovoked attack was drowned out as other sparks of battle magic erupted elsewhere in the crowd.

Daniel stopped himself from wading in and breaking them apart. He stepped back from Noah and Dawn, bringing up his personal shields to full strength, carefully setting Dawn and Casey as exceptions in his intentions should he need to show his hand and protect them.

"It's locked!" a panicked shriek carried over the hubbub from a woman who had tried to step through the Threshold. Daniel's hope for a peaceful resolution sank with his stomach as a few more patricians threw themselves at the Threshold to no effect.

More snatches of words—some accented or touched with translation magic—tumbled over each other and the chaos that ensued.

"He was right! It's a trap—"

"If anything happens to me, my people had orders to lay waste to you Spanish. You've always had it in for us—"

"Could we Skip back? I can't sense the direction from here—"

"I'll kill you. I'll fucking kill you all. You were the one who told me to come—"

A scream momentarily dulled the roar of the crowd, and everyone turned to it. Centered among the other fights Xiao Sheng stood, panting and grinning, over the crumpled form of the Slavic former Councilor. Daniel felt frozen as he watched Xiao Sheng wrap his magic around the fallen man and squeeze until the Councilor's own magic winked out.

"Enough!" Daniel sent a concussive wave out through his aura, wincing when it bounced off the obsidian cliff a heartbeat after he'd stopped bracing for it. It had the desired effect of ending the dozens of direct altercations that were sending magic arcing across the black-pebbled beach, but arguments and whispers persisted.

"Enough," he said again, but when Xiao Sheng turned, Daniel fell back a step. His eyes, murky green with the magic of his aura, were fixed on Daniel. The bickering and sizzles of magic picked right back up, and Xiao Sheng stepped forward, his expression elated and murderous.

Daniel reached for him with his own aura, hoping to incapacitate the Cantonese leader just long enough to regain control of the situation, but found with a horrible sense of losing his grip that his magic couldn't find purchase. Dawn and Casey were both shouting at a swarthy man who seemed to have attacked them, and as Daniel looked around, he realized that no one was paying him the slightest bit of attention.

He backed away as Xiao Sheng advanced on him until the other man stopped, pointing at Daniel's feet. "I should never have let a Councilor live. Not when I knew their faces. Especially not a murderer like you. Renard is wrong. Far more blood is owed. Now I'll spill yours right where you spilled Cartwright's."

Daniel glanced down at the obsidian pebbles beneath his leather shoes, and the world seemed to slow around him. *He was right.* At the edges of his vision, Daniel saw an olive-gray net of magic expand between Xiao Sheng's hands, but didn't react. *Murderer.*

The word didn't cut like it used to. Especially not from such a hypocrite. Daniel looked up and lunged forward, grabbing Xiao Sheng's wrist in a gloved hand, his bright-yellow shields strong and layered with light as the Threshold in the corner of his eye rippled.

"Not today."

Chapter Thirty-Three

A ngie landed not in the Council world with Daniel as she'd expected, but on the steel mesh of a shadowy walkway high up in an industrial or military building, looking down over a bustle of activity. The air smelled like fuel and plastic, and was filled with the loud grind of massive engines and wheels. Seth's red hair caught the light a little way along the suspended catwalk she stood on, just below the steel beams of the ceiling, and Angie's eyes narrowed.

Her mouth went dry when she reached for the tether of Daniel's watch once more, but realized that arriving where she had wasn't a mistake. She cast around, but Daniel was clearly nowhere to be seen through the jungle of pipes and grating she'd landed in, nor in the massive silo command center below, leaving her to the concerning conclusion that Seth indeed had Daniel's watch.

Nausea overwhelmed Angie as she did a double take down below. She didn't generally mind heights, but the sight of the narrow, circular room disappearing down into the earth—and the massive, polished nose cone rising from it—made the world shift beneath her.

Angie dropped to her knees, grabbing the handrail, and swallowed the bile that rose. The radio had mentioned nuclear bombs. She hadn't expected to land right on top of one.

When the quality of light around her shifted, her disorientation eased as her attention was pulled back up to the rafters. The moment the grinding sounds stopped, the sunlight filtering down into the bunker became flat and smoky. Seth stood a hundred feet away with his back to her, a man with a bushy brown mustache at his side, and one arm stretched high overhead.

"Perfect." Seth was smiling when he turned away from whatever he'd done, tucking something into his jacket pocket, and froze when he saw Angie. "What the hell are you doing here?" He glanced back up behind him, then frowned at her, moving closer along the walkway. "How did you know to come here? Who told you when we would be firing? I didn't even tell Fawl..."

Angie stood, trying to hide how scared she was without a plan or her usual magic. "Why the hell would I tell you that?" She didn't even know who had been behind the cryptic radio message but wasn't about to reveal that. "My contacts aren't who you think, and I'd rather keep it that way." She went to stuff her hands into the pockets of her denim jacket before remembering she'd taken it off, and instead crossed her arms, pointedly looking past Seth at the other man.

Seth followed her gaze, glaring at the man behind him, then throwing himself against the railing. The whole catwalk juddered with the impact, and Angie grabbed the railings on either side, dropping her stance an inch. Seth leaned out to scan over the people below with the same look of angry panic. "The auxiliaries..."

Both men Voyaged away, and Angie rushed to where they'd been standing, peering up. The entire yawning opening in the roof where thick doors had been hauled open was filled with a Threshold of black smoke, dimming the light of the setting sun outside. Daniel had gone through to the Council half-world. Seth had his watch. And now a nuclear bomb was aimed straight through a Threshold. "No. Oh no..."

Angie Voyaged, once more following the tether of Daniel's watch, and landed in the center of the control room, built in a crescent-moon shape against the wall of the missile silo. A dozen soldiers had guns leveled at her head in an instant, the metallic rattling chilling her. Refusing to react, Angie grabbed Seth's shoulder and spun him to face her.

Seth bared his teeth, backing away. He waved a hand dripping with red flames at Angie. "Fuck off, Forester. Or my soldiers will shoot you where you stand."

"Stand down," Angie demanded, ignoring the threat. "Whatever you're doing here, wherever you're planning to send that nuke, I won't let you." She readied her stance just enough to be noticed, and carefully kept her aura placid as smoke. She knew she didn't have the power to bring her flames up—at least not with any stability or force. All she had was the bluff that she didn't even need to, relying on what Seth had heard and seen of her magic in the past. The weight of the gamble sat heavy on her chest.

Seth raised a hand, and Angie's awareness felt every imperial soldier nearby lean in. Her breathing became shallow as Seth conjured a ball of black flames, and she braced herself to Voyage, since there was no way she could trust her ability to shield or fight back when he hurled it.

"I wouldn't do that if I were you," Angie bluffed, hearing the lie in her own voice.

Seth hesitated, arm still raised, and frowned. It slowly morphed into a smile as his head tilted to one side. He lowered his arm, his flames winking out, and Angie swallowed. "Nor would I," he said, and Angie finally glanced around nervously at the other patricians and plebeian auxiliaries nearby. "Not when I don't have to. Tell me," Seth said, pulling out a handkerchief and wiping the soot from his hand. "How are your parents, *Angelica*?"

Angie's blood went cold. "So you *were* involved..."

Seth looked satisfied, and unexpectedly signaled for the soldiers to lower their guns. A shade of suspicion covered his pale face as he looked around at them, but disappeared when he turned his attention back to Angie. "Of course. Garrett has been a loyal part of my network since the beginning."

"What did you do with them?" Angie's fists balled at her sides, and her heat finally rose. It flicked and breathed with the rise and fall of her ribs, unhappily resisting her attempt to haul it back under control.

"I gave them what they wanted most." Seth's infuriating smile just sat there smugly on his face until Angie was ready to smack it off.

A sinking feeling filled her until she couldn't hold back from asking exactly what she knew Seth wanted her to. "Which was?"

"I took them to Eden."

"Bullshit." Angie knew the retort was an unthinking attempt to argue against a reality she simply didn't want to believe, and her face fell. Her insides joined when Seth pulled a heavy gold sigil ring from his pocket.

"Not at all. The plebeian families of patricians were always allowed to join the refugees there, and your dear parents were only too eager." He tossed the ring high in the air, and Angie lunged to catch it. "Call it an insurance policy against my death. I have loyal friends there, too. If this evening goes as planned, they'll be well taken care of for the rest of their long and comfortable retirements. But if anything should happen to me, or if you meddle in my affairs, then by tomorrow morning they'll both meet, shall we say, unfortunate ends."

Angie's heart pounded loud in her ears as she scanned the command center staff. Half weren't even paying attention, issuing commands or working at the banks of computers and dials. The rest were either blank-faced soldiers or expensively dressed patricians she didn't know—and who wouldn't meet her gaze. "What are you doing here? What, exactly, am I not supposed to meddle in?"

Seth moved to the inches-thick plexiglass window overlooking the massive silo, tilting his head for Angie to join him. She did, folding her arms tightly over her churning stomach. "These are my pride and joy." He gestured out at the gigantic missile, then down at the floor it was standing on, which had a large seam running through the middle. "The second is below, ready to fire as soon as the first launches—and once I've had a chance to set the second destination."

"Through Thresholds?" Angie could barely see the circular opening high overhead, the film of smoke across it distorting the light in a way that was still deeply unsettling.

"Yes. I've made them even more effective with magic." He wiggled his fingers. "Now each can destroy a whole continent. The last nuclear bombs in existence, so I thought they should act the part."

Angie felt nauseous. "And which continents do you intend to destroy? Which half-worlds?"

"That's for me to know, and you to find out once I'm done." Seth started to turn back to the launch preparations Angie tuned out, but she caught his arm.

"I don't believe you really have my parents. And so help me, I won't let you do whatever it is you're about to." She shoved the gold sigil ring she knew all too well into the front pocket of her jeans, trying to ignore the lie she spoke. *I could find them before tomorrow morning. He wouldn't actually... I could...*

"It will only take you an hour or so to check," Seth said when a woman in a lab coat wordlessly tapped his shoulder, then returned to her monitors. Just as Angie was about to ask how he expected her to do so, Seth pulled a key from another pocket and dropped it into Angie's hands before she could even register. "I'd hurry, though. Their time is almost up."

Angie cradled the large jade key in her cupped palms, entranced by the maroon, yellow, and white magic pulsing in watery patterns across it. It was, without question, the key to Eden. Finally in her hands. And she didn't want to use it.

A cry outside of the command center, presumably coming from the workers below the missile, made everyone not glued to monitors rush to the window. They were all looking up and pointing, and Angie's heart swelled when she saw the cause of their alarm.

Jasper Rose. The nonbinary patrician looked older by at least a decade since Angie had last seen them, as they descended slowly in a cloud of pale-yellow light from the massive Threshold stretched across the top of the silo. *Of course the key to the world they'd been trapped in had been taken by Seth.* She glanced at him, wondering if she could grab the key from his pocket, but quickly dismissed the idea. Angie looked around for Daniel, wondering if it was his magic surrounding the former Councilor and slowing their fall, but gave up when Jasper drifted past the window of the command room, seemingly without noticing it.

Angie Voyaged to the closed hatch below the missile, her heart pounding hard in her chest. She watched Jasper descend, hope she barely dared to name thundering through her blood.

Seth appeared on the other side of the silo, swiftly followed by the other patricians present, and more soldiers joined those already pointing their firearms at Angie through a service door off to one side. Jasper turned, marking them as they cleared the lower swell of the missile supported on its sleek fins, but didn't linger their attention on the minister or his equally unhappy looking cronies.

"Jasper," Angie breathed happily as the older adept touched down on the slab of steel beside her. The moment they stood on firm footing, the cloud of yellow light that surrounded them seemed to split apart like the petals of a flower, each taking shape into something almost humanoid but still connected to Jasper's feet along the floor.

"Inferi?" Angie stepped back, torn between excitement and dread. She swallowed hard when one of the pale, light-formed figures stepped forward. She grasped her necklace, spinning the stem of the silver key so the three decorative interlocked rings at its handle brushed faintly against her chest. A darted look at Jasper's pleased expression prevented her from retreating further, but Angie's every fiber was still balanced to fight or run when the creature spoke.

"Yes. We are Inferi. We bring you greetings of good will and hope for a rekindling of the alliance between our two peoples, ambassador."

Angie smiled weakly, trying to catch up with the wildly unexpected turn of events. The being of light was vaguely human, even vaguely masculine, but lacking more concrete features Angie could discern. Angie didn't even reach for the copper coin she now knew held another Inferi, but the strangeness at meeting more, the confirmation of their respectful and intelligent greeting, twisted guilt through her thoughts. Her eyes refocused past and through the demon who had just spoken when Seth strode toward them, his friends close behind, and she swallowed again.

"Thank you, ambassador. Erm." Angie gave Jasper an uncertain glance. "Earth welcomes you in return. I welcome you." Behind the creature she spoke to, Seth raised a hand crackling with black flames, and Angie felt the blood drain from her face. "But they probably don't."

The Inferi leader followed Angie's gaze, the rest following suit, and Jasper stepped toward Seth, hands raised in appeasement.

"Seth, stand down." Their tone was lighter and gentler than Angie thought was called for, and she nearly called to them to step back, to not trust the red-haired man, as they went on. "These beings are our friends." Jasper gestured behind them at the sentient demons standing in front of Angie, not a trace of stress in their face or posture. "I've put my faith in you. In teaching you, guiding you, and entrusting many of the half-world keys taken from the old vaults to your care. Now, please, continue your faith in me." They turned their back on Seth, beaming at the Inferi. "Today we start a new age."

Seth had dropped his magic when Jasper had addressed him directly, but the moment he turned away, he did something Angie couldn't quite see.

"No, we don't." Seth's voice was a dark bark, and before Angie could step forward, Jasper turned back to him, only for him to step in close, making them go rigid. "Humans and demons will never mingle!" Seth shouted, pushing Jasper away from him, and several people gasped as Jasper slumped to their knees, Seth's right hand stained scarlet. "Did you hear me?" His face was twisted with rage, and the Inferi Angie watched him through warped and swelled, one condensing down to Jasper's side. "We are God-fearing people in this world. And will wipe out every. Last. *Fucking.* Demon, if it's the last thing we do."

"Stop," Angie said, breaking out of her frozen shock. She glanced up at the smoky Threshold high overhead. "You can't just nuke their world. That's..." Angie looked at Seth, silently pleading for him to show any remorse, hesitation, or humanity she might appeal to. "You just can't."

"Watch me." Seth sent a ball of red flames hurtling toward Angie, and the Inferi leader expanded in front of her, protecting her from the blast with a thundering screech that made every hair on Angie's body stand on end.

Chaos exploded. Angie managed to bring a shield up in front of herself as several soldiers fired at her. She backed away from the patricians descending on her and the Inferi, who scattered. Just as the mustached man lifted a net and spear of eggplant-colored magic, one of the armed soldiers turned their raised rifle away from her, aiming it at the patrician, and fired.

The man screamed and toppled, clutching his leg, and the gaggle of Seth's friends lost their shared focus as each looked around fearfully in every direction.

"You shouldn't have betrayed us," the only Inferi who remained before Angie said, and she could have sworn that raw emotion shook their words. "You'll pay for giving us such a welcome."

People scattered all around her. Plebeian technicians sprinted out of sight behind doors and hatches while legionnaires shouted commands and counter commands that Angie barely registered. She watched as the Inferi detached from the tether connecting it to Jasper, who gasped and heaved on their knees, then shot like an arrow into the nearest soldier wearing the fancier gray uniform of a legionnaire.

He grunted, his body shuddering, and when he drew his pistol, holding it level at Seth's head, his eyes were no longer brown, but light yellow. The shot he turned on his nearest comrade set off a ripple of gunfire in its wake, and Angie ducked, desperately holding her small bubble of shields together, before she saw if it met its mark.

"Angie..."

She only looked up when the faint word drifted through the melee, and she found Jasper's eyes locked to hers. Seth had moved away from the former Councilor, unscathed by the bullets aimed for his transparent black shields, and Angie crawled forward.

"I'm here," she said, taking in the gash in Jasper's side and the small drip of blood from the corner of their mouth. "Can you heal yourself?" She knew it was unlikely, even for the most skilled natural healers.

"No. Angie." Jasper grasped her hand, their eyes wide, and their long, gray curls splayed across the floor. "Don't worry about me. You need to stop them."

Angie turned her attention up, flinching when a bullet whizzed an inch over her head through her failing shields. She strained to spot any weakness or break in the Threshold high overhead, undoubtedly strengthened by the moment of power of sunset on the equinox. She didn't have the key that had created it, and a glance at Seth—protected by shields, experienced patricians, and well-trained legionnaires—dashed her hopes of getting it. "If you could summon a key for me, or tell me where to Voyage to get one..."

"I'm sorry." Jasper's words were slurred, bubbling with blood, and when Angie looked back down at them, their eyes were closed, and their dusty-pink magic faded in and out of sight. "I'm sorry I put my faith in the wrong person."

"No," Angie sobbed, shaking Jasper's shoulder. "I need help. I don't know where Dawn or Daniel are, or if they have keys, or if they'd understand. Please. No, not yet." She leaned in close when the adept muttered something more, but the dying prayer they whispered was in a language Angie didn't understand, the gentle, ancient sounds of it lost on the only ears that bore witness.

Angie wasn't allowed even a moment to grieve. An auxiliary crashed to the ground and slid past her, his empty eyes staring vacantly ahead, and Angie leapt to her feet. The light-formed Inferi that had inhabited him rose like a ghost, shrieking and speeding into the next nearest auxiliary, who instantly turned on the comrades she'd been fighting alongside without a shred of hesitation.

Looking around, she saw that Seth had been separated from his friends, and he Voyaged away with a snarl when a possessed soldier got through his shields from behind, leaving his jacket in its grasp. Angie followed without hesitation, once again tracing the tether of Daniel's watch. She needed to know why Seth had it. What he'd done with her friend, her lover, the only person in existence she couldn't imagine living without.

When she landed in the control room, three rifles cocked at her head immediately, and Angie froze. She couldn't trust her shields to protect her, nor her flames to kill them before they fired.

She watched, horrified, as Seth, in unison with a patrician technician, turned a large plastic key in the console and reached for a big red button. Before he could press it, Angie Voyaged away up to the catwalk where she'd first glimpsed Seth creating the Threshold.

Digging in her pocket, Angie pulled out the heavy jade key. Every fiber of her being screamed against what she knew she had to do, making her chest heave and her hands shake as clicks and groans of machinery began to build below. She couldn't let it reach Daniel. Couldn't close the Threshold entirely and let it land who knew where in her world.

"I'm so sorry," she sobbed, pressing her eyes closed for an indulgent second as the recently refreshed images of her parents' faces swam into her mind, and the memory of words that weren't her own, spoken to her in anger, answered.

It's better for my world if I let you go.

A deafening crack and thunderous rumble forced Angie's hand. She reached for the film of the massive Threshold overhead, and the moment the jade Eden key touched the membrane of magic, it wavered and turned from black smoke to silver.

The impact of the launch blast from below sent Angie slamming into the ceiling of pipework over her head, the jade key spinning away into the gantries lining the silo. Angie's magic bloomed hot and acrid around her, utterly out of control and fueled by the shock, horror, guilt, and desperation of what she'd just done. She surrendered to it, curling up on the grating where she'd landed, letting all thought abandon her to the all-consuming inferno as the nuclear missile hurtled past her, up and into Eden.

When Angie's senses returned in its wake, she could barely believe it. *I'm alive. How the hell am I alive?*

Her ears were ringing too much to hear her own panting breath, and Angie slowly pushed herself up from the catwalk floor, which had been coated in a thin film of soot by the launch blast fifteen seconds before. A dribble of blood fell into her eye as she stood, and she wiped it away with the back of her hand, realizing that every stitch of her clothing had burned away but somehow, miraculously, her skin was untouched.

One glance below reminded her that she wasn't done. There were two. The heavy blast doors from which the first missile had launched were rolling apart, the rumble of the engines more noticeable through the soles of her feet than her ears, and they were nearly open.

Angie wanted to hesitate, wanted to think, but knew with one look at the silver Threshold overhead that she had no such luxury. *Two nukes. Two half-worlds.* Seth would have to come up to change it and would see that Angie had foiled him.

Stumbling forward, Angie Voyaged into the control center below. If guns once more threatened her, she didn't hear them over the numbing ringing in her head. Seth stood before her, another key in his fingers, his face twisting in rage as he screamed words at Angie she couldn't hear.

Angie let her thoughtless muscle memory take control, and socked Seth so hard in the jaw that he dropped on the spot, the little key skittering under a bank of computers. Angie stepped over him and slammed the heel of her hand into the second large, red button marked LAUNCH. It sank into the console with a satisfying, heavy click that echoed through her bones.

The world swam around her as a door to one side opened, several possessed soldiers spilling in, their figures illuminated by the second blinding launch blast in harsh, washed-out clarity.

Someone struck Angie from behind, and the world went black.

CHAPTER THIRTY-FOUR

The world seemed to reverberate with the first step Seth Laufey set upon its shores. "Did you send her?" Black and orange flames peeled from him, and the in-fighting among the adept leaders ceased.

Xiao Sheng twisted his wrist free from Daniel's grip as both tried to keep their footing on the pebbles shifting beneath them. The Gael didn't resist, his arms splayed wide for balance. The two men stepped apart as the crowd parted before the glowering minister's approach, and Daniel braced himself when all attention locked on him.

The ground stilled as Seth stopped inches from Daniel, the younger man's face twisted with anger. "Did. You. Fucking. Send. Her."

Daniel remained impassive, summoning his cane with a flourish in case he needed it. "Send who where? Was your magic affecting magma far underground just now? Impressive."

Seth ignored the attempted change in topic, poking Daniel hard in the chest—then yanked his hand back when a tendril of Daniel's aura smacked it with air cold enough to damage skin. "Angie, of course. Do you know how she knew where and when to find me? Did you tell her what to do?"

Daniel scoffed and let his confusion show through his skeptical expression while hiding the cold flash of worry that shot through his limbs. "I've never been able to tell that woman what to do. I have no idea what you're talking about."

"Not this again," Casey Easton called over the silent watchers, waving a tattooed hand at Daniel with a look of contempt. "Cartwright himself never got that bullshit accusation to stick. Drop it already." Daniel smiled. Not with mirth, but with dark, pleased satisfaction. Seth backed off a pace, splitting his accusing attention between Daniel and Casey as the latter looked around, seeming to gather a few silent supporters before speaking again. "Minister Laufey, please. You promised us a new lock. One built to protect the innocent, and nothing more. That's the only reason any of us are here. What can you teach us about that? Exactly what breakthrough have you had?"

Seth barked a laugh, and Daniel's smile vanished. "I lied. You stupid, gullible *children*." A ripple of unease fluttered across the listeners beneath Seth's bright, scathing glance as he turned in a circle, and a fresh flutter of activity at the obsidian Threshold was short-lived when it remained impassible. "I will never help a single one of you selfish traitors that refuse to bow to the empire." He laughed again, making the hair on Daniel's arms stand on end. Judging by the uneasy glances exchanged around him, he guessed that many others felt the same way.

Daniel shook his head, his heat rising. *Selfish? Traitors? Hypocritical bullshit.* Perhaps Seth was simply too fickle to expect consistency from. Either in who he saw as his enemies, or in the justifications he believed in for his actions.

"I will never bow to the empire again," Xiao Sheng said, stepping forward. "You named no such price when you convinced us all to come here. You must keep your word. If you don't"—the man's hands balled into fists at his sides, and Daniel saw his aura ripple—"you will have to answer to every Cantonese-speaking adept, now and in the future, as my forces rip from you what you owe us, only stopping when there's nothing of you left." Seth simply skewered him with a look that could kill, and Xiao Sheng swallowed hard, his bullying bravado visibly faltering. "What's your price, less than returning to the empire? What are your demands?"

"I have none, you presumptuous nobody." Seth's aura flared, scorching Daniel's and forcing him and a dozen others back a few paces.

Daniel waited for something more, anything he could formulate a plan around, and darted his eyes to Dawn. However, the black woman's attention was held by something past Seth.

"Release her!" Dawn shouted, and all eyes turned to see what she was talking about. Marissa had stepped through the Threshold, and someone fell to their knees beside her. It took Daniel a stretched moment to realize it was someone he knew, bound and gagged.

Hannah Crowther.

Seth ignored Dawn's demand. "Bring her." Marissa obeyed, hauling Hannah to her feet, and dragged her across the black beach.

"What's this?" Daniel asked, stepping forward and giving Dawn a subtle signal to stand down.

Marissa threw Hannah down at Seth's feet, and he dragged her head back, forcing her face up to Daniel's. "You've been naughty," Seth purred, pressing his face close beside Hannah's and looking up at Daniel with mock pleading. Straightening, Seth dropped Hannah's dirty hair with disgust. "So very naughty. Not wanting to take my lead, not doing as you're supposed to." He twisted his fist, forcing Hannah's mouth an inch from his own, his eyes still locked on Daniel. "The problem is, I can't tell if you're just stubborn or actually trying to undermine me. So I have a test for you. Fail it, and I kill every person who's ever been witnessed speaking to you." He pulled a handkerchief from his pocket, cleaning the soot off his hands, and waved casually between Daniel and Hannah. "Kill her."

Daniel couldn't move, and no words would come. He swallowed, looking between Hannah's pleading eyes and Seth's ruthless ones. Gripping the head of his black and gold cane, he wished he'd never picked it back up. Had never stepped back onto the path that led him to the choice now set before him. He was out of the loop, lacking in friends, and had no idea what he stood to lose in not taking the bait—let alone what he might gain.

"Fuck that," Dawn said, low and loud, and sent a whip of gold magic cracking toward Seth's head.

Daniel stepped in front of her in a flash, taking the considerable brunt of the blow on his shields, and wished with his whole being that Dawn could read his thoughts as Seth reared back just behind him. "Stand down, Renard. Or did you not already know she betrayed you long before you chased her away?"

Dawn pulled her auric whip back, coiling it like a living snake back into her palm. "I don't care. She's one of mine, no matter what she does, and I have to do what I can to protect her against people like Laufey." Her dark eyes darted frantically between Daniel's, and he hoped he correctly understood her meaning as she drew back the barbed length of golden magic once more. "If an evil bastard like you wants to stand in my way, then so be it, Councilor Fawl."

Daniel raised a hand wrapped in thick, solid layers of his pale aura as the lash flew at him again, full of the raw, frantic emotion blazing from Dawn, and it wrapped around his limb harmlessly. Gripping it, Daniel yanked it, and Dawn gasped, stumbling toward him.

"You're weak, Renard." *I told her she needed to rest.* Daniel centered his balance when the whip in his fist disintegrated and reformed in Dawn's, onlookers scattering to outside the pile of rubble that had once been the Council thrones.

She shouted wordlessly as she flung her magic at him once more, and Daniel caught it in a stream of his Air aura, redirecting it away from himself. He barely caught the secondary attack Dawn launched at him—a spinning dagger of solid gold magic—and deflected it with his cane, turning as it passed within an inch of his face. He watched as Seth deftly caught the dagger, dropping Hannah on a pile of rubble where he'd pulled her back to. *Damn.*

Daniel spread his arms wide, gathering all the air his expansive aura could reach into him, and Dawn's new whip sputtered out as her lungs tried but failed to expand. Tighter and tighter, he brought it into a raging cyclone between his gloved hands, and with the slightest wince of apology at Dawn, sent it blasting at her in a rush that made other leaders shield their eyes.

Dawn was blasted back, crashing into the nearest line of adepts, and Daniel wasted no time in Voyaging ahead, bending over her and grabbing her by the throat, still withholding all air from her lungs as she struggled back to her knees. "Enough," he snarled as people fell over each other to get out of the immediate range of his aura. *Enough,* he willed her to read in his eyes as he silently searched hers for the consent he needed for what he was being asked to do. He couldn't risk saying any more with so many listening.

Dawn clawed his wrist weakly, careful not to touch the sliver of bare skin between the shirt cuff and leather glove. She mouthed the empty air, her eyes bulging, and she held Daniel's gaze with deep sorrow before finally dropping her hands away in surrender. Her eyes closed, a single tear falling across her dark-brown cheek, and Daniel took it as the signal he sought.

He dropped Dawn with an exaggerated expression of contempt. Stepping back and leaning heavily on his cane,

Daniel combed back his sandy hair, which was barely long enough to warrant it. Turning back to Seth, his breath was deep but even. "Is that enough proof for you?"

"No." Seth's face was set in a mask, his hand firmly gripping Hannah's hair, where she silently sobbed around her gag.

"Too bad," Daniel replied, straightening his tie and risking a bluff. "I have no interest in playing your games. Kill her yourself."

"Stop." The single word was dangerous, barely moving Seth's lips, and Daniel obeyed in spite of himself. "The point, Councilor Fawl," Seth said, yanking Hannah to her feet, "is not for her to be dead. But for you to prove you will kill someone you're sentimental about if I tell you to." Seth licked up the side of Hannah's face, and revulsion shivered down Daniel's spine at how unhinged the man before him truly was. "If you don't, there will be nuclear consequences."

Daniel's whole being contracted, his aura losing color as it sped up around him. "Nuclear?"

"With a bit of my own magic attached, and a deadman contingency with"—he checked the watch on the wrist gripping the back of Hannah's neck—"three minutes left on it." Seth shoved Hannah forward, where she stumbled and fell to her knees, catching herself with bound hands. "Each can take out a continent. One to take out Boston and the eastern seaboard of the Americas, and one to take out western Europe."

Daniel desperately looked for a lie, a bluff, in Seth or a rather dormant Marissa, but he'd never shared Angie's certainty in reading such things. He stepped toward Hannah and quickly assessed his options. A deadman contingency meant he couldn't risk attacking Seth. The Threshold home was locked, and there was no way in Hades he'd risk trying to Skip home. *Angie.* Maybe, if he beaconed for her, together they could—

Seth plunged one hand into his pants pocket with a dark smile and casually added two sentences that made Daniel's heart stop. "Did I mention Angie failed when she tried to stop me? I've left her carefully sedated exactly where the first bomb will fall." Marissa, beside him, was watching Daniel closely, but was unreadable. When Seth withdrew his hand, it held an ornate silver lock Daniel recognized, and he knew his cards were played out.

Daniel raised a gloved hand to Hannah. Her eyes met his, silently pleading, and time slowed without the need for magic. *She was Jon's wife. The mother of his soon-to-be-orphaned children. What would his ghost say?* He shoved the thought aside and frantically wondered how he might fake what he needed to do, but every idea was a dead end. Seth would almost certainly check both her body and her magic. *I can't let Angie die. Hannah is no loss for me.*

Bile rose in his gullet from the guilt and grief that answered, but he quelled them with the briefest thought about how many lives were at stake. "It's for the greater good," he told the woman before him, and nearly believed it. Surely he could convince himself he was sparing her from the suffering of life. And sparing her children her twisted desire to catalyze their magic through pain.

The horror of what he needed to do sent his internal compass spinning, and it took everything Daniel had to not let his head go with it. Letting his thoughts fall back into the indifference of his military days, Daniel forced a dark smile to stretch his mouth wide and held Seth's eyes.

With a flick of his wrist, Daniel summoned the gun from the safe in his Boston home. At least that proved Boston had yet to be turned to slag. He prepared the loaded gun he'd last fired only a few feet away in swift and practiced motions, forcing his magic far away from feeling the aura or emotions of the woman kneeling before him. "For the empire."

He lifted the sleek black pistol and fired a single shot. He barely notices the rush of noise and movement that erupted and fragmented around him like the bullet had broken far, far more than just the man he'd fought so long to become. That part of himself was leaking away with the blood of the corpse at his feet, and neither could be stopped.

Daniel barely registered Seth's wide grin as he tipped his hand, and a dribble of molten silver that used to be the lock seeped into the black pebbles with the dark blood at Daniel's feet. "Right choice."

Daniel didn't want to be himself. Didn't want to think or feel or care. "I'm glad." *Now where the hell is Angie?*

CHAPTER THIRTY-FIVE

T he world seemed to reverberate with the first step Seth Laufey set upon its shores. "Did you send her?" Black and orange flames peeled from him, and the in-fighting among the adept leaders ceased.

Xiao Sheng twisted his wrist free from Daniel's grip as both tried to keep their footing on the pebbles shifting beneath them. The Gael didn't resist, his arms splayed wide for balance. The two men stepped apart as the crowd parted before the glowering minister's approach, and Daniel braced himself when all attention locked on him.

The ground stilled as Seth stopped inches from Daniel, the younger man's face twisted with anger. "Did. You. Fucking. Send. Her."

Daniel remained impassive, summoning his cane with a flourish in case he needed it. "Send who where? Was your magic affecting magma far underground just now? Impressive."

Seth ignored the attempted change in topic, poking Daniel hard in the chest—then yanked his hand back when a tendril of Daniel's aura smacked it with air cold enough to damage skin. "Angie, of course. Do you know how she knew where and when to find me? Did you tell her what to do?"

Daniel scoffed and let his confusion show through his skeptical expression while hiding the cold flash of worry that shot through his limbs. "I've never been able to tell that woman what to do. I have no idea what you're talking about."

"Not this again," Casey Easton called over the silent watchers, waving a tattooed hand at Daniel with a look of contempt. "Cartwright himself never got that bullshit accusation to stick. Drop it already." Daniel smiled. Not with mirth, but with dark, pleased satisfaction. Seth backed off a pace, splitting his accusing attention between Daniel and Casey as the latter looked around, seeming to gather a few silent supporters before speaking again. "Minister Laufey, please. You promised us a new lock. One built to protect the innocent, and nothing more. That's the only reason any of us are here. What can you teach us about that? Exactly what breakthrough have you had?"

Seth barked a laugh, and Daniel's smile vanished. "I lied. You stupid, gullible *children*." A ripple of unease fluttered across the listeners beneath Seth's bright, scathing glance as he turned in a circle, and a fresh flutter of activity at the obsidian Threshold was short-lived when it remained impassible. "I will never help a single one of you selfish traitors that refuse to bow to the empire." He laughed again, making the hair on Daniel's arms stand on end. Judging by the uneasy glances exchanged around him, he guessed that many others felt the same way.

Daniel shook his head, his heat rising. *Selfish? Traitors? Hypocritical bullshit.* Perhaps Seth was simply too fickle to expect consistency from. Either in who he saw as his enemies, or in the justifications he believed in for his actions.

"I will never bow to the empire again," Xiao Sheng said, stepping forward. "You named no such price when you convinced us all to come here. You must keep your word. If you don't"—the man's hands balled into fists at his sides, and Daniel saw his aura ripple—"you will have to answer to every Cantonese-speaking adept, now and in the future, as my forces rip from you what you owe us, only stopping when there's nothing of you left." Seth simply skewered him with a look that could kill, and Xiao Sheng swallowed hard, his bullying bravado visibly faltering. "What's your price, less than returning to the empire? What are your demands?"

"I have none, you presumptuous nobody." Seth's aura flared, scorching Daniel's and forcing him and a dozen others back a few paces.

Daniel waited for something more, anything he could formulate a plan around, and darted his eyes to Dawn. However, the black woman's attention was held by something past Seth.

"Release her!" Dawn shouted, and all eyes turned to see what she was talking about. Marissa had stepped through the Threshold, and someone fell to their knees beside her. It took Daniel a stretched moment to realize it was someone he knew, bound and gagged.

Hannah Crowther.

Seth ignored Dawn's demand. "Bring her." Marissa obeyed, hauling Hannah to her feet, and dragged her across the black beach.

"What's this?" Daniel asked, stepping forward and giving Dawn a subtle signal to stand down.

Marissa threw Hannah down at Seth's feet, and he dragged her head back, forcing her face up to Daniel's. "You've been naughty," Seth purred, pressing his face close beside Hannah's and looking up at Daniel with mock pleading. Straightening, Seth dropped Hannah's dirty hair with disgust. "So very naughty. Not wanting to take my lead, not doing as you're supposed to." He twisted his fist, forcing Hannah's mouth an inch from his own, his eyes still locked on Daniel. "The problem is, I can't tell if you're just stubborn or actually trying to undermine me. So I have a test for you. Fail it, and I kill every person who's ever been witnessed speaking to you." He pulled a handkerchief from his pocket, cleaning the soot off his hands, and waved casually between Daniel and Hannah. "Kill her."

Daniel couldn't move, and no words would come. He swallowed, looking between Hannah's pleading eyes and Seth's ruthless ones. Gripping the head of his black and gold cane, he wished he'd never picked it back up. Had never stepped back onto the path that led him to the choice now set before him. He was out of the loop, lacking in friends, and had no idea what he stood to lose in not taking the bait—let alone what he might gain.

"Fuck that," Dawn said, low and loud, and sent a whip of gold magic cracking toward Seth's head.

Daniel stepped in front of her in a flash, taking the considerable brunt of the blow on his shields, and wished with his whole being that Dawn could read his thoughts as Seth reared back just behind him. "Stand down, Renard. Or did you not already know she betrayed you long before you chased her away?"

Dawn pulled her auric whip back, coiling it like a living snake back into her palm. "I don't care. She's one of mine, no matter what she does, and I have to do what I can to protect her against people like Laufey." Her dark eyes darted frantically between Daniel's, and he hoped he correctly understood her meaning as she drew back the barbed length of golden magic once more. "If an evil bastard like you wants to stand in my way, then so be it, Councilor Fawl."

Daniel raised a hand wrapped in thick, solid layers of his pale aura as the lash flew at him again, full of the raw, frantic emotion blazing from Dawn, and it wrapped around his limb harmlessly. Gripping it, Daniel yanked it, and Dawn gasped, stumbling toward him.

"You're weak, Renard." *I told her she needed to rest.* Daniel centered his balance when the whip in his fist disintegrated and reformed in Dawn's, onlookers scattering to outside the pile of rubble that had once been the Council thrones.

She shouted wordlessly as she flung her magic at him once more, and Daniel caught it in a stream of his Air aura, redirecting it away from himself. He barely caught the secondary attack Dawn launched at him—a spinning dagger of solid gold magic—and deflected it with his cane, turning as it passed within an inch of his face. He watched as Seth deftly caught the dagger, dropping Hannah on a pile of rubble where he'd pulled her back to. *Damn.*

Daniel spread his arms wide, gathering all the air his expansive aura could reach into him, and Dawn's new whip sputtered out as her lungs tried but failed to expand. Tighter and tighter, he brought it into a raging cyclone between his gloved hands, and with the slightest wince of apology at Dawn, sent it blasting at her in a rush that made other leaders shield their eyes.

Dawn was blasted back, crashing into the nearest line of adepts, and Daniel wasted no time in Voyaging ahead, bending over her and grabbing her by the throat, still withholding all air from her lungs as she struggled back to her knees. "Enough," he snarled as people fell over each other to get out of the immediate range of his aura. *Enough,* he willed her to read in his eyes as he silently searched hers for the consent he needed for what he was being asked to do. He couldn't risk saying any more with so many listening.

Dawn clawed his wrist weakly, careful not to touch the sliver of bare skin between the shirt cuff and leather glove. She mouthed the empty air, her eyes bulging, and she held Daniel's gaze with deep sorrow before finally dropping her hands away in surrender. Her eyes closed, a single tear falling across her dark-brown cheek, and Daniel took it as the signal he sought.

He dropped Dawn with an exaggerated expression of contempt. Stepping back and leaning heavily on his cane,

Daniel combed back his sandy hair, which was barely long enough to warrant it. Turning back to Seth, his breath was deep but even. "Is that enough proof for you?"

"No." Seth's face was set in a mask, his hand firmly gripping Hannah's hair, where she silently sobbed around her gag.

"Too bad," Daniel replied, straightening his tie and risking a bluff. "I have no interest in playing your games. Kill her yourself."

"Stop." The single word was dangerous, barely moving Seth's lips, and Daniel obeyed in spite of himself. "The point, Councilor Fawl," Seth said, yanking Hannah to her feet, "is not for her to be dead. But for you to prove you will kill someone you're sentimental about if I tell you to." Seth licked up the side of Hannah's face, and revulsion shivered down Daniel's spine at how unhinged the man before him truly was. "If you don't, there will be nuclear consequences."

Daniel's whole being contracted, his aura losing color as it sped up around him. "Nuclear?"

"With a bit of my own magic attached, and a deadman contingency with"—he checked the watch on the wrist gripping the back of Hannah's neck—"three minutes left on it." Seth shoved Hannah forward, where she stumbled and fell to her knees, catching herself with bound hands. "Each can take out a continent. One to take out Boston and the eastern seaboard of the Americas, and one to take out western Europe."

Daniel desperately looked for a lie, a bluff, in Seth or a rather dormant Marissa, but he'd never shared Angie's certainty in reading such things. He stepped toward Hannah and quickly assessed his options. A deadman contingency meant he couldn't risk attacking Seth. The Threshold home was locked, and there was no way in Hades he'd risk trying to Skip home. *Angie.* Maybe, if he beaconed for her, together they could—

Seth plunged one hand into his pants pocket with a dark smile and casually added two sentences that made Daniel's heart stop. "Did I mention Angie failed when she tried to stop me? I've left her carefully sedated exactly where the first bomb will fall." Marissa, beside him, was watching Daniel closely, but was unreadable. When Seth withdrew his hand, it held an ornate silver lock Daniel recognized, and he knew his cards were played out.

Daniel raised a gloved hand to Hannah. Her eyes met his, silently pleading, and time slowed without the need for magic. *She was Jon's wife. The mother of his soon-to-be-orphaned children. What would his ghost say?* He shoved the thought aside and frantically wondered how he might fake what he needed to do, but every idea was a dead end. Seth would almost certainly check both her body and her magic. *I can't let Angie die. Hannah is no loss for me.*

Bile rose in his gullet from the guilt and grief that answered, but he quelled them with the briefest thought about how many lives were at stake. "It's for the greater good," he told the woman before him, and nearly believed it. Surely he could convince himself he was sparing her from the suffering of life. And sparing her children her twisted desire to catalyze their magic through pain.

The horror of what he needed to do sent his internal compass spinning, and it took everything Daniel had to not let his head go with it. Letting his thoughts fall back into the indifference of his military days, Daniel forced a dark smile to stretch his mouth wide and held Seth's eyes.

With a flick of his wrist, Daniel summoned the gun from the safe in his Boston home. At least that proved Boston had yet to be turned to slag. He prepared the loaded gun he'd last fired only a few feet away in swift and practiced motions, forcing his magic far away from feeling the aura or emotions of the woman kneeling before him. "For the empire."

He lifted the sleek black pistol and fired a single shot. He barely notices the rush of noise and movement that erupted and fragmented around him like the bullet had broken far, far more than just the man he'd fought so long to become. That part of himself was leaking away with the blood of the corpse at his feet, and neither could be stopped.

Daniel barely registered Seth's wide grin as he tipped his hand, and a dribble of molten silver that used to be the lock seeped into the black pebbles with the dark blood at Daniel's feet. "Right choice."

Daniel didn't want to be himself. Didn't want to think or feel or care. "I'm glad." *Now where the hell is Angie?*

Chapter Thirty-Six

Daniel couldn't help but fear the worst. Angie wasn't at their Boston home, nor was she answering his beacons or calls. The meeting had ended in chaos barely an hour before, and Daniel wondered if Seth's failure to keep them trapped after the gunshot rang off the obsidian cliffs was accidental or intentional. The cackling Fire aura had Skipped away as soon as the first gaggle of panicked leaders had stumbled through the Threshold, and no one had dared to jostle Daniel as he'd strode through among them.

Now standing in the very last place he could think to look for her—the prison where her abuser and rapist had once been held—the possibility that he still couldn't save her, wherever she was, loomed large enough to crush him. He checked his watch, wishing he'd thought to stop time at any point in the last few hours when doing so might have brought him to a different end, and was surprised to find his wrist bare.

He checked his other wrist, then his pockets, to no avail. With a flick, he summoned it from wherever it had gotten to, only a moment more of confusion lingering. He was sure he'd put it on that morning, and a quick check as he secured it revealed no damage or issue with the clasp that would have allowed it to fall off.

All other thoughts abandoned Daniel when Seth's Voyaging beacon lit in his mind. Knowing it was his only chance of finding Angie or negotiating her release, he didn't hesitate to follow. Hopefully, his proof of loyalty could at least buy him her location.

"I thought you'd shielded it!" Seth screamed the moment Daniel landed in the chaotically disturbed recording studio within the Roman imperial palaces, and it took him a beat to realize he wasn't the target. Seth had Moretti cornered against a camera the size of a man, both of their faces flushed and contorted, although Seth's aura seemed to be more contained than normal.

"I did!" Moretti shouted back, and his eyes sliced to Daniel. "It's not my fault that bitch got in. Maybe she planted a token on you that she could follow?"

Seth turned to see what the other man was looking at, and his Voyaging beacon in Daniel's mind went silent. "Fawl. I assume you've been looking for Angie. Did you find her?"

Daniel's mind raced as he summoned his cane and shifted an inch further out of the path of plebeians and patricians alike running past him in every direction. "Don't you have her?" he asked in reply, and watched in puzzlement as Marissa threw herself at Seth. Her hand dipped into his trouser pocket, and she covered the motion by dramatically clutching his arms.

"You saw him. You saw what he did to prove himself to you. Please, please trust him already!" Marissa's eyes darted to Daniel's wrist when she turned to him, and something clicked in his mind. Had she stolen his watch and planted it on Seth? Where had that gotten Angie into, and how and why? He doubted he'd get the opportunity to ask any time soon.

Daniel took a chance and carefully kept his tiring aura from betraying his true feelings. "Why not ask her whatever it is you need to? Where are you keeping the bitch?"

Seth barked what might have been a laugh and shook Marissa off, clearly gathering himself. "I never had her. I was bluffing. I had to know you weren't in league with her."

The relief and anger that surged through Daniel nearly broke free of his control, making him perspire beneath his black silk suit. "And what do you believe now?" he asked as levelly as he could.

Seth fixed him with a long stare as the room around them became less frantic. Furniture was being re-arranged into something resembling order, and the noise died down as chairs and papers were collected. "Did you lie to me? Are you still in love with her? In league with her?"

"No." Daniel wondered if he'd answered too quickly and drew in a deep breath. "As I've said before, I'm simply sentimental about my former recruits." He lifted a gracious hand to both Marissa and Seth, who seemed pleased with the answer. "And in this case, with Mrs. Crowther, the price for such sentimentality was an easy one to pay." Bile rose fast in Daniel's gullet, and he shrugged as nonchalantly as he could while he forced the urge back down.

Seth nodded, lifting a hand and turning it in front of him in a pattern of shifting black and red flames. "Just as well. I'm not done with her yet." Daniel raised a quizzical brow, and Seth's smile when he answered left no doubt that he wasn't done baiting Daniel, either. "I connected her magic to mine a few months ago," he said, and Daniel braced himself. "Stupid bitch walked right into the trap I set for her with a bunch of plebeians in Nevada. Since then, I've been sapping her flames to feed my own." He sent a gout of flames toward the ceiling, and Daniel felt sick. "Natural gift of a Fire aura, according to Cartwright. Consuming whatever we want. Burning through magic not our own."

Daniel almost smiled, despite the grotesqueness of the confession. Of course Milton was still tormenting Daniel and trying to hurt him from beyond the grave. *The world almost wouldn't feel right without that hanging over me.* "I see. Very well done."

Seth looked past Daniel, and both men stepped aside as a large, antique projector was brought past them. Daniel noticed the civilians in the room were slowly being replaced by legionnaires as two more bearing large cardboard tubes followed past.

"So tell me," Seth said, looking Daniel up and down. "Can I truly trust you to be a loyal soldier under my command going forward?"

Daniel chewed on the bitter responses that rose fastest to his lips, then bowed. "Of course, Lord Laufey."

The improvised title had the desired effect, and Seth smiled. "And will your family, your cousins and whatnot, interrupt your devotion to my causes? Will the little orphan betray his empire when his sore spots are prodded?"

Daniel bared his teeth. "Hardly. I proved that today, as well."

Seth's smile widened with every moment Daniel stood, fixed in place by his unrelenting attention. When Seth spoke, triumph finally bolstered Daniel's faltering desire to remain. "Excellent. Then welcome, welcome." Seth stepped forward, clasping Daniel's gloved hand and clapping him on the shoulder. "Let me show you what we'll be about."

Seth turned and strode toward the massive table, which had been set up in the middle of what Daniel suspected was rapidly becoming another war room. He trailed behind, not yet ready to abandon his search for Angie. "What about the last nuclear missiles? If I may ask, Minister, why did you intend to target Boston and the English Conference site with them? The latter are neutral, are they not?"

Seth's aura juddered and thickened around him unhappily, but the man laughed as he reached the table strewn with maps and ledgers. "Ha! No reason. I just pulled that out of the hat. Though I wouldn't mind recruiting a natural resource producer like Lord Braithwaite, given half a chance." Seth beckoned Daniel to stand beside him, but a disturbance by the door interrupted whatever he'd been preparing to say next.

Daniel barely had time to register the legionnaire who had burst in—a young, broad man with a tattoo of crossed spears on his stubbled cheek and wild eyes—before he fell, screaming, to a bolt of Seth's magic that reduced him to a pile of ash and scraps of metal in the time it took the room to gasp.

Seth jerked his arm back as if recovering from the recoil of the magic he'd just used, and the smile that flashed across his face before settling into a smirk was dark and self-satisfied.

"Why did you do that?" Daniel asked.

"He was one of the soldiers who got possessed," Seth replied, and Daniel's shock turned to horror. "He might still have been."

Daniel gaped, wrapping one hand around the anti-possession sigil tattooed to the inside of his other wrist. He almost questioned if Seth knew that killing the host could have just sent a demon jumping lethally from host to host, but remembered he'd taught Seth as much himself when the younger man had been his recruit. Seth knew perfectly well and didn't care.

"Right," Seth said, turning back to the table and the collection of patricians—most in uniform—gathered around it, and Daniel wrestled his attention away from what little remained of someone he would have loved dearly to question further. "We've gotten the proof I've hoped was coming for some time. Demons are real, and they're coming for earth."

Every listener shifted uncomfortably, including Daniel. *It's because I'm out of the loop, and know that demons are always bad news*, he told himself firmly, but couldn't deny that some small part of him had started to question if his blanket belief in that was still warranted after meeting the demonic ghost of Jonathan.

"So, it's time to move ahead with our holy mission." Seth slapped his hands on the table before him, his eyes alight with bright, fervent energy as he looked around at everyone standing silently around the tall, wide table. "I'll catch some of you latecomers up on this more thoroughly in the coming days, but for now, just know that it's my intent to take the fight to them." Seth's eyes lingered on Marissa. "A righteous crusade against the forces of the devil, killing them in their nests before they can ever threaten God's creation here in our world."

"Demons from—" Daniel began, but cut himself short when every single other person in the room shot him an enraged or warning look. *Surely Seth knew that demons from half-worlds weren't the same as those in Christian mythology? Surely he knew there was no Satan?* Outwardly, Daniel winced his apology for the interruption and pressed his lips tight together.

"Our missionaries," Seth went on a bit too loudly and rather pointedly at Daniel, "will carry our might against these foes. Together we will eradicate the unclean and stake our claim in every world that might nourish and strengthen God's Chosen. To that end"—Seth nodded to Moretti, who stood, glowering, as he rubbed what Daniel suspected was a bullet hole in the fabric of his blood-stained trousers—"I intend to ramp up recruitment and call our network of the faithful back to Rome."

As Seth began questioning another patrician about how golem production was going, Daniel's thoughts slipped more and more inward. *I'll only stay until I think of another place to look for Angie*, he promised himself. *And only with Seth long enough to stop him for good.* Forcing himself to continue following the onslaught of new information he was behind on being privy to, he folded both hands across the gold-handled cane he now knew he'd be forced to keep carrying for the foreseeable future.

Not forever, only as long as it takes.

Chapter Thirty-Seven

W hen Angie returned to the missile silo from the courtroom, she found it abandoned. A titanic groan of steel buckling and cracking as it cooled made her flinch, ready to Voyage away immediately. She looked around, then up at the nearly pitch-black sky, barely visible through the opening high overhead. Was it possible she'd only been gone a few hours?

Angie realized she was twice as far down as she'd been before during her first visit, and craned to see the blast doors between the lower chamber she stood in and the one above. Somewhere on those doors, now retracted into the sides of the silo, would be the charred remains of Jasper Rose, mingled with those of their indiscriminate attackers.

She dropped her head in shame, feeling none at the sight of her bare flesh in comparison. Angie couldn't begin to name what she might have done better—or differently—to have chosen a path that wouldn't have gotten Jasper killed without losing even more. Yet the feeling that, at some point, she must have had that choice would not abate.

Wondering what had become of the ashes of her clothes only made her spirits drop further. She'd thankfully not been wearing her late sister's precious jacket, but the phone she'd had clipped to her belt was almost certainly destroyed, and her heart sank as she remembered what else she'd held in her pocket.

Dropping to her knees, Angie peered down through the grated floor, ignoring the protests from her feet, knees, and hands, and frantically searched for any sign of her father's signet ring.

To her shock and relief, it took less than a minute to spot a glint of gold down in the belly of pipework and gantries beneath her feet. Memorizing the location, Angie jogged to the nearest access hatch, not trusting her Voyaging.

It took her several more to barge, burn, and pick her way down to the lower floor, still warm beneath her feet from the launch blast. When she found the glint of gold she'd seen, she darted for it and scooped up the fat gold ring like it might slip further from her grasp if it saw her coming. The band was slightly misshapen, lumpy where it had clearly melted a little, but the sigil of Silvanus was intact.

Angie cradled it to her bare chest. Her mind seemed to resist thinking about what had become of her parents, guilt and shame making her thoughts slip to one side every time she tried to face what she'd done. The words *I'm sorry. I'm so, so sorry* played over and over through her whole being.

As if to mock her, the moment Angie rose to her feet, another glint of something that didn't belong caught her eye. The jade Eden key, still wrapped in white, yellow, and maroon magic. Angie looked away, not wanting to face what might lay beyond the doorway it could open, but the thought of someone else confirming the devastation for her made her collect it, too, before heading back the way she'd come.

As she reached the last heavy door she'd left open onto the grated floor of the lower missile bay, the sight of a black-suited figure standing with his back to her nearly made her stumble. *Daniel.* She opened her mouth to cry out to him, desperate for all he could offer, but the realization of what he'd see when he turned silenced her.

Angie stared for a long moment at the coveted, despised jade key in her hand before placing it deep inside the track for the massive pneumatic door, stepping through silently and pressing the button to close it behind her.

The grind of machinery almost drowned out the crunch of shattering jade that made Angie sway where she stood, and Daniel whipped around at the sound.

The expressions that chased each other across his face were wild and disjointed, and Angie held her long auburn curls back from her own as his aura whipped up in a cyclone around them. "Angie." The word seemed to fall from him without his consent, and she felt his eyes over every inch of her like a predator as he limped forward over the strange footing. "What happened to you?"

He pulled off his long gray coat, and she gratefully let him drape it around her, breathing in his nearness and the familiar scent of beeswax and frankincense hungrily.

"It's—" She swallowed hard, dropping her father's ring discreetly into the pocket of the coat and buttoning it closed around her. "It's a really long story. How did you find me here?" She stopped herself before asking how long she'd been gone, hoping her three-week stay under the care of the Inferi might have gone unnoticed, buying her time to process and decide how to tell anyone about it, and how it happened.

"You're lucky I was able to compromise the magical tripwire alarms Seth set up all around here in case you came back," Daniel replied, lingering close to her, his dark eyes searching. "Why have you been ignoring me for hours?"

Only hours? Good. Angie smiled weakly to hide the way she winced at the lie she told. "I stopped him from killing you and all the other adept leaders with one nuclear bomb, and Gods know what other world with the other. The aftermath took some..." She trailed off, rubbing the back of her head where she'd been struck. "Well. I'm feeling pretty lucky I survived at all."

Daniel reached for her cautiously, and Angie fell into the hug he wrapped around her, burying her face in his shirt and thoughtlessly avoiding touching his skin lest it ruin the moment. "I'm so glad you're alright."

"And you," Angie replied, her words muffled but full of the relief and guilt she tried to hide. She pulled back enough to look up at Daniel's dear, expressive face, full of worry and gratitude. "*Were* you in the meeting with all the adept leaders? Please, I—I need to know for sure."

The lines in Daniel's forehead deepened a degree. "Yes, I was. And Dawn, and Casey, and everyone else." He nodded slightly, his Adam's apple bobbing. "I'm not surprised it was supposed to be deadly for all of us." He removed an arm from around Angie to pull a hand down his face as a veil seemed to fall behind his eyes. "I guess my position with that bastard is still more tenuous than I'd like."

Angie felt a line of tension slide off her shoulders with the confirmation that she'd made the right choice. She started to speak, to explain everything, but found she couldn't bring herself to tell Daniel the price that had been paid for his life. Daniel, too, seemed to hold back from saying something, and she shared in the weak sigh of release he breathed instead.

"Listen," Daniel said, releasing Angie and stepping back. "I think we both have a lot to tell the other, but I can't take the time to do this now." He glanced at the gold token-bonded watch on his wrist, and Angie was secretly glad he didn't suggest stopping time instead. "I need to make sure my cousin and his family stay safe, and get some vital information passed along before it's too late. Including your confirmation of Seth's true intentions behind the meeting, and what became of the last two nukes. Would you be willing to meet me at the Boston house in about an hour to..." His wide mouth stretched, and he lifted an apologetic hand that shook slightly. "Catch up?"

Angie nodded emphatically. "Yes. Please."

Daniel clearly hesitated for a stretched few breaths before turning and Voyaging away, and Angie followed suit, the need to return to the world she knew well enough to predict screaming through her.

When she landed on the empty upper floor of a parking garage in Salt Lake, the world dropped out from under her. Her car was nowhere to be seen. She frantically Voyaged to the floor above, then the next few below, knowing with absolute certainty that the shields she'd left protecting it would, if anything, make it easier for her and her alone to spot.

When the memory of leaving the parking garage and heading for her parents' home two-hundred miles west caught up with her, Angie felt more frustration with herself than relief. She found it undisturbed at the Salt Flats waystation where she'd left it and took ten minutes to change before Voyaging away once more.

—◦❖◦—

Landing on the Pacific clifftop, the midday sun warmed the air and mixed the scent of pine heavily with the brine of the ocean below. Angie walked right up to the edge, the toes of her boots sending a bit of loose dirt tumbling into the surf several hundred feet below.

She glanced over her shoulder, gauging exactly where she'd stood the last time she'd visited, and after shifting a few feet to one side, began her slow and careful climb down.

Over the next ten minutes, Angie descended, searching every inch, every crag, for a gleam of copper. She dearly wished she could fly or hover. But there was no way she would risk astral projection, the only option for that she had in her current state. *Not after last time.*

When she inevitably fell, her instinct kicked in, and Angie Skipped to the next nearest half-world, landing in a pile of dry, purple leaves coated in fine, deep-blue powder that made her sneeze. Frustrated, she Skipped back to the top of the cliff, then Voyaged back to just above where her search had been interrupted, glad that her natural affinity for the skill aided her accuracy.

Extending a hand, she tried to summon the coin over and over but nothing happened. Angie wasn't surprised. The magic had only ever worked for her a handful of times even when her magic was at its peak. So she resumed climbing.

The spray of the ocean was a cold mark of failure when she reached it, the first brush of it against her cheek and the bare skin of her arm wiping away the last hope she had of finding the copper sigil coin bearing the last remnants of her dearest friend.

Angie scratched at the scar over her elbow she'd earned fighting in the battle Jonathan had died in and stumbled to sit on a kelp-slicked rock nearby, wrapping her fingers tight around it.

His presence—whether in memory, ghost, or demon impersonation—had held her grief at bay, but acknowledging that she had thrown that comfort—that sentient, caring, vibrant remnant of him—away, broke open the walls she'd built around that tender part of her heart. She had no one to blame for losing him permanently but herself.

"Jonathan," she called into the crash of waves with the first sob that doubled her over, expecting no answer and not knowing if she hoped that his spirit, his ghost, or simply the memory of him in her own mind heard her. "I'm so, so sorry."

"I know."

Angie gasped, bolting straight up, and found Jonathan's ghost looking at her with gentle, guarded compassion that matched his tone. Her aura blossomed into yellow flames, illuminating him even more clearly. Scouring the cliffs and water around them, she gasped again, this time with a desperate question. "Where?"

Jonathan pointed at a tide pool tucked against the edge of the cliff a few yards away, and Angie scrambled toward it, ignoring the bruises and scrapes she collected in doing so. When she found it, the familiar weight and solidity of the carved copper sigil coin felt ecstatic and heart-wrenching as she snatched it up with a shriek.

Collapsing to the ground, Angie cried. Time lost all meaning, and the world fell away as the sun tracked slowly overhead, sparkling off the water in shifting patterns of light.

Her bruise-colored aura swelled with mugwort smoke and the smell of wet ash, and she released any thought of controlling it, afraid she might fall apart if she tried. Jonathan's ghost bent over her, his form blocking some of the spray from the waves, and when the raw emotion owning her subsided enough for thoughts to form once more, Angie looked up at him, feeling every inch a confessing child before a parent. "Jonathan, I've done something unforgivable. I—I can't tell anyone. I just can't."

"Then don't. For this moment, Angie, just breathe."

Angie pressed a hand tightly over her mouth, thoughts of Lucia, her mother, her father, and Jasper swirling in layers of sickly black dread through her heart and head. If only she believed in Gods, she'd ask one to strike her down just to end how she felt in that moment, but nothing greeted her when she reached for such faith. When she spoke again, the words cut like glass between her trembling lips. "I just want to die. I just want to be done."

She knew the concern on Jonathan's face too well to need to look. She imagined all the things he was thinking in the silence that followed and wished she hadn't burdened him in her moment of weakness.

"I'd miss you terribly," he finally said, and Angie felt her own burden grow. "If there's a specific reason you feel that way, I'd be honored if you let me help you address it. Or if I can't, I'm sure Dan, or Casey, or one of the other people who love you, would want to do anything they could to stop you from hurting yourself as well."

The thoughts that answered, unspoken, made Angie's head ring. *Casey hates me now, and I don't even know why. And there are no other people. Not anymore.*

"Does this have anything to do with whatever you've been keeping from me for the last few months?" Jonathan asked, and Angie forced herself to sit up straighter, rubbing her eyes with the heel of one hand to clear them. "Are you ready to talk about that yet?"

"No, and... yes, I suppose." Compared to the losses and stresses of the last few days, her worries about Hannah's accusations regarding her relationship with Jonathan barely registered, and the thought of easing even one small part of the weight on her shoulders was sweet.

"Your wife told me she thought—or knew or whatever—that you and I were more than friends." Angie glanced up at Jonathan, relieved to see him look shocked and affronted, and didn't wait for him to reply. "She got in my head. I wasn't thinking straight, I don't think. But Jonathan, I never felt that way about you. Not romantically or more than that." She pressed the coin deeper into her palm. "I did love you. But never as more than a friend. And I never felt like you weren't on the same page with me when you were alive." Angie dropped her head, her voice falling with it. "I just let her get to me because you were dead, and I knew I couldn't ask *him*, the living Jonathan who I'd interacted with over those years, if it was true."

"I understand. And you're right, I've never seen you the way Hannah claimed. I'm sorry she caused you distress." Angie breathed deeply with relief, and Jonathan mirrored her with a small smile.

Angie was delighted by the clarity her state of distress lent her, and the peace of her certainty undercut the reaction she might once have had to Jonathan's firm reassurance. "I think, in retrospect, part of me hoped it could have been true, just to justify how much your death hurt. And it festered because I don't trust that I currently know what other people are thinking and feeling when my own emotions are involved." Angie had to blink, processing the words she couldn't believe she'd spoken. *Had that really been true?* The second part certainly was.

Angie pushed up from the rock she sat on, unwilling to let her thoughts spiral into wondering if a healthy love, devoid of strife or strain, was another factor, something she'd wanted to imagine her way through with the excuse of the accusations. "Never mind." Her voice broke, and she cleared it, tucking the coin deep into the pocket of her jeans. "Guess I just let my darkest thoughts win for a little while there. We should head out. I promised Daniel I'd meet him." The thought of returning to him gave Angie the strength she needed, and she pulled her aura back under her control, the thick, dark smoke heavy and sluggish as she prepared to Voyage.

Jonathan stepped forward, holding out an ephemeral hand, and Angie reached for it, letting the wisps of his digits brush through hers, still dusted with blue powder from the half-world. The same dark blue his living magic should be.

"Angie. Don't let a spark of darkness rule your heart. It's only a spark. Don't feed those flames. If you do, there's no telling what you'll become."

CHAPTER THIRTY-EIGHT

L ess than a minute after leaving Angie in the empty missile silo, Daniel opened the small safe bolted
and magically obscured inside the kitchen cabinet by
the front door of his sleek Boston home. He'd seen no
evidence of tampering, but still released a breath when
he confirmed the contents were untouched. He wasn't
sure if he should believe that Seth's threat against Boston
was truly the random choice he'd claimed. The paranoia
that he shouldn't wouldn't relent, despite having other
things he needed to do.

Inside the safe, a small, ancient book bound in rough
animal skins stood against the back, faintly saturated
with an uncountable number of magical signatures from
its many owners before Daniel had stolen it from Milton
Cartwright. In front of it lay a fancy pen steeped with
Jonathan's azure magic and a black chess queen wrapped
with Dawn's signature gold.

Removing the gold watch from his wrist, Daniel held it
close to his eyes, tracing the heat shimmer and faint, silvery wisps of Angie's magic bonded into it before carefully placing the token with the others. It was too precious
to risk being stolen, as he suspected had nearly happened

earlier that day. Next time, it might be warded against him summoning it back.

Before he closed the safe, he plucked up the leather shoulder holster for the pistol tucked into the back of his belt and a single replacement bullet from a cardboard box. The safe latched with an electric whir and mechanical click as he closed the cupboard door bearing his first aid kit over it, and Daniel readied himself for what was to come.

—◦✦◦—

"No, I already warned them," Daniel said to the Hellenian patrician leader, Miss Doukas, as a dozen people scurried around them and the freestanding Threshold through the clearing. "Byrne is still angry with me, despite having only defended myself against him, but one of his lieutenants, Bailey Johnson, received me and I believe she took my warnings seriously."

The mountainous pine air was unusually cool for the Mediterranean midnight, and the heavyset woman pulled a knit sweater tighter across her curves. "Good. Very well. Do you want me to pass along what you've told me to the leaders I know wouldn't listen to you?" Another bronze-skinned adept, Demitria, caught her eye, gesturing happily at the Threshold they were preparing to test and explore, and Miss Doukas gave her a nod before returning her attention to Daniel.

He nodded gratefully. "Please. Though from what I've heard, the plebeian general who appears to be hunting for adepts is only a concern for your part of the world. I can't recall his name. For the rest, hopefully knowing there are no nukes hanging over their heads will embolden them, and if Laufey is going to start a colonizing push, we all should as well."

"Agreed. I assume you'll tell Renard yourself?" Daniel nodded, and the Hellenes woman pursed her lips. "Then please, do me two favors. First, please tell her that Nikolaos and Demitria have settled in well with the children they've taken in, but we've had to increase the magic we're collectively using to keep his Sight at bay and his sanity intact."

Daniel's insides squirmed. *One more thing to figure out, if I can. One more reason we need a new lock, and we still have no idea how to build one.*

"Second, tell her she'll need to tell the Cantonese leader all of your information by herself. He's not welcome anywhere near my camp, and has been causing large problems between us and our allies. I have no intention of going anywhere near him."

"Are you serious?" Dawn shook her head, looking out the small window at the recently returned recruiting platoons he'd found her debriefing, thankfully with far fewer casualties than the first he'd witnessed in their camp months before. "You want us exploring half-worlds when we can't even keep up with everything happening in our own?"

Daniel had Voyaged discreetly to her office, sending the first adept he saw to fetch her, and the smell of dust and faint spices lingered despite the light breeze from his Air aura. He rubbed the back of his neck, holding his aura under tight control in the confined space.

"I'm not telling you that you have to do anything. Just keeping you in the loop. I'm hoping that by spreading the information about where we are most likely to find more high-value half-world keys and the rest, we might get all the language leaders to go back to at least being open to alliances with you and each other down the road. Rather than all being at each other's throats like we last left them. We now know we can't grab the half-world keys en masse before anyone else does, so we need to brace for them to be handed out among your—*our* enemies, bargained with, and possibly used against us."

"I know. Sorry."

Daniel reined in his exhausted temper. "The only thing I'm actually asking you to do is use this information as leverage of your own and tell the Cantonese, since Xiao would probably try to kill me on sight. It sounds like they have few other friends willing to warn them."

The woman across the desk from him closed her dark eyes, and Daniel double-blinked to read the currents in her thin gold aura. "Fine. I will, in a few days." Weariness was etched across her face, and guilt joined it as she pulled a hand down it. "Don't tell anyone, but I think you may have been right about him. He truly wants to be our ally. I believe that. But he's done far more harm than good to our efforts since he joined up."

Daniel's tongue played at the corner of his mouth, repressing his urge to say, "I told you so."

Dawn sighed, tapping a worn plastic pen on the lined notebook open before her distractedly. "I'm just"—she huffed a weak laugh, darting Daniel an amused glance and throwing her weight back in her squeaking chair—"burned out."

Daniel's failure to join in her humor disappointed even him. "What could I do to help?"

Dawn slowly shook her head, her gaze dropping to the scuffed and dirty floor. "Whatever the hell you can or want to. Just take something off my plate. Anything to give me one more friend and one less enemy."

Daniel chewed on his retort that he was, again, only trying to help by bringing her more information to be aware of, but ultimately swallowed it. "As you wish."

Daniel spent the next twenty minutes hunting. As he Voyaged again and again—sometimes landing where he'd hoped to and sometimes not—he looked through records and questioned anyone he thought might be both willing and able to point him in the right direction.

Anything for a distraction from the bitterness that his old scrying ability had become all but useless. He'd crossed a line he'd hoped he'd never have to, and the thought of using the excuse it gave him to act proactively felt enticingly close to justification for what he intended to do.

As he pawed through yet another record office in Tianjin, Cathay, he wondered what he was going to tell Angie. When he imagined how she'd react to him telling her that he'd shot Jonathan's widow in the head to prove a point to a power-drunk madman, the sight of her silently tucking the demon of Jonathan back into her pocket, kept rising in answer. She'd been unwilling to let go of even a memory when he asked her to for her own sake. *No. I can't.* It all made him feel sick. Until he thought of a better way to explain what he'd done than he could currently conjure, he couldn't bear the thought of telling her.

Finding what he was looking for, Daniel studied the sale slip carefully and willed his concentration to focus on where he wanted to go.

A scream greeted Daniel when he Voyaged yet again, and he dropped a few inches, his arms coming up as he cast about for the source. He found it almost instantly. A woman with a thin nose and straight black hair was awkwardly bent backward against the wall behind him, pleading and shouting in a language Daniel didn't understand with the large Cathayan man towering over her.

Daniel lunged forward, appalled, and grabbed Xiao Sheng by the shoulder, spinning him into the fist he slammed into the other man's jaw. The other man stumbled back, clearly taken by surprise. The woman tugged a terrified child out from behind her, both of their faces bleeding and bruised, and they darted through a curtained doorway and out into the street beyond.

Using the moment it took for Xiao Sheng to recover, Daniel ensured that the strong, complex shields of his aura obscured his presence, and would continue to hide his actions from any prying eyes, magical or not. When the Cantonese straightened, enraged, Daniel added a layer to prevent Voyaging away and slammed his full weight into the larger man with a forearm across his chest.

"What the hell were you doing to them?" Daniel demanded, letting his pent-up sense of injustice pour from him unchecked. When Xiao Sheng just bared his brown and chipped teeth, Daniel pulled a layer of easy translation magic over his words and repeated the question, adding, "What were you going to do to them if I hadn't stopped you? Kill them?"

Xiao Sheng grinned wider, his eyes full of anger, and the movements of his lips out of alignment with the words Daniel heard. "Nothing you wouldn't do in my place, Fawl. Merely ensuring that my legacy continues in more than blood by making sure my magic is passed down with it. Creating new soldiers from slaves who will never wear chains again."

Horrified, Daniel rocked his weight forward, knocking Sheng's head back into the rough-daubed wall. "I would *never* torture someone into magic! Especially not a child. Not someone I loved. Who the hell told you about that possibility?" The thought of the emperor trying to torture himself into magic rose, unbidden, and Daniel pushed it back away with a stifled gag.

"I've known since the beginning," Xiao Sheng replied, licking dry lips. "And I've been passing little secrets like that along. You see, networks of faithful informants go *both ways*." The emphasis on the last few words made Daniel's blood run cold.

"Seth?" Daniel glanced around what had clearly been built as slave housing and stepped back a healthy pace, drawing his gun in case the other man had any ideas about repeating their last encounter. "You're one of his?"

Xiao Sheng rubbed his chest, his gaze lingering on the sleek black pistol. "Why would I tell you? Fuck off and mind your own business." He turned away dismissively, but Daniel stepped in his path, raising the gun to his hip. "You wouldn't kill me," the Cathayan taunted, glancing down at the firearm. "I'm under the protection of that negro bitch, and you know it."

Daniel let his arm drop straight, hoping it appeared to be out of hesitation or surrender, and lied about his reaction through a cool buffet of his aura. "So?"

Xiao Sheng puffed his chest, looking Daniel up and down. "Don't doubt for a moment that I'll return the favor of sticking your nose in where it doesn't belong. What was the name the minister used to make you kill that woman? Angie Forester? If you can hunt me, I can hunt her. And there's nothing you can do to stop me."

Daniel stepped back, the soles of his leather shoes tapping on the packed dirt floor, and leveled his pistol at the other man's head with a wicked grin. "Not at all. I needed an excuse to make sure you stopped sabotaging Dawn's efforts, and you just gave me one." He felt the draw of it, the control and certainty wash through him from his scalp to the soles of his feet, and his breath hitched.

Drawing a deep breath, he steadied his aim. "This gun has taken two lives before yours. You witnessed both. The first, I had to take to save my world. The second, I was forced to end to save my heart. The third life it takes—which will be yours, you pompous, hypocritical ass—will save my cause and the last true friend I have left on this earth."

Chapter Thirty-Nine

When Angie had changed for the second time in as many hours, wiping away the blue dust from her skin and hair, and felt that she had composed herself enough to face another living creature again, she Voyaged to Daniel's home in Boston.

The sound of running water greeted her, and she hung the long gray coat he'd lent her on the hook by the door. She found Daniel in the kitchen with his sleeves rolled up, scrubbing his arms up to the elbow with medical thoroughness. She watched his frowning concentration as he ruthlessly scoured his skin, just drinking him in.

"Hey," she said, leaning against the edge of the counter by the fridge, and he turned with more surprise than she'd expected. "Didn't you feel me come in? I was surprised the wards let me Voyage right through."

Snatching a pristine hand towel from the door of the dishwasher, Daniel dried his hands with a tight smile. "I was distracted. And I keep them open to you."

Angie chewed her lip, every tick of the grandfather clock in the living room chipping away at the veneer of fragile calm she'd collected since the Oregon beach. Unable to bear the silence, she reached for any question she might ask to justify lingering in the elegant, spotless house. "So... What were the last five hours like for you?"

Daniel's aura paled and stirred, reminding her why he left no papers, no curtains, nor a single lamp set out to be disturbed by such expressions. Angie watched his angular face twist, saw his chest rise and fall erratically as his eyes darted between hers.

He seemed to start to speak a dozen times, each attempt more charged and raw than the last, but it all fell away when he sighed, draping the towel back over its perch. "Stressful. And a bit scary in patches. All around a day I'd rather forget." He leaned against the counter opposite Angie, crossing his arms over his waist.

"How's your family? They come through okay?" Angie asked, regretting it instantly. That was the last question she herself wanted to answer.

"Yeah. My cousin's daughter will probably need therapy, but they're okay, and I'll be relocating them under new names when I can, so Seth can't get to them again."

"Do you think it's just a coincidence that they live so close to my parents?" Angie winced and tried to plan how she could change the topic at the next opportunity.

"Coincidence..." Daniel's gaze slid away, unfocused. "Who knows. They've all been there since before you were born, since before I ever met Cartwright..." He seemed to shake himself, his tired attention returning to Angie. "Maybe. Probably. Speaking of, are they alright?"

In a heartbeat, Angie's aura fled in toward her skin, but she turned her full attention to it, forcing it back out into less distressed currents of purple-gray smoke. She hoped

Daniel couldn't smell the burned plastic stench leaking from it like she could. "Don't know for sure. Looks like they left their place with the money I gave them of their own accord. I haven't found them or heard from them since." *Not technically a lie. I just need some time...*

Daniel nodded, and thankfully didn't press. "Anything else from the last few hours on your end worth asking about?"

Angie blinked and swallowed, trying to produce more answers that could protect the tender ball of shame knotted tightly beneath her heart. Ideally without directly lying to someone she desperately needed to be honest with. "Yeah." Her voice broke on the single word, and she swallowed again, finding it easier to speak if she studied the floor rather than the dear face watching her intently. "I listened to the radio like you said, and I followed the instructions the announcer gave in code. I found Seth preparing to send a nuclear bomb through to a half-world..."

Angie pushed away the image of Jasper Rose descending from on high and chose to name a different death, despite knowing Daniel would misunderstand the context. He already knew to blame her for Jasper's first disappearance. "Lucia died." She couldn't help wishing she had the Wyrd thread she'd helped Bailey make or the key to the Norns. Wishing she could bargain her way back out of her crushing guilt over the deaths she'd witnessed and caused. Before she could wonder which life she'd choose over the others, she reminded herself it probably wasn't even possible, and she'd have to live with the weight of them all—including her own parents—until her dying day.

Angie pressed a hand over her mouth and held her tightening breath as tears blurred her vision. When she blinked them away Daniel was within reach, his hands by his sides.

"Oh Angie, I'm so sorry."

Angie nodded, trying to force herself to resume breathing, and Daniel helped by redirecting the topic of conversation. "But you saved so, so many lives. You know that, right?" Angie nodded again and sucked down an audible breath, which made Daniel smile kindly. "How did you stop him? How did you find him and get through the shields around the place?"

Angie blinked. She hadn't given that much thought amid the chaos. "The radio told me to follow your watch. Didn't you tell them to say that? It led me right to Seth. He must have had it on him, and the token-bonded tether bypassed the shields."

It was Daniel's turn to blink, first in surprise, then in what appeared to be confusion, before a slow smile won out. "No, I had no idea what message you might get. I was playing a hunch. But that explains a lot, and I think my hunch was right." He glanced at the cupboard Angie knew held his safe. "I think Marissa sent me the letter warning me about the imperial broadcasts starting back up, back in July. And that she pinched my watch and planted it on Seth earlier today so that you could follow him."

The mention of the woman's name made Angie heat with anger, and she scoffed. "Doubtful." There was no way that bitch had done anything good, or helpful, or selfless. Not in a million years.

Daniel seemed ready to argue, but the spark in his countenance died quickly. He took half a step closer, brushing the backs of his fingers against the front of Angie's hip through her jeans, his eyes lingering on the contact, and Angie heated in a wholly different way. "No matter. All that matters is that we both somehow, miraculously, survived in one piece." His hand dropped back to his side, and Angie tried to ignore the momentary electric thrill of his touch. "And what of the hours between your triumph there, which is when I presume Seth came to the meeting in the Council world, and when I found you there hours later?"

Angie thought back over everything Daniel had said on the empty Coliseum stage and chose to say nothing of the Inferi. She reached for her pocket, risking the lesser offense, and guiltily pulled out the large copper coin. "I retrieved something I threw away in anger and regretted losing every moment since."

When Daniel's eyes fell on the sigil coin, he held out a hand and stilled hers, grief flashing across his face. "Please, no."

Angie hesitated, needing one last nail in the coffin of her doubts before she'd let the topic drop. "You never thought there was anything between us, right? There never was on my end, and the ghost says the same on his, but... I'm worried you might have heard rumors, or... something."

Daniel tilted his head, looking disbelieving. "Is that why you never told me about the coin or the illusion before I pressed?"

"Yeah, in part. And because he—*it*—had asked me not to tell you, and I just really couldn't bear to lose him a second time." Angie dropped her gaze to the coin, unable to watch whatever further admonishments were to come, but none did.

"Okay. I understand. Then no. And there was nothing in his journals to contradict what you know. But I don't want to see it—*him*—again. Can you understand that?" There was no anger or rebuke in his Caledonian voice, and Angie simply nodded, glad he at least hadn't asked her to get rid of it again.

"Yes. Of course." She had Jonathan back. If Daniel didn't want the same, she wouldn't force him to take comfort from where she intended to keep drawing it. *What now?* she almost asked, as the clock in the living room once more became the only sound to be heard, but she couldn't bear the thought of the answer being *leave.*

"Do you remember what you said to me a long, long time ago, in Hawaii?" she asked instead, stuffing the coin back out of sight. "Just before we showed the world that I was still alive?" Daniel seemed confused but amused, and he nodded. "I'm not sure I was supposed to hear, but you said you didn't like who you'd be without me." Angie crossed her arms, unconsciously defensive against what she feared might incite rejection, and Daniel copied her, his dark eyes fixed on hers. When she spoke again, it was barely a whisper. "I don't like who I am without you, either."

In the silence that followed, the Air and Fire auras filling the room seemed to take up all the space, all the oxygen, building a tangible, physical pressure that consumed Angie whole. She couldn't tell him everything she was terrified of coming to light. And although she had pushed him away in the first place, had asked for the space that had nearly broken her spirit, she couldn't bring herself to take it all back and fall into his arms, as every fiber of her being was screaming to.

Daniel's face and aura conveyed matching conflict, and he, too, seemed to fight back unknown fears before speaking, his voice low and gruff. "Then does this mean we're done with the break?"

Angie smiled, caught between joyful delight and guilty hesitation. "Yes, Daniel, please." Her voice cracked, and she stood up straight from where she had been leaning, squeezing her arms tighter across her middle.

"We'd need to go back to being a secret," Daniel added with a wince, not moving. "With Marissa bending Seth's ear, and the lengths he's gone to in order to force me to prove I'm loyal to him alone..." Daniel's throat bobbed, and Angie inched closer to him, wanting to soothe the raw emotion that momentarily twisted his features. "There's no knowing who might report back to him, so no one can know."

Angie nodded, afraid to speak in the face of the fragile, tiny glimmer of hope shining between them. When Daniel's arms unfolded to reach for her, she fell into his arms, clinging to him like he'd be torn from her forever if she didn't. "I missed you."

Daniel buried his face in her hair, the vibration of his skin achingly familiar and comforting. "And I, you." His fingers trailed lightly down Angie's spine through the thin fabric of her T-shirt, and she shivered against him. Daniel's breath hitched, and he squeezed her a little tighter. When Angie looked up at him, his expression of cautious relief held a spark of something more deep in his eyes, and Angie barely had to lean toward him before his lips brushed hers, and all her worries spun away.

When Daniel's hand cupped the side of her face, he kissed her deeper, harder, and Angie's knees buckled. Half from the glorious feeling of falling into him once more, which laced her silvery aura with rosewood smoke, but half from the dizzying way the vibration of his skin curse ramped up in her awareness, tingeing the sweet fragrance with a whiff of cigarettes.

Angie braced herself against the latter, and nearly fainted from doing so when it spiked in response. Hurriedly, she relaxed as much as she possibly could, utterly releasing any and all control over her magic that had tried to harden against the intrusion, and was rewarded with instant relief.

Daniel's grip was firm and commanding as he lifted her, not seeming to notice the cause of her near faint, and pulled her to him.

Angie wrapped her legs around his hips as he carried her out of the kitchen and down the hall toward his room, his mouth not releasing hers for a second. The moment her boots touched the carpet, Daniel's strong fingers were at her hips, tugging her shirt over her head and deftly releasing her bra to slide it off. Intoxicated by long-held need and desperation for the comfort of Daniel's touch, Angie didn't hesitate in removing his dark clothes with equal eagerness.

Daniel pushed her back onto the bed, unlacing her boots and pulling them off, followed by her jeans, and Angie sighed happily. She spared another thought to releasing all control of her aura. Daniel's was wrapped around hers, and seemed more than content to soothe and contain the flare of singeing heat that accompanied each brush of his sharp nose against the sensitive flesh of her inner thigh.

When she reached for his belt, he pushed her back and she didn't resist, watching hungrily as he tore off the rest of his clothes, pried off his shoes and stepped up against the side of the bed at Angie's knees. One of his nudged hers apart, and her breath hitched, growing more labored as he repeated the move with her other leg, leaving her splayed before him.

Her legs were forced wider still as Daniel slowly crawled onto the bed, the sight of his lean, slender tor-so bending over her in the near-total dark making her mouth go dry. One of his hands slipped beneath her head, gripping her hair in a fist, and Angie let her head fall back in ecstasy to his control.

Daniel shifted to one side, and his other hand found her apex in an instant. His fingers pressed firmly to her clit, and when she bucked, he pushed her knee back apart with one leg, tutting wickedly in her ear. "Now, now, none of that." His mouth dropped to her neck, and Angie gasped as his fingers dove inside her.

Little by little, she melted under his touch, and when she tried to lift her head against his hold on her hair, she found herself flipped onto her stomach. "Daniel," she moaned as he once more nudged her knees apart, and his answer was a brush of warm breath on the shell of her ear.

"Angie."

She arched her back for him, and his cock brushed against her, making her shiver with pleasure. Rocking at her entrance, Daniel tilted her head almost to the point of discomfort and kissed her deeply, bracing on both elbows over her. Angie gripped his arms hard when he entered her fully, gasping against his parted lips, and Daniel breathed into her until she thought she might burst.

He'd never done such a thing before, and Angie's mind reeled from the deep, intimate heat of it as he lifted away, still holding her head still as he set his pace. The feeling of him filling her again after so long was utterly blissful.

"Fuck," Angie muttered when Daniel shifted his angle, and her eyes rolled back in her head. Stroke after stroke, she could barely think, her breath all but stopping, and when he sped up, his balls slapping her clit with every thrust, it only took a dozen more for her to build, strain, and break over the edge.

Daniel grunted behind her, his pace becoming more frantic, and he pulled the fistful of hair he held at the base of her skull, sliding her face along the coverlet until her throat was exposed. "Is that what you wanted?"

Angie tried to nod but couldn't, settling for a wide grin, and relished the feeling of him slamming into her over and over until he shuddered, contracting in spasms over her, grinding to a stop, buried in her to the hilt.

The moment Angie's spasms tapered off into the last of Daniel's, his fingers released from her hair, and he gently, shakily, separated from her, which she protested against with a teasing moan. Chuckling, he rolled her toward him as he collapsed beside her, and she obliged eagerly.

Nestling into his chest, she tangled her legs with his, and as his arms wrapped around her, holding her tight to him, she melted into the safety and comfort of his embrace. Oh, how she'd missed it.

"Thank you," she whispered to him as the world outside her blissful moment began to seep back in, and she desperately tried to hold it at bay. *I made the right choice*, she reassured herself, each word bolstered by the resounding beat of Daniel's racing heart beneath her. *In all of it. Especially in coming back to this.* Some part of her tried to argue back, lifting her lies, fears, and uncertainties to the surface, but the kiss Daniel pressed to the top of her head silenced it.

"Thank you for coming back." Angie could hear the rough emotion in his voice and pushed up to gaze down into his dear, beautiful, expressive face. She caressed his sharp cheekbone and traced the line of his jaw hidden behind his short beard. "I love you," she whispered, and deep-yellow light blossomed around them.

"I love you, too." Daniel's dark eyes glittered, and he pulled Angie down into a tight embrace. "And please, whatever happens next, don't ever tell me goodbye again."

THE END

⊷⊶✦⊷⊶

Did you enjoy this book? You can make a big difference! I would be very grateful if you could scan the code below and spend just five minutes leaving a review on this book's Amazon page. Honest reviews of my books are the most powerful tool in my arsenal when it comes to getting my books in front of more readers, and it helps me write more of what you want and like!

A Spark of Darkness

Want to follow Angie and Daniel's next adventure and get updates on the next installments in the series? Or become an ARC reader, or just chat? I love hearing from my readers, so scan the code below to stay connected on Facebook!

www.facebook.com/rebeccamaeve.hartwell

ALSO BY REBECCA MAEVE HARTWELL

Continue the adventure with Angie and Daniel in the next book in the Unlocked series, coming in 2024!

~

Want to catch up on their story so far? Check out the earlier books in the series!

A Heart of Flame
A Soul of Light
A Mind of Smoke

~

A Heart of Flame – The Unlocked Series Book 1

Is magic all she's ever wanted, or one more dangerous gift?

When fire erupts within Angie, she's snatched away into a glittering new world, leaving behind her suffering and turmoil under the boots of the Empire. As beautiful facades burn away, Angie fights to fix a world even more broken than she is.

Daniel's assignment proves far more dangerous than he bargained for. Angie transforms his life in one impossible way after another, ripping away his masks. As she does, he fears for the secrets they conceal. Salvation, trap, or ruin; he's only certain of one thing—she changes everything.

Caught in a web of beautiful lies and painful truths, secret passions battle against deep wounds. Will Angie and Daniel find enough healing in each other to overcome their darkness with light? Or will they succumb to the demons in their lives and tumble beneath the deadly currents of the magical world...

A *Heart of Flame* is the first book in the dark-romantic urban-fantasy series Unlocked, featuring complex characters, immersive worlds, and high-stakes magic. If you like rebellious hope, dizzying luxury, and spicy connections, you'll love this dazzling new action romance! Unlock A *Heart of Flame* to start this captivating series today!

Grab it here!

A Heart of Flame Paperback

~

A Soul of Light – The unlocked series Book 2

A lock is broken, the world is cracked, and time is running out.

Angie dreads the consequences she didn't think she'd live to face when she defied the patricians and released their ancient, hoarded magic. But the doorways she's opened are being crossed from both sides, and she may be the key to unlocking secrets long kept safe. If her flames illuminate the truth, anyone standing beside her will face a high price from those who want her dead.

Daniel's dreams of relief, belonging, and hope for everyone he loves are tantalizingly within reach. He tries to keep his balance as worlds collide, reveling in his restored magical and political power. But he must bargain what's dearest to him as disruption threatens to give way to desperation, and may lose as much as he hopes to gain.

Angie and Daniel must return to the opulent, corrupt community that nearly broke them, falling into a maze of betrayal and warping power, and treacherous encounters with malicious creatures threaten to cut the threads of their existence short. Can they prevail through their ever-changing world of political scandal and forbidden magic? Or will they lose each other—and themselves—to the currents of fate which threaten to rip them apart...

A *Soul of Light* is the second book in the dark-romantic urban-fantasy series Unlocked, featuring complex characters, immersive worlds, and high-stakes magic. If you like rebellious hope, dizzying luxury, and spicy connections, you'll love this dazzling new action romance! Unlock A *Soul of Light* to continue this captivating series today!

Grab it here!

A Soul of Light Paperback

~

A Mind of Smoke – The Unlocked Series Book 3

The old world order clings savagely to control. Battling to usher in a just society, will a traumatized couple triumph over cruel autocracy?

Angie Forester aches to end the masses' suffering. Though battered, bruised, and heartsick, the determined young woman refuses to let the brutal ruling magic class regroup and reassert their sadistic stranglehold. Resorting to blackmail and threats, she forces the scheming puppet masters to elevate her beloved to greater power and sets up a deadly confrontation.

Daniel Fawl sees secrecy as safety. Disguising his true intentions under layers of subterfuge, the careful manipulator leaves nothing to chance in his war against the nemesis who makes his life a living hell. But though every step he takes moves him closer to his goal of bringing down the twisted status quo, the cunning air elementalist fears those he holds dear will be caught in the crossfire.

As deportations and massacres plague the land, Angie reels from a betrayal that may cost her the man who fills her heart. And even as Daniel gathers talismans to defeat the patrician order, he feels unanchored and reckless in the face of dangerous odds.

As each decision compromises their ideals, will they become the very thing they fight?

A *Mind of Smoke* is the breathtaking third book in the Unlocked contemporary romantic fantasy series. If you like deeply realized characters, relentless adversaries, and realistic relationships, you'll love Rebecca Maeve Hartwell's rollercoaster ride to revolution.

Buy A *Mind of Smoke* to enter a coup for the ages today! Grab it here!

A Mind of Smoke

Also available in the Unlocked Universe:

A Life of Stone - A prequel novella in the Unlocked series.

Frozen in stone is torture beyond imagining. Returning to life is worse.

Demitria has been sleeping in stone for two and half thousand years. The centuries pass, barely noticed, until someone touches her with a spark of familiar warmth, and her blood quickens beneath her skin of marble. Her desire to live pulls her on, even as the trials of her past—and the fears of her future—push her to stay safe, cold, and solid.

Nikolaos is forced to set aside the revenge that has driven him into the life he now leads when he sees a familiar face at an auction. Not among the sea of wealthy bidders, but on an implausibly lifelike statue. He becomes its caretaker when his employer purchases it, both men hoping it will bring their dreams to life.

When the man who holds them in his unforgiving fist demands what he cannot have, chaos tears through the beautiful facade of the isolated world he rules. Will Demitria and Nikolaos overcome their ancient wounds, finally claiming their own destinies? Or will they lose everything to the hard fate the Gods—and other magic users—have dealt them...

A *Life of Stone* is a teaser taste for the dark-romantic urban-fantasy series *Unlocked*, featuring complex characters, exciting alternate worlds, and high-stakes magic. If you like rebellious hope, dizzying luxury, and spicy connections, you'll love this captivating new action romance! Unlock A *Life of Stone* to start exploring this captivating series today!

To claim your FREE ebook copy of A *Life of Stone*, scan the code below, Or visit: www.rebeccamaevehartwell.com/a-life-of-stone

A Life of Stone

About the Author

Rebecca Maeve Hartwell grew up unschooled on a horse ranch in the Nevada mountains, immersed in her own world of fantasy. Playing dress-up with elaborate back-stories, building forts and inventing entire fictional wars in which to defend them, devouring library books, or even directing friends in plays and home movies she scripted, everything was a story, and everyone was a character in them.

Despite this, she never considered a career in writing until her mid-twenties, instead indulging her love for plots and magic through re-enactment, acting, and escaping bad situations through daydreams. It was in the darkest moments in her life that the seeds for the first novel she wrote were planted, and she became an author in the hopes of helping others to escape, survive, recover, and thrive, just as the stories of others helped her to.

Rebecca lives and writes in Maine with her two cats. She enjoys Lindy Hop swing dancing, sewing costumes, and long drives in the dark with just the right music playing.

Learn more about Rebecca Maeve Hartwell and her books by joining her newsletter through her website:

www.rebeccamaevehartwell.com

Many, many thanks to every single person who encouraged and supported me in writing. I love you all dearly.

Book Cover by Faera Lane

Developmental Editing by Isla Elrick

Line Editing by Alex Moyer (OMG I love you)

Copy editing by Natasta Smith

Proofreading by Nicole Simpson

Further editorial thanks to:

Greg Marbais

Linda Laird

Mary Pel

Vic Brocquard